THE
BOOKSELLER
OF
PARIS

BOOKS BY SUZANNE KELMAN

A View Across the Rooftops

When We Were Brave

Under a Sky on Fire

When the Nightingale Sings

Garden of Secrets

We Fly Beneath the Stars

THE PARIS SISTERS SERIES

The Paris Orphans

The Last Day in Paris

SUZANNE KELMAN

THE
BOOKSELLER
OF
PARIS

bookouture

Published by Bookouture in 2024

An imprint of Storyfire Ltd.
Carmelite House
50 Victoria Embankment
London EC4Y 0DZ

www.bookouture.com

ISBN: 978-1-83790-530-0
eBook ISBN: 978-1-83790-524-9

Dedicated to the memory of Adele Kibre, who saved thousands of books and produced over 3,000 reels of microfilm, smuggled from Nazi-occupied territories during World War Two.
Her legacy is a reminder of the enduring power of words and the indomitable human spirit that seeks to preserve them.
May this story, inspired by her profound bravery, serve as a tribute to all that she cherished and fought for.

Perhaps all the dragons in our lives are
princesses who are only waiting to see us act,
just once, with beauty and courage.

— RAINER MARIA RILKE

PROLOGUE

Madeline

She gasped awake in a panic, her body rigid with fear as she fought to free herself from the oppressive, weighty darkness. Her chest strained and her muscles quivered as she realised she couldn't move, and the heaviness compressing her was a solid, cold embrace of concrete and steel.

Her mind moved through a weighted fog, consciousness returning to her slowly as a relentless, mechanical wail pierced her entire body, triggering a sense of familiar dread, making her pulse race with terror.

With a sudden jolt of recognition, she realised what it was. An air-raid siren. She had been caught in a bomb blast.

Panicking, she struggled to pry her eyes open, but salty tears mixed with the sting of dust that also clogged her throat as heat and acrid smoke burned her lungs.

Terror engulfed her as a new reality seeped in – she remembered nothing from before this moment. Not where she was, or even her own name.

As she rapidly blinked her eyes her vision began to clear,

but her surroundings were a maelstrom of unfamiliarity, and a nameless terror filled her body with ice.

Desperately, she clawed at the blankness, seeking any clarity.

As she peered through the hazy darkness, pinholes of light stretched like fingers towards her, and clouds drifted above her head. But she wasn't outside. With frightening awareness, she realised she was looking up at a gaping hole in a precariously hanging ceiling.

As the air-raid siren's relentless wail continued to vibrate through her body, she focused through the clouds of dust as a battered metal sign swam into view, dangling dangerously above her, shuddering back and forth like a disgruntled pendulum.

She desperately tried to decipher the words through the haze, and slowly spelt them out until a chilling sensation spread rapidly through her body.

The words were in German. The nameless terror morphed into gut-wrenching clarity – she was in enemy territory.

A face materialised out of the chaos, and the voice in the dreaded grey uniform sliced through the darkness.

'*Bist du verletzt? Kann ich dir helfen?*'

He was asking her if she was hurt and if he could help her.

'Where am I?' she asked, seamlessly speaking the language of her adversary.

'At the Berlin Central Station. There was no warning before the bombs hit.'

'I can't move,' she spluttered, gasping for every breath.

He gave a curt nod before he began to carefully extract her from the wreckage.

All at once, agony, a searing white-hot pain, crackled through her leg like electricity. She screamed out in anguish, her cries echoing off the concrete walls and reverberating through the debris-laden building.

Her blood, a vivid contrast to the grey dust, seeped from a

deep wound in her leg. The pain unlocked fleeting memories – a Parisian street bathed in sunlight, the aroma of new books, a hint of laughter...

As the soldier stemmed the bleeding, the sound of ambulance bells closed in.

'You will need to go to hospital,' he informed her.

This triggered a burst of fear, a need to protect. She panted, to bear the pain, as fragments of memory teased her again – as her own name hovered on the edge of consciousness, tantalisingly close...

As he lifted her onto the stretcher, her hand brushed against something beneath her shirt – a shape that was foreign, another flash of memory, a man's face. She fingered her dirt-caked waistband to examine what it might be pressing against her skin.

And then all at once, a name surged up from the darkness, familiarity resonating from the void – *Madeline Valette*. Her own name was like a beacon in the fog. She closed her eyes with relief. Then wrenched them open again – she couldn't go to hospital; they would find out what she had strapped to her body.

Madeline was a bookseller from Paris, a French spy, and beneath her clothes she was smuggling banned Jewish literature.

Battling the agony, she desperately tried to sit up, only to be taken by more searing-hot pain that coursed through her veins like liquid fire, as the memory of Jacob's voice still rang in her ears, begging her to get the books to safety.

Madeline Valette's body writhed violently as the agony became too much to bear, and, in a final act of rebellious protection, she clung desperately to the books at her waist, before being consumed again by the thick, murky darkness.

1

Olivia

Livi's cream-coloured Mini Cooper glided through the large iron gates as the Elizabethan manor came into view. Its half-timbered structure, a testament to the grandeur of earlier centuries, stood resilient against time's relentless march.

She turned down the radio so the 80s disco beat faded, and rolled down her window, letting the warm, newly cut grass and rose-scented air wash over her.

'How the other half lives,' she mused, her gaze sweeping over the lush, green lawns of the estate.

Today was a break from her usual routine, a rare outing from her Lewisham flat and the digital confines of her job. As an antiquarian bookseller, she lived her life either in a tiny shop or at home entrenched in endless hours of online research and acquisitions, with Tommy, her beloved cat, as her sole companion.

But today she revelled in the thrill of a real auction, surrounded by tangible history that sent a tingle of excitement through her weary, road-travelled bones.

Livi checked her reflection in the rear-view mirror. She loved how her new pixie cut accentuated her green eyes and heart-shaped face. It had been a brave choice to cut her shoulder-length blond hair, but this new look seemed to give her a newfound confidence. Taking a deep breath, she stepped out of the car, and spotted a familiar battered blue Ford Fiesta. Damien, her friend and fellow dealer, strolled over with his usual ease.

'Escaped the city, did you, Olivia?' he teased, their long-standing friendship evident in his tone.

She chuckled as she locked her car. 'Mr Milner is tied up with a nervous client,' she informed Damien, speaking of her boss. 'Too much babysitting for my taste.' With a bright smile, she hugged Damien warmly. 'We couldn't miss this one, though. How did a French collector end up in Oxford with such a trove of World War Two German works? There's a story here, I'm sure...'

Inside the manor, Livi was struck by the coolness and old-world charm of the foyer. The estate was packed, buzzing with eager bidders, each vying for a piece of the late owner's extensive collection. Rows of auction lots, from historical artefacts to valuable art pieces, were all available to buy.

In the library with its now emptied shelves were boxes upon boxes of books. Livi's stomach tightened with excitement; she knew that within one of them might lie rare and most cherished German works. Exactly what she was looking for.

As she sifted through, she felt a twinge of unease. There were many books that were disturbingly sympathetic to Hitler's ideologies, including a worn copy of *Mein Kampf*. This collector had obviously been a Nazi sympathiser.

She meticulously checked each book for signs of damage, aware that Milner's clients were very particular collectors.

Damien reappeared, his curiosity evident. 'Find anything good?' he asked.

'Just the usual,' she replied. 'What about you?'

'A group of rare Meissen figures. Bidding's starting soon. Save you a seat?'

'Great.' Her attention was drawn back to a box she hadn't yet explored. 'I'll see you out there.'

She worked her way through the next lot, stopping to consider a first edition of *Steppenwolf* by Hermann Hesse. Knowing it would be too expensive for Milner to consider, she was about to move on when her eyes caught something at the bottom of the box – a book of poetry. Poetry books, she knew, were specialised and harder to sell. She hesitated, debating whether to open it. But something drew her in. It had a dark blue cover embossed with golden letters: *Für Die, Die Ich Liebe*. For the One I Love. She skimmed the verses. Their beauty was a stark contrast to the sinister nature of the other books. As she read, she felt her usual feeling of cynicism rising. She didn't believe in love. Well, not anymore.

As she closed the book, something slipped from the pages. A black and white photograph. She was going to place it back in when something familiar about it caused her to move to the window to scrutinise it. *It couldn't be, could it?* She turned it over and read the inscription, and her stomach clenched into a tight ball.

To my darling Ada, I will never forget this day.

She sucked in breath as she flipped it back over, unable to believe what she was seeing. But she knew this face as if it was her own.

A heavy feeling of foreboding began to unravel her once-coherent world. Persistently, she delved deeper into the box, discovering more photographs that left her gasping. Beneath them, a bundle of letters beckoned. She pulled the top one from its envelope, dated 1936. Skimming it, she let out an involuntary 'Oh God,' as a wave of light-headedness washed over her. The bell signalling the auction's start jolted her back to reality.

She clung protectively to the box, not wanting to let it go. She yearned to unravel the mystery immediately, but there was no time.

Reluctantly, she jotted down the lot number and hastened into the main hall, her purpose clear. She had to win this lot at any cost. She needed to uncover the full story behind these revealing and shocking photos of her great-grandmother, photos that threatened to change everything she had ever known.

2

PARIS, MARCH 1940

Madeline

Madeline Valette unlocked the weathered door to L'Élégance de l'Encre, her bag of morning pastries in hand. As she stepped inside, the tiny brass bell chimed gently, signalling her arrival. The familiar, comforting scent of aged leather and paper mingled with the subtle aroma of the fresh pastries she brought in every morning. It was a warm embrace that always welcomed her into her quaint little bookshop nestled at the corner of rue de la Pompe and avenue Foch.

Inside, she paused, taking a deep and lingering breath, as if absorbing the welcome from her old friends – the books that had been her confidants since childhood. This bookshop was more than just a place of business; it was her sanctuary, her anchor, a small island of stability in a sea of uncertainty.

Gathering a stack of envelopes from the mat and moving to the counter, the morning sun cast mismatched shadows across the oak floor that creaked under her high heels. Each step echoed softly in the quiet space, while the gentle hum of the city outside provided a comforting backdrop.

As she organised the letters into an orderly pile, Madeline relished the anticipation of her daily ritual – reading letters from friends at the end of the day with a cup of tea.

Her morning routine continued as she embarked on the task of restoring misplaced books to their rightful spots. Madeline straightened a line of classics that had fallen forward, and one book fell to the floor with a thud. *Les Misérables*. It was her late husband's favourite book. Even though Alex had been American, he had been fluent in French, and memories of him reading it to her at night flooded her thoughts. As she reached down to pick it up, her throat tightened with grief, and she blinked back tears. Even after two years, the pain of his loss to cancer lingered like an open wound, refusing to heal.

The young bookseller whispered softly to the empty room, 'Good morning, my darling. I miss you too.'

She returned the book to its place, the simple act of shelving it a painful reminder of Alex's absence. The ache in her chest was a constant companion, a dull throb that never quite faded, echoing the lingering sorrow of her grief.

She ran a finger down the worn spine. This was all she had left of him – a bittersweet reminder of her lost love. But as long as she had the books he loved and their bookshop, the memory of her husband would live on forever. Madeline closed her eyes, finding solace in the silence and the ghosts that lingered with her.

Her reverie was interrupted by the familiar chime of the bell above the door.

'*Bonjour, Madeline!*' Monsieur Deveaux, her elderly neighbour, poked his head through the doorway. He was impeccably dressed, his twinkling blue eyes framed by bushy white eyebrows and a neatly trimmed white beard.

'*Comment allez-vous aujourd'hui?*' Madeline greeted him warmly, asking him how he was today while wiping away a stray tear. She was delighted to see the old man, who hadn't visited the shop in a long time.

Monsieur Deveaux shrugged, the lines of his weathered face deepening. 'I had a little stay in the hospital and the bones are aching again.' He glanced around the shop, his eyes glimmering with memory. 'It's good to see the old place again. Brings back happy times.'

'I'm so glad,' Madeline replied softly. 'The books and I have missed you.'

Monsieur Deveaux cleared his throat and fished a few coins from his pocket. 'The usual, please.'

'But of course.' She retrieved his copy of *Le Matin* and rang up the sale, bidding him goodbye once she had done so. *'À bientôt!'*

'À bientôt, Madeline.' He tucked the newspaper under his arm and exited into the brightening day.

Silence descended upon the shop once more. Madeline leaned against the counter, taking in the lingering scent of Monsieur Deveaux's woodsy cologne. She had known the old man her whole life and had watched his health decline with sadness. Although he had numerous options for purchasing his daily newspaper, and as a rule she didn't sell a lot of them, she always ensured one was set aside for him. Their shared routine was a small, yet meaningful, daily exchange.

She shook off her melancholy; there was work to do.

Madeline opened the wooden shutters with a creak, flooding the shop with golden light. She caught a glimpse of herself in the reflection of the window. She loved the ease of her new bobbed haircut, inspired by the female pilot Amelia Earhart, which framed her oval-shaped face and accentuated her large brown eyes.

She continued with her tasks, dusting each shelf, straightening every book and giving the floor a quick sweep. The gentle tinkle of the bell alerted her to a new customer. She turned towards the entrance and noticed a woman she had never seen before.

Her attire was impeccable. She wore a charcoal-grey tailored suit made of soft, rich wool. A pale lavender blouse, crafted from delicate silk with a subtle sheen, peeked from beneath the jacket. Perched gracefully upon her head was a hat, wrapped with a satin ribbon in a shade of soft, muted lavender. Her entire ensemble exuded timeless sophistication, elevating the shop by her presence. Despite her poised appearance, there was a subtle undercurrent of worry in her demeanour.

She approached the counter with a quickened stride, and Madeline greeted her warmly, 'Welcome to The Elegance of Ink. How can I help you?'

The new customer arrived at the counter as her fingers played with the delicate silver bracelet on her wrist, her touch light and hesitant, revealing her anxiety.

'Do you have a copy of *The Sun Also Rises*?'

'Of course,' Madeline responded, showing her the Hemingway collection.

'I'm so glad you still have them,' the woman replied, her voice carrying gratitude and a hint of apprehension. 'My name is Dominique. I am originally from the South of France but I have just come from Berlin where it was impossible to get any of Ernest Hemingway's books.'

Madeline sucked in a breath at the mention of Germany. 'I am guessing you are relieved to be here. How was it when you left?'

Dominique's voice carried a hint of her southern French accent, adding a musical lilt to her words as she shared snippets of her life before arriving, painting a vivid picture of Berlin during a time of growing unrest. As she spoke, her eyes reflected the weight of the challenges she had faced. She recounted the oppressive atmosphere, the ever-present fear, and the heartbreaking decisions she and her husband had to make to ensure their safety.

'Berlin was becoming more and more dangerous,' Dominique explained, her fingers continuing to play with the silver bracelet. 'Every day brought new threats and uncertainties. My husband's position as a diplomat offered some protection, but it also placed us under constant scrutiny.'

Madeline's heart went out to her as she listened to the woman's story. She admired the courage it took to uproot her life in such tumultuous times.

'You are most welcome here, Dominique. If you ever need guidance about the city or a friendly face, do not hesitate to reach out,' Madeline said with empathy.

Dominique offered a small, appreciative grin. 'Thank you. Books have always been a source of comfort. Transporting me to different worlds, offering solace in times of uncertainty. Back in Berlin, I used to spend hours in the library there, surrounded by the words of countless authors. It was my refuge. I miss that sense of belonging and the hardest part was saying goodbye to the friends and colleagues we left behind, knowing many of them faced an uncertain future.'

Madeline could see the pain in Dominique's eyes, the weight of the choices she had made still heavy on her heart.

'Coming to Paris was a difficult decision, but we had no other choice. My husband's work brought us here, and while I am grateful for the safety we have found, I feel adrift, disconnected from the life I once knew.'

The young woman's eyes glistened with unshed tears, but she quickly composed herself, her resolve evident. 'Now that I am here, I am committed to building a new life, to find a sense of purpose and belonging. Paris is a city of culture and history, and I want to immerse myself in it, to become a part of this vibrant community.'

Madeline felt a deep connection to Dominique, recognizing

in her the same desire for a fresh start, the same longing to find meaning in the midst of upheaval.

As she slowly wrapped Dominique's parcel of books, a familiar thought surfaced. She liked this woman and wanted to help. 'I know this sounds sudden,' she began, 'but I've actually been thinking of hiring someone here for a while. Since my husband passed away two years ago, I've been working alone. I don't suppose you would want to work here in the bookshop? I couldn't pay much, but I've been looking for someone who would be the right fit. It might be the perfect opportunity for you to stay busy, meet fellow book lovers, and find that sense of belonging.'

Dominique's eyes widened with surprise and appreciation. 'That's a wonderful idea.'

'It's time,' Madeline continued. 'I have been struggling with moving on...' She paused, swallowing down the grief that threatened to expose itself.

Even without elaborating, Dominique sensed Madeline's pain. 'That must be hard for you,' she responded empathetically.

Madeline acknowledged her words with a nod, not wanting to break down in front of this new customer.

'Are you interested?'

'I would love to work here. As books have always been a passion of mine, I can't think of a better place to start building connections in Paris.'

Madeline felt a sense of excitement at the prospect of having a new person around in the shop.

'I'm delighted to have you join me. It's more than just a job though; my customers are a family here. We're a close-knit community of book lovers.'

They arranged for her to start the following Saturday, and Dominique left with her parcel of books.

Madeline's bookshop continued to hum with the energy of a

bustling morning, as customers weaved their way through the shelves.

Among the vibrant clientele, Marcel stood out with his quiet tenacity. A man of average height and wiry build, his face bore the marks of past struggles. His dishevelled clothing hinted at the financial hardships he was facing.

Noticing his skittish demeanor, Madeline approached him carefully, her steps slow and deliberate, the wooden floor creaking beneath her.

'Good morning, Marcel,' she greeted softly, yet warmly. 'It's always good to see you. Is there something specific you're looking for today?'

Marcel quickly shoved a book back onto the shelf and eyed her warily. As she approached, a subtle sour scent hung in the air, and she couldn't help but wonder if he had been sleeping rough.

'I was just looking,' he replied hastily, obviously guarded in his demeanour.

Understanding Marcel's predicament, Madeline decided to extend her assistance. She moved back to her counter, her fingers lightly grazing the worn wood, as an idea began to form. 'I'm glad you stopped by. I have this bag full of books that are not selling. You are welcome to take them, if you think you might enjoy them.'

Marcel's eyes briefly brightened, only to cloud with distrust. 'I don't want *charity*,' he insisted with a hint of defiance. 'I've managed on my own for a long time.'

Madeline raised an eyebrow, her expression conveying surprise. 'Charity?' she exclaimed, genuinely incredulous. 'I just need to get rid of them; I don't have room for every book, especially if they are not selling. There's no shame in accepting something freely offered.'

Marcel hesitated for a moment longer before nodding slowly, his guard lowering. 'All right,' he murmured, his voice laced with discomfort.

Madeline strode to the back of the shop and returned with a canvas bag filled with books, a mix of novels, poetry collections and non-fiction titles.

She handed the bag to Marcel. 'Consider it a gift from one book lover to another. I hope you find some gems in there.'

Marcel accepted the bag, his fingers gripping it tightly. 'Thank you,' he said with real sincerity.

With a nod, Madeline watched as Marcel shuffled out of the shop. As the brass bell chimed softly, she couldn't help but feel a sense of fulfilment. She loved how her bookshop was more than just a place of commerce; it was a haven for souls seeking solace, connection and the magic of literature.

The thought of welcoming Dominique into the bookshop infused Madeline's work with a newfound vitality. While the decision to bring on an assistant was a step forward, it also stirred a poignant ache in her. Her mind drifted to Alex, whose exuberant spirit once filled the shop, blurring the line between a bookshop and a lively café. His passion had been infectious, shared generously with customers and saved in special moments just for her. He had been the most exciting man she had ever known. His absence now left a void no newcomer could hope to fill, his memory a constant companion amid the shelves and stories he once animated with such fervour.

The day passed in a flurry of activity, unfolding with its usual rhythm. She assisted customers, restocked shelves, and enjoyed the quiet haven that had been her world for so long. As the sun dipped below the horizon and the day's final light crept away, Madeline closed the bookshop's heavy oak door with a sense of accomplishment.

She ascended the creaky wooden stairs to her apartment and entered her cosy home. It was a space imbued with memories of the life she had once shared with Alex. The worn armchair by the window, the soft lamplight and the faint scent of her own books all provided her with comfort and familiarity.

Her evening ritual began with the soothing process of making a cup of tea. The kettle whistled, and as she poured hot water into a cup, it released a cloud of steam that carried the aroma of chamomile through the small kitchen. She settled into her soft chair, the warm glow of the lamp illuminated the small stack of letters she had picked up and brought with her from downstairs.

As Madeline sifted through the pile of envelopes, one leapt out – it bore Alex's name in a foreign hand she didn't recognise; the postmark was German.

A letter for Alex? After all this time? Who didn't know he was dead? Her mind raced with questions. Her heartbeat quickened, and her fingers trembled as she sliced open the letter.

A feeling of unease settled into the pit of her stomach.

My Darling Alex: these first words pierced her chest like a dagger and plunged her into a whirlwind of confusion and dread. Who was writing to her husband in such an intimate way?

She braced herself as she continued.

I hope this finds its way to you, and that you are well. This letter is my last hope, a desperate plea to you for help. I find myself in a time of great peril, with nowhere else to turn. The world around me has grown dark, and my days are filled with fear and uncertainty. Oh Alex, I hope you can help me even though I know our marriage was a tumultuous chapter in our lives.

Madeline stopped reading and gasped as the word 'marriage' leapt off the page, stabbing her with an untold fear. She reread the words over and over again, feeling them suffocating her with disbelief.

What marriage? Who was this person? Alex had never been married except to her. A thousand questions whirled through her mind her pulse thrumming in her ears as she flipped over the letter to read the name of the sender. Ada. The name meant nothing to her, but it felt like a dagger that twisted in her gut.

A wave of pure terror crashed over her, cruelly assaulting her mind with a barrage of horrific thoughts. How could she have not known about this wife in Germany? Why had Alex kept this secret? These thoughts led to darker questions. Had Alex led a double life? Had her own marriage been a sham? Her heart constricted painfully against her chest as she grappled with the terrifying possibility of her new shattered reality.

The questions made her stomach plummet as she frantically combed through her memories, searching for any hint or clue that Alex had been harbouring such a monumental secret. However, the more she thought, the deeper Madeline's feelings of betrayal and confusion became. She questioned if she had truly known her own husband. The man she had loved, built a life with and shared all her hopes and dreams with.

Madeline's mind was already reeling from this first shocking revelation when she was hit with another one, this time even more devastating.

Alex, I hope you are sitting down because I have something sensitive to share with you – you have a son, and his name is Kurt.

Madeline gasped, unable to believe what she was reading – her husband had a son?

The pain of this was unbearable; the one thing she had wanted to give Alex was a child, and now she found out he had one with another woman. This had to be a cruel joke.

She was numb now as she read on, floating somewhere above herself as the words on the paper blurred and she attempted to absorb the series of blows that continued to rain down upon her fragile heart.

Do you remember that one last time we were together, for old times' sake we joked, right before the divorce was finalised, my deepest regret is that I never told you about him, but I was already engaged to another man and it didn't seem fair to you as we had both moved on in our lives.

You would be so proud of Kurt, he is a bright and kind-hearted boy, full of life and innocence. But being your son makes him half Jewish. In the eyes of this merciless regime, his very existence is an offence. Every day, I fear he will be found out. In Nazi Germany, innocence is no shield against the madness that has descended upon us.

I am in constant fear, each day more harrowing than the last. Alex, your strength, your protection is sorely needed. The love you once professed for me I hope will now extend to your son. I wanted to tell you about him the last time we met but couldn't bring myself to do it. I hate asking you for help, knowing it's been so long since we last spoke. But I must try, for Kurt's sake.

Alex, our son's life hangs in the balance, and I am powerless to shield him from the horrors that surround us. Please, if you ever truly loved me, if you have an ounce of kindness left in your heart, find a way to save our son from this living nightmare.

I am leaving this letter in the hands of a trusted friend, one who can ensure its safe delivery. I pray that it reaches you, and that you will consider helping him. I cannot give you an address because of fear of this getting into the wrong hands. But if you manage to make it into Germany, go to the place we first met; you can contact me through the person there, they are a friend.

With the deepest of regrets and the most love and gratitude,

Ada

Madeline collapsed back into her chair as waves of dizziness washed over her, the shocking words in the letter seared through her body. She felt like she was drowning in a sea of disbelief, desperately trying to cling to any shred of her shattered truth.

Tears of grief and shock flowed down her cheeks, flooding the neat little world she had meticulously built. A turmoil of emotions ripped through her in waves; deep sadness for what should have been Alex's joy in the news of fatherhood, confusion, anger and betrayal at the revelation of her husband's hidden marriage.

It was some time later, when her body ached from crying and there were no more tears to shed, that she began to think about what she should do.

All at once the incident from the morning flashed in her memory – the book fallen from the shelf. She was normally unswayed by superstitions, but now it stood out as a peculiar occurrence, as if Alex was communicating with her from beyond the grave. A chill ran down her spine as she considered the possibility. Could it be her husband's cryptic way of urging her to act?

Wiping away the tears from her cheeks, she reread the enigmatic letter. Its urgency was palpable. She knew, no matter what had happened in the past, or what Alex had done or not done, she couldn't ignore it. If this letter was true, a little boy, Alex's son, was in danger. She had to find this woman and uncover the truth. But how?

She reread the end of the letter.

The place they first met.

She had no idea where that could be. But as she absorbed this shocking revelation, Madeline knew she had no choice.

Because somewhere in Nazi Germany was a woman who had the answers and a young, vulnerable Jewish boy, Madeline's stepson, whose life was in danger, and now that Alex was dead, she was the only person left who could help him.

3

Olivia

The manor house buzzed with anticipation as people gathered inside the large ballroom for the auction. Ancient tapestries hung limply against the walls, fluttering slightly as the heat from the closely packed bodies filled the room.

Livi's body tingled as she took her seat next to Damien, clutching her paddle in a white-knuckled grip. Her mind was a whirlwind of thoughts, all centred on the shocking pictures of her great-grandmother that she had stumbled upon. Could this dusty box hold the answers to the questions about her family that had tormented her for years?

Her knowledge of her family history was scant. Her grandfather had been a war orphan who had been brought to England and adopted. He very rarely talked about his past, and had remained tight-lipped about his birth parents, including his mother, Ada, who Livi was sure was the woman in the pictures she had just found. She knew this because the only other photo of Ada she'd ever seen was displayed on her mother's mantelpiece. Besides that, her family's history was shrouded in mystery.

As the auctioneer's gavel struck the podium, signalling the start of the bidding, Livi's palms grew hot and clammy. Time seemed to slow down as she anxiously waited for her lot to come up.

Finally, after what felt like hours, they reached the box of books that Livi so desperately coveted. Adrenaline coursed through her body as the bidding began, and she noticed straight away the intense interest the lot had garnered. It was likely due to the presence of the rare Hesse book within the collection. She braced herself for a fierce competition.

Her stomach churned as someone opened the bidding at ten pounds and three other bidders immediately responded. Livi desperately tried to decide if she should join in, or wait for her moment.

The tension in the room was palpable as bids continued to fly back and forth between serious collectors. Sweat beaded on Livi's forehead as she watched intently, fear and hope warring inside her. She couldn't let this opportunity slip away, even if it meant spending more than she could afford.

The bidding slowed down as people, reaching their limit, shook their heads. The bids were high, at the top of a comfortable amount for Livi, but she could still afford it. She bit her bottom lip as the auctioneer called for any more bidders. This was her chance. She was just about to raise her paddle when a new bidder entered the fray. She snapped her head back round to see a tall, impeccably dressed man in a tailored navy suit who stood out, his silver hair lending an air of distinguished sophistication. He exuded confidence, the kind that only comes from years of successful bids. Livi recognised him from previous auctions; he was a regular, with a penchant for acquiring antique literature.

Damn the Hermann Hesse book. It had to be that, because the other books were almost worthless.

The auctioneer's voice rang out: 'Two hundred and fifty-five.'

This was it. Her heritage was at stake. With a deep breath, she calculated the meagre amount in her bank account and prayed it would be enough. Because this wasn't just about money, it was about a question that had haunted her for years...

'Two hundred and seventy-five,' she managed to say, her voice shaking with nerves.

'Two-ninety,' came the quick response from the suave man across the room. He didn't even break a sweat as he casually flipped through his catalogue, only concerned with how much profit he could make.

Summoning all of her courage, she raised her paddle again. 'Three hundred.'

But he effortlessly countered with three-twenty-five. Panic began to set in as she frantically added up her credit card limit – an option she hated but might have to resort to. She could feel Damien squirming beside her, but she was laser-focused.

Livi kept her gaze fixed on the older man, hoping against hope that he would shake his head. When he did, she felt a surge of relief.

However, it was short-lived, as another voice spoke up from the back of the room. A woman and a new challenger. This was starting to feel like a nightmare and her nerves were now completely frayed.

'Four hundred,' Livi declared, thrusting her paddle into the air with desperate resolve. The room fell silent as the auction-eer's gavel hung in the air.

She strained to listen for the other bidder, but all she could hear was the pounding of her own heart, drowning out any other sound. She locked eyes with Damien. Both of them were holding their breath in anticipation.

'Going once.'

Her mind raced with thoughts as she drew in breath.

'Going twice.'

She willed the hammer down with every fibre of her being.

With a final bang, the hammer fell, and Livi let out a loud sigh of triumph, her body going completely limp as she realised she had won it.

But it had come at a cost; she wasn't quite sure how she would pay for it. But she had to have that box.

As they waited for the next lot and people discussed the bidding frenzy that had just occurred, Damien turned to her with a look of incredulity on his face.

'That was exciting. I'm guessing you have someone with deep pockets who really likes Hermann Hesse? I had it valued at less than that.'

'It wasn't the value I was interested in; it was something else,' Livi said, her breath thready from all the excitement.

He looked at her quizzically, but she didn't elaborate.

Livi couldn't wait for the auction to be over. She had bid everything she had, and she hoped selling the Hermann Hesse book might help offset the cost.

She collected her lot and, paying with her credit card, crossed her fingers that it wouldn't get rejected.

The crowd's chatter felt distant as she considered the weight of what she had found. The photographs of her great-grandmother tucked in the poetry book were a stark contrast to the image Olivia held in her memory – in one minute, these photographs had upended everything she knew about her family.

The cashier pulled the receipt from the machine and handed it to her to sign. She offered a wobbly signature, then hurried from the ballroom, clutching the box close as if it were a fragile piece of her own soul.

Damien gave her a knowing nod, his eyes reflecting his

curiosity. Livi managed a smile that didn't quite reach her eyes as she confirmed the arrangements to meet him at a local pub. She would need both her friend and a stiff drink to process this one.

With the box secured in her Mini, Olivia didn't immediately start the engine. Instead, she allowed herself the moment she had been denying – the moment to feel the full brunt of her discovery.

Gingerly opening the box, she lifted the small book and extracted the photographs, shuffling through them, her body shuddered as she shook her head in disbelief.

Finally, she started the car, the purr of the engine a comforting reminder that she was still grounded in the present.

Driving through the Oxfordshire countryside to the pub, the scenery was a blur. All she could see was the photographs, her great-grandmother's eyes, reflecting a story Olivia had yet to fully understand.

After a brief drive, she arrived at the Whispering Oak, a quintessential English pub that seemed plucked from the pages of a storybook. Its centuries-old stone walls bore the marks of history, and its ancient roof gave it an idyllic, fairy-tale charm.

Inside, it was a cosy realm of dark mahogany beams and whitewashed ceilings and walls. Rustic lanterns cast a soft dance of light across the tables and old tools and photographs whispered of bygone days.

The air carried the melded scents of oak from the hearth, aged whisky, and hearty fare, creating a symphony of tradition and comfort.

Scanning the room for her friend, her gaze passed over a group of jovial farmers sharing a raucous laugh over pints of bitter ale. They were clearly regulars, guardians of the bar and local lore, deep in convivial debate.

She found Damien at a table nestled in the corner. He

seemed to sense her agitation as she approached, and glanced at the box she carried in her arms.

'So, what on *earth* is in that box, Liv?' he asked, furrowing his brow as he lifted his pint to his lips.

Livi leaned closer, her voice tight with her discomfort.

'Damien, you won't believe what I discovered.'

Taking a sip of the white wine Damien had already ordered for her, she handed him the stack of photographs and watched his expression change as he processed the images.

'Whoa,' he exclaimed as he shuffled through them.

The photographs revealed a deeply unsettling scene. Every detail was already etched into her memory.

The setting was a grand, opulent garden, reminiscent of a historical manor house. Lush, meticulously maintained shrubbery framed the background, and intricate stone sculptures dotted the landscape. Vibrant flowers bloomed in a kaleidoscope of colours, contrasting sharply with the disturbing nature of the photographs.

In the centre of one of the images sat her great-grandmother, a striking woman with a sense of elegance in her every gesture. She wore a flowing, silk dress that cascaded in ivory waves, but it was who sat next to her that had prompted Livi to spend next month's food money on this box.

Seated next to her beautiful great-grandmother, with the same eyes and face shape as Livi, was a Nazi officer. He was wearing a sharply tailored uniform, bearing the emblem of the Third Reich, his rank insignia visible. His black SS cap rested beside him.

What was most disconcerting in the photographs was the interaction between them. In one, Livi's great-grandmother held a bunch of grapes and fed one to the Nazi officer. Both of them were captured in an unabashed moment of laughter, their expressions carefree and devoid of the world's horrors outside the frame. The Nazi officer's arm was outstretched, fingers poised to accept the grape, and Livi's great-grandmother leaned in close, their eyes locked in mutual amusement. In another the Nazi kissed her neck as she laughed, her head thrown back.

It was the stark contrast between the serene garden setting, the elegance of her great-grandmother's attire, and the chilling Nazi officer's uniform, combined with their shared laughter, that brought a chill to Livi.

'Who is this?' Damien asked with interest.

'This is a picture of my great-grandmother, I'm sure of it. My mother has a photo at home that obviously was taken on the same day, she is wearing the same clothes and is in the same place, but in that one she is alone.'

Damien downplayed it. 'You don't know the story behind these photographs; it could just have been a group of friends getting together. I bet half of them were in the army during that time...'

Livi reached into the box once more, this time producing a small bundle of love letters tied with a faded ribbon. 'It's not just the photographs, Damien,' she said, her voice heavy with dread. 'I found these letters as well. Love letters between my great-grandmother and a Nazi officer, Frederick Mueller.'

As Livi translated one of the letters, dated 1934, Damien's eyes widened. Their correspondence indicated a serious relationship.

She lowered her voice. '*I will never forget last night,*' she quoted, highlighting a passage. 'This implies that my great-grandmother was sleeping with a Nazi not long before the start of World War Two.'

Damien leaned forward, his voice urgent with intrigue. 'Did you have any idea?'

Livi shook her head. 'But what's even more disturbing is that my grandfather was born the year after these letters are dated, which raises a horrifying question, Damien. Am I the great-granddaughter of a member of the Gestapo?'

4

PARIS, MARCH 1940

Madeline

Madeline sat in the dimly lit room, a cold cup of tea forgotten on the table. She stared at the letter that had unravelled her world, its words echoing in her mind. Finally, girding herself with the courage she needed, she approached her husband's desk. With an unsteady hand, she caressed the polished wood, a touchstone to a happier past she longed for.

Reverently, she opened the lid, the creaking exhale echoing in the room, a ghost of a sound from the past. He had always promised to oil the hinges but had never found the time, and her heart ached with the absence of the man she still loved. As angry as she was about all these secrets, she so desperately wanted to feel his arms wrap around her right now, reassuring her, making all these unknowns go away.

'Oh, Alex,' she whispered, her voice laden with sorrow. 'Why aren't you here to help me understand this?'

Inside the desk, she found letters and photographs, and the usual jumble of papers and remnants of his past, offering her a glimpse into his manic yet organised mind.

Madeline's fingers lingered on a leather-bound journal, a repository of her husband's thoughts and memories. She had read it countless times during the lonely nights since his passing, seeking solace in his words. But now, she sought answers.

She settled into Alex's favourite mahogany desk chair and opened the journal. She gently flipped through its pages, aching to find any clue, any hidden truth that could unravel the mystery of his past. She paused on one entry dated after they were married, noticing something she hadn't noticed before: an 'A' at the top of the page, underlined. Could that refer to Ada? She read the extract below it.

15 August 1936

The streets of Berlin beckon with whispers of history and promises of adventure. Today, I wandered into the heart of the city, near the sprawling Tiergarten, where a quaint coffee shop nestled quietly amid the cobbled lanes. The aroma of freshly brewed coffee embraced me as I stepped inside.

The interior, bathed in the soft glow of vintage lamps, was warmed with antique furnishings, each piece whispering stories of a bygone era. The wooden chairs creaked with age, and the tables bore the marks of countless conversations. A soothing murmur of voices floated through the air, mingling with the gentle strains of a street musician's melody drifting in from outside. A bulletin board cluttered with vintage postcards and pictures added a unique charm to the space.

Overseeing it all was a quirky metal cat, perched high above, watching as we sipped our coffee. It was as if time had stood still in this place, a sanctuary of tranquillity within a bustling world.

I met a friend there from my reckless youth. As we delved into deep conversations and sipped our coffee, I observed the people around me. Friends gathered at nearby tables, sharing stories and laughter, a stark contrast to the serious tone of our discussion. In both instances, there was an undeniable sense of connection, of lives intertwining for a fleeting moment. Others revelled in joy, while ours was in a more serious vein. It was a beautiful tapestry of humanity.

Yet, amidst the serene ambiance, a tinge of melancholy crept in. An unspoken longing hung in the air, as if our conversation remained unfinished, connections unfulfilled. I couldn't quite put my finger on it, but the ache of it lingered, hidden beneath the surface.

After my friend and I parted ways, I was reminded of the mistakes made in my wayward past. The weight of unsaid words and unfulfilled promises pressed upon me. It's strange how the simplest of moments can stir such complex emotions.

She stared at the date at the top of the entry, August 1936. Just a year after she and Alex had married. Despite the warmth in her apartment, her whole body trembled with cold as she considered her husband's potential infidelity.

As Madeline reached the end of the entry, the subtle melancholy was now so apparent, the cryptic undercurrent to her husband's narrative. She couldn't ignore the unanswered questions that lingered in the margins of his words. Her gaze returned to the words 'mistakes made'. Was he talking about the last time he had slept with Ada *for old times' sake*, as she had mentioned in her letter, or about a marriage to a woman he had never told her about – or, worse still. She had read stories of men having wives in different countries. Surely, not her husband. But she had to face facts; he had travelled so much while they had been married. It was a possibility...

Fresh tears sprang to her eyes; grieving him had been so hard. Now, this new unanswered pain struck her to her core, and more than anything she didn't want to face the memory of her marriage with this crippling thought that maybe the husband she had held in such perfect regard may have deceived her.

In the days that followed, Madeline tried to maintain a semblance of normalcy in her beloved bookshop. The routine comforted her, but the unanswered questions kept her awake at night. Then, on Saturday, Dominique arrived in the bookshop, her presence a bright spot in Madeline's emotional week.

'I'm here and ready to go!' Dominique announced, her enthusiasm infectious.

Madeline welcomed her new employee warmly. Under her guidance, Dominique's progress was rapid, her natural charm and elegance, leaving an indelible impact on the customers. It was as if her genuine love for books had a magical way of enchanting all who walked through the door.

At the end of the day, Madeline turned to the young woman.

'Would you like to join me for some tea? Unless you need to rush off?'

'Not at all,' Dominique assured her. 'My husband is very busy with this looming war, so he is often gone until late into the evening. I have no one to rush home to.'

Madeline closed the shop and led Dominique upstairs. As they sat in the cosy front room, the fragrance of freshly brewed Jasmine tea mingling with the delicate scent of Dominique's exquisite perfume.

They talked of books and Paris, finding comfort in shared interests.

'Is it just you and your husband?' Madeline asked as she took a sip of her tea.

Dominique's eyes clouded with sadness. 'Unfortunately, though we have tried, we haven't been blessed with children.'

Madeline felt a pain in the pit of her stomach.

'I understand. I so wanted to give Alex a child, too. A lovely little boy with my husband's dark wavy hair and handsome features. When I had my first miscarriage, I was very sad, but the second one left me... devastated.'

Dominique reached for Madeline's hand, a silent understanding passing between the two women. Their shared grief bonded them in a way that words could never fully express.

'I'm so sorry, Madeline,' her new friend whispered softly, her eyes brimming with empathy. 'It is a silent grief, isn't it? One that people don't want to talk about. But it doesn't change the desperate ache that the loss of that child brings.'

Madeline's eyes misted with tears as she continued. 'Once I was feeling well enough, Alex took us on a short holiday to Vienna, saying it would be a new start. He held me in his arms on the balcony overlooking the Danube River, and we watched the sunset as he said, "*We will get through this together, my love. We will create new memories to fill the loss in our hearts.*" And for a brief moment, amid the grandeur of Vienna, I felt a glimmer of hope that maybe, just maybe, we could heal from our pain and find joy again.

'But when we arrived home, he had a cough that quickly grew worse... Six weeks later, he was dead from cancer.'

Dominique's eyes widened in shock and sorrow as she listened to Madeline's heartbreaking story. 'Oh, Madeline, how you must have suffered through it all alone... losing a child and then your husband in such a short span of time.'

Madeline paused for a moment, scooping a lock of her dark bobbed hair over her ear. Her ebony-brown eyes glistened with tears as she swallowed down her own emotion and decided to share her secret with her new friend. 'I had a shock this week that brought all of this up again for me. I received a letter from Germany, addressed to my late husband, saying he has a son he never knew about with another woman.'

Dominique gasped in astonishment. 'A *son?*' she breathed, her eyes wide with concern.

Madeline approached her desk and found the letter, handing it to her new friend to read.

'I cannot imagine the emotions you must be feeling,' Dominique said softly as she finished.

'I knew nothing of this woman. Why didn't he tell me? I have been consumed with a whirlwind of emotions since this arrived: betrayal, hurt, confusion... The thought of my husband maybe having an affair with this woman is tearing me apart. How could he do this to us? To our marriage? When we were so in love. It's hard to believe he would betray me. It makes me question if I ever truly knew the man I spent all those years with. And yet, a part of me still wants to deny it and hold on to the happy memories we shared, because that is all I have left.

And I have so much anger about him not being here to explain himself, to apologise, or deny it all. Then I feel guilty for feeling this way, questioning his memory, without even knowing the truth.'

Dominique's smile was tinged with bittersweet sympathy. 'People often have complex lives, and we may not know every aspect of the person we love. And to be fair to your husband's memory, you don't know who this woman is or even if this son is your husband's child. Things are very desperate in Germany. People will do anything to get their children to safety.'

Madeline sighed. 'I can't risk ignoring this. This woman clearly knew my husband and our address. And while I try to make sense of all this, one thing remains clear – an innocent child's life hangs in the balance. If he is truly my husband's son, he deserves to know the truth about his father... my Alex.' Her voice trembled, tears threatening to spill over.

Dominique squeezed her hand. 'I will help you in any way I can. I can take care of the bookshop, if you have to go to Berlin.'

'Thank you. Though, to be honest, I don't know if I can

afford to keep travelling back and forward to Germany, trying to find this woman with such little information,' Madeline fretted.

'We will find a way,' Dominique declared with unwavering assurance.

Madeline felt a sense of relief, knowing she had her new friend's support. Despite the unresolved questions surrounding Alex's mysterious past, they were both adamant about finding a way forward. Their personal struggles with infertility only strengthened their resolve to fight for the life of an innocent child.

5

LONDON, OCTOBER 2011

Olivia

When Livi arrived home, Tommy, her white fluffy cat, was waiting at the door, his plaintive meows conveying his obvious displeasure at her prolonged absence. Dropping her keys onto the hall table, she caught her reflection in the mirror – her short fair hair was unkempt, and her green eyes were mascara-streaked from the long, taxing day.

'All right, hold on a moment,' she said softly to Tommy, who demanded attention as he weaved between her legs. She carefully placed the weighty box on the coffee table and scooped Tommy up for a hug, kissing the top of his head.

She flicked on her lamps and the soft lighting in her cosy front room cast a warm glow over her sanctuary. Muted earthy tones, mismatched shelves filled with books, antique globes and framed vintage maps welcomed her home.

Exchanging her leather boots for fluffy pink slippers, she sighed with relief.

The traffic from Oxford had been a nightmare, turning a

short trip into a long exhausting journey. With a comfortable shuffle, she entered the cosy kitchen and settled Tommy on the floor. She set the kettle to boil, craving the comfort of a soothing cup of tea as Tommy clawed at her legs, demanding his dinner.

As she went through the motions of their evening ritual, her gaze kept drifting back warily to the box on the table. Countless thoughts raced through her mind. All the way home, she had been trying to put the pieces together. How had this poetry book, written in German and with pictures of her great-grand-mother with a Nazi slipped inside it, ended up in an estate sale in England that had come from France? None of it made sense.

Settling herself on the worn sofa with a cup of tea, she steadied herself. 'Okay, I can do this,' she whispered.

She started with the aged poetry book. Trained in research, she knew that anything out of the ordinary could be a clue. As she read the words of love in their faded golden lettering, she had to stop herself from being cynical. She struggled with the idea of romance herself, but how could she not? Married at nineteen, she had thought she would be safe with a man she'd loved since secondary school.

She and Graham had had a good relationship while they were young. But things changed almost from the first day after they married, when he became possessive and demanding. That went on for three years of incredible hardship before it turned violent, and she'd finally left home with just the clothes on her back.

People didn't talk much about spousal abuse back then, so she had felt terrible feelings of failure for not meeting his unrealistic standards, and her confidence had taken a fatal blow. And now here she was, in her thirties, and she had not been able to commit to another relationship, since the fear of it happening all over again terrified her.

She returned her thoughts to the book. She removed the

delicate dust jacket and it revealed a book that had clearly been cherished over the years, bearing signs of age with endearing charm. She meticulously scrutinised each page, running her eyes over the text, but there were no underlined passages or marginal notes to offer any hints. Her attention then shifted to the photographs. There was the familiar image that had graced her mother's sideboard for as long as she could remember. However, the rest of the images, with the beaming Nazi, added an eerie and unsettling element to the scene.

Livi was overwhelmed. She needed a break. She reached for her phone and dialled her mother's number. After a few rings, Stephanie's airy voice greeted her, launching into an animated monologue about her mischievous dogs and their latest escapades.

'Mum,' she began, pausing slightly, unable to just blurt out what she had found, 'I have something I want to show you, and I was wondering if I could come over tomorrow. Are you around?'

'Of course, love. Come over for lunch,' her mother responded, warmly, but with a hint of exasperation. 'Although I must warn you, your father has decided to redecorate yet again. He claims that retirement was a brilliant idea, though I'm not entirely convinced it was a wise move for me or our poor house.'

Just then, a chorus of barking erupted in the background, and Livi had to pull the phone away from her ear.

'Sorry, darling!' her mother's voice crackled through the receiver. 'I have to go. Some woman is here to drop off jumble for the Scouts, and I promised to help with the sale.'

With that, the phone on the other end clicked off abruptly. Livi closed her own phone and widened her eyes. She loved her mother dearly but, as a confirmed introvert, the whirlwind of her mother's busy social life always left her feeling drained after their interactions.

Livi decided to continue her research and reached into the box. The revelations she had encountered so far had been unsettling, but nothing could prepare her for what she was about to uncover. She pulled out another one of the letters, dated 1939, and began to read.

My dearest Ada, it began, filled with longing and affection. The letter spoke of shared moments and dreams of a future when Germany would reign in glory. Frederick's pride in serving the Führer and the prospect of promotion were clear. But it was the end of the letter that chilled her to the bone:

I will not be able to see you for a while as I have been given a new appointment. We are finally going to address the Jewish problem, and are looking at a potential site and I will be going to Oświęcim in Poland to work on this. I will miss you and see you again soon.

Much love, Frederick

Livi felt a wave of nausea. *Oświęcim*. 'Why does that name sound familiar?' she wondered aloud as she tried to piece together the fragments of her hazy recollections from her school history class. The disconcerting sense of recognition nagged at her, compelling her to find out more.

Quickly, she turned to the internet, her fingers typing the name Oświęcim with a sense of urgency. As the search results returned, she was jolted to her core.

Her voice quivered as she cried out, 'Oh my God!' Tommy looked at her curiously, sensing her distress.

As she stared at the screen, a wave of emotions engulfed her – shock, horror, and a profound sense of betrayal. On the website was a black iron gate with the chilling words, *Arbeit macht frei,* Work Sets You Free. It was a haunting image of

Auschwitz, one of the most notorious death camps in Nazi history.

Struggling to process the weight of this discovery, staring at the photos of her great-grandmother in the arms of this Nazi, Livi knew one thing: she would never be able to rest until she uncovered the whole story of her family's past, no matter how painful it might be.

6

***

PARIS, APRIL 1940

Madeline

A few weeks later, Madeline met Archie McLeish, an old friend visiting from America, at a small pavement bistro in the centre of Paris. Tall, dark, and striking, Archie retained his timeless dapper charm as he stood to greet her with the customary double-cheek kiss.

'I was so glad to get your letter. It has been quite some time since you were last in Paris, hasn't it?' Madeline remarked with enthusiasm.

Archie was thoughtful as he pulled out the wrought-iron chair for her, its familiar groan echoing against the tiled floor. 'Yes,' he acknowledged, his voice tinged with sad nostalgia. 'It was for Alex's funeral.'

She felt a punch to her gut, having forgotten that had been the last time he had visited. Memories of that sorrowful day surged back, making her catch her breath. It took her a moment to refocus her thoughts, and she was glad of a familiar menu to bring her back to the present.

Before long, they were catching up as old friends do. Amid

the soft hum of conversation and clinking of cutlery, they shared family news, and inevitably the subject of Alex came up.

'How are you holding up?' Archie asked, sipping his wine.

Madeline thought of the blow Ada's letter had dealt her, making her doubt her husband's fidelity, but replied, 'You know, good days and bad.'

Archie's eyes glistened with affection as he reminisced about his time at Yale with Alex, sharing tales of mischief and adventures. Madeline laughed at his stories, feeling a familiar blend of nostalgia and pain.

She wanted to talk to him about Ada, but couldn't bring herself to ask outright, so, as she sipped at her wine, she asked, 'Did Alex date much at university?'

'Oh yes, I remember one time when Alex got himself into a bit of a romantic tangle,' Archie replied with a laugh. 'Dating two women at the same time.'

'Really?' Madeline's stomach tightened as she felt the weight of her secret.

Archie chuckled at the memory. 'Alex suggested that the best course of action was to talk to both women, be honest with them, and let them choose. So, that is what he did, and he got a slap on the cheek from both of them for his honesty. He didn't end up with either of them, and I ended up dating one for the rest of my time at Yale.'

Madeline paused, forcing down a bite of her chicken, before deciding to broach the topic weighing on her mind since the mysterious letter.

Madeline's voice took on a serious note. 'Archie, did he often date two women at the same time?

Archie, noticing the shift in her tone, raised an eyebrow, concern flickering in his eyes. 'No, not at all. Why do you ask?'

Madeline met Archie's gaze, steeling herself. As they continued their lunch, she recounted the entire story of Ada's letter, each word laden with the weight of her discovery.

Archie listened intently, his expression growing more serious with each detail. She concluded her account with a simple but loaded question.

'Did you know anything about this woman? I know he was in Germany after he left Yale. Did you two keep in touch that following year?'

Archie shook his head, his concern mirroring hers. 'No, Madeline, I went on to study law while Alex embarked on his sabbatical. But I must say, this situation doesn't sound like him at all. Would you mind if I had a look at the letter?'

She agreed, and after settling the bill, they headed back to her apartment. Archie read the letter, his brow furrowed in thought while Madeline poured him a brandy. The weight of the situation settled between them as she waited anxiously for his opinion.

Nervously filling in the weighted silence, Madeline said, 'I don't know if what this woman says is true, but I need to find her, to get some answers. And if this boy is Alex's son...' Madeline's voice trailed off, choked with emotion.

Archie leaned forward and covered her hand with his own. 'You don't know all the circumstances. Are you sure you want to get involved?'

Madeline was unwavering in her reply, her voice steady despite the turmoil inside.

'I have to. The problem is I don't really have the money or the resources to go there. Also, I need a valid reason to travel without alerting the Nazis. I still have my American passport, which Alex got for me after we married. As long as America stays out of the war, I could travel there freely. But how?'

Archie leaned back in his chair, deep in thought. 'I might be able to help you.'

She felt a pang of guilt. 'No, Archie, I don't want any money from you. That is not why I am sharing this. I just wondered if he had told you anything about this woman that could help me.'

Archie assured her, his tone gentle but firm. 'No, I wasn't thinking of anything like that.' He rose from his seat and approached the apartment door. 'You are alone up here, aren't you?'

Madeline was puzzled by the sudden shift in the direction of their conversation. 'Yes, of course. Why?'

He returned to his seat, his voice hushed. 'I'm not here in Paris on a social visit. I was asked to set up a literacy service in the US to help protect literature from all over the world. With Hitler's advances in Europe and the burning of books, there's a real concern about preserving knowledge. Roosevelt firmly believes that knowledge is power, and Hitler aims to control that narrative.

'I've heard about the burning of books and the suppression of literature in Germany. It's a terrible situation,' Madeline responded.

Archie continued, 'We believe that Hitler intends to do this in every country, strip them of their own narrative. In response, we're recruiting individuals to collect information: books, newspapers, manuals, technical papers – anything that documents our era. I've been tasked to put together teams to go out and achieve that, and we have been training librarians, archivists, document specialists, and anyone who has that kind of knowledge, and then sending them out around the world, especially Germany. When the war ends, this knowledge will be invaluable.'

Madeline was puzzled by the suggestion. 'How would the work you are doing help me find Ada?'

'You're the perfect candidate; you can be trusted. You speak multiple languages and have an extensive knowledge of literature, both of which are significant assets. It's wise you've reverted to your maiden name; your married name, Friedman, might attract unwanted attention.'

'Me?' Madeline scoffed. 'I've hardly ever left Paris; I'm just a *bookseller*.'

'There is no *just* Madeline. Are you familiar with the new microfilm technology?'

'I think I read something about that. It's a new, easy way to record information, very helpful for scholars.'

'If you are willing to be trained, I would love to have your expertise – and, while you are in Germany working for me, you could continue searching for this woman and her son.'

Madeline gulped down a swig of her brandy as she listened. 'Is it... dangerous?'

'It's Germany, but as a bookseller with an American passport, you can legally acquire various materials for your shop. At least this way, you'd be doing some good.'

Madeline smiled wistfully, thinking of her late husband. 'This sounds like something Alex would have been fascinated by. He loved anything related to espionage.'

Archie's eyes twinkled with understanding. 'I know, he was quite the adventurer. He always thought highly of you, and he often mentioned that you were the bravest person he knew.'

Memories of her husband filled her with a bittersweet ache. 'I can assure you I am no braver than the average person you know. In fact, I think Alex's death has made me more fearful.'

Archie leaned forward and took her hand. 'It takes a lot of courage to get up every day after the loss of a partner and keep running a business. I think you are braver than you realise,' he said gently. 'I think you are perfect for this role, but of course it is up to you.'

She drew in a breath as she considered his words. At least this way she would have the resources and a legitimate reason to travel to Germany, and maybe she could do some good.

'Okay, I'll do it,' she said, feeling her stomach clench with the nervous anticipation.

'Alex would be proud of you,' her friend encouraged, before

revealing more about the role. 'You'd be tasked with collecting information and microfilming it. And you would also rendezvous with a contact in Germany and one here in Paris to hand over what you've collected. You can't share what you are doing with anyone, even close friends or your family; it is for their own safety. It will take a little while to organise, but we will get an operative over to the shop to train you in the microfilm technology once everything is in place.'

Taking a deep breath, Madeline felt a weight of the situation settle on her shoulders. 'I will do what you need, but just until I find Ada. I'm not so sure I'm cut out for espionage.'

Her friend chuckled. 'You may surprise yourself.'

Madeline was driven by fierce commitment. She knew this mission could be dangerous, venturing into unknown territory both literally and figuratively. But no matter the cost, she also couldn't ignore the pull in her heart and the dangerous plight of a small boy.

7

LONDON, OCTOBER 2011

Olivia

The following morning, Livi arrived at her parents' cosy farmhouse to the enthusiastic barking of their Irish red setters, Duffy and Delilah. Her mother waved to her from the garden, where she was busy trimming her rose bushes.

As she exited her car, Livi admired her mother's grace. Though their facial features were very similar, Livi had inherited her sturdy, square frame from her father, in stark contrast to her mother's slenderer, graceful physique. Stephanie, a former dancer, now a full-time homemaker, still exuded the grace and elegance of her former career.

Stephanie greeted her daughter with a warm hug and led her into the farmhouse. The air was filled with comforting scents of freshly baked bread, lavender and wooden furniture polish.

Her mother paused. 'Olivia, you've cut your hair.'

Livi instinctively smoothed her hand through her newly shortened waves 'Oh, yes, I forgot to tell you.'

Her mother's excitement couldn't be contained as she

probed further: 'Have you met someone special?'

'No, nothing like that,' Livi responded hurriedly, cheeks colouring. 'Just a whim. I needed a change.'

'Oh.' Stephanie's voice carried a touch of disappointment. 'You know I'm always hopeful.'

Calling out to her husband upstairs, from where muffled banging sounds emanated, Stephanie rolled her eyes playfully at Livi, her frustration at her husband's preoccupation with decorating obvious. Meanwhile, Duffy and Delilah showered Livi with their exuberant welcome.

Steven entered the kitchen in his work clothes, specks of white paint in his wispy hair. He gave Livi a warm embrace, and she felt herself ease into the security that was home.

'You look like a little pixie!' He grinned.

They settled around the pine kitchen table and her mother served them home-made ginger biscuits as Livi pulled out the book she had brought from her bag and laid it in front of them. Stephanie examined the German poetry book with curiosity. 'This is lovely,' she remarked, turning it over in her hands.

Steven inspected the cover, nonplussed. 'Is there something unusual about it?'

'Not so much the book,' Livi said carefully, knowing her mother could be easily upset. 'But what was *inside* it.'

She reached into her bag and handed her mother one of the photographs of her great-grandmother alone standing in the garden, her fingers cupping a rose.

Stephanie's expression furrowed as she examined it, then let out an exasperated breath. 'Well, this is incredible,' she remarked. 'This was inside the book?'

'Yes,' Livi confirmed.

She showed it to her husband. 'my grandma Ada,' she stated, even though he must have seen a similar photo a thousand times in his own living room.

'Where did you come across it?' Steven asked.

'I was at an estate sale yesterday for my work. I was going through one of the lots, and this book was in there, along with this photograph.'

Her mother appeared incredulous. 'It seems unbelievable.'

'I know, that's exactly what I keep thinking.' Livi responded.

'Was the previous owner of the estate German?' Her father asked.

'No, actually, the man was from France.'

Stephanie strolled into the front room and returned with the photograph of her grandmother from the sideboard. Holding the two pictures side by side, they scrutinised them closely. It was undeniably the same person in the same location, and she was wearing the same outfit.

'How much do you know about what happened to Great-Grandmother Ada during the war?'

'I know very little about her,' her mother admitted, smiling at the photo in the silver frame. 'Your grandfather escaped Germany before things got worse, but he never shared much. Whenever I asked, he'd say he didn't remember. He was very young, and it deeply affected him. I always thought he knew more but chose to keep it to himself.' She sighed heavily as she added, 'As you know, I haven't seen your grandfather in a long time.'

'There is more,' Livi said, fumbling in her bag again and pulling out the letter and the other photographs.

The room fell into an eerie silence as Livi's parents stared down at the picture of Ada cavorting with a Nazi, their expressions a mix of bewilderment and distress. The weight of the new discovery hung heavily between them as Livi shifted in her seat with nervous anticipation.

Stephanie shattered the silence, her voice trembling as she struggled to put her thoughts into words. 'I can't believe this...'

Livi's father, usually buoyant, now wore a grave expression as he reached out and clasped his wife's hand.

'Could there be a link to this... Nazi officer and *our* family?' Livi asked, her tone guarded.

'Absolutely not!' Stephanie snapped, her tone sharp and defensive, a reflex to protect the ideal world she clung to. 'Dad would've mentioned it. She probably just attended a party.'

Livi ventured further, her eyes searching her mother's face for any hint of understanding. 'Or perhaps he felt too much shame.'

Stephanie recoiled, her features hardening at the suggestion.

Undeterred, Livi pressed on. 'There are love letters, too, referencing... *Auschwitz*.'

The word clearly struck Stephanie like a slap. 'No, I refuse to accept my grandmother associated with such monsters. You should destroy it all,' she declared, her typical way of dealing with anything she found unpleasant.

Shocked by her mother's quick dismissal, Livi stood her ground. 'But these letters are from before my grandfather's birth. This man might be my great-grandfather.'

Her mother sucked in a sharp breath. 'Even so, there's no proving it,' she retorted, pushing the letters away as if they were tainted.

'Do you think Grandfather Kurt might know something more?'

'He won't see you. You know that,' her mother responded sharply.

Livi's heart sank. The chasm between her and the reclusive grandfather had always been a silent source of sorrow.

Stephanie rose, her voice clipped. 'Nothing more to discuss,' she declared, sweeping the table clean and depositing the dishes in the sink. 'Some mysteries must be accepted as they are.'

'*Should* we accept it?' Livi asked softly. 'I could at least try to contact him.'

Stephanie's denial was quick. 'He hasn't seen you since you were a child; who knows if he'd even remember you.'

After the tense exchange, a heavy silence settled among them, that signalled to Livi that her mother considered the conversation concluded. Stephanie's movements were methodical as she began serving dinner, a homemade chicken pie, Livi's favourite.

They ate in silence, the uncomfortable tension in the room thickening as they grappled with the weight of this new revelation.

But as they wrapped up their lunch and Livi prepared to leave, she knew she simply couldn't just bury this. It was too unsettling to be ignored.

At the door, she faced her mother. 'I need to explore this, Mum.'

Stephanie became stern. 'Livi, what if you unearth terrible things that are better left hidden? This could mean shame and guilt for *all* of us.'

Livi felt the weight of her warning. But what choice did she have? She knew she would never sleep easy until she knew what had happened to her family, consequences be damned.

8

PARIS, JUNE 1940

Madeline

Three months later, the bright sunshine and azure skies of June painted a stark contrast to the sombre mood in Paris.

The once vibrant rhythm of the city had been replaced by an oppressive silence, pierced only by the heavy rumble of Nazi tanks crawling along the cobblestones, their swastika flags casting sinister shadows amid the beauty of the Parisian morning.

Amid the many shuttered storefronts, Madeline's bookshop stood defiantly open, a sanctuary in a city on the brink.

Watching through the window, the sight of the German soldiers – stark, methodical – marching past the shop felt surreal. The tumultuous roar of the invading force shook the ground, while the red-white-and-black banners of hate fluttered in the cool breeze.

Inside, the dimly lit bookshop was filled with the tense murmurs of Madeline's regulars. Monsieur Deveaux, his face lined with worry, clutched his hat against his chest as if seeking comfort in its familiarity.

'Madeline,' he whispered, barely above a breath, 'I never thought I would witness such a sight. What will this darkness do to the Paris that I love?'

Madeline placed a reassuring hand on his arm, her own heart heavy with the weight of his words.

A memory floated to the surface. How Alex would take her by the hand on rainy days, when the Parisian streets were empty, and dance with her among the book aisles as a favourite song played on the wireless. Their own little world between the rows of literary classics and the faint smell of leather-bound history. '*The evils of the world can never touch us in here,*' he would whisper into her ear as they twirled together, their laughter echoing through the quiet shop. And she would believe him, in those moments of stolen magic, feeling as though the weight of reality had momentarily lifted from her shoulders.

She wondered what he would make of all this. And if they would have found their own safety amid it all.

The shop bell jangled discordantly as Marcel barged in, his jovial countenance and dishevelled appearance a stark contrast to the sombre group.

'Why do you all look so sad?' he barked, a defiant gleam in his eye. 'The Germans will run this place better than we ever did.'

The other customers shifted uneasily as Monsieur Deveaux's face flushed with anger and disbelief.

Appalled by the suggestion, the old man spluttered out, 'How can you say such a thing? An enemy never comes to make a place better. They want to steal the Paris we know and make it German.'

'And what's wrong with that? You speak from a place of privilege, Monsieur,' Marcel snapped back, his resentment clear. 'I've had nothing but the backhand of this city, and now, maybe I'll have a chance to rise.'

The bookshop's patrons exchanged uneasy glances, each weighed down by the gravity of Marcel's bitter words.

Madeline felt a pull to respond. 'I understand your frustrations, Marcel,' she said, her voice calm yet resolute. 'But we must remember that these invaders are not here to uplift Paris or its people. They seek power and control, to extinguish the spirit of our city and its vibrant culture. We need to remain united; we cannot let that happen.'

Marcel harrumphed. 'I think we should at least give them a chance. It can't be any worse than what we have now.' The young man continued to mumble as he prowled around the shop. 'You are all ignorant of the struggles that people like me face every day. The Germans might bring change – maybe it won't be the change you want, but it could be the change *I* need.'

With that, he stormed out of the shop. Madeline watched him go. She knew a little of his background, and it was very dire. He had been brought up in the worst type of poverty, at the hands of an abusive father. She knew that Marcel's anger stemmed from a place of deep resentment and desperation. But despite all of his hardships, she had managed to reach him with books.

But now, she feared he could be easily influenced by the allure of power, even if it came from an occupying force.

After Marcel had left, Monsieur Deveaux rested his hand gently on Madeline's arm. His expression was grave, and his voice tight with concern. Leaning in, he whispered, 'Madeline, there's something I need to tell you, alone, something of the utmost importance.'

She pulled him into her back room so they could have some privacy. He spoke in a hushed tone. 'I am Jewish.'

The words hit her hard, not only because of what it meant in these tumultuous times but also because her late husband, Alex, had been Jewish. She had often wondered how much danger his life might have been in if he had lived through this time.

The older man continued. 'I fear for my safety, as you know I no longer have any family; they have all left me now.'

He was always so private; Madeline was taken aback by her friend's candour, and she ached for the weight that he carried.

She looked at the photo of his beloved family that he had pulled out from his pocket, and her heart swelled with empathy and understanding.

Monsieur Deveaux continued, 'I need to know that, if anything happens to me, there's someone I can trust with something very valuable. Can I count on you?'

Madeline lowered her voice, soft and reassuring: 'You can count on me, Monsieur. I'll do everything in my power to help you, I promise.'

Monsieur Deveaux returned to the shop one hour later, holding a wrapped box tightly. His eyes filled with anxious gratitude as he handed it to Madeline.

'If anything happens to me, Madeline, promise me you'll keep this safe until I return.'

Madeline agreed solemnly and tucked the box away securely; her mind raced with the responsibility she had just accepted. She looked up to meet his gaze, her eyes brimming with conviction. 'I promise you. This will remain safe with me. Whatever happens, I will not let you down.'

9

LONDON, OCTOBER 2011

Olivia

For the next two weeks, Livi's life revolved around a singular mission – locating her elusive grandfather, Kurt Armstrong.

It proved to be far more challenging than she had initially thought. She knew his name had been changed from something German when he had been adopted after the war, but he was hard to find. First, she tried the number her mother had given her, but it was disconnected. Then, an internet search yielded no results. Livi felt like she was searching for a ghost, a man who existed only in the memories of his estranged family.

Just when she was ready to give up, a flicker of hope emerged. She was phoning around her extended family, and a cousin informed her that he did have another number for Kurt. Hurriedly, she scribbled it down on a piece of paper.

She hung up the phone, and eyed the number warily as she reached for her coffee mug. Bringing it to her lips, she closed her eyes and inhaled the soothing aroma before taking a sip. The warmth spread through her chest but did little to calm the fear jumping in her stomach. She could do this, she told herself. He was her grandfather, after all.

Livi paced the kitchen, her steps echoing on the cool tiled floor. She clenched and unclenched her hands at her sides, fighting against the fear churning inside her stomach. As she gathered her courage to make the call, Tommy weaved between her legs, offering a comforting distraction in the midst of her anxiety.

She stopped pacing and drew in two deep breaths. Soft morning light poured through the windows, casting a warm, welcoming glow on the white kitchen countertop. Beyond the windowpane, the joyful sounds of children on their way to school wafted in, their laughter and chatter forming a poignant contrast to the heaviness Livi felt. 'He's family, for goodness' sake,' she rebuked herself.

The words of the therapist she had seen after her divorce echoed through her mind; '*Olivia, you can do hard things; you are stronger than you think.*'

Livi flipped open her phone and dialled the number.

The phone rang once, twice, and Livi's heart thudded louder with each ring. On the third ring, she bit her lip and braced herself for disappointment. The fourth ring came and went, and Livi prepared to leave a message, a prospect she despised more than talking to someone. But on the fifth ring, a sudden, abrupt voice answered.

'Yes?' The response was so gruff that it caught her off guard, and she momentarily forgot her rehearsed words. 'Who is it?' the voice on the other end demanded, its tone harsh and impatient.

'Hello. Is this Kurt Armstrong?' she finally squeezed out.

'I don't do sales calls,' the voice retorted, the irritation clear in the words. 'Don't call me again.' Her grandfather had a strong Scottish accent, but she could still detect the hint of a German accent beneath it.

'No, no, this isn't a sales call,' Livi hurried to explain before the connection was severed. She heard a frustrated sigh from the other end, signalling her grandfather's reluctance to engage in any conversation.

'My name is Olivia Stapleton; I'm your...' She paused for a minute and took a breath. '...*granddaughter*,' she finally managed to say, her voice quivering.

An uncomfortable silence followed, so profound that Livi wasn't sure if her grandfather had hung up, or if he had even registered her words.

'Hello?' she faltered, her voice barely more than a whisper. 'Can you hear me?'

'I can,' came the quick reply, dispassionate and devoid of emotion.

'My name is Olivia, and I'm your—'

'I heard you,' he cut her off, his impatience evident. 'I was just wondering why you're calling me.'

Livi struggled to find her words. 'Well, it's... I have something I wanted to talk to you about.'

'Go ahead,' her grandfather said, still unyielding in his tone.

'It's delicate,' Livi continued, her throat dry. God, this was worse than she had imagined. 'I was wondering if we could meet?'

'I don't have any money if that's what you want,' he responded abruptly.

'Oh, no, it's nothing like that,' Livi hurried to explain.

'Got yourself into some trouble, have you? Credit card that needs paying off? Boyfriend thrown you out? Believe me, I'm not the person to turn to. Go and get yourself a job.'

'I swear it's nothing like that!' Livi assured, regret for calling him already filling every inch of her being. She couldn't fathom how anyone could be so dismissive, especially when it concerned family. 'I just have a family situation that I wanted to talk to you about, to do with your mother,' Livi finally revealed.

The mention of his mother seemed to catch her grandfather's attention. His voice, almost a whisper, betrayed a hint of curiosity. 'I can't imagine there'd be anything about my mother you'd want to talk about.'

'I have items I believe belonged to Great-Grandmother Ada. I want to talk to you about them and I was wondering if I could come and see you—'

'I don't think that would be a good idea,' he interrupted, his voice growing colder. 'How did you get this number?'

'My cousin Bill gave it to me.'

'Well, he shouldn't have done that without talking to me first.'

Livi felt like she was clutching at straws, but asked, 'Could I give you my number in case you change your mind?'

'No,' he responded, his reluctance clear. 'I can't see when I would need it.'

With that, he abruptly ended the call, leaving Livi stunned, her mouth open. She had laid herself bare, reaching out to a family member who had shown no interest in connecting. She couldn't understand how a grandfather wouldn't want to see his grandchild, even out of curiosity. Her other grandparents on her father's side had been so wonderful, devoted figures in her life until their passing. It was incomprehensible to her that anyone could be this cold.

As she placed her phone down, tears stung her eyes and a familiar feeling of rejection gnawed at her, reminding her of her ex-husband's cruelty and disdain. The cold indifference of her grandfather stirred up memories she had tried hard to bury. That feeling of being completely unloved, powerless in the face of a forceful person.

Her ex-husband's words echoed in her mind. *'You're nobody, Olivia, utterly worthless.'* She forced them away.

Well, she would have to do this without her grandfather's help. She couldn't turn back now; the quest to uncover her family's secrets had consumed her, and she felt compelled to press on despite the emotional toll. But the pain of his rejection was jolting. The picture of the Nazi swam into her mind; was her grandfather the son of that evil regime? Was that where he got his cruelty from? She didn't know, but she would never call him again to find out.

10

PARIS, JULY 1940

Madeline

One afternoon while Madeline was organising her shelves, her youngest sister, Gigi, surprised her at the bookshop. Her body moved with its usual elegant way, betraying the fact she was a dancer. Madeline welcomed her sister with a warm embrace. 'I thought I'd see you at Benjamin's party!' she cried, giving her youngest sister a hug.

Gigi's impish grin lit up her face as she pulled out a box and placed it on the counter. Madeline stepped back a little cautiously. Giselle was well known for her high jinks and just the expression on her younger sister's face was enough to make Madeline a little wary.

Gigi urged her sister to open it. Inside was a little colourful tin music box, and, when she turned the handle and the familiar notes of an old French nursery rhyme filled the room, she felt a surge of love for her sister's kind gesture. However, her joy was short-lived as a bouncing clown suddenly sprang out of the box, causing both sisters to react with screams and laughter.

'You *wretch*!' Madeline exclaimed, catching her breath.

'I think he will love it, don't you?' Gigi responded, her face full of its usual mischief. 'I can't wait to give it to him.'

As they left the shop, Giselle and Madeline walked arm in arm. There was something special about the youngest and oldest sisters. Madeline had always felt it, ever since Gigi was a tiny baby and had been brought home to the small, crooked house in Montmartre, where a tumble of children had filled the space. Giselle had seemed so perfect, like a little doll asleep in her sun-filled crib, and Madeline had known at that moment that she would always be special to her.

They passed a censored newspaper stand, and Madeline bought a copy of *Paris-Soir* for her father and scanned the headlines, shaking her head in disbelief. It was nothing but a glorification of Hitler and his accomplishments.

'The new ballet is opening!' Giselle exclaimed with excitement, peering over her sister's shoulder at the paper. 'How exciting!'

Her sister pointed at the bold headlines. 'You're not concerned about the censorship of this news?'

Giselle waved a hand dismissively. 'Oh, this war won't last. Someone will see sense and deal with him before long.'

Madeline tucked the newspaper under her arm as they strolled toward their parents' home.

The sun cast a warm glow over the neighbourhood, painting the houses in hues of gold and amber. Birds chirped merrily from the branches, their songs weaving through the gentle rustle of leaves in the breeze. Laughter echoed from nearby gardens where children played, their voices carrying on the wind like delicate melodies.

'Benjamin is growing up so fast,' her sister remarked.

'I know,' Madeline agreed, her mind drifting back to the shock of Antoinette's secret marriage and surprise pregnancy. Antoinette, the most spirited of the Valette sisters, had always pushed boundaries.

'Isn't he a similar age to when we lost Pierre?'

The sudden shift in conversation caught Madeline off guard, mirroring her own grief from earlier that morning. She felt a pang at the mention of their brother. Born a year after their sister Isabelle, the two of them had been inseparable. His death in a fire in their mother's art studio had left a void in all their lives, especially Isabelle's. Madeline's heart clenched as she recalled a vivid memory: Pierre's laughter echoing through the house as they played hide-and-seek, his small hand clutching hers tightly as they raced through the garden. The memory, once a source of joy, was now tinged with sorrow at the thought of what could have been.

'He was four,' Madeline replied softly, pushing the pain of their brother's death to the back of her mind. She couldn't bear to recall his impish little face. 'But let's focus on happier things today,' she assured, squeezing her sister's arm.

The scent of their mother's pink roses greeted them from the top of the street and, as they opened the little gateway, Gigi snapped off a rosebud to sniff as they made their way to the open door.

'We're here!' Giselle shouted down the hallway.

'Who is here?' Called back their father from his little reading study.

'Your daughters!' responded Madeline playfully.

'Which ones?' He played along, knowing full well who it was by their voices.

'The *best* ones!' retorted Giselle, popping her head into the study; and then, spying her father curled up in his favourite armchair reading, she rushed to cover his face with birdlike kisses.

Their father, Bernard, chuckled and placed the book onto his little mahogany reading table, overflowing with a stack of them.

Madeline followed her sister into the study and, as the

tallest sibling, matched her father's height as they hugged tightly, then planted a loving kiss on both his cheeks. He was a kind, dignified man with a twinkle in his eye that seemed to have been passed down to all his daughters.

'Papa, how are you?' Madeline asked, her concern evident in her tone. This ongoing war had left everyone on edge.

He sighed and glanced at the newspaper that Madeline handed to him. 'Thank you for this work of fiction,' he said, shaking his head. 'Benjamin is waiting for you in the garden.'

The two sisters entered the little walled garden at the back of the house. It was a serene oasis of greenery and fragrant flowers, sure evidence of their mother, Delphine's, green fingers – a place of security and a stark contrast to the uncertainty of the world beyond the walls. Antoinette was sitting on a wrought-iron bench, her son, Benjamin, playing at her feet.

'You're here!' Antoinette exclaimed as she stood up, her long curly blond hair glowing in the sunshine. She embraced her sisters warmly. 'I'm so glad you could make it. Benjamin has been asking about his aunts all morning.'

Benjamin, a cherubic little boy with Antoinette's blond hair and mischievous blue eyes, looked up and beamed when he saw his aunts. 'Aunt Maddy! Aunt Gigi!'

Madeline scooped Benjamin up into her arms feeling the warmth of his tiny body against hers and showered him with kisses, while Giselle produced the colourful music box from her bag. Benjamin's eyes lit up with delight as he turned the handle and the familiar melody filled the air.

'Thank you, Aunt Gigi! It's wonderful!' he exclaimed, clapping his hands in glee.

It wasn't long before the rest of the Valette sisters joined them. Charlotte, the second youngest, who still lived at home, and Isabelle, who worked at the Louvre.

After they had eaten and cut the cake, Madeline left her sisters talking and laughing around the table. The warm aroma of the amazing meal still hung in the air as she gently knocked at her father's study door before entering.

Inside, Bernard sat in his cosy armchair, pipe in hand and glasses perched atop his nose, surrounded by walls lined with books. The rich, earthy scent of pipe smoke wafted through the air, mingling with the comforting aroma of aged paper and leather bindings. This was the place where Madeline's love for books and reading had begun on her papa's knee, evoking feelings of nostalgia as she entered the room.

She brushed past his desk and took a seat in one of the armchairs opposite him. Taking a deep breath, she handed him the letter from Ada without saying a word. As he read it, his face grew more serious.

'We can't even imagine what people are dealing with in countries worse than here,' he said. 'Did you know anything about this first wife?'

Madeline shook her head. 'Not until I got this letter. I have business for the shop in Berlin, so I'm going to try and find her. Though, I have no idea where to look.' She didn't elaborate on the real reason for her trip. She remembered Archie's clear instructions on secrecy.

Her father tapped his finger against his lips as he thought. 'You know, people are creatures of habit. Wherever this is, I bet he went back often – a man in a strange city who doesn't speak very good German would stay close to places he knew.'

His eyes lit up as he got up from his chair and went to his desk. He returned moments later with a stack of postcards, which he handed to Madeline. The worn edges felt smooth against her fingertips as she flipped through them, each one a tangible connection to her late husband.

'Alex knew how much I liked getting postcards,' her father said softly, a hint of nostalgia in his voice. 'Whenever he travelled he sent me some. They might help.'

Madeline hadn't even considered that idea before. As her

father's words sank in, hope swirled in her chest. She rose from her chair, her mind racing with unanswered questions.

'Madeline.' Her father's voice cut through the sounds of laughter and conversation at the party, drawing her attention. She turned to face him, feeling a knot tighten in her stomach at the solemnity in his gaze. He moved closer, his concern evident.

'Please be careful.'

She furrowed her brows and took a step back. 'I have my American passport. I'm not worried about getting in and out of Germany.'

'I wasn't talking about the Nazis,' her father replied softly.

Confusion clouded Madeline's features as she tried to understand his words.

'I'm talking about your *heart*,' he said gently, placing his hand on her arm. 'When we lose somebody, we will do anything to bring them back. Make sure this woman is telling the truth. The dangerous man she talks about could very well be the child's father.' He paused for a moment, then added with emphasis, 'It is very suspicious that she only just decided to tell Alex. Please promise me you won't be blinded by your grief.'

Tears welled up in Madeline's eyes as the weight of her father's words settled upon her. She blinked them back, fighting to maintain composure in the face of uncertainty. With a stuttering breath, she stepped forward, enveloping her father in a tight embrace.

'I will be careful, Papa,' she acknowledged, her voice barely above a whisper.

As she returned to the party, she knew she hadn't been entirely honest. Deep down, she wanted this to be Alex's child, and denying that desire was impossible.

The family spent the afternoon in the garden, celebrating Benjamin's birthday. There was more food, a picnic with delicious French pastries and sandwiches, and laughter filled the air as the sisters reminisced about their own childhood and shared stories of their adventures.

As the sun descended, Bernard unveiled a vintage gramophone, and the garden was filled with music. Delphine and Bernard swayed gracefully around the garden, their hearts entwined in a timeless waltz. Meanwhile, Gigi endeavoured to teach her sisters the Lindy Hop, an American favourite. Amidst their stumbling steps, infectious laughter continued to reinforce the sisters' unbreakable bond.

Catching her breath, Madeline observed them all with affection, her gaze shifting from Charlotte twirling Benjamin in circles to her parents and the others mastering the dance steps. As the night grew darker and the stars began to twinkle overhead, Madeline couldn't help but feel a deep sense of gratitude for the moments of happiness that life offered, in such challenging times.

But even beneath the soft glow of lanterns lit by their mother, amidst the music, laughter, and safety of her family home, Madeline's mind couldn't rest. The warmth and joy around her only heightened the stark contrast to the turmoil within as her thoughts kept drifting back to the letter. Anticipated danger cast a shadow over her happiness. Madeline knew that no matter how precious these moments were, a daunting journey awaited her beyond this familiar embrace.

11

LONDON, OCTOBER 2011

Olivia

When Olivia answered her phone two days later, the voice on the other end was instantly recognisable – her grandfather's rough baritone. He sounded oddly subdued and she could almost hear him squaring his shoulders as he spoke.

'Olivia, it's Kurt, your grandfather.'

As if she wouldn't recognise him. She'd been haunted by their last conversation.

'Yes,' she replied, her stomach knotting as she braced herself for whatever was to come.

'I have reconsidered,' he stated bluntly. 'If you still want to talk to me, you can visit me this weekend. But I want you to understand, I'm a private person, Olivia. I don't want you snooping around. And I will only talk about my mother in a way I am comfortable with.'

'Yes, of course,' Livi replied, her mind racing to understand his change of heart. 'I just have something to show you and a few questions.'

The phone call ended abruptly, and the weight of the

conversation settled in her stomach like a stone. His lack of an explanation left her puzzled. She couldn't shake the feeling that something was amiss, that maybe there was a hidden agenda behind his invitation.

Livi dialled her mother's number and anxiously waited for the call to connect. When she answered, the warmth of Stephanie's voice was reassuring.

'Mum,' she said, struggling to keep her voice steady, 'I just got off the phone with my grandfather. He called and invited me to Scotland for the weekend.'

Her mother sucked in a sharp breath of concern. 'Olivia, no! What did you say?'

'I agreed to go.'

She waited as her mother relayed the news to her father, who must have heard the concern in Stephanie's voice. He mumbled something in the background.

'Are you still sure you want to dredge up all this past?' her mother said with exasperation. 'Your father and I are worried about this. You know he can be difficult, and after what you've been through I'd hate to see you take a step back.'

Livi reflected on the overwhelming feelings of depression and anxiety that had consumed her after her marriage ended. However, she was committed to not letting those emotions hold her back.

'I'm okay,' she replied firmly, 'I need to do this – not just for myself but for our family.'

'Well, if that's your choice. I hate the thought of you going alone. I would go with you, but we have that blasted jumble this weekend, and your father and I are manning the white elephant stall...'

'I'll be fine. I'll just stay an hour or so, then get a little bed and breakfast for the night and come home the next day.'

She hung up the phone and took a deep breath. She could do this.

. . .

On the day of her departure, Livi's anxiety was heightened, but she resolved not to let it deter her as the mantra *You can do this, Livi* played on a loop in her mind.

At the station, she took a hesitant step onto the bustling platform, and was immediately engulfed in a sea of unfamiliar faces and frenzied movements. The air was charged with an electric energy that made her mind spin and her heart thrum against her chest. She hadn't left London in years, and the thought of venturing beyond its familiar borders terrified her.

She clutched the straps of her bag, the weight of it grounding her in the midst of the chaos as she forged ahead towards the train, knowing once onboard there would be no turning back. Entering the compartment, she sank into one of the comfortable seats and let out a sigh of relief as the train departed on time.

With her head resting against the train window, Livi took in three deep breaths as she gazed out at the passing landscape. The countryside flew by in a blur of vibrant greens and golden fields interrupted only by quaint villages and grazing livestock. Despite her elevated fear, a sense of calm washed over her as she watched nature's beauty unfold before her.

But as they crossed into Scotland, the scenery transformed into rugged mountains and valleys, and her thoughts returned to apprehension as she prepared to meet the grandfather she had only heard stories about. Would he be welcoming or distant? Would he even recognise her?

In an attempt to distract herself, Livi carefully sifted through the assortment of items she had brought to show her grandfather: the collection of old photographs, handwritten letters, and the worn poetry book. As she studied the photographs in more detail she noticed something she hadn't seen before. She had been so engrossed in studying the people captured that she hadn't noticed the tiny detail in the corner of one image – the name of the estate. Excitedly, she turned it towards the window for better light and squinted to make out the words. She spoke the words out loud – 'Herrenhaus Eichen-wald,' which translated to Oak Forest Manor in English. A spark of interest ignited within her and she reminded herself to look up the history of the estate when she got back home.

As Livi carefully placed each item back into her bag, her mind wandered back to the enigma of her great-grandmother's life, a woman shrouded in mystery. And her grandfather's tight-lipped demeanour and refusal to divulge information only intensified her curiosity and fuelled her need to unearth the truth of what had transpired so many years ago.

12

PARIS, JULY 1940

Madeline

Since the beginning of the occupation, Paris had been holding its breath, watching with fear the streets lined with the ominous grey uniforms and the dreaded Nazi flags. Day by day, the city was unravelling, its spirit threatened by the impending shadow of Hitler's vision. The hearts of the Parisians remained resilient, but fear gripped them, causing them to hold their breath, uncertain of what lay ahead.

Madeline's bookshop, once a hub of bustling literary activity, had fallen silent since the announcement of the occupation. It now served as a quiet refuge for mothers seeking stories to soothe their children's fears before bedtime, and a few faithful patrons in search of an escape from the grim reality. Everyone was busy, their thoughts fixed on survival.

One morning a young woman, clad in an olive-coloured coat entered with a cautious yet tenacious air. She stood as tall as Madeline, yet her build was robust compared to Madeline's slender frame.

She approached the counter, her hazel eyes meeting Madeline's with an unspoken understanding. The young woman didn't waste time on pleasantries. Her nervous gaze skipped around the room and she spoke in a hushed tone.

'Madeline Valette?'

'Yes.'

She handed her a small book.

'This contains instructions and details for your training.'

Every inch of Madeline tingled with alertness as she realised this was a Resistance agent.

'I will be back in a few days to work with you. To keep us safe we will use codenames. I am Falcon, and your codename will be Story Keeper.'

Madeline's pulse raced with the seriousness of the covert exchange, as she remembered that the information she recovered would aid the fight for the Allies.

As the young woman prepared to leave, a dark figure emerged in the bookshop doorway, and Madeline's breath caught in her throat at the sight of the unmistakable uniform of a high-ranking Nazi officer. Clutching the book, the agent had entrusted to her, Madeline felt a bead of sweat form on her palm. She glanced anxiously at the Resistance agent nearby, whose tense expression mirrored her own apprehension. The rhythmic click of boots on the hardwood floor reverberated through the shop as the Nazi advanced, his sharp gaze sweeping over the shelves. Time seemed to slow to a crawl as he approached the counter. Falcon discreetly pressed her hand against Madeline's, her fingers grazing the book. Her message was clear – hide the book containing the vital information. She then said in a nonchalant way, 'I will be back on Saturday afternoon to see if the book is available then.'

Madeline's heart hammered in her chest as she hurriedly stashed the forbidden book beneath the counter. In the reflection of the glass doors, she caught sight of her wide, horrified brown eyes, mirroring the turmoil within. With trembling hands, she brushed a strand of her bobbed brown hair behind her ears, attempting to regain her composure. Leaning on the counter for support, Madeline watched as the agent discreetly slipped away, leaving her alone to face the enemy.

The Nazi's rigid posture was a stark contrast to the warmth that once filled the shop.

'I am Commander Von Smit,' he introduced himself with an air of cold detachment.

She responded cautiously, her voice betraying a hint of unease. 'How can I help you?'

The Nazi officer moved with purpose towards the bookshelves, his gaze fixed on certain titles. 'We in the Nazi Party have strict standards for reading materials,' he explained, his tone cold and authoritative. 'We expect many of our soldiers to visit your establishment, so we must ensure that the books you carry meet our requirements.'

'Standards?' Madeline echoed, her apprehension growing.

'Books that are not Jewish, that promote healthy homes and families,' he continued, sliding a piece of paper towards her with a list of books to be removed from her shelves.

Madeline's heart sank as she read each forbidden title. 'Helen Keller?' she protested, her voice tinged with disbelief. 'What could you possibly have against Helen Keller?'

The edges of Herr von Smit's mouth turned downward, his expression unwavering. 'She is disabled and outspoken. She is to be removed from your shelves.'

Madeline shook her head slightly as she continued down the list, each item a blow to her love of books. Removing so many, including popular ones that had a hold on the hearts of many, would be a devastating loss.

'It will take me a while to do this,' she finally admitted.

Von Smit replied smoothly. 'If you need any assistance,' he said, his eyes narrowing, 'I can always provide help.'

Madeline struggled to maintain her composure, recognizing it as a veiled threat and understanding the need for caution.

After he left, Madeline's heart ached as she carefully removed each forbidden book from the shelves. The familiar titles taunted her, reminding her of the freedom that was being taken away. Tears streamed down her face as she tenderly packed them into boxes, and her mind raced with memories of her own love for reading and how many of these books had shaped her into who she was today. With newfound conviction, Madeline vowed to do whatever it took to preserve knowledge and fight against the oppressive regime. As she worked, she couldn't shake the thought of Ada and Kurt; if books were such a threat to the Germans, what chance did those deemed undesirable have?

Later that evening, as she delved into the pages of the book given to her by Falcon, her codename, 'Story Keeper', echoed in her mind like a battle cry, fuelling her desire to protect the written word at all costs. And even though the fear of what lay ahead still clawed at her, she drew strength from the memory of her husband and the bookshop they had built together. She was committed to staying strong and fighting for what she believed in, no matter the danger that awaited her.

13

SCOTLAND, OCTOBER 2011

Olivia

The grey, pebble-dashed semi-detached houses stood in neat rows along the narrow street. Among their uniform structures stood Livi's grandfather's home, its unkempt garden and creaky gate setting it apart from the rest. It wasn't lost on her how well this mirrored the neglected ties within their family.

She was anxious about confronting the reclusive man who had always been a shadowy figure in their lives, especially armed with the revelation that he might not even know he was the son of a Nazi. Olivia's resolve wavered.

As she approached the doorstep, a knot of anxiety tightened in her stomach. She hesitated for just a moment before mustering her courage and lifting the stiff brass knocker on the seemingly abandoned house. Did anyone even visit? Time stood still as she waited, wishing she was at any other door in the neighbourhood.

Finally, she heard a faint shuffling in the hallway, and the door slowly creaked open. The man who stood framed there had a stout figure, cropped grey hair and a sharp jawline, and the same shaped eyes as her mother. His attire was neat but modest – a tweed jacket in earthy tones over a white shirt, with trousers that had been tailored for easy comfort. He surveyed her with impatience, removing his glasses and fixing his gaze. An uncomfortable silence settled between them and there was a hint of irritation when he finally spoke.

'So, you decided to come then?'

She gave him a meek smile.

'You had better come in, I suppose,' he said, reluctantly stepping aside.

The interior of the house had no warmer welcome for Livi. Inside was a hollow void where life had seemingly retreated. Not a single family photograph marked the walls, no decorations breathed character into the space, and scarcely any furniture occupied the rooms. It was as if the essence of life had been stripped bare, reflecting a person who had no desire to create any warmth or comfort within its walls.

He gestured towards the cramped front room, and she followed him inside, feeling the weight of their strained reunion. They stood in awkward silence, until he broke it with a subtle sniff.

'You look just like my mother,' he said decisively before quickly changing the subject and offering her a drink, which she accepted obligingly. As he made tea, she lingered in the entrance of the kitchen, trying to maintain a disingenuous smile as she gripped her bag.

He turned and eyed her quizzically. 'You have somewhere to stay?'

'Oh, I haven't arranged any accommodation yet. I was considering a nearby hotel.'

'You can stay in the spare room,' he said, looking towards the kettle.

'I don't want to put you out,' she replied.

'Don't be ridiculous,' he said, almost sounding disappointed. 'You'll stay with me. It'd be wrong for you to go to a hotel.'

Despite her initial urge to reject his offer once again, she found herself agreeing. It wasn't merely out of politeness or from any desire to spend more time in the overbearing silence and cold that filled the house. It was something in his eyes when she had talked of a hotel – a glimpse beyond the detached façade he presented to the world. For an instant, she spotted a spark of longing for a genuine connection, and it was this fleeting glimpse that piqued her curiosity and swayed her decision.

After stowing her suitcase in the spare bedroom, she stood at the window, gazing out at the Scottish landscape. Its stunning beauty contrasted with the sadness that shrouded her grandfather's life. She lingered in the room longer than necessary, apprehensive about the impending uncomfortable silence in his company. She pondered how to breach his aloofness and establish a connection with him on some level.

The kettle's whistle prompted her to cautiously descend the creaking stairs, not wanting to disturb the ghosts that seemed to inhabit every corner of this house. She sat on the edge of the hard, grey sofa in the living room, surrounded by a stark white backdrop and dark grey furniture.

Livi swallowed down her anxiety, which was now starting to rise from her tightened stomach and constrict her chest. *You can do this*, she kept reminding herself.

Her grandfather appeared and handed her a chipped mug, and sat across from her, sipping his tea wordlessly. As if to explain his silence, he muttered, 'I'm not big into family, as you've probably noticed. I had my work, as a bookkeeper, which was very important to me, and now I'm retired. I like a quiet life.'

'Of course,' she said, 'I didn't mean to interfere in any way. I promise you I won't be here very long. I have a few questions and something I wanted to show you.'

'To *show* me?' His eyes narrowed and he appeared defensive.

Livi had wanted to postpone revealing what was burning a hole in her bag until he warmed up. But he demanded to see it immediately. So, with a sense of apprehension, she pulled out the book she had brought with her.

'I have this book,' she said, feeling uneasy as she handed it across to him. He stared at the cover.

'It's written in German,' she continued.

'Yes, I know. I still understand, though I haven't spoken that language for many years.'

'Have you seen it before?'

'A book of love poems,' he said, his tone implying she was wasting his time.

'It's what's inside I wanted to show you,' she continued, her voice faltering.

The moment he opened it and his eyes fell upon the photograph of his mother with the Nazi officer, his reaction was immediate and intense. He inhaled sharply, the air growing thick with his emotion. His face paled as he stared at the image, and for a heart-stopping moment it seemed as if he might collapse under the weight of the past.

'I thought you might be able to help. Tell me more about my great-grandmother,' she said, as her words spilled out in an attempt to bridge the awkward silence.

He raised a firm hand to stop her. It was as though he could bear no more than the haunting image before him.

Slowly, he lifted the photograph, his fingers quivering, and brought it closer, pulling out his reading glasses to scrutinise every detail. As his gaze lingered on the picture, it was obvious his thoughts were transported back to a time marred with pain.

Finally, he broke the silence, his voice heavy with emotion. 'Where did you get this?' he asked.

'At an estate sale in Oxford.' Her voice was tense, mirroring the emotional turmoil in the room.

He lowered the photograph, his gaze now fixed on the window as though seeking solace in the world beyond. She could sense the emotional storm churning within him and she longed to escape the heavy atmosphere that enveloped the room, leave this house and never come back. She had been so intent on getting answers, she hadn't really thought through how this might affect him.

As she watched him, a sense of foreboding washed over her, as if she had just handed him Pandora's box. In that moment, observing this man, who had been so indifferent to her, a grand-father she had never known, she glimpsed his vulnerability, and her heart actually ached for him. She wished she had never come to bring him so much pain.

14

PARIS, AUGUST 1940

Madeline

Paris in August should have been aglow with the last of summer's warmth. But the war had cast a shadow that even the sun couldn't dispel. Madeline's days were consumed now with preparations, learning the intricacies of microfilm photography – a skill that felt worlds away from her life as a bookseller.

In addition to her undercover work, Madeline harbored concerns for her business. The sight of vacant shelves, once adorned with cherished banned books, pained her deeply, and that, along with the threatened shortage of paper, added to her worries. Nevertheless, she viewed keeping her doors open as her own quiet act of resistance.

Monsieur Deveaux entered the shop, and as she watched him, she worried for the older man. He had lost a lot of weight and lived in constant fear. As he approached the counter for his usual newspaper, they exchanged friendly conversation while she retrieved his copy of Le Matin.

Engrossed in their discussion, she didn't even glance up when the bell rang.

But when Marcel arrived at the counter, sporting a new fascist armband, Madeline's muscles tensed. Monsieur Deveaux visibly cowered beside him. Marcel then demanded she display a propaganda poster, but she firmly refused, citing the bookshop's commitment to neutrality and the promotion of knowledge and freedom of expression.

Marcel's eyes narrowed, and his lips formed a thin line. 'Principles!' he scoffed, his voice dripping with disdain. 'Your principles won't save you when the Germans have won this war and punish those who didn't support them.'

Monsieur Deveaux, now visibly pale, mumbled something about needing to get home and hastily exited the shop.

Madeline stood her ground, meeting Marcel's gaze with defiance.

'Suit yourself,' he muttered, shoving the crumpled paper back into his pocket. 'This will not end well for people like *you!*'

Exhausted, Madeline closed up the bookshop early. As she waited for Falcon, thinking of all the hate around her, she couldn't help but feel unprepared for the dangerous world of espionage she was about to enter.

It was late afternoon when the agent finally knocked on the shop door. As well as her usual olive-green coat she had on a light cotton headscarf that concealed most of her face, hazel eyes and blond hair, allowing her to blend in with the crowd and maintain a low profile as she moved through the city's streets.

Though she appeared unassuming, Madeline always sensed an air of confidence and self-reliance radiating from Falcon. She reminded her strongly of her younger sister, Antoinette. Her devil-may-care attitude that blazed brightly in her eyes, made Madeline admire the young woman.

Madeline re-locked the door and ushered the spy upstairs. 'Would you like a drink?' she asked apprehensively, not sure of the protocol.

Falcon dismissed the idea with a sweep of her hand. 'I can't be here long; I have other stops to make this evening.' She pulled a small leather bag from her coat pocket and placed it on the table. 'Here is everything you need for your mission,' she said, her voice serious. 'The camera, and the film. Did you get a chance to read the book?'

Madeline affirmed she had and, taking the bag from Falcon, sifted through its contents. The camera was small and compact, with a leather cover that made it easy to hide in her pocket. The film was wrapped in a protective casing, and the instructions were written in small, precise handwriting.

'Here is a list of literature that is of high priority for you to collect while you are in Germany. Memorise and destroy the list once you have read it. You don't want there to be any trail. We are liaising with the British as well as the Americans on this. They are currently training up operatives and will help get the films to the Allies once you return. You should find a safe place to hide the books, papers and film in the bookshop until we collect them.'

Madeline looked around uneasily. She hadn't realised she would be keeping items in her home.

'We can also give you some special espionage weapons training, etc, before you go.'

Madeline's jaw dropped open. *Espionage weapons training?* She hadn't considered that aspect of her mission, and the thought of handling weapons made her stomach churn.

'I... I don't know if I'm ready for that,' she stuttered, feeling overwhelmed.

Falcon confirmed her understanding. 'We won't pressure you into anything you're not comfortable with. As a bookseller, you have a right to buy papers and collect books in other countries; make sure you are discreet when using your camera. But keep in mind that the more skills you have, the better equipped you are to handle any situation that may arise. You will be travelling to Germany, after all.'

Falcon's words landed heavy, as Madeline packed away the camera, remembering she was going into the very heart of Hitler's regime.

'How do I contact you if I need to talk to you?' she asked apprehensively.

'What is your favourite book?'

Madeline went blank momentarily, before thinking of Alex's face and answering hesitantly, '*Les Misérables*.'

'Good choice,' Falcon responded thoughtfully. 'Nice and thick. I'll stop by once a week, on Thursdays. If you have a message for me, leave it in that book using the code.'

'There is a code?'

'I can teach it to you now.'

Madeline responded eagerly, grateful for the offer. Falcon showed her how to use certain letters and numbers to represent different messages and instructions. It was complex, but Madeline was a quick learner, and she practised with Falcon until she felt confident enough to use it independently.

'Remember to be careful, and always be on the lookout for suspicious activity, and, most importantly, trust *no one*. You never know who might be an informant for the Germans,' Falcon warned as she prepared to leave. 'Finally, here is some money for your trip. When are you planning to leave?'

'I haven't decided yet,' Madeline replied truthfully. 'In the next week, I think.'

'Just remember to keep calm and blend in with the crowd,' Falcon said, sounding very motherly. 'And if things get too dangerous, leave the mission and come back. Your safety is our top priority.'

Madeline agreed, feeling a sense of reassurance from her words.

Leading her down to the back entry of the shop, the young agent bade her goodbye. 'See you Thursday,' she said with a wave. her dark clothes blending into the darkness outside. She was brave, confident and fearless, everything Madeline aspired to be.

Madeline returned to the darkened bookshop to make sure she had a copy of *Les Misérables*, and a memory came back to her. Finding little notes her husband had hidden for her between the pages of the book she was reading at the time. Each note was a tender expression of love, sometimes a quote, other times a new place to go for dinner or a reminder of an inside joke shared between the two of them. She still found these notes from time to time, a sweet whisper from the past that never failed to bring a tearful smile.

As she stood alone in the dimly lit room, the book in one hand and the list clutched tightly in her hand, she wished once again that Alex was here. His boisterous laughter and bright spirit would have been a welcome presence in this solemn moment. She could almost feel his arm round her shoulder, his lips brushing against her neck as he whispered words of encouragement. '*We will make an incredible team, my darling, you just need to trust yourself, Maddy,*' he would have said with his signature charm.

A pang of bittersweet loyalty surged through her as she thought about all they could have accomplished together. Alex would have been one of the first to eagerly join the underground Resistance movement, using his wit and bravery to outsmart their enemies.

But now, as she stood alone with only memories and a mission at hand, she knew that she had to carry on without him. She straightened her posture and took a deep breath, channelling Alex's unwavering courage.

Together or apart, she was committed to fighting for their country and his son.

15

SCOTLAND, OCTOBER 2011

Olivia

Livi's grandfather fell into silence for the rest of the evening, his emotions never more evident than when he carefully replaced the photo of his mother in the book. Dinner passed with minimal conversation, despite Livi's attempts to breach the walls he had erected. His gaze, laden with unspoken turmoil, spoke volumes, signaling his reluctance to delve into the past.

Respecting his need for space, Livi retired to bed after dinner, the chilly room and stark white sheets amplifying her feelings of isolation. As she lay awake, she pondered her grandfather's enigmatic past, longing for a deeper connection with him beyond the painful memories that haunted him.

The following morning, Livi got up and dressed for the day. Descending the stairs, she could smell and hear the sizzling of bacon and plates being moved around the kitchen. She was grateful for her grandfather's effort to make them breakfast. Reflecting on their strained interaction the night before, she hoped for a more open dialogue today, understanding that her grandfather's guarded demeanor was likely a result of years spent alone, shielding himself from the world. She wished, she understood him more. What had happened to him that was so terrible that he could barely talk about it?

In the kitchen, she found Kurt standing over the stove. His back was turned to her, his shoulders hunched, and she could see the tension radiating off him. As he nudged at the meat, he seemed a million miles away in his thoughts.

'Good morning,' she said softly. She wanted to say 'Grandfather', but it just felt too familiar for the current state of their relationship.

Startled from his thoughts, he turned around. 'Good morning, Olivia,' he replied, his voice tinged with weariness. 'I made breakfast for us. Would you like coffee or tea?'

'Tea would be great,' she replied.

Sliding down onto one of the chairs at the kitchen table, Livi watched as Kurt poured steaming water into the teapot with practiced ease; Livi struggled to find the right words. The atmosphere was heavy, closer to being alone with a stern headmaster rather than a family member. She longed to bridge the gap and find a connection, but she was unsure where to start or what to say.

She noticed there was a daily newspaper lying on the table; it looked as if he had already read it. There was a stack of newly paid bills beside it. He must have been awake for hours.

She watched as he deftly plated the crispy bacon on toast and set it down in front of her.

He then sat down beside her to eat. As they started their breakfast, the only sound was the scraping of their cutlery on their plates. The silence was unbearable, as Livi tried desperately to think of something to say.

Her grandfather cleared his throat. 'It is going to be cold today; I hope you brought warm clothes.'

She confirmed she had, and they returned to their breakfast in silence.

Livi finished eating, and was just trying to decide what was a polite amount of time to stay before excusing herself from the table when all at once he started to speak.

'It was a shock what you brought me yesterday. I wasn't prepared for how it would feel to see photos of my mother again after all these years.'

Livi watched his face intently as his voice trailed off, the words hanging in the air between them. She could see the pain grooved deeply in his face. It was clear that her grandfather was wrestling with a lifetime of emotions, memories and regrets. She wanted to offer comfort, to express her understanding, but the weight of their shared silence and distance held her back, especially after the way he had shut down the night before. So, she spoke tentatively.

'I'm sorry,' she began, her voice soft and sincere. 'I didn't mean to bring up painful memories for you.'

Her grandfather responded slowly, his gaze fixed on the table. 'It's not your fault, Olivia. It's a time in my life that I've tried very hard to forget.'

She wanted to ask a hundred questions: how his mother had died and when he had left Germany; but she sensed that pressing him further would only push him away.

He drew circles with his finger on the table anxiously as he continued.

'And there were other terrible things that happened during the war, things I have regretted for the whole of my life. Some pain never goes away, Olivia, and some pain is as raw today, even for me in my seventies, as it was when it happened in the 1940s.'

Suddenly, he stood up. 'I have something to show you.' He declared.

He ascended the stairs, the creaking indicating his climb toward the attic.

Upon returning, he cautiously opened a small dusty box,

revealing its contents. Carefully spreading them out on the table he cleared his throat.

'This is all I have left from that time.'

Livi looked down at the meagre pile: a battered book, a grainy picture of his mother, some old ticket stubs and a map, obviously drawn in a child's hand, and what looked like a good luck charm.

He sucked in air as he continued, not taking his gaze from the ketchup bottle, which he fidgeted restlessly with as he spoke, asking her again to show him the pictures.

He shuffled through them until he came to the photo of his mother and Frederick Mueller with the grapes.

His words were heavy, laced with both bitterness and sorrow, as he began to speak.

'I remember this man. His name was Frederick Mueller, and he was in the Gestapo. We lived with him.'

As the weight of his words settled between them, the room seemed to grow colder. She needed to know, even though she was afraid of the answer.

'Does that mean... he's your *father*?' she asked.

He looked at her with conviction. 'No!' he spat out. 'I will *never* accept that!'

Livi, more confused than ever, waited, hoping for him to elaborate. But when she finally asked for clarification, he just bristled.

Reluctantly moving on, Livi found another picture of her great-grandmother and held it towards him.

'How did your mother die?' She inquired.

All at once, he leapt to his feet. 'I don't want to talk about that,' he snapped, his voice raw with anger and pain.

He had seemed so calm talking about Mueller; she didn't expect his sharp response to her question. His eyes hardened and his jaw clenched as he nervously paced the kitchen.

Livi recoiled, shocked at the sudden shift in his demeanour.

She had unknowingly crossed into a forbidden territory, touched a wound that ran deeper than she could have imagined.

His forceful response shut Livi down, memories of her ex-husband's anger making her retreat, creating an impenetrable silence between them.

Her gaze returned to the photograph, as she gathered herself, and tried again.

'But—' She was about to say that it might be healing for him to talk about it.

He cut her off. 'No, Olivia, I told you before you came not to push me for answers. I have a right to my privacy.'

'I-I just want to understand,' she stammered, tears welling up in her eyes. 'I want to know about my family, about my roots. I want to know the truth.'

Sometimes the truth is a painful thing,' he spat out, his voice filled with bitterness. 'Sometimes it's better not to know. Rather than living with a terrible truth.'

His words landed like a devastating blow, crushing her hopes of uncovering more and leaving her no closer to unraveling the mysteries of her great-grandmother's past and the truth of her allegedly cursed heritage.

16

PARIS, SEPTEMBER 1940

Madeline

In the early morning light, on her day of departure, Madeline meticulously finished checking her suitcase. Inside, as well as a change of clothes, there was her husband's journal and Ada's letter; and, in an inconspicuous side pocket, she had carefully placed the tiny microfilm camera. Lastly, she clicked open the clasp on her handbag, checking inside one more time that she had the money Falcon had given her for the trip.

As she snapped closed her suitcase, she did her last scan of the list of most endangered literature, before striking a match and burning it in her fireplace.

For weeks she had carefully planned her trip, putting on a brave face while secretly battling her inner fears.

As she made her way down the stairs and cast one final glance at her dimly lit bookshop, a wave of terror washed over her in an icy chill.

She had entrusted Dominique with the running of the bookshop, but the thought of leaving Paris for an unknown amount of time, knotted her stomach. She hadn't left the city in so long, and the uncertainty of it all only heightened her dread.

As she stood in the darkened building, the memory of the last trip she had taken stung her; it had been with Alex just before he fell ill. Tears sprang to her eyes as she remembered their trip to Austria. She had loved Vienna's graceful blend of ancient and modern architecture. He had persuaded her to go for ball season. Her husband had been such a romantic.

They had danced the night away in a grand ballroom, lost in each other's arms. The way he twirled her around the floor made her feel like she was the only woman in the room. They had spent their days wandering the streets, hand in hand, taking in the sights and sounds of the vibrant city.

But then, Alex had fallen ill. It had started with a cough, and then quickly turned into something more serious. They had rushed back home to get him medical attention, but it was cancer. The doctors had done all they could, but he had passed away quietly in his sleep.

The memory of that trip was bittersweet for her now. She longed to go back to Vienna, to relive those moments with Alex once more, but she knew that could never happen. She wiped away her tears, trying to shake off the painful memory. It was time to move on; she had his son to find, now.

At the bustling station, Nazi soldiers stood guard at every corner, their cold, unfeeling eyes scanning every passenger with suspicion. Every inch of her body felt tense as she avoided eye contact and quickened her pace, knowing that this was just a foreshadowing of what was waiting for her in Berlin. Madeline refused to let fear paralyse her. She squared her shoulders and boarded the train, determined to see her mission through to the end, no matter the risks.

As the train rolled out of the station, Madeline pulled out her husband's journal, his words, as always, comforting her.

The train journey to Berlin was a never-ending nightmare;

her identity was repeatedly checked and at each station troops of German soldiers boarded the train, their heavy boots echoing down through the carriages. She tried to keep her composure, avoiding eye contact with any of them. It was warm on the train and the sweat glistened on her forehead beneath the brim of her hat as she gripped her handbag tightly.

When she finally arrived in the city, she felt suffocated by the atmosphere of fear and oppression that surrounded her. Everywhere she looked, Nazi flags were flying and propaganda bombarded her senses, a constant reminder of the danger she was in. She blended into the crowds, walking through the bustling city in a desperate attempt to avoid drawing any attention to herself.

She moved cautiously towards the guesthouse her friend had recommended, following the directions that Dominique had given her. But instead of the woman in her thirties that Dominique had described, a rather stern-looking older woman who eyed her suspiciously was behind the reception desk. Sitting next to her on a stool was a young man with the same stern-looking eyes. Madeline imagined he was probably the woman's son.

'Frieda is away,' the woman said cryptically when she asked about her. 'I am in charge of the guesthouse, now.'

Madeline felt a sense of unease wash over her, and she wondered if it was safe to stay here. She tried to remain calm and composed, not wanting to alert the woman to the fact that she was concerned. 'I'm just looking for a place to stay for a few nights. I have some business to attend to in the city.'

The woman studied Madeline for a moment before saying brusquely, 'We have a room available.'

Madeline followed the woman up a flight of stairs and down a narrow hallway. The room was small and modestly furnished, but it was clean. Madeline thanked the woman and settled in for the night, her mind racing with thoughts of her mission.

. . .

The next morning, she was preoccupied as she got dressed. First, she had to contact the agent Falcon had told her about, then she had to start her work for Archie.

Madeline left the guesthouse her strides purposeful as she navigated her way towards the designated meeting spot. She was terrified as she walked through the crowded streets, knowing that if she was caught with her camera the consequences would be dire.

At the café, she sought out Swift. She spotted a young woman sitting at a small table, wearing a red scarf and reading a newspaper, just as Falcon had described.

The woman wore an expression of cool detachment, her stunning features reflected a steely resolve, evident by the subtle tightening of her lips. Her short blond hair was neatly cropped, framing piercing green eyes that seemed to miss nothing.

As Madeline approached, Swift remained engrossed in her newspaper, a subtle gesture that belied her astute awareness of her surroundings. As she slid nervously into the seat next to her, Swift acknowledged Madeline with a mere flicker of her eyes, before returning her gaze to the printed page.

Without looking up from her newspaper the agent spoke quietly. 'You must be the one Falcon sent.'

'I'm Story Keeper, yes.'

Swift lowered her newspaper before gesturing for a waiter to take their order. Once he was gone, she spoke again a sardonic smile playing on the corner of her lips. 'Welcome to hell; what do you need from me?'

Madeline took a deep breath and recalled the list of literature and newspapers she needed to collect. Swift listened carefully, taking notes in a small notebook. When Madeline had finished, she handed her a slip of paper with a few addresses and names scrawled on it.

'Those are the shops and places that may have what you need.'

Madeline hesitated for a moment, but couldn't miss this opportunity. This woman was obviously knowledgeable.

'There is one other thing.'

Swift raised an eyebrow.

'I am trying to find someone,' she whispered, her voice steady despite her fear, her fingers twisting nervously in her lap.

The agent studied Madeline with curious eyes as if weighing her up. She leaned in closer, the hum of conversations around them fading into the background. 'Finding people in Germany these days is a lot more difficult than books; they go missing all the time.'

Madeline matched her movements, also drawing closer. 'A young child's life is at risk.'

Swift's expression softened, a flicker of empathy crossing her face. Scanning the café for any signs of eavesdroppers, Swift spoke again. 'Tell me everything you know. Every detail could be crucial.'

As Madeline recounted Ada's story, Swift lit a cigarette, her face a mask of concentration. When Madeline finished, Swift considered her words and there was a heavy silence between them, broken only by the subtle clinking of cups and saucers nearby.

'I may be able to help,' Swift finally said, exhaling a large cloud of smoke and crushing the remains of her cigarette into an ashtray. 'I have a friend who works in the records department. She may be traceable, unless she has changed her identity and gone into hiding.'

Hope surged within Madeline at Swift's words, only to be dashed by her next comment.

'You should know, if the Gestapo is involved she is probably dead or in a camp, and if she is alive and hidden away it will be dangerous. They have spies everywhere, and tracking someone who is in deep hiding is nearly impossible.'

'I understand,' Madeline responded, her voice cracking with raw emotion.

Swift's gaze softened as she looked at Madeline, her tone wistful. 'You loved this man deeply, didn't you? To risk so much for his child.'

Tears welled up in Madeline's eyes as a wave of grief washed over her taking her unaware.

'Yes, I still love him,' she confessed, her voice pulsing with the heartache of loss. 'I'm committed to the war effort, but this is my real reason for being here.'

Swift nodded, 'love can drive us to do the most courageous things, especially in the darkest of times," she stated, philosophically, before affirming her support. I will do everything I can to help you. Meet me back here the day after tomorrow, same time.'

Madeline took the list of bookshops, thanked Swift and left the café, her mind racing with thoughts of what lay ahead.

Over the next few hours she travelled to various parts of Berlin, collecting the literature she needed. She had to be careful at each stop, keeping her guard up. But despite the risks she managed to collect most of what she needed literature, newspapers and books.

At the end of the day, she had one final stop. Pushing open the heavy wooden doors, she stepped into the Berlin central library. The air was thick with the mingled scent of sweat and ammonia, overwhelming her senses. Despite her efforts to remain composed, her skin prickled as she absorbed the vast, unwelcoming space. Towering shelves lined the walls, filled with German titles that loomed above her, evoking a sense of intimidation despite her fluency in the language. The symbols of the Reich were ubiquitous, from the abundance of swastikas to a large portrait of the Führer himself, all serving as a stark reminder of her presence in Hitler's domain.

She combed the library, scanning for the elusive business directories she required. But amidst the towering rows of books, her search proved futile.

With no alternative, she summoned her most charming smile and approached the information desk. An elderly, balding man was looking down at a pile of books and stamping methodically inside the front covers. She waited for a few seconds before, finally, he slowly closed the last book and pushed his spectacles up his nose before acknowledging her.

'Yes?' he asked, his tone sharp.

'My husband asked me to look up a business address for him. But, unfortunately, I only just remembered, and my home is far away. And now he needs it urgently. Do you have, by chance, business directories here?'

Blinking from behind his spectacles, the librarian responded, somewhat affronted. 'Of course, we have them. The business section is at the back. I'll show you.'

He slowly moved from behind his desk, opening and shutting the hinged counter that kept him apart from everyone else, and ambled towards the back of the room.

She noticed that he was meticulously dressed and radiated authority. This was his empire. She could tell by how he checked for dust or moved a chair back into the correct position as he travelled through the room. He tutted when he saw that some books had been left out on a table, and picked them up and replaced them on the shelf before he continued on his way.

Madeline's heart was now pounding so hard she could hear it in her ears. She knew what she had requested was innocent, but it could mean everything to the Allies as they began collecting targets to bomb.

The man escorted her to the back of a set of shelves in a dark corner.

'What is the business you are looking for?' he asked bluntly.

Madeline stuttered out the first thing that came to her mind. 'Haberdashery.'

'Haberdashers are on the bottom to the left,' he informed her, 'in the book under "H"; you can't miss it.' He said it as if he was speaking to a small child.

He shuffled away, and she waited until his footsteps had quietened before she looked over her shoulder and pulled out the actual directory she wanted, German industrial manufacturers. She opened it slowly, looking over her shoulder again, and turned to the first page. She nervously pulled out her camera that she had concealed in her bag, but it slipped from her shaking hand and clattered to the floor. She swore and looked around again as the sound echoed up and down the chambers. She waited another couple of seconds, but nobody came.

Quickly, she lifted the camera and started to take photographs of the manufacturing company addresses.

Archie had made it clear that they would need these to help locate targets. They wanted to know not only where were the warehouses that contained ammunition, something that would be kept top secret, but more importantly the location of manufacturers that produced materials used in ammunition production.

She continued to flick through the directory, photographing page after page, looking over her shoulder every few minutes to ensure she was alone.

When she was finished, she carefully placed the directory back, knelt down and picked up the haberdashery directory. She copied down a random number, then placed the book back. Checking her camera was concealed again, she took in a deep breath before cautiously navigating her way back through the room.

The same man behind the counter looked up and watched

her intently, his eyes peering from below his glasses as she held up the piece of paper towards him with a smile, not believing what she had just done.

When she got outside, she was sweating, her hand cramping, and she felt light-headed. This mission would be far more taxing than she had anticipated, but it was a sacrifice she was willing to make to find Ada. Yet, as she made her way down the street, a prickling sensation crept up her spine, a nagging feeling that she was being followed.

17

BERLIN, SEPTEMBER 1940

Madeline

Madeline awoke to a disconcerting unfamiliarity and as the weight of her mission in Germany settled back upon her shoulders, she braced herself for another day navigating the complexities of Hitler's Germany. Her initial experiences had been deeply unsettling. It wasn't just the propaganda, or swastikas on every corner that had most disturbed her, it was the atmosphere, the pervasive sense of fear and oppression that hung in the air that was in such juxtaposition to the arrogance and bravado displayed by the Nazi regime.

In France, the Nazis' unwelcome presence was just as looming, but the French resisted with a fierce tenacity that seemed to challenge the occupying forces. But here in Germany it was different; the very essence of the people seemed to have been suffocated as if they were just resigned to their fate.

As she prepared for the day, Madeline's thoughts lingered on Alex, the heart of her mission. Today, she would seek the coffee shop he had chronicled in his journal. With the city just beginning to stir, she ventured out. Even this early the oppressive regime was on display, from the intimidating soldiers patrolling the sidewalks to the propaganda posters plastered on every wall.

Despite the chilling atmosphere, Madeline pressed on. Her journey took her across town to The Tiergarten, the park Alex had written about in his journal.

Here, her mood shifted dramatically. The entrance gate welcomed her into a serene oasis, offering a tranquil respite from the city's oppression. The scent of freshly cut grass and the distant laughter of children playing enveloped her, offering a fleeting moment of solace amidst the chaos of war.

Yet the vastness of the park only served to remind Madeline of the difficult task ahead. Finding Alex's coffee shop amidst the labyrinth of city streets felt daunting.

Taking a break on a weathered park bench, she sifted through the postcards from Alex's travels, hoping for a clue. Each one depicted a different part of Berlin, with colourful pictures, and each one contained heartfelt messages from her husband. But none had a picture of a coffee shop. She scanned the words he had written, her stomach clenching as she recognised the familiar voice of her husband echoing through the handwritten cards. As she enjoyed the carefree loops of his handwriting and quirky observations, memories flooded back, bittersweet moments of their life together. He had so loved to travel, and had been in awe of new places and experiences.

She swallowed down the lump in her throat, pushing aside the ache of longing as she focused on the task at hand. She couldn't afford to get lost in her emotions now; there was too much at stake.

She was just gathering the postcards to put them back in her bag when she noticed something. One was dated just a day after the journal entry about Ada. Excitement began to seep in as she realised, he could easily have sent it after his visit to the coffee shop.

She shuffled through the other postcards, searching for any that had been sent at the same time, but none of them matched. There was something else, too: all the others had been posted from one post office except for this one. She remembered her father's words about people being creatures of habit. This post office might be nearby.

She looked around and spotted a young couple walking hand in hand through the park, their gentle laughter filling the air. She approached them, mustered her confidence and asked for directions.

The post office was nearby, and Madeline thanked the couple for their help, her mind buzzing with anticipation. She soon spotted the old post office, its weathered exterior standing out among the modern buildings surrounding it.

'Okay, Alex,' she said out loud to herself as she scanned the area, 'where is your coffee shop?'

There wasn't one to be seen, but there was a little side road that seemed to lead to a quieter part of the city. She decided to follow her intuition and turned onto it.

As she walked further, the noise of the bustling city gradually faded away and was replaced by a sense of tranquillity. The buildings became smaller and less grandiose, with quaint shops and cafés lining the streets. She noticed a sign for a coffee shop.

Madeline's pace quickened as she approached it. She noted it had a charming exterior. She peered through the window, her eyes scanning the interior for any trace of familiarity from the journal entry. But it was clear that this was not the place Alex had described. It was cold and austere, with large gold-rimmed mirrors and marble countertops. Customers sat in cold isolation, and it lacked the warmth and cosiness that Alex had described as she recollected his words.

The interior was warmed with vintage furnishings, each piece

telling a story of its own. The wooden chairs creaked with age,
and the tables bore the marks of countless conversations.

Disheartened, she continued down the street, searching. There was a second coffee shop further down. This one had a more modern aesthetic, with large windows and small metal tables. But once again the sleek and minimalist design of the coffee shop was a far cry from the warmth and nostalgia Alex had described.

Madeline started to feel discouraged. How many coffee shops could there be in Berlin close to The Tiergarten? She was just about to double back and try one of the other streets close to the park when she saw a tiny sign.

The third coffee shop had an old-fashioned charm that seemed to resonate with the description in Alex's journal. Its exterior was covered with window boxes bursting with vibrant flowers, and the smell of freshly brewed coffee wafted out onto the street. Madeline's heart skipped a beat as she pushed open the door and stepped inside.

The interior was warmed with vintage furnishings, just as Alex had described. The wooden chairs creaked with age, and the tables looked as if they bore the marks of countless conversations. The soft glow of dimmed lights cast a warm ambience over the cosy space, and the sound of quiet chatter mixed with the gentle clinking of coffee cups filled the air. Madeline felt an overwhelming sense of familiarity wash over her. This was just the kind of place Alex would have loved.

She stepped fully inside, but her feet froze in place as she caught sight of the majority of the clientele.

Many of them were dressed in Nazi uniforms, their presence casting a dark shadow over the once inviting atmosphere Alex had described. Madeline's heart sank as she realised that she had stumbled upon a coffee shop frequented by German soldiers. Fear clung to her skin, threatening to overwhelm her, but she advanced further inside, not wanting to look as if she had something to hide. As she searched for a table, the soldiers cast curious glances in her direction.

She could feel their eyes boring into her back as she searched for a seat. Every step she took felt laden, the weight of their gazes suffocating her. She finally found an empty table near the corner and quickly took a seat, trying to blend in with the few civilian patrons scattered around the room. She was desperate to occupy her hands and divert attention away from herself, so she reread the postcards.

As she waited to be served what passed for coffee during the war, the aroma of stale tobacco and bitter chicory filled the air as Madeline glanced around the room, observing the interactions between the soldiers and the civilians. It was clear that tension filled the air, yet there was an unspoken understanding between them. The soldiers seemed to keep to themselves, engrossed in their conversations and occasional bursts of laughter. The civilians, on the other hand, appeared wary and cautious, casting furtive glances in the direction of the those in uniform. That's when she saw it. In the corner was a bulletin board, though now it was far from overflowing with vintage postcards and pictures, as Alex had described it. She drew in breath as she saw a tiny metal cat above it. This must be the right place. Tears welled up as she realised her husband had sat in this room. But she would not ask about Ada here. Everything inside her screamed danger. Something had obviously changed since the time Alex had written about it. Now, the atmosphere was heavy with an undercurrent of fear and unease.

Her *ersatzkaffee* arrived, a coffee substitute. She took a cautious sip, attempting to calm her nerves while planning her next move. Aware of the soldiers' presence, she felt uneasy lingering too long. Two of them, their uniforms disheveled and hats pushed back, sat nearby, occasionally glancing in her direction. Wisps of smoke curled from their cigarettes as laughter punctuated their hushed conversation. Getting the distinct feeling that they might be discussing her, Madeline decided to hasten her exit.

Just as she settled her bill, she caught a snippet of conversation between the waiter and an older couple behind her.

'But I have always ordered schnitzel here; Herr Braun makes it especially for me.' The older man implored.

The waiter's response was cold. 'He no longer works here. We have new management now.'

She heard the couple gasp in disbelief, the woman's voice tight as she asked why. She turned to see the waiter simply shrug, and shove a new menu at them. Madeline started to put the pieces together. There was a new manager, which explained the change in atmosphere and the presence of German soldiers. The absence of Herr Braun was an unfortunate example of the shifting dynamics of the city in a town under Nazi rule and it was clear that this was no longer the haven Alex had described.

Stepping back outside of the coffee shop mentioned in her husband's journal, conflicting emotions surged within her. Feelings of betrayal at the thought of her late husband meeting another woman here mixed with her unwavering commitment to finding his son. She pushed down her own desire for answers in light of the needs of a little boy as she strode away. "I'm sorry, Alex, she murmured, tears welling up, 'But I promise you, I will find them.'

18

LONDON, OCTOBER 2011

Olivia

Livi's mind wandered as she rode the Underground to work the following day, the rhythmic rumble of the train offering a backdrop to her thoughts. As she glanced out the window, she noticed a solitary, older man standing on the desolate platform, his silhouette cast long by the dim light. Memories of her grandfather's lonely existence resurfaced, tugging at her heart with a heavy hand. She couldn't shake the image of him, surrounded by his meager belongings, his solitary life so isolated.

Something uncomfortable stirred in Livi. She had been trying to ignore it, but the truth was she harbored a deep-seated fear of ending up the same way.

When she had left Graham, she hadn't planned to be single this long, but now she feared she would never trust anyone again. She remembered Kurt's words the night before she left Scotland, as he pushed the dusty box he had shown her into her hand. 'Take these things, I have no reason to look back.'

Sensing his pain, she had leaned forward and covered his hand with her own and had been shocked when he'd flinched at her touch but he hadn't removed it and she had wondered with great sadness when was the last time someone had touched him.

Pulling out the things her grandfather had given her, she looked at them again. A faded, crayon-drawn map tugged at her heartstrings. It was hard to imagine a young Kurt sketching it. What had compelled him to draw it? Opening the battered book, Livi noted that it was written in Yiddish, and was perplexed. They weren't Jewish – how had it come into young Kurt's possession, especially with the wartime book burnings?

Inspecting the book more closely, she noticed an official-looking nameplate. She strained to read the faint printing, and gasped at the name Herrenhaus Eichenwald – the same manor she had seen in the old photograph of her great-grandmother. Could this manor be where Kurt grew up, and possibly where Ada had lived?

The Underground stations flashing by the window dimmed, replaced by haunting images of a dark manor entwined with her family's past. Staring again at the photo of her great-grandmother with Mueller, Livi realised there were many questions that needed answers. Did this German manor hold some of them?

Stepping out the Tube, Livi transitioned from the hustle of modern-day London into the timeless charm of Cecil Court, and made her way towards the antiquarian bookshop where she worked. Nestled between Charing Cross Road and St Martin's Lane, this hidden alley in the heart of London was like stepping back in time. The well-used path beneath her feet, slightly uneven and worn down by centuries of footsteps, echoed with a history that seemed to whisper through the air.

The Victorian shopfronts, with their wood-framed windows and inviting displays, housed an array of antiquarian bookshops, each with its own unique personality.

Known as 'Booksellers' Row', this enclave, which seemed insulated from the city's chaos, was a haven for bibliophiles and collectors, a sanctuary for those in pursuit of rare first editions, obscure titles and beautifully bound works.

Approaching the shop where she worked, Livi admired the ornate sign that hung above the shop door. The gold lettering, slightly faded but still elegant, announced the name of the bookshop, Quill & Quire. This was a place she had come to cherish as a second home. Despite its compact size, the shop was a treasure trove of literary history, with every inch occupied by books arranged on towering shelves. A display case under lock and key held the most precious volumes, while a cosy nook offered a plush armchair and Persian rug for readers.

The owner of the shop and Livi's boss, Mr Milner, had a quirky and offbeat taste and the interior reflected that. The walls were adorned with vintage posters, handwritten letters and ageing prints of famous authors. Her boss was already behind his desk, engrossed in a thick volume of Voltaire plays. His wiry build and unkempt silver hair gave him an air of wildness and wisdom and he was the kind of older person that you just couldn't quite age. Though she was sure he was way past retirement age, he had an energy and enthusiasm that was much younger and defied his years. His passion for his work radiated from him, making the bookshop feel alive.

'Good morning,' Livi greeted him as she approached the desk.

Mr Milner looked up. 'Ah, good morning, Olivia,' he said, setting the book aside. 'So, where's this book from your grandfather you told me about on the phone yesterday?'

Livi began to chuckle. 'Let me at least get settled,' she teased, slipping out of her woollen coat and hanging it on the rack beside the desk. 'I have quite a story to share.'

As she hadn't been in the shop for a while, she began at the beginning, telling him all that had happened at the auction and then the visit to her grandfather's. She was careful to leave out the part about her maybe being related to a Nazi. She still wasn't quite sure how she felt about all that. It was crazy to feel guilty, but she did.

He listened intently, shaking his head in disbelief at certain parts of the story.

'I can't believe you went all the way to Scotland. I am proud of you and I do have some good news for you, about the Hesse you told me about. I think I have a *very* eager buyer.'

When he mentioned the price he had negotiated, her mouth dropped open in astonishment. It was a substantial sum, far more than she had ever anticipated. Relief washed over her. The weight of her financial worries suddenly felt lighter.

'Now your the book,' he said impatiently, his fingers wiggling with anticipation and his eyes gleaming. Livi reached into her bag, careful not to crush the delicate package, and pulled out the small, leather-bound book with faded gold lettering on its cover.

'This is it,' she said, placing the book gently on his desk. 'My grandfather brought this back from Germany.'

The elderly shop owner's eyes sparkled as he took the book from Livi and gently opened it to inspect the contents. His fingers brushed lightly over the delicate pages. As he slowly moved through the book, there was the slight smell of paper and leather. Livi's favourite.

'It is in Yiddish,' he whispered, his voice filled with awe. 'A rare find indeed. How did this escape the Nazis during the 40s, I wonder?'

'I'm not sure; my grandfather is reluctant to talk about his time in Germany. But he must have held on to this book for a reason, hidden away in his attic, for all these years. But look at this,' Livi said, turning to the front pages. She pulled a reading lamp closer, as Milner pulled a magnifying glass from his drawer.

He read out the words slowly. 'Herrenhaus Eichenwald.

Herrenhaus is "manor", isn't it? But you're the German speaker – what is Eichenwald?'

'The translation is Oak Forest,' Livi said. 'I looked it up. The manor is in Berlin.'

'Interesting,' Milner mused, his eyes narrowing in contemplation. Then he sighed. 'I'm actually due to go to Berlin this month. I have to hand-deliver a very fragile book to another dealer. I'm not really looking forward to it.'

He narrowed his eyes at Livi as he thought. 'I don't suppose you would be interested in going instead, would you?' Then, apparently remembering her anxiety, he shook his head. 'Of course. Though my fellow antiquarian may know a lot more about books from that area than I would.'

'Yes,' she said before she could stop herself. 'I'll go.'

Mr Milner looked at her with surprise and delight. 'Are you sure, Livi? Two trips out of town in one month? That's more than I have known you do since I've met you.'

Livi hesitated for a moment, her mind racing with thoughts of the unknown and the possibilities that lay ahead. But deep down she knew that this was an opportunity she couldn't pass up. Milner would pay all her expenses – and, now she had money coming from the Hesse, she had a little extra herself.

'Yes,' she said with newfound conviction. 'I'm sure. I want to go.'

But as she travelled home that evening on the crowded Tube, Livi couldn't help but feel a tinge of apprehension. She hadn't left England in years before and the thought of going to a strange country on her own terrified her. But beneath all the fear she had an overwhelming, burning need to find out all she could about her family's dark past.

That night she woke up after a terrible nightmare of being lost in a foreign city, unable to find her way back home or speak the language. The dream left her feeling shaken and uncertain about her decision and doubts crept into her mind like shadows, whispering words of caution and fear.

In the darkness, her ex-husband's face flashed into her head. And she felt tears begin to well up in her eyes. It had been years since she had last seen him, but she could still hear his voice in her head as if it was yesterday. '*You'll never be able to do anything on your own, you're just too weak. You're pathetic, Olivia!*'

Livi's hands formed tight fists. Those old, haunting words wouldn't hold her back any longer. She had carved out a new life, finding strength she never knew she had. Berlin was her chance to prove she could stand on her own two feet.

The thought of boarding a plane and diving into the unknown sent a jolt of anxiety through her. But she couldn't let fear win, because she had to get to the bottom of her great-grandparents' story in order to find out who she really was.

Livi resolved that she was going to do this – and she was going to do it on her own.

19

BERLIN, SEPTEMBER 1940

Madeline

As Madeline rushed back to her room at the guesthouse, she patted her coat pocket, making sure her camera was still hidden. But as she unlocked her bedroom door, an uneasy feeling flooded over her. The room felt slightly off; something wasn't right. Then she saw that her suitcase wasn't closed, as she had left it.

Madeline combed through her belongings. Nothing seemed to be missing or out of place, yet the feeling of being violated persisted.

Her gaze landed on Alex's journal. One of its pages was carelessly turned over. She tried to rationalise what she was seeing. Maybe the maid had accidentally knocked over her suitcase and quickly tried to tidy it up? But, deep down, Madeline knew there was more to it than that.

Clutching the journal tightly, she felt a surge of protectiveness for Alex's words. This was their story, their memories. Someone had invaded her privacy.

Then, with a chill, she remembered passages in the journal

discussing Jewish holidays they had celebrated together. Whoever had read this journal now knew of her late husband's Jewish heritage.

A memory resurfaced from the previous day – the unsettling encounter with Frau Kaufmann, the owner of the guesthouse. The way she had stared at Madeline with piercing, distrustful eyes. Was that who had read the journal? What would the woman do with what she had found out?

An hour later, Madeline went down for dinner, hiding the journal beneath her clothes.

The dining room was bleak, with heavy wooden furniture and dimmed lighting. The other guests were scattered sparsely across the room, their hushed conversations creating an eerie atmosphere.

Frau Kaufmann entered the room, her steely gaze fixed upon Madeline. Their eyes met for a split second, but in that brief moment Madeline sensed a deep hostility emanating from the woman.

Dinner was a tense affair, with Madeline hyperaware of everybody in the room and a cold pit of dread growing in her stomach as a clock slowly marked time in the corner.

What had made her think she could do this? She suddenly felt very foolish for taking on this mission. She wasn't a spy; she was a bookseller. Even with Archie's encouraging words ringing in her mind, she felt vulnerable. Then she thought of Ada and Kurt. Maybe she would find them this week, and then she never had to come back to Germany again. She would go home and lock her door and do what she did best. Sell books.

The food arrived but Madeline could barely swallow even a few bites before she left the table in search of an early night.

Hastily, she locked and bolted the bedroom door, before undressing and curling up in bed, clutching Alex's journal close. As she lay there in silence, images of Frau Kaufmann's suspicious eyes haunted her; also, that feeling of being followed. Was she imagining it all?

Sleep would not come easily; the events of the day had left her feeling anxious and exposed. Thoughts raced through her mind as she lay awake listening for any sound that would hint at danger lurking beyond her door. She wished she was home in Paris.

She had to be careful from now on. With its information about her life, the journal was a risk, and she couldn't let it fall into the wrong hands. She needed to leave the guesthouse as soon as possible. It wasn't safe for her to stay.

Madeline lay in bed, her thoughts racing as she tried desperately to stay awake and alert. Fear ravaged her mind as imagined shadows took on new shapes and crept through the room, filling her with dread. All at once, she remembered the words Alex had once said to her, when she had been heartbroken after the loss of their second baby.

'*We need the darkness and shadows to truly appreciate the light, my darling, and only in the midst of our darkest moments can we find our greatest strength.*'

She took a deep breath, steadying herself with the memory of her husband's reassuring words. Drawing upon the inner strength she had felt from his love.

Exhaustion finally won out and pulled her into a fretful sleep, filled with turbulent dreams and menacing visions.

When Madeline awoke the next morning, she felt drained. She had so foolishly underestimated the immense risks here in Germany, and she wished she had paid greater attention to Falcon's offer of weapons training – it had seemed so extreme at the time, but now fear of the unknown was gripping her tightly and she realised just how dangerous it was here.

Adjusting her brown felt hat atop her head, she scrutinised

her reflection. The fatigue was evident in her brown eyes, and her usually vibrant chestnut hair hung lifelessly. Twisting slightly in the mirror, ensuring the seams of her stockings were straight, she noticed how her skirt was now draping loosely over her diminishing waistline. The stress concerning the war was visibly taking its toll, reflected in her weight loss.

She didn't go down for breakfast, but packed and left her room early to check out.

'You are leaving us already?' Frau Kaufmann asked suspiciously. 'I thought you planned to be here another day or two. I hope it isn't anything we have done?'

Madeline shook her head, her thoughts centred on the journal tucked deep in her bag. 'I just have some urgent business to attend to back home,' she said weakly, trying to hide the fear that was still churning in her gut.

Frau Kaufmann's eyes lingered on Madeline, a hint of scrutiny in her gaze, before she finally spoke. 'Very well, I hope your time here was comfortable.'

With a terse nod, Madeline murmured her thanks, then hastened out of the guesthouse, a surge of relief flooding her as the building faded from view.

With each hurried step, the weight of Ada's desperate words bore down on her, and one urgent thought hammered in her mind: she must locate Alex's child – and soon.

Because now she understood the fear in Ada's letter and the danger that Germany posed to anyone who was an enemy to the Reich.

LONDON, NOVEMBER 2011

Olivia

A couple of weeks later, Livi looked around her flat, ensuring everything was unplugged. Tommy was safely with the neighbour who always spoiled him, and she was packed and ready to go.

She couldn't believe she was going to fly. Since her divorce she had a real fear of being trapped and experiencing a full-blown panic attack. As she thought of being on the plane, her mind raced with a thousand 'what ifs', imagining scenarios where she was trapped at 30,000 feet, anxiety coursing through her, with no escape.

Her emotions threatened to overwhelm her, and she closed her eyes, focusing on her breathing. Slowly, her heart rate began to calm, and her hands stopped shaking. She pictured her grandfather's face. She was not just doing this for herself but also for *him*. To find out anything she could about what happened to him during the war so she could help heal the wounds that still tortured him. The book he had given her could be a clue to unlock his past.

With renewed commitment, Livi picked up her bags and headed to the airport.

Onboard her plane, a picture of Graham flashed into her mind, the last time she had been on a plane had been with her ex-husband for their honeymoon. She couldn't believe it had been that long. It was before things had gone wrong for them. Before his controlling behaviour had stolen all her self-confidence. She felt her chest tighten and panic overtake her as thoughts of Graham loomed large. Fear starting to grip her, she pulled out her phone and called Damien.

He answered on the first ring. 'Hey, Livi, I was wondering how you were doing.'

She spoke quickly. 'I'm on a plane to Germany.'

The silence on the other end was palpable. Eventually he spoke.

'I'm sorry – for a minute, I thought you said you were on a *plane?*'

'I am, to Germany.'

'Oh my God, Livi, did you have a *stroke?* I can't get you to go on a boat trip down the Thames with me and you're flying to another country. Are you alone?'

'Yes, and I'm panicking.'

Damien let out a sigh. 'Okay, okay. You're going to be fine. Take some deep breaths, and count to ten. You got this, I can't believe you're doing this, Livi. I love that you are taking all these new risks. First going to Scotland, now this. I think finding out you might be the great-granddaughter of a Nazi has actually been good for you.' He chuckled.

'Very funny,' she responded flatly.

'Livi, you are doing this for all the right reasons. If you just stop resisting, this could be an amazing adventure. And it was time for you to move on after Graham. I know this trip will involve being in a lot of dusty bookshops, talking about people that have been dead for hundreds of years with ancient old men, because I know how you get your kicks. But promise me you will try and get out a little, do something *fun*. Meet a few people under a hundred, maybe? And then call me when you get back. I want to hear all about it.'

After Damien hung up, Livi followed his advice and, even though she fought her anxiety the whole way, the flight went smoothly, and before she knew it they were landing to a cityscape that stretched beyond her plane window, revealing the patchwork of Berlin's history.

Modern glass buildings and historic façades surrounded the Spree River that snaked through the city like a silver ribbon, while the lush greenery of The Tiergarten offered a burst of nature amid the urban expanse.

After landing, she collected her bags and practised her language skills with a friendly taxi driver who drove her to the boutique hotel she had booked close to the bookshop where she was meeting the client.

After checking in and taking a quick shower, she settled in and relaxed with a book.

But as she read, Livi's thoughts kept wandering back to her grandfather. She pulled out the photographs of his mother with the Nazi, laughing and frolicking in the garden of the manor, and wondered what could have been so horrendous that he couldn't even talk about it.

She didn't know what had happened to him, but coming here was the first step in finding out.

21

BERLIN, SEPTEMBER 1940

Madeline

The following morning at their usual café, Madeline and Swift exchanged a tense nod. The agent passed her an envelope, and Madeline's heart raced as she read the contents: a marriage certificate with Ada's name linked to Frederick Mueller, a high-ranking Nazi officer. The realisation hit Madeline like a cold wave; Ada, the woman she'd been tirelessly searching for, was entwined with a monster.

Swift's voice was low and urgent, cutting through the murmur of the café. 'This man isn't just any officer—he's Gestapo.'

Madeline could barely believe it. She had never imagined that Ada's 'powerful man' would be someone so inherently dangerous. 'Are you sure this is her?' Madeline asked, her voice thin with the shock.

'Everything matches—including a first marriage to Alex Friedman...'

Madeline cut her off, her voice breaking, 'My husband.'

The grief was raw, as piercing as the days following Alex's death.

Swift continued, 'And she remarried Mueller shortly after her divorce.'

Madeline's mind raced. Ada's plea in her letter echoed in her thoughts, a desperate call for help that Madeline could not ignore, especially when it involved Alex's son. 'I must find her, Swift. Her little boy is in grave danger.'

Swift nodded, her eyes reflecting her concern. 'Your bravery is commendable, but please be cautious. Mueller's notoriety is well-earned, and if he discovers your intentions...'

Madeline absorbed the warning, steeling herself for the challenges ahead. The risks were immense, but the stakes were even higher. She could not—and would not—turn back now.

Swift scribbled an address on the back of an envelope and gave Madeline a map. 'The manor is called Eichenwald. It was formerly owned by a Jewish family but is now occupied by Nazi officers and used for socialising with Hitler.'

The two women locked eyes, the gravity of Madeline's decision ever present as the waiter placed their drinks on the table. Swift lit a cigarette, the smoke curling into the air, and offered one to Madeline, who declined with a shake of her head.

'I will be careful,' Madeline assured Swift, her voice firm, once the waiter had moved away. She suppressed the overwhelming desire to be back in Paris, safe within the familiar walls of her bookshop.

They sipped their drinks in silence, each absorbed in her own thoughts, the air heavy with the unspoken risks of Madeline's mission.

As they left the café, Swift wished her luck, and Madeline pocketed the envelope. The two agents acknowledged one another one with a subtle nod and parted.

. . .

That afternoon, Madeline stood outside the manor, her palms sweating, as she took in the stone pillars that framed an ornate iron gate. Above the gates the sign clearly read HERRENHAUS EICHENWALD. Slowly she pushed them open; they groaned heavily on their ancient hinges, the metallic echo slicing through the silence. Taking a deep breath, she stepped inside. Her feet crunched over the gravel of the circular driveway as she walked slowly towards the house.

The building was imposing in its grandeur, its towering stone columns and elaborate iron embellishments casting stark shadows in the late afternoon sun. Her body tensed as she contemplated what awaited her inside; would Alex's son be there? Would he resemble her husband? And what of his ex-wife, would she welcome her or view her with suspicion?

Bracing herself for what might come, Madeline rang the doorbell. Its strong chime echoed through the hallways beyond. On the doorstep, she rehearsed the ruse she had planned for this unexpected visit in case Ada's abusive husband was at home. She clutched a couple of books she had bought on her way, hoping they would lend credibility to her story.

After a few moments, heavy footsteps sounded from within, and an intimidating figure answered. A severe-looking butler dressed in a starched uniform looked down his nose at her through narrowed eyes.

'Yes?' he said gruffly.

She cleared her throat and tried to steady her trembling voice. 'I would like to speak with Mrs Mueller.'

The butler regarded her suspiciously. 'On what business?' he asked, his tone sharp.

'I'm here to drop off some books for her husband,' Madeline said hastily, not missing the flash of mistrust on the butler's face.

Behind him in the centre of the hallway hung a huge swastika flag rippling in the breeze from the open door, a distraction in itself, never mind what it represented. This would be her first introduction into a Nazi's home, someone who lived here in Germany, somebody who had the power to have her thrown into jail – or worse – for any reason he wanted.

'Is she at home?'

The man hesitated, and his nostrils flared as he took in Madeline's request. He finally gave in with a resigned sigh.

'Come in and wait here,' he said brusquely, and shut the door with a resounding thud. Madeline held her breath, listening as his footsteps faded down the hallway.

After what felt like an eternity, the butler returned. 'Mrs Mueller will see you in the library for a few minutes today. She's raising funds for the Führer's new art gallery,' the man informed Madeline with pride.

Traversing the marble hallways, Madeline tried to avoid looking up at the swastika flags that loomed overhead. The library was opulent, with floor-to-ceiling bookshelves carved from dark wood, a view of the gardens, and plush velvet furniture.

Feeling suddenly out of place in her simple clothes, Madeline nervously clutched the package in her hands.

While waiting, the distant chatter of one of the maids discussing a teashop she planned to visit later that day drifted through the air.

A few minutes later, Mrs Mueller swept into the room with practised grace. She was petite and flawlessly put together; her well-coiffed hair curled just so with not a strand out of place. Her lips were bare of red lipstick – Madeline had heard the Führer had a deep-seated loathing for it – and instead she wore a dainty pink shade the same as her nail polish, all complementing perfectly her powder-blue twinset. A fawn jacket hung loosely off her shoulders, adding a touch of refinement to her already impeccable look. She moved with the effortless grace of someone who was born into wealth and power, and on entering the room looked Madeline up and down with surprise.

'Mrs Mueller?' Madeline asked.

'Yes,' she answered, holding out an elegant white hand with beautifully manicured nails. 'I believe you have something for my husband,' she said as she studied Madeline with piercing eyes.

She handed the books to Mrs Mueller, who was impressed that she had travelled all the way from Paris. Madeline explained she was already in Germany on business and had offered to drop off the books for Herr Mueller.

Madeline had been certain that revealing her origins to Ada would signal her purpose in visiting, prompted by Ada's letter. However, the woman appeared oblivious, displaying no sense of urgency. It was all bewildering.

'Please,' Mrs. Mueller said, motioning towards an ornate chair, 'sit down. Let's have some tea.' Gracefully, she seated herself and summoned her butler, who promptly entered the room with a silver tray.

From the outset, it was evident that the woman was staunchly aligned with Hitler's ideologies, leaving Madeline puzzled as she awaited the opportune moment to broach the subject of the letter.

Maybe this act was how she survived? After all, she didn't know that Madeline was there to help. Madeline had anticipated glimpsing the woman who had captured Alex's interest, yet this woman appeared too refined for his tastes; he typically preferred a woman's intellect over her appearance.

The woman poured the tea and, as she handed Madeline a cup, remarked, 'My husband is occupied with crucial work alongside the Führer. His role is of utmost importance.' Her tone resonated with pride.

'Of course,' Madeline said, feeling weary of the pretence.

She took a breath and leaned forward, lowering her voice. 'I'm here to assist you. I've arrived from my bookshop, once owned by my late husband, Alex.'

The woman's teacup froze in mid-air, shock and distrust flickering across her face. She studied Madeline with caution, trying to understand her words.

Suddenly, the sound of tiny running feet echoed in the hallway.

'That must be Nanny and my little one,' the woman exclaimed, turning away.

About to meet Alex's child for the first time, Madeline stood up nervously. Suddenly the door to the library burst open, and in rushed a little girl with blond hair and green eyes. Madeline's breath caught in her throat. This wasn't Kurt. This wasn't Alex's son.

'Do you have only one child?' Madeline asked, her voice tight as her palms started to sweat and her stomach cramped as she searched for answers.

'Just my little girl,' the woman replied, kissing her daughter's blond head.

Shocked, Madeline wondered what had become of her son. Was this truly Ada?

Panicking, she excused herself, pretending she had forgotten an appointment and left, her cheeks still flushed with embarrassment. Her footsteps echoed through the hallway, as she berating herself for not heeding her instincts about this woman from the outset.

As she exited through the front door, her stomach still tight with tension, Madeline struggled to catch her breath. Relief washed over her that she hadn't exposed her true intentions, yet beneath that veneer lay a deep well of disappointment. With a sinking heart, she acknowledged the crushing truth: how perilously close she had come to being discovered. It was a stark reminder of her ill-preparedness and the magnitude of the task before her. As she strode back down the driveway the realization weighed heavily upon her – she was in over her head and ill-equipped for this search. Worse still, she was no closer to finding Kurt.

22

BERLIN, NOVEMBER 2011

Olivia

Livi emerged from the elevator into the cosy hotel's lobby, happy to have found such a hidden gem far from the bustle of the city. The lobby exuded old-world charm, with intricate wood carvings hanging on its walls and a chandelier studded with crystals casting a warm glow, illuminating the space with a soft, inviting light.

She paused for a moment, allowing the inviting surroundings to ease the tension that had knotted her shoulders since her arrival.

The aroma of freshly baked bread and brewed coffee lured her to the dining area, where she indulged in a simple, comforting breakfast of buttery rolls, sliced cheese and cured meats.

With each sip of coffee, her resolve strengthened, the liquid courage warming her from the inside out. She was proud of herself for making this courageous first step abroad and alone.

With the help of a friendly concierge highlighting her destination on a vibrant map pulled from baskets filled with tourist brochures, she set off into the crisp Berlin morning, as the city was awakening with the soft blush of dawn. She noted that every city had its own smell and this one was no exception. The scent of freshly baked pretzels from a nearby bakery mingled with the earthy aroma of autumn leaves, creating a comforting atmosphere that felt very different from the London she had just left.

Clutching the package for the dealer, Livi strolled through the streets, her grandfather's book tucked securely in her backpack. The possibility that it might unravel the threads of her family's connection to a Gestapo officer, who could be her great-grandfather, was both terrifying and compelling.

The bookshop was nestled in an old brick building, small and unassuming. Its modest sign swayed gently in the morning breeze. Inside, the familiar dusty aroma of old paper filled the air as her eyes adjusted to the dim light, a stark contrast to the burgeoning daylight outside.

Otto Beckmann, the proprietor, emerged from behind a fortress of towering books on his counter, his short white hair, which merged into his scraggly beard, was haloed by ring of white light from an overhanging lamp. The warmth in his kind brown eyes offered Livi a silent welcome as he adjusted his glasses, peering curiously at her.

Livi fingered the package in her hands as she navigated the labyrinth of bookshelves, weaving through the stacks of books towards the counter.

She always felt more anxious meeting strangers, and her throat tightened as she introduced herself to the man behind the counter and explained her presence.

Otto's demeanour transformed with the mention of his fellow bookseller, Mr Milner. His excitement was obvious.

'How is my old friend? Is he well?'

'Yes, he wanted to come himself, but he's very busy right

now. I had another book-related reason for being in Berlin, so he sent me with this.' She placed the package on the counter.

Otto's eyes gleamed with anticipation as he reached out to pick it up. 'Ah, I know what this is. Come, let's go into my little back office to chat and have a cup of coffee while I open it. I don't always get a chance to talk to another book dealer.'

Livi followed Otto through a heavy velvet curtain and into the cramped back office that already smelled of coffee, squeezing past piles of books that threatened to topple at any moment.

He called upstairs, and an older woman appeared on the landing. He informed her of Livi's arrival and asked her to watch the shop. The woman made her way carefully down the stairs, followed by a little stout dog who walked as awkwardly as she did into the shop.

The old man beckoned Livi over to a well-worn armchair with its own side table stacked with even more books. As he prepared fresh coffee, Livi sank into the chair, the soft leather creaking under her weight. Once seated, Otto carefully unwrapped the package Livi had brought. And his eyes widened as he revealed the ancient book Mr Milner had placed in there.

The leather cover was weathered and worn, its deep-brown hue showing years of handling. His breath caught in his throat, and a sense of reverence filled the room. Livi watched in awe as Otto opened the book, revealing pages yellowed with time.

'Ah, this is a rare find indeed. I have a client here who is dying to get his hands on this, the last one for his collection.' He drew her attention to the frayed binding. 'As you can see, it is very fragile, and very valuable, so we didn't want to risk putting it in the post,' he murmured as he brushed his fingers over the embossed lettering on the cover.

After setting the package aside, he served them coffee and

they settled down to talk. 'You mentioned you were here on other book-related business. Something else for Milner?'

'No, not for work,' Livi replied, taking a cautious sip of the hot coffee, trying to decide where to start. 'This is for a personal project of mine. I've been researching my family history, and I have recently come into possession of a book from this area.'

Otto leaned forward, his eyes bright with curiosity. 'Do you have it with you?'

Livi pulled out her grandfather's book and handed it to the bookseller, who drew in a breath in awe as he took it from her.

'Where did you find this?' he asked, flipping through the pages with delicate fingers.

'It belongs to my grandfather. He brought it to Scotland from Germany during the war.'

The older man turned to the bookplate in the front.

He brought the book close to his eyes, and his eyes narrowed as he thought for a moment, whispering the name written inside. 'Herrenhaus Eichenwald, that is very odd...' he murmured in a way that produced a queasy feeling in Livi's stomach.

She watched Otto intently, her curiosity piqued by his reaction to the name.

'You know this place?'

'Oh yes,' he said, peering up at her over the rims of his glasses. 'It was notorious during the war, a Nazi playground. It was a place often frequented by Hitler.'

Livi's chest tightened as she leaned in closer. 'Do you know the officer that lived there during the war?'

'I don't remember his name, but the Nazi who lived there was well known for being responsible for many atrocities against the Jews. Which is odd because this is in Yiddish. And I can't believe it survived the burning of the books from that manor.'

Livi looked down at the battered cover of the book, wishing

she had asked her grandfather more about how he had acquired it. He had seemed so fragile at the end of her visit; she hadn't wanted to press him for more details before she'd left.

'Can you tell me anything more about the estate?' she asked, eager for any information she could gather.

Otto shifted in his seat, his eyes flickering over Livi's face. 'It's not a place you really want to know about, though it once housed an extensive and beautiful library.'

Livi knew that he was trying to spare her the dark history of Eichenwald. But he had no idea why it was so important for her to know the truth.

'Anything you know would be helpful,' she encouraged.

Otto eyed her for a moment, as if weighing up whether to share what he knew. Then, apparently making his mind up, he cleared his throat.

'Before the war, Herrenhaus Eichenwald was a beautiful estate, owned by a wealthy Jewish-German family. They were avid collectors of literature and had amassed a vast library over the years. But when the Nazis took power the family was forced to flee, leaving behind their beloved home and all their possessions. The Nazis converted the estate into a secret base for their operations. They used it for meetings, training, and the library that once held the family's beloved collection was used to house propaganda and other vile works of literature.'

Livi listened intently, her heart heavy with the weight of history. She couldn't help but imagine the pain and loss that the Jewish family must have felt, leaving behind everything.

'What happened to the family?' she asked.

Otto took a moment before answering. 'Unfortunately, the family did not survive the war. It is rumoured that they were captured and sent to concentration camps. Their fate, like so many others', was sealed by people who stole their home.'

Livi's eyes welled up with tears as she absorbed the gravity of Otto's words. The book in her hands suddenly felt heavy with the legacy of her own family.

'Where is it?'

'On the outskirts of Berlin. I have only been there once, to look at a collection. It's a very beautiful estate, but with such a dark history. It now serves as a museum dedicated to preserving the memory of the Holocaust, a painful reminder of the atrocities committed during that time.'

Otto's wife appeared from behind the curtain, asking him a question about a delivery. Otto, who had seemed lost in his thoughts, pulled himself to his feet.

'Excuse me for a minute,' he said to Livi.

He left her alone digesting all that he had said. The little stout dog wandered into the back room and stood staring at her as if he sensed the tumultuous emotions she was going through.

When Otto came back, the spell between them seemed to be broken. 'I'm afraid I have had a large shipment of books arrive; it is clogging my very narrow aisle, and I need to unpack it. So, I will need to cut short our little visit. But it has been wonderful to meet another antiquarian, and I am so grateful for the package you brought me.'

Recognising the regimented manner that Germans often had, she knew their time was over, and stood up. 'Of course. If you think of anything else you want to share with me about this book, I am staying at the Metro Hafen Inn.'

He lifted the book towards her, then withdrew it again, as though thinking about something. Turning it over, he stared at the cover.

'Is anything wrong?' she asked.

'It sounds strange, but it is as if the book is off balance somehow.' He shook his head dismissively. 'Probably just its age.'

She took the book from him, only half listening, still reeling from all she had heard.

It wasn't until she was back in her hotel room later that she thought about his words again. Pulling the book out of her bag, she held it up in her hand and turned it over. He was right; it felt bulkier at the back than the front. But she couldn't see any water damage, or anything else that might explain why the back would be different. Pulling down her desk light, she examined the binding closely – it seemed okay – then the endpapers. That was when she noticed it, a slight bulge in the back of the book. Going against everything she would normally do as an antique book handler, she took out a little penknife attached to her keyring and carefully pried up the bulging edge.

Shining the lamp on the desk onto the book, she carefully pulled out what was hidden under the endpapers, and sat there staring at it in shock.

23

BERLIN, SEPTEMBER 1940

Madeline

As Madeline stepped out of the imposing iron gates of Herrenhaus Eichenwald, a shiver coursed through her whole body – not just from the bone-chilling air, but also from a palpable sense of uncertainty. She stood at the kerb, the manor's grim shadow looming behind her, her mind racing. She couldn't leave Berlin without answers; *someone* in that house must know Ada's fate.

Suddenly, she remembered what the maid had said about finishing her duties at four o'clock to have a cup of tea in town. It was a slender thread, but Madeline had to follow it.

She retreated to a hidden spot behind a pillar at the gate, wrapping her coat tighter against the biting wind, and waited.

She constantly checked her watch. The hands inched past the appointed hour, and doubt crept in. Perhaps the maid had changed her plans. But then, right when Madeline's hope began to wane, a side exit creaked open. The old maid, swathed in a thick woollen coat, her arms clutching a sizable bag, stepped out onto the path. The woman was heavyset with grey hair, strands escaping from her bun in wisps that framed her weathered face. She moved with an uncomfortable swagger that hinted at years spent on her knees, scrubbing and cleaning floors. Madeline followed her from a safe distance as the woman entered a quaint teashop nestled at the road's end. Madeline hesitated outside, peering through the fogged glass.

Inside, the teashop buzzed with the quiet din of conversation, its walls adorned with lamps casting a warm glow over small, intimate tables. The maid sat alone, her attention buried in the folds of a newspaper.

Taking a fortifying breath, Madeline pushed open the door and stepped into the warmth. She approached the table and, after exchanging courteous nods with the maid, asked if she might join her, citing the crowded space. The maid's eyes showed a flicker of suspicion before she assented.

As Madeline sat, the waitress brought her a steaming cup of tea, and she began the delicate dance of casual conversation, a thin veil for her true intentions. 'It's getting so cold outside, isn't it?' she ventured, her voice betraying a hint of her nerves.

The maid offered a slight nod, then her gaze returned to the paper. Madeline pressed on, 'It's colder than Paris. I'm here on a buying trip. I'm a bookseller, you see,' she said, trying to sound breezy. The mention of Paris seemed to pique the maid's interest, and her eyes lifted briefly from the print.

'What kind of books?' she asked, her tone carefully neutral.

Madeline recounted a few titles from the Führer's list of approved reading, watching the maid's reaction closely.

'What about you, what do you like to read?'

The woman looked up from her newspaper, her eyes narrowing suspiciously, and then, seemingly reassured by Madeline's friendly demeanour, she began to relax. 'I enjoy all kinds of books,' she said, 'especially mysteries.'

Now Madeline was on familiar ground and soon they were talking about the mystery books that they both loved while they drank their tea. She could sense the woman softening towards her, and felt relief wash over her as the conversation flowed more naturally.

After her second cup, Madeline decided it was time to take a chance. Lowering her voice so no one else in the teashop could hear, she asked tentatively, 'Actually, there was something else I wanted to talk to you about. I know you work at the manor; I went there earlier. I was looking for a friend. I heard that your employer had been married to someone called Ada. I'm a friend of her family, and I was hoping to see her while I was here.'

The maid's demeanour changed instantly, the grip on her teacup tightened, and her eyes widened, and she scanned the room quickly before leaning in, her voice dropping to a whisper. 'Where did you hear that?'

The waitress came over to check if they needed more tea. Both women tensed, their eyes flicking nervously to the waitress as they waited in silence until she moved on.

'She sent me a letter,' Madeline told the maid, her voice steady despite the anxiety gnawing at her.

Seizing on the opportunity to gossip, the maid leaned in closer. 'Ada has gone. Herr Mueller married again, and his new wife and stepdaughter live there now,' she divulged as she scanned the teashop.

Her instincts were correct. The woman she had met was not Alex's ex-wife. Madeline felt a flicker of hope. 'Do you know where she went?'

The maid hesitated, her gaze shifting to the door as if expecting someone to walk in at any moment. 'There are rumours,' she said in a hushed tone. 'Some say she fled to the countryside, others believe she might be in hiding somewhere in the city. No one knows for sure.'

She had got away, there was hope yet. Madeline hadn't realised until then how much she had braced herself for the worst, believing Kurt had been taken away for being Alex's son, and for being discovered as half-Jewish. The maid, now with her guard down, became nostalgic.

'Kurt was such a lovely boy. And I liked Ada. I was sorry to see them leave.'

Madeline took a sip of her tea. 'What was the reason for their departure?'

The older woman went on to tell a story of the night Ada left that revealed the painful circumstances of their departure from the manor after a huge argument and accusations of an affair.

A knot formed in Madeline stomach as she acknowledged how much pain Kurt must have gone through.

The older woman continued, now warming to her topic as she sipped at her tea, the newspaper discarded. 'Someone said he was already seeing his new wife while Ada was still living with him and was just looking for an excuse to get rid of her. Ada lived there for many years and barely left the manor; she could never have had an affair with another man. It was all just a lie.'

Madeline's mind was reeling. Was it as her friends had suspected? That this boy wasn't Alex's son, but this Nazi's, and this was a desperate plea from a mother to find her a home for Kurt? When had Ada and Alex slept together if she was living with this other man for years?

The older woman continued as Madeline silently pieced together the story.

'Yes, he brought his new wife here and claimed that Ada had gone away of her own accord; it was rumoured that he wanted to kill her. She knew a lot about his work with Hitler, so as far as I know she was forced into hiding. But what woman would leave this manor and all that wealth to go on the run with a small boy?'

Madeline's mind raced as she listened to the woman's story,

each new detail making her chest tighten with fear. She pressed her further. 'Is Ada's life still in danger?'

The woman sniffed. 'I don't know much about my employer,' she said, her eyes darting around anxiously, 'but I do know one thing: he can be a cruel man. He travels a lot to Poland for the Führer, and the things I overhear in that house, about what is going on there, are...it's terrible.'

Suddenly, the maid stopped short, her face contorting with fear, understanding she may have said too much.

'You won't tell anyone about this, will you?' she whispered with concern.

Madeline placed a reassuring hand on the woman's arm, hoping to calm her down. 'Thank you for sharing all of this with me,' she said softly. 'I promise I won't tell anyone. I just want to find Ada and get her to safety.'

The woman nodded slowly. 'I understand,' she whispered, 'but please be careful. You never know who might be listening.'

Relief washed over Madeline at the thought that Ada hadn't been killed before leaving the manor. The sound of Mueller's threat only strengthened her resolve to find Ada and get her out of Germany before it was too late. As she prepared to leave, a peripheral movement caught her eye – a man studying her intently. Recognition dawned; it was Frau Kaufmann's son, from the guesthouse. He averted his gaze and vanished into the crowd outside before Madeline could confirm her suspicion.

A wave of unease crept into the pit of her stomach. Was it a mere coincidence, or had he been following her? Madeline stood, rooted in fear, as the reality of the dangers surrounding her – and Ada – settled in.

With each passing moment, Madeline's wariness of the danger she faced in this land under Hitler's shadow deepened.

24

BERLIN, NOVEMBER 2011

Olivia

Livi squinted in the dim light, carefully extracting the worn, yellowed pages tucked inside the endpapers of her grandfather's book. They were handwritten – and a poem in German. The carefully crafted lines and delicate language immediately captivated her, and she admired the beautiful handwriting and imagery.

However, as she delved into the poem, about a man revisiting all the places of his lost love, Livi felt an unsettling strangeness. Why was this poem hidden in a Yiddish book, taken from an estate's library?

She pondered this mystery, her gaze drifting out of the hotel room window to the Berlin cityscape below, with the faint orange glow of streetlamps piercing the dark night. An eerie cold and expectant stillness filled the air, causing her to shiver and wrap her jumper tighter around herself. The words of the poem seemed alive, hauntingly familiar, as if from a dream or a half-forgotten memory.

Her flight wasn't until later in the afternoon the next day. She toyed with the idea of renting a car to visit the manor. Could she do that? Maybe, since she had felt so emboldened since leaving England alone...

After tucking the poem back into the pages of her grandfather's book, she sought refuge in a comfortable routine – taking a hot shower, ordering room service and, finally, surrendering to the embrace of crisp white sheets. Sleep claimed her before she could ponder the poem any further, the warmth of the down duvet lulling her into a deep slumber.

The next morning, as dawn's chill snaked up Livi's arm, she sensed something was amiss.

Even for the quiet street her hotel was on, the stillness was uncharacteristically profound, the sounds from outside muted in an unusual way. Stirred by concern, she reached for her dressing gown and opened the curtains. Outside, the world had transformed; a pristine blanket of snow enveloped the city, the morning light casting a pearlescent sheen over the untouched powder.

Panic fluttered in her chest, a frantic bird beating against the cage of her ribs. She had been managing her fears well until now, but the thought of navigating to the airport through the snow brought on a fresh wave of anxiety. She dialled the airline while pacing in the chilly room, only to have her fears confirmed – all flights were cancelled due to the unexpected storm.

She called her mother. Stephanie's voice was soothing, urging Livi to embrace the situation. 'At least you speak the language,' she reassured. 'Go and socialise, meet some people. It will all turn out fine.'

After hanging up Livi took long, deep breaths as she let her mother's words sink in, and reluctantly accepted her circumstances. Resolved to make the best of her extended stay, she dressed and ventured down for breakfast. Afterwards, she planned to occupy herself with work and reading back in her room. Once there, she made the necessary calls – to her neighbour caring for her cat, and to her boss, who was expecting her timely return. To her surprise, Mr Milner was in a good mood, buoyed by the success of a recent client meeting. It turned out that the family he had been assisting through the process of acquiring their library had just finalised the sale.

'Take your time, Livi. There's no need to rush back. Everything is going fine here,' he said breezily before ending the call. Livi hung up the phone and looked out of the window with a tense sigh. Watching the candy-floss-like snowflakes fill the grey sky, she reluctantly reminded herself there was nothing she could do.

The unexpected knock at her door that afternoon jolted her from her cocoon of blankets and books. Peering through the peephole, she saw a small, round figure clad in a thick fur coat, with a hat pulled down low over his face. As she leaned closer to the door, she recognised Otto Beckmann, the antiquarian bookseller whose shop she had visited the day before.

'Ah, I did get the right hotel!' he said cheerfully. 'You are still here. I thought you might not have been able to fly out. Your boss would never let me live it down if I didn't make sure you were all right. My wife thought it only right to invite you over for dinner tonight since you're so far from home. Some of my family will be there, and there will be food and wine; it's simple but lovely, especially if you brighten up the room.'

Otto's kindness touched Livi deeply and, after only a brief hesitation, she agreed. Being among people would offer a welcome distraction from her anxiety.

'Well then,' he said jovially, 'you know where we are – just a few streets from here. See you at seven.' Then, with a wave of his gloved hand, he waddled off down the corridor.

Livi closed her door and took a deep breath; she was grateful to have plans for the evening. She hadn't brought any clothes specifically for going out, so she rummaged through her suitcase and found a warm sweater and jeans that would suffice.

That evening, she ran her fingers through her messy hair and stepped out into the snow-covered street. Walking towards the shop, an icy chill brushed her cheeks, and the cold, crisp air filled her lungs. The snow sparkled under the streetlights, transforming her surroundings into a winter wonderland and momentarily dissipating her anxiety.

Otto's apartment above the shop exuded a warm and inviting atmosphere along with the aroma of a home-cooked meal.

However, Livi's anxiety flared anew as she entered the crowded room. It seemed like his entire family was there, and they all stopped and stared at her as she stood in the doorway.

She resisted the urge to run, planting her feet firmly on the ground.

Otto quickly came over to her, his face bright with excitement, and proceeded to introduce her to everyone. As her host rattled off all their names, which she knew she would never remember, he poured her a large glass of red wine.

As she navigated her way around, making polite conversation, the room felt chaotic, filled with laughter and loud conversations. The warm glow of lamps and the clinking of glasses created a lively but overwhelming atmosphere.

She regretted her decision to come. It was also very warm in his home, and it was unfortunate she was wearing the thick sweater.

Feeling awkward and out of place, she backed away from the rowdy crowd and edged her way towards the bookshelves. As she surveyed Otto's collection the sight of familiar titles like old friends gave her a sense of comfort. The little dog she had met the day before trotted over and stared at her, its inquisitive eyes adding to her unease.

She had just pulled out a first edition of a poetry book by Friedrich Schiller when someone tapped her on the arm.

'So, your name is Livi; is that short for something?'

'Olivia,' she said, turning to meet the gaze of the most captivating blue eyes she'd ever encountered. The man before her looked to be in his early thirties, with a cascade of blond waves that hung just below his ears, and she felt her heart skip a beat, acutely aware of her thick lumpy sweater hugging her frame and the flush on her cheeks from the indoor heat. She suddenly felt dishevelled, her hair a wild, untamed contrast to his own.

'My name is Markus,' he introduced himself, with a warm smile, his voice a smooth tenor that seemed to resonate with confidence, giving him a Jude Law vibe. He was tall, with broad shoulders, wearing an ironed cobalt-blue shirt that brought out the colour of his eyes perfectly. The shirt did nothing to hide the contours of his well-built form, with sleeves rolled up to the elbows that revealed strong forearms. Form-fitting, black denim jeans paired with polished oxfords completed his look, one that whispered casual elegance.

'I just arrived, and my grandfather insisted I come to introduce myself,' he continued. 'So, you're here on a visit?' His question hung between them, punctuated by a casual tilt of his head, his hair catching the light framing his face in a halo of gold that screamed *Adonis* to her.

'Yes,' she stammered. 'That's right. I'm here from England.'

'You like Schiller?'

She furrowed her brow, wondering if she had misunderstood him.

He pointed at the book still in her hand, which she had completely forgotten about.

'Oh, I was just looking at your grandfather's collection.' She felt foolish as she carefully placed the book back on the shelf.

He didn't draw attention to her reddening cheeks as he asked her if she wanted some more wine.

'That would be wonderful,' she lied, seeking anything to divert attention from herself. As he filled her glass, the aroma was sweet and inviting, with hints of berries and oak. 'Thank you,' she said, trying not to blush again. She took a sip, letting the rich, velvety liquid coat her tongue, its warmth spreading through her chest and easing her nerves slightly.

The air was warm, almost stifling, and as she held the wine glass, its smooth surface felt cool against her palm, oddly comforting.

She wasn't sure if it was the wine, the fact that she was away from her life and its carefully maintained barriers, or the fears she'd harboured about being alone after leaving her grandfather's, but she found herself unexpectedly drawn to Markus. He was warm and engaging without being overbearing, and his genuine interest made her feel seen and valued. Their conversation flowed effortlessly, as if they had known each other for years, helped perhaps by the fact that they seemed to be the only people there under fifty.

As the night wore on, Livi found herself laughing and smiling more than she had in weeks. The wine had a pleasant, soothing effect, blurring the edges of her anxiety. Markus was a captivating storyteller and his gentle charisma was refreshing and disarming, capturing her full attention. She still felt awkward, though, as she so rarely talked to men her own age – especially men as attractive as Markus – and she was painfully out of practice. She reminded herself that what happened here wouldn't matter – they were two people from completely different countries, likely never to meet again. Yet, whether it was reassuring herself of this fact or the influence of the second glass of red wine on an empty stomach, she found herself emboldened to speak openly and honestly with him, a level of candour she hadn't shared with any other man, except Damien, in a very long time.

As they sat together at dinner, he offered her a seat by an open window, the cool breeze a welcome relief against her warm skin. Their conversation naturally drifted towards their relationship statuses.

'Are you married?' he asked, as they began eating.

'Divorced,' she replied with unexpected confidence, surprising herself.

'Me too,' he replied. 'It wasn't an easy decision, but Annika and I realised we wanted different things. It was better not to hold each other back. How about you?'

'Same,' she lied. Although slightly tipsy, she wasn't prepared to share the true details of fleeing a marriage with nothing but the clothes on her back and the ensuing messy divorce with a stranger.

Their conversation continued, and as they finished dessert, it shifted to the reason for her visit.

'How fascinating,' he remarked, his interest evident, possibly heightened by the wine. 'Do you have the book with you?'

She retrieved it from her bag and handed it to him. He thumbed through it attentively and as the musty scent of history filled the air she explained what she knew of its journey.

'What's this?' he asked, extracting the fragile papers tucked between the pages.

Livi's heart raced at the sight; she had been sure she had left the poem at the hotel. Now she was embarrassed by its romantic nature.

'Oh, it's just something I found hidden in the book. I'm not entirely sure of its significance.' She stumbled over her words.

He began to read it aloud to her, reciting each stanza with a clarity and passion that nearly took her breath away. She kept her gaze fixed on the page as he spoke, but found herself sneaking glances at him. She was deeply attracted to his intense blue eyes and the way his blond hair draped forward as he read.

'You read like a poet,' she commented after he had finished.

'I am an actor; though I'm not doing very well at the moment, I have to be honest. It's hard to find work, but I'm trying.' His voice wavered slightly, and Livi could sense his vulnerability even in this brief exchange.

'Something doesn't quite work with this poem. The cadence is off,' he observed.

'I noticed that too,' she mused, reflecting on the poem's words. Though understanding poetry wasn't her forte.

He slipped the poem back between the pages, and the book fell open to the bookplate.

'Ah, Herrenhaus Eichenwald. I know where this is. It's not far from here.'

'I was hoping to visit today, but the weather had other plans.'

'I have some time off tomorrow. I could take you, if you like? Maybe there are more clues to your grandfather's past there,' he responded casually then took a sip of his drink.

She paused, a sudden nausea bubbling in her stomach. 'Oh, that's impossible. I'm sure I'll be flying out tomorrow.'

But he shook his head, gesturing outside to the blizzard raging through the night sky. 'I don't think you will be able to leave tomorrow. It is somewhat unusual for us to have snow this early in November, but they say more snow is coming tonight,' he declared with a confident nod. 'We could go on an adventure instead, if you're up for it?'

Normally this would have prompted a definite 'no' from her. But her usual guard was down, a combination of being out of her familiar environment, the wine and the ease of their interaction, and she found herself agreeing instead.

'But how would we get there?' she asked nervously.

'They will clear the roads; people need to get to work. But I'm not so sure about the planes. I think they will be backed up.'

He handed her back the book and grinned, his blue eyes sparkling with excitement.

'I can pick you up tomorrow morning, if that works for you? You will love Eichenwald.'

Though she felt a little self-conscious, she was secretly relieved; she had not been excited about navigating her way to the manor on her own in a foreign country.

She studied his face for clues about his expectation. Was this a date, or just a friendly outing? His warm smile and easy demeanour offered no obvious answers.

After the dinner party, Otto insisted that Markus walk her back to the hotel. The cold night air nipped at her cheeks, but the conversation and his presence kept her warm. They spoke with ease about winters from their own childhoods as the enchantment of the snow-covered streets drew them back to simpler times. The crunch of snow underfoot and the crisp, refreshing air felt invigorating. She studied him when he wasn't watching, calming herself with the knowledge that even if he did consider it a date, she would be gone as soon as the snow had cleared. She decided to simply enjoy the company and not overthink anything.

In the hotel lobby, he took her hand in his. It was warm and soft as he bade her goodnight. He looked adorable with the snowflakes dusting the shoulders of his grey wool coat and scattered throughout strands of his blond hair. She felt a flutter in her chest as their eyes met one last time before he turned to leave.

She didn't get into the lift right away, but watched him stride away, his tall, toned body moving with easy rhythm.

As she undressed in her room she remembered the depth of their conversation, smiled at the jokes he had shared and contemplated the warmth of connection she very rarely felt outside of her inner circle. It had been so nice to spend time with a man her age with such ease; it had been a long time.

As she reflected on her evening she was so relaxed that, for the first time in as long as she could remember, she drifted off to sleep without remembering to take her evening anxiety medication.

25

BERLIN, AUTUMN 1941

Madeline

It had been nearly a year since Madeline began her undercover work for Archie. Travelling back and forth monthly, she had filled suitcases with books and newspapers, and microfilmed thousands of documents, handing it all off to Falcon in Paris.

But even with her success as a spy, there had been no further word of Ada, and she had begun to fear that Ada had been arrested – or, worse still, that she was dead.

She met Swift at their usual café in Berlin one morning, and they traded information over coffee. The café had gone through a noticeable change. The clatter of cups and the murmur of conversations were now underscored by the weariness etched on the faces of the patrons. Rationing had taken its toll – the chicory coffee was weak and served in chipped cups, and the pastries, once abundant, were now replaced by meager slices of stale bread. The air was thick with the smell of burnt coffee substitutes and the lingering scent of cigarette smoke.

'How do you feel about the fact that the Americans are

staying out of the war?' Swift asked, lighting a cigarette glancing around in her usual observant manner.

Madeline took a sip of her coffee and sighed, her gaze fixed on the wisps of smoke spiralling upward from Swift's cigarette. 'It's disheartening,' she replied, her voice tinged with a hint of frustration. 'People in Paris are becoming very discouraged. Though it is better for me. It means I can still travel in and out of Berlin relatively easily.'

Swift exhaled a cloud of smoke. 'Yes, it does give you an advantage,' she admitted. 'But at what cost? The longer the Americans stay out of this war, the more emboldened Hitler becomes. It's as if he believes there is no real threat from the outside world. And in the meantime, people are fighting and dying, shortages are becoming worse and people are stretched to their limit. It is enough to make you want to give up.'

'I feel like that about my search to find Ada,' Madeline mused, her eyes clouding with sadness. She glanced at a nearby table where an elderly man sat alone, his hands trembling as he nursed a cup of thin soup. The sight deepened her sense of despair and helplessness. Swift followed her gaze, which seemed to trigger a memory.

'I almost forgot,' Swift said, stubbing out her cigarette. 'I might have something to encourage you on that score. We have a new Resistance contact in the network. He is the caretaker of Eichenwald, the place she used to live. He lives in a cottage at the back of the estate. If you want, I can take you to meet him.'

Madeline felt a rush of encouragement, struggling to process this unexpected glimmer of hope.

'We will have to travel by bicycle, but I have some Resistance business over in that area later today and I know a way to get into the manor without being detected by the Nazis. Meet me here this afternoon so we can be back before the curfew. I will get you a bike so we can ride out together.'

Later that afternoon, they cycled out of the city. It was a gorgeous day with the sun shining brightly, casting a warm golden glow over the countryside. Madeline pedalled alongside Swift, the wind rushing through her hair, a sense of expectation building within her. The air was crisp and filled with the earthy scent of the fields they passed, a welcome contrast to the grim atmosphere of the city.

As they approached Eichenwald, the grand manor's towering structure emerged from behind a curtain of trees. She remembered the last time she had been here and the disappointment she had felt. Then she had travelled by bus, but now, because of the war, so many of the services were no longer operating.

Swift led her down a road to the back of the mansion. There they bumped and jostled along a narrow, uneven dirt path that led them deeper into the woods, away from the prying eyes of the main house.

They abandoned their bicycles and Madeline followed Swift through a dense thicket of bushes. The air was thick with the scent of pine and damp earth as they manoeuvred through the undergrowth, their footsteps the only sound on the leaf-covered forest floor.

Emerging from the foliage, they found themselves at the edge of a clearing. The sun cast soft, dappled light across the well-manicured lawns leading to the back of the manor.

In the centre of the clearing stood a charming cottage, its stone walls covered with flowering vines. Smoke billowed from the back of the house, where someone tended a fire. The sweet scent of burning wood and the crackle of leaves filled the air.

Swift led her towards the cottage, as a sense of hope welled up inside Madeline.

The caretaker was in the back garden placing branches onto the flames.

At the sound of their footsteps, he turned around, and a rush of something unfamiliar fluttered in Madeline's chest. This was not the weathered old gamekeeper she had pictured; instead, a handsome man stood before her, his age mirroring her own. His dark hair was a sharp contrast to the pale sky and neatly framed a slender face that spoke of both strength and gentleness.

His eyes, kind and unexpectedly reminiscent, met hers, tugging at a memory of her late husband's warm gaze, which had held the same gentleness. For a second, the war-torn world around them seemed to fall silent. In that brief moment, something shifted in her heart, a spark of connection that felt almost destined. She quickly averted her gaze, feeling suddenly vulnerable, her emotions stirred by the unexpected tenderness of the moment.

As Swift introduced Jacob Weiss, Madeline surreptitiously studied this stranger with hands calloused not by war but by working the land, who seemed to mysteriously bridge the gap to a life Madeline once knew.

'I have business with someone further down the lake,' Swift informed them. 'I will be back in an hour.'

Jacob ushered Madeline into his cosy cottage and led her into his comfortable front room, where an undeniable sense of awkwardness hung between them. It was clear he wasn't used to having visitors, and she felt equally out of place in a stranger's home. The room was airy, filled with the comforting scent of pine and the delicate fragrance of pink and cream roses, carried on a breeze from an open window. He hurriedly cleared a stack of books from the only armchair and nervously fidgeted with his hands.

They exchanged shy smiles, and then he offered to make her a cup of tea. As he moved into the kitchen, she picked up a poetry book balanced on the arm of the chair. To her surprise, the page was open to one of her favourites – 'Bright star, would I were stedfast as thou art' by John Keats. She had a copy of Keats' works by her bedside at home, and seeing this poem brought her a sense of comfort and connection between them in a way that only books can.

Upon re-entering the room with a tray of tea, Jacob noticed her reading the poem, and a faint glow spread across his cheeks. Not wanting to draw attention to his embarrassment, Madeline quickly placed the book back and accepted the cup he offered with a gracious smile. The air between them seemed to lighten ever so slightly as they settled into a companionable silence, sipping their tea and stealing glances at each other when they thought the other wasn't looking.

'So, how can I help you?' he finally asked.

Madeline took a deep breath, and told the whole story of her search for Ada and her son.

Jacob listened attentively. 'Of course, I knew Ada when she lived on the estate, and Kurt was a lovely boy.'

'Do you know what happened to them after she left Eichenwald?' Madeline asked anxiously, excitement brimming at the thought that she might finally have a lead as to their whereabouts.

Jacob's expression turned sombre. 'I wish I did,' he replied. 'But after she disappeared, rumours circulated that she had gone into hiding. The night she left, she brought me some of her belongings, the things she could not carry with her, and said she would be back for them. But she never returned. I haven't seen or heard from her since that night.'

Madeline's heart sank at Jacob's words. Yet another dead end. She felt the familiar weight of disappointment pressing down on her chest.

As they awaited Swift's return, their conversation turned to their Resistance work and books, and they found common ground in their shared passion.

Jacob showed Madeline his extensive collection of poetry

books, each one well-worn and filled with annotations. They discussed their favourite poets, sharing lines and verses that had resonated with them over the years. It was a welcome distraction from the weight of their conversation about Ada.

There was a vulnerability in him, and a depth, both of which she found captivating. He was very masculine but there was a tenderness in the way he spoke, a sensitivity that drew her in, and his companionship seemed to evoke memories of a time in her life when solitude was not her constant companion. His presence, so unexpectedly similar to her husband's, filled her with a poignant mixture of comfort and an aching nostalgia.

Time stood still in the cosy cottage as they chatted, and she found herself lingering in the warmth of his eyes, observing the set of his strong jaw, noticing the way his whole face lit up when he spoke about something he was passionate about.

'Tell me,' she began as she sipped her tea, attempting to sound casual despite her growing curiosity, 'how did you come to be the caretaker of this remarkable manor?'

'Both my father and grandfather worked on the estate, and in the end, I couldn't resist the pull of this place. The history, the stories that have unfolded within these walls... it called to me. And so, when the opportunity arose to become the caretaker, I couldn't say no.'

Madeline's eyes lingered on the walls lined with books, each volume representing a story, a fragment of the past meticulously preserved. 'It's amazing how our personal stories have power, just like books,' she mused. 'They connect us to the past and remind us of who we are. This is why I became a bookseller, to help preserve the legacy of story. Books are our testament to having lived, loved, and learned.'

Jacob's expression softened. 'The Jewish family who owned Eichenwald felt the same, and deeply believed in preserving their collection. They saw it as a bridge to their heritage. When they were forced to leave, I felt an obligation to protect their legacy.'

'I wish I could have known them,' Madeline said softly. 'Helped them somehow.'

Jacob seemed thoughtful, as if weighing something more important he wanted to share.

Madeline watched him carefully, waiting as he gathered his thoughts.

'I actually do have a situation you may be able to help me with...'

His eyes met hers, reflecting a mixture of hesitation and hope. He continued, his voice taking on a more earnest tone. 'In my efforts to preserve the legacy of this place, I've come across several items of significant historical value. These aren't just any books; they're irreplaceable treasures of literature and history, many of them belonging to the family.

'Some are so precious that I need to get them out of Germany. I know this is asking a lot. But do you think there's any way you could take them back to Paris with you?'

Madeline's eyes widened in surprise at Jacob's request. She hadn't anticipated being asked to take such a risk, but the thought of preserving these important books stirred something within her. It was a chance to protect something valuable, to ensure that the knowledge contained within those pages would survive.

'I... I would be honoured to help,' Madeline replied, her voice filled with conviction.

His whole face relaxed with relief.

He left the room and returned with three books, one of which was small, aged and leather-bound. He gently placed it in Madeline's hands.

'This,' he began, his voice carrying an undertone of reverence, 'is one of the family's most treasured heirlooms. It's written in Yiddish, and I'm certain it would not survive if left behind.'

As Madeline caressed the weathered leather cover, she felt the pulse of its importance in its weight, a precious piece of history in her hands.

'I will keep it safe,' she promised him, her voice resolute yet gentle, aware of the trust he was placing in her.

In the quiet moment that followed, Jacob's eyes met hers, conveying his depth of gratitude and a flicker of something more, a tender kinship that neither of them had anticipated.

'Thank you,' he murmured, the emotional weight of his words mingling with an unmistakable note of affection. 'You don't know how much this means to me.'

As their gazes lingered, a silent acknowledgement passed between them, the air charged with the promise of something burgeoning, something neither could yet define.

When Swift arrived back at the cottage, Madeline's mind was still alive with all that she and Jacob had talked about. She turned to him, with assurance.

'I promise you, I will do everything in my power to protect these books, and once this is all over they will be waiting for you.'

Jacob's eyes were filled with relief. 'Thank you, Story Keeper,' he whispered. 'And I will do everything I can to help you find Ada.'

Swift and Madeline left the safety of the cottage, weaving their way back through the thicket of bushes. The sun had shifted in the sky, elongating the shadows that stretched across the forest floor.

Madeline clutched the precious books close to her in her bag and made a silent vow to herself and to Jacob. Her journey, she realised, was more than a quest for Ada – it was a battle to preserve the echoes of a past threatened by oblivion.

The stakes were higher now, another crucial chapter in her fight against darkness. Little did she know the challenges ahead would test her in ways she could never have imagined, pushing her deeper into the heart of the conflict, demanding her utmost resilience and courage.

26

BERLIN, NOVEMBER 2011

Olivia

Fresh flurries of snow began to fall as Livi and Markus drove up the winding road that led to Eichenwald. The sprawling estate was a grand spectacle, nestled on the banks of Wannsee lake, amid lush greenery. Its grand three-storey structure resembled an ancient Greek temple, complete with cream pillars and large windows that let in streams of natural light. As they navigated the circular driveway, Livi couldn't help but admire the well-manicured gardens – a symphony of contrasts, with the stark white snowflakes dusting the deep greens of ancient trees, weaving a tapestry of nature's beauty.

'Breathtaking,' she sighed, her eyes wide with wonder, as they parked the car.

She took a moment to survey the grounds. Her chest tightened as she caught sight of some of the sculptures she had seen in the photographs of her great-grandmother. With sadness, she remembered that Ada had spent time in this place; it still seemed surreal.

'It's hard to believe that such a beautiful home has such a dark history,' she said with a touch of sorrow.

'Indeed,' Markus agreed, his blue eyes reflecting the marvel before them. 'Though now it's a museum, and they also teach the truth about the Holocaust. All the money raised by the estate goes to Jewish foundations.'

As he was distracted locking the car, she allowed herself the luxury of admiring him unobserved for a moment. His blond curls were slightly damp from his morning shower, and whenever he turned his head, the gentle fragrance of mint from his shampoo mingled with the lime and bergamot of his aftershave, evocative of a crisp sea breeze.

Today he was wearing blue jeans that contoured his hips perfectly and a cream jumper that broadened his shoulders, highlighting his athletic build.

A museum worker exited the building and stole a glance at him, and Livi admired how Markus carried his appeal with an easy confidence, seemingly indifferent to his own looks. In their conversations, he had downplayed his appearance with a touch of self-deprecation that only endeared him more to her. He had explained the night before that in some way he wished he had a less classic look so he could tackle more character parts in his acting career.

As if sensing Livi's gaze, he turned to her with a nervous smile, his blue eyes meeting hers with warmth.

'Are you okay?' he asked, the concern obvious in his tone. 'You look really thoughtful – with all you have found out, this isn't too hard for you, is it?'

She shook her head. 'No, I was just miles away,' she responded, not about to divulge the fact that she had been studying him.

As they approached the entrance, the snowfall intensified, swirling around them like a living force, pushing them forward as though even the weather was driving them inside to learn more.

They quickly ascended the steps and entered through the solid wooden double doors.

Inside, a dimly lit foyer was decorated with elegant, antique Bavarian-style furniture and green faded wallpaper. A large antique grandfather clock marked time in the hallway. With each swing of its large golden pendulum, the clock infused the room with a sense of stability and grandeur.

Livi shivered, not from the cold but from the fear of what might be waiting for her in here. As she looked around, the echoes of its dark history seemed to pulsate from the walls.

The silence was suddenly broken by the echo of footsteps as a man wearing a volunteer's badge approached them.

'Welcome. We didn't expect anyone today, with this weather. So you will probably have the place to yourself,' he said, cheerfully.

As he took their money, he gave them a potted history of the manor and a shiny brochure highlighting places of interest in each room.

As they began their tour, Livi studied the first sombre display detailing the Blumenthal family, who had owned Eichenwald before being forced to flee Nazi control. It spoke of their desperate flight as Hitler's dominance reached further and further across the fatherland, ending in the tragic death of the whole family at Auschwitz during the Holocaust.

Livi's eyes filled with tears as she slowly studied the photos, one black and white image after another. Each photo showed a family in a moment of everyday happiness. She was drawn to one in particular. The Blumenthals were taking a break from a game of croquet. Mallets were propped up against the table while they took time to share tea and cake around a table laden with food. Men slouched back against decorative iron chairs, wearing bushy moustaches, and women beamed in wide-brimmed hats that cast shadows over their faces. In front of the table, seated on the lawn, children were dressed in starched sailor suits with pressed skirts and trousers.

As she read about their ultimate fate, she studied each face, and she could feel her throat constricting as guilt welled up inside her chest for maybe being related to those responsible for the atrocities that robbed this family of its life. It was hard to believe that days like this could have preceded so much pain and sorrow. And yet here she was – standing on grounds where her great-grandfather may have given orders for their execution. She knew it was irrational, but still she couldn't seem to stop the feeling of shame and guilt that washed over her in an icy wave.

As they continued through the estate Markus strode ahead, and she felt so grateful to have his support as she delved into this dark place in history. His tender kindness and calm demeanour made her feel at ease.

They passed through an arched doorway into a long gallery hall, their footsteps muffled by an ancient carpet runner. Faded portraits in gilded frames lined the walls, stern faces staring down at them as they walked. Many were in Nazi uniforms.

Markus paused before a series of paintings depicting the estate's former inhabitants. 'It's incredible to think about how the Nazis used this place during the war,' he remarked.

Livi's stomach churned as she studied the faces rendered on the canvases. The lives that had once thrived here were now nothing more than ghostly shadows on the walls, their stories silenced by the passage of time. But still, their formidable images cast a foreboding shadow.

She forced herself to keep walking. The next portrait depicted the estate's ballroom, lit by crystal chandeliers, filled with swirls of dancers – Nazi's in uniforms and in their arms, glamorously dressed women. A chill went through her, imagining the laughter and music that once echoed here.

'It's sickening,' Livi murmured, her gaze lingering on the

scene. But still she couldn't help but stare with a macabre fascination at each of the faces, looking for the one that would be familiar, the face of her great-grandmother.

As she did, she shivered involuntarily, the hairs on the back of her neck standing on end.

Markus seemed to notice her discomfort and placed a reassuring hand on her arm, which intensified her shiver for a much different reason.

'Are you sure you're okay? You've been very quiet since we got here.'

'I don't know,' Livi admitted, her green eyes clouded with doubt. 'Being in this place is harder than I thought it would be. It makes it all so real. Reading about the war in a history book at school is very different from being somewhere like this. It brings it all to life.'

'Perhaps that's what makes places like these so powerful?' Markus suggested, his expression thoughtful. 'They serve as a reminder of the past, no matter how painful or disturbing it may be. Places like this have been preserved so we don't forget,' he continued wisely.

She studied his handsome face for a moment, thinking of the contrast between this kind friend and all she was witnessing. He was a German with that perfect Aryan look that Hitler had admired so much; but how different he was to the people she was reading about here. They moved on, and stepped into the library.

Livi finally felt a sense of relief. Books were her friends, and she felt her heart starting to calm as she perused the bookshelves, her antiquarian book dealer's heart always looking for the next great find. But she was surprised to see a couple of the shelves empty.

Her gaze lingered on the inscription engraved into a plaque on the wall beside one of the bookcases. Her brow furrowed. 'Apparently this used to be full of unique and rare books,' she murmured, her voice barely audible. 'But so many of their most precious works were lost during that time.'

'Such a tragedy,' Markus agreed solemnly, his blue eyes darkening with sorrow. 'And yet it's remarkable that this estate has managed to preserve any of its history from before the war.'

Below the inscription was the story about the caretaker of the estate, who had stayed on after the Blumenthal family had left, to try to protect as much of their heritage as possible. There was a shadowy picture of the man, slender with thick dark hair and one of the groomed moustaches that were fashionable back then. He was in a tweed jacket and knickerbockers, with a hunting gun relaxed at his side.

But it was the look in his eyes that drew Livi's attention. Gentle, kind eyes that made her feel that he cared deeply for what he believed in. She read more about him. He had studied literature at school and had even had ambitions of being a writer, before his love of the outdoors had guided him to take work at the estate in the 1920s. It outlined how he had worked with the Resistance during the war to preserve as much of the personal belongings from the estate as he could, including some of the books that were now displayed in the library. And it was because of his efforts that so much of the Blumenthal family history was recovered after the Nazi leaders went into hiding.

As they continued up to the bedrooms, Livi tried to imagine her great-grandmother and grandfather living here.

'How much do you know about your family's involvement with this house?' Markus asked.

'My great-grandmother died during the war,' Livi replied. 'Though I don't know any of the circumstances of her death. I have only just started to spend time with my grandfather, Kurt. According to my mother, who also was estranged from him after her parents were divorced, he never spoke of his life during the war.'

'Perhaps he believed it was for the best?' Markus replied

softly, as they ascended to the second floor. 'The things people did to survive... sometimes the truth is too much to deal with. I'm sure it was all so traumatising for him, and I'm guessing your grandfather was a young boy during that time.'

'He was, and for some reason he left Germany and was taken to France. I don't know any more about his story except he was orphaned and was adopted by a British family. Which is how he ended up in Scotland.'

At the top of a very long and winding staircase with gilded banisters, they were met with a long corridor with many bedrooms off a narrow hallway. They entered the first bedroom, and Livi gasped in awe as she stepped inside. The walls were decorated in an intricate gold leaf design, and a child-size four-poster bed dominated the centre of the room. 'This must have been one of the Blumenthal girls' rooms,' Markus said, pointing to a faded portrait hanging over the fireplace. It was of a young woman with raven hair and piercing, blue eyes. 'I believe I saw a picture of her in the first photo collection,' he added.

Livi felt a strange connection to the girl in the portrait, as if she was whispering to her from beyond the grave. 'She was a stunning young woman,' she said, her voice barely above a whisper. 'It's so sad to think about what happened to her.' She strolled to the bedroom window, her arms folded as she looked out across what seemed to be a beautifully manicured garden, now covered in snow. As Livi gazed out of the window, she couldn't help but imagine the young woman from the portrait walking through these gardens, the sun shining down on her raven hair. It was hard to reconcile the beauty of the estate with the atrocities that had occurred.

Markus approached her, and his presence felt so warm and comforting as he stood slightly behind her in silence, both of them admiring the winter landscape. The sun had finally broken free from the clouds, illuminating the garden with a soft light that glinted off the fallen snow like a river of diamonds.

As they stood there, enveloped in the tranquility of the moment, Livi felt a wisp of Markus' breath on the back of her neck. It sent a shiver down her spine, igniting an overwhelming wave of attraction for him. Heat radiated from her body, and when she looked down, she noticed that tiny hairs were standing up along her forearm. She knew she found him attractive, but she couldn't remember the last time she had felt such a strong physical reaction to someone, and it was both exhilarating and disconcerting.

All at once, she had the most irrational feeling to just turn around and place her arms round his neck and kiss him.

She quickly blinked her thoughts away. The gentle way Markus had woven himself into her life had disarmed her, slowly allowing her to open up a sliver of her guarded heart. Feeling uncertain about this new development, she quickly stepped away from him with a stiff smile as they continued on.

As she battled these new brimming feelings, they descended the staircase and entered what would have been the main family room. Livi was glad the tour was nearly over; her stomach had started to relax and she had started to wonder if her initial ideas were correct. Had Ada's love affair with Frederick Mueller resulted in a marriage? There was nothing here to confirm that was the case. Just because Ada had been in love with this man didn't mean they had married, or that Kurt was his child. She was sure Nazis had affairs all the time. Her grandfather had been a young boy when he had lived here, and he may not have understood all that was going on around him during that time.

As if to laugh in the face of her optimism, Livi's gaze fell upon a portrait above the fireplace that sent a jolt of shock coursing through her veins. There, nestled among the shadows and secrets, was a young boy, with her grandfather's chiselled chin and expressive brown eyes, seated on the lap of the notorious Nazi. But it was their expressions that held Livi transfixed. In the awkward embrace, the look in the little boy's eyes was frozen in a haunted expression, and the darkness in Mueller's eyes seemed a chilling testament to the horrors he had both witnessed and perpetrated.

'Markus,' she whispered, her voice tight with tension. She drew his attention towards the portrait, and her body began to tremble involuntarily.

He followed her gaze and his own eyes widened with shock as he took in the image before them. The inscription beneath the painting read:

Frederick Mueller with his son, Kurt.

'Your grandfather?' Markus asked, his voice heavy with the burden of understanding.

Livi nodded mutely as she stared at the portrait, the breath stolen from her lungs as she struggled to come to terms with the revelation that confirmed the knowledge that had upended her entire world. Her mind raced, her thoughts tumbling over one another like waves crashing against a rocky shore.

As she stood amidst the ghosts of her family's past, Livi felt the ground shift beneath her feet. The air grew heavy with the weight of generational secrets, and a sense of foreboding suffocated her. There was no way she could deny it now. She had unearthed a truth that would forever change her perception of her family.

And with these new revelations, the dark legacy that haunted Herrenhaus Eichenwald was now forever intertwined with her own bloodline.

27

BERLIN, AUTUMN 1941

Madeline

Clutching the worn leather suitcase close to her side, Madeline pushed her way through the sea of anxious faces. With each step her heart pounded in rhythm with the jarring thud of hurried footsteps that echoed through the Berlin station. The acrid scent of train smoke and sweat hung thick in the air as she weaved through the bustling crowd, each jostle and shove threatening to reveal Jacob's books hidden beneath the waistband of her skirt. They pressed at her ribcage, a constant reminder of the risks she was taking.

'*Entschuldigung*,' she muttered, sidestepping a woman carrying a wailing child and narrowly avoiding a collision with a hasty Nazi soldier.

With relief, she saw her train was already at the platform. Soon she would be home in Paris.

Suddenly an air-raid siren pierced the clamour, its shrill warning slicing through the chaos like a knife. Before anyone could react, a deafening explosion shook the station, sending shockwaves through Madeline's body.

The response was instantaneous. Panic surged, a tidal wave of terror that swept throughout the crowd. Voices merged into a dissonant chorus of screams, drowning out all reason.

Another blast tore through the platform, shattering windows and sending glass shards flying.

'Run! *Run!*' someone shouted, panic rising in their voice. Screams filled the air as people ducked for cover or fled. The shockwave knocked Madeline to her knees, heat washing over her. Dust and debris clouded her vision, choking her lungs.

A second blast made a direct hit on one of the walls, knocking Madeline flat on her back as rubble rained down and trapped her beneath it Instinctively, she clutched at the books, pain and terror shooting through her body.

Desperately, she called out, pleading for help. *'Bitte... bitte helfen Sie mir...'* Her voice was barely a whisper, the words choked by the dust and rubble that threatened to bury her alive. But everyone was bent on saving their own lives.

As she lay trapped, the siren screaming in her ears. She was fought for every breath, her whole body shaken by the explosion, and her nose and throat burned with the heat of fire and the stench of burning wood. She could taste the metallic tang of blood in the back of her throat. The symphony of cries, moans and whimpers from the injured intensified her sense of urgency.

Her head swam as a darkness overwhelmed her – a heavy, warm blanket of fatigue that threatened to pull her into its depths. Struggling to cling on desperately, she closed her eyes, resolved not to surrender without a fight. She began to feel light-headed and all the chaotic sound around her seemed to echo into a darkness that was pulling her forward.

She had to protect Jacob's books. She would close her eyes just for a minute, just until she could get her breath, and as she slipped away her hands continued to protectively cradled the books bound at her waist...

28

LONDON, NOVEMBER 2011

Olivia

Livi gently turned the key in the lock, savoring the reassuring click, then nudged open her front door.

The familiar scent of home greeted her– the comforting aroma of freshly brewed coffee mingling with the delicate hint of lemon air freshener. Leaving her suitcase by the door, she shed her coat in the hallway.

As she ventured into the living room, her gaze landed on the box from the auction she had left on her coffee table, and it stirred a whirlwind of emotions within her.

Her thoughts instantly returned to Markus, and thoughts that were like a warm blanket of comfort wrapped around her. The memories of their time together flooded her mind. The weight of the revelations at the estate still hung heavy, but somehow the connection she had formed with new friend had provided a sense of safety and security amid the stark, raw reality of her family's past.

She still couldn't shake the image of the portrait showing her grandfather as a young boy with Frederick Mueller. The darkness of her family's past now loomed larger than ever, casting a long shadow over her understanding of who she was and where she came from. But Markus had been there to support her. On their way back from Eichenwald, he had been sensitive, giving her space to process the shocking revelations. He had offered to take her to dinner, but Livi had declined, opting instead for quiet reflection in the aftermath of the tumultuous visit. On the journey back from the manor, she had received a call from the airline informing her that her new flight would leave early the next morning, and she and Markus had agreed to keep in touch.

As they parted ways, a lingering hug conveyed unspoken sentiments, igniting a further spark of connection between them. Livi knew that the longer she remained in Germany, the stronger the pull towards Markus would become. Amidst the turmoil of her family's history and the complexities of her own feelings, she hesitated to embrace this newfound complication.

Sinking into her favourite armchair, Livi realised she was exhausted from the travel and feeling vulnerable. Amid all this turmoil, she faced a new, daunting fear: the prospect of revealing this grim truth to her estranged grandfather.

How could she confirm that he was definitely Mueller's son, that a portrait existed capturing him in the embrace of such a monster? The thought of confronting him with this knowledge threatened to shatter the tentative relationship they'd begun to build.

After collecting Tommy from her neighbour and brewing a soothing cup of tea, Livi settled at her kitchen table with her laptop. Since the first day she had found the pictures at the auction, she had put off doing any major research about Mueller, wanting to wait until she was sure she was related. But her newfound knowledge had ignited a morbid curiosity within her, and it was now driving her to uncover everything about his past.

Her fingers flew over the keyboard, navigating through a labyrinth of gruesome Holocaust images, and the history that had once felt distant now engulfed her, intimately personal.

She gasped when she finally found Frederick Mueller's, his sharp face staring out from the screen with eyes that seemed to reflect the darkness of his war record.

But then came more Holocaust pictures – innocent children's faces huddled together in makeshift scarves – and Livi could take no more. The threat of a full-blown panic attack began to build in her chest, each image intensifying the weight of her emotions

She pushed back from the table and stood up unsteadily. She felt the cold press of the wooden floor against her bare feet as she paced the room, trying to breathe deeply and calm herself down. She wished more than ever that she had never bid on that lot. If she had known then where it would take her, she would have just walked away. Now she understood fully what the statement 'ignorance is bliss' meant.

Her mobile phone rang, startling her. She answered it, tight-lipped and harried.

'Livi? Are you okay?' It was Damien's voice.

'Yes.' Her high-pitched breathy response reflected the anxiety attack she was attempting to recover from.

'No, you're not, what's wrong?'

She told him about her trip and what she had found out.

'I'm coming over,' he said firmly. 'John has gone out for the night, so I am home alone anyway. I'll bring wine!'

Thirty minutes later, Damien was knocking on Livi's door with a bottle of red wine cradled in one arm and a large block of dark chocolate in the other.

'I want to hear everything,' he said decisively as he marched past her. 'But first, where's your corkscrew?'

After a few moments of small talk as they uncorked the

wine and filled glasses, they settled down in the front room and Livi started to tell her story in more detail.

Damien sat there, captivated, his mouth often hanging open in shock as he interjected with the occasional exclamation of 'Oh my God!' when she shared particularly striking details of her trip to the estate.

When she had finished, Damien sat back in his own chair, face carefully composed in what Livi called his war mask – the same face he made when attempting to outbid someone at an auction.

'Would you like my opinion?' he asked.

'Yes,' Livi said wearily, suddenly worn out from all she'd been carrying.

'I know you understand that none of this is your fault, and we know that you're already a sensitive person who can carry the weight of the world on their shoulders. But I believe that, once you've processed all the shock, this experience will make you even stronger. Since you and Graham divorced you have spent so much time avoiding pain – now you have to face it head-on. Look at what has already come out of it; you've started travelling and building a stronger relationship with your grandfather. And you've even stood up to your mother – who I love, by the way, though we have to admit she can be overly protective at times...'

Livi chuckled thinking of that side of her mother as he continued imparting his wisdom.

'This horrible thing is going to somehow end up as a good thing. I just know it, I feel tingly, and you know what I'm like with my spidey-sense.'

To demonstrate how he was feeling, Damien did a peculiar body shiver that made the corners of her mouth turn up in amusement.

'And it is better that you know,' he concluded firmly.

'That's what Markus said,' she muttered absently.

Damien's eyebrows rose and he sat forward in his chair. 'Err, *who?*'

She felt warmth spreading to her cheeks, a sudden awareness washing over her that she hadn't intended to bring up her new acquaintance.

'Oh, no one. Just a guy I met in Germany; he drove me to the manor.'

'Just a guy?' Damien asked sceptically. 'Then why are you *blushing?*'

She responded too quickly for it to seem true. 'I am not! It's just the wine.'

She attempted to play down the connection, but Damien was not easily dissuaded and kept pressing until she finally admitted to being drawn to Markus.

Damien spoke conspiratorially. 'This is quite an adventure you are on.'

Livi then showed him the poem she'd found inside the book and he looked it over, shaking his head with astonishment. 'This is what I love about the business we are in – we never know what we're going to find with antiques. Why do you think it was in there?'

'I have no idea, it's not dated, but it had to have some significance. Someone went to a lot of trouble to make sure it was well hidden.'

'So, what next?' Damien asked, breaking off a piece of the chocolate.

'Well, my grandfather deserves to know his own history,' she said, her voice wavering slightly. 'No matter how painful it may be. So, I am going to see him again. I don't want him to be alone when I tell him about the portrait. I could tell by the way he talked about his past that he hoped his memories of Mueller were wrong.

So, I will call him tomorrow, and go up and see him again this weekend. He is very bitter, but when I stayed with him there was a sadness to him that broke my heart. He lives with so much pain from his past. He seemed to go through so much trauma during the war he could barely talk about it or his mother. I still don't know how or where she died.'

They then went on to talk about other things until it grew late.

As Damien left, he gave her a big hug. 'I think you are very brave and I'm proud of you. I know how hard all this is for you with your anxiety, but you are doing so well.'

Tears pricked Livi's eyes as she allowed her friend's words to sink in.

Damien swept off down the hallway with his parting comment: 'Call me if you need anything.'

The next morning, Livi did her usual nervous pacing of the kitchen before she finally plucked up courage. Steeling herself, she picked up her phone and dialled her grandfather's number, her pulse quickening as a memory of the portrait at Eichenwald flashed into her mind – the image seemed branded into her very soul.

She tapped her nails nervously on the counter while she waited. At the window, raindrops slid down the glass like tiny rivers, the gentle pattering matching her own drumming beat. The sky was a heavy grey, mirroring her own sombre emotions.

'Hello?' Kurt answered, his usual wariness evident in his tone.

'It's me, Livi,' she said hesitantly, swallowing hard against the lump that had formed in her throat. The short silence that followed was deafening, and she anxiously twisted a strand of her short, wavy hair round her finger.

'Ah, hello, Olivia,' he replied, his voice softened by his Scottish brogue.

Livi took a deep breath, her green eyes fixed on the rain-splattered world outside.

'There's something important I need to discuss with you,' she managed, her voice trembling ever so slightly. 'I've just returned from Germany, and I came across some information about our family history that I think you should know.'

'*Germany?*' Kurt's voice sharpened, suspicion creeping into his words. 'What were you doing there?'

'I was there for work but also searching for answers,' Livi replied, her tone resolute. 'About our past.'

She could almost hear the gears turning in Kurt's mind, the weight of his unspoken thoughts heavy in the silence that stretched between them. When he finally spoke, his voice was hushed, tinged with emotion.

'What have you found?'

'Something interesting,' Livi confessed, her heart aching with the knowledge of the pain her discovery would bring.

'Oh really?' Kurt retorted, his voice strained with disbelief and something else – fear, perhaps?

'I would like to come and see you again.'

Kurt was silent for a long moment, and Livi held her breath, anxiety gnawing at the edges of her thoughts. She knew she was asking him to confront a past he had buried.

'Very well,' Kurt finally agreed, his voice barely audible above the sound of the rain. 'Come to Scotland. We will discuss this further.'

'Okay,' Livi whispered, relief washing over her. 'I'll see you at the weekend.'

As she hung up the phone, Livi stared out at the rain-soaked landscape, her heart heavy with the knowledge of what lay ahead. In seeking the truth, she had unearthed a past that threatened to shatter everything she had built with him. And yet, she could not ignore her family's history, and the dark secrets that tied it all together. But she was not looking forward to the journey ahead.

29

BERLIN, AUTUMN 1941

Madeline

Madeline awoke to the sterile smell of antiseptic and the unfamiliar chill of a hospital gown on her skin. Panic flooded her senses, Jacob's books were gone, her skirt obviously discarded somewhere during her hasty treatment. Her heart raced, her breath was shallow and ragged; had the nursing staff found them? Would they turn her in?

'Excuse me,' she whispered to a passing nurse, her voice wavering. 'Where are my things?' Her voice sounded hoarse and strained.

'Your clothes have been removed. Your injuries needed tending to,' a nurse replied, her tone brusque but not unkind. 'Do not worry. They are safe.'

Madeline's eyes scanned the busy hospital ward. In its sterile confines, she felt more vulnerable than ever. Her thoughts raced with uncertainty and fear, her fingers clenching the thin sheets that covered her trembling form.

She could not shake the terror of being exposed, nor the

overwhelming responsibility of safeguarding the precious literature she had risked everything to save.

She seemed to lie there for hours, the incessant ticking of a
wall clock punctuating the oppressive silence that enveloped
her thoughts. Each tick seemed to amplify her mounting terror
as doctors and nurses bustled about, racing to save the lives of
those injured around her.

'Ah, Fraulein.' A crisp voice finally pierced the oppressive
air. A tall man in a pristine white coat approached her, his right
arm circled by a swastika armband. 'You are awake. Good. My
name is Dr Schultz. Please, sit up.' His command was harsh,
leaving no room for objection. With great effort and a wince of
pain, Madeline complied, sitting upright on the bed. The doctor
began his examination, his hands prodding her injured leg with
mechanical detachment.

'Does this hurt?' Dr Schultz enquired, pressing on a tender
area near her wound. Madeline clenched her jaw, stifling a cry,
unwilling to reveal her true vulnerability.

'A little,' she lied.

'Your leg is severely injured, but it appears no bones are
broken,' he stated coldly, making notes on his clipboard. 'You
were fortunate,' he remarked without emotion. 'The nurse will
dress it. You can stay here tonight to recover, but you must avoid
putting weight on it for a week, or you risk further injury.'

'I was planning a train journey. I have to leave,' she asserted,
her fear of being trapped overwhelming her.

'Not this week.' He shook his head. 'You will make things
much worse if you do. I suggest you call your husband and get
him to take you home.'

His words sliced through her, sharper that she could have
imagined. A longing for Alex surged within her, a yearning for
his guidance and the comforting strength of his presence. He
had always been at his most attentive when she was unwell,

bringing her food on a tray in bed, accompanied by a little bunch of cream or pink roses, her favourites, in a bud vase.

But he was gone, and in this foreign land his absence enveloped her more profoundly than ever, leaving her adrift in a sea of her own grief. And somewhere in this hospital were Jacob's books, just waiting for the wrong person to find them and have her arrested.

'Get some rest,' Dr Schultz ordered, then turned on his heel and left her without another word.

He had barely left when another figure appeared at her side, her presence offering a stark contrast to the chill Dr Schultz had left behind. The nurse, clad in a crisp white uniform, approached Madeline. She had gentle eyes and an air of quiet resolve that immediately caught Madeline's attention, stirring hope within her.

As she adjusted the bedlinens the nurse leaned in, her voice a whisper barely rising above the ambient noise of the ward. 'My name is Elsa. I was the one who undressed you while you were unconscious,' she disclosed, locking eyes with Madeline in a moment charged with tension. Madeline braced herself, fearing that the next words might seal her fate.

'I know what you were hiding,' Elsa continued, her tone neutral yet laden with significance. 'They're... Jewish.'

Madeline drew in a sharp breath as their eyes met. Was this woman about to tell her she was turning her in to the authorities?

But her eyes were kind. 'I managed to hide them before anyone else arrived. They are safe for now.'

'Thank you,' Madeline sighed, clasping the woman's hand, her voice trembling as a sense of relief and optimism washed over her. 'I was so afraid they'd been discovered.' With a heart full of thankfulness and renewed hope, Madeline whispered her gratitude, feeling the burden of her secret momentarily lifted. Elsa's reassuring squeeze of her hand was a silent pledge of solidarity.

'We must be cautious,' Elsa warned, and outlined a plan to return the books discreetly.

'Dr Schultz...' Madeline began hesitantly, her thoughts drifting back to the cold, calculating man who had examined her just moments before. 'Do you think he suspects anything?'

'Dr Schultz is a loyal servant of the Reich,' Elsa replied, her disdain, obvious. 'But he is also a man of medicine, and his focus remains on treating patients – for now, at least. I go to my Resistance meeting tonight. I will inform them of your situation, and they will help.'

'Thank you, Elsa,' Madeline said quietly, her voice filled with newfound resolve.

After Elsa left her, Madeline lay in the sterile hospital bed, her body aching and her mind reeling from the events that had transpired. The sharp smell of antiseptic filled her nostrils, an unwelcome reminder of her current predicament. She stared at the ceiling, the stark white tiles providing no comfort or distraction from the turmoil within, until she drifted off into a fitful sleep.

Her sleep was filled with nightmares. Thoughts of the bomb blast flooded her mind – screams echoing through the air, the ground shaking beneath her feet, and the suffocating weight of the rubble pinning her down. Her heart raced as she remembered the German soldier who had helped her, unaware of the banned books strapped to her body. How close she had come to being discovered.

The following morning brought little relief. Sunlight filtered through the cracks in the curtains, casting stark shadows on the sterile walls. Madeline's injuries throbbed with renewed intensity, anchoring her to the hospital bed against her will.

Elsa visited her that morning, and told her that someone was coming to the hospital that afternoon to pick her up.

Madeline was asleep when that someone arrived in the afternoon. And was shocked when she opened her eyes to see Jacob Weiss bending over her, his eyes filled with concern.

Instantly, a flurry of conflicting emotions washed over Madeline – relief at seeing a familiar face, trepidation about what his presence might mean, and a spark of something else entirely – a remembrance of the inexplicable connection from their first meeting.

'Jacob.' She gasped, drawing in a sharp breath of surprise. 'What are you doing here?'

'I heard from my cell leader about the agent caught in the bombing and knew it was you, so I came to see how you are,' he replied, his voice tinged with worry.

'Thank you,' she managed, feeling vulnerable and acutely aware of her scant attire.

'Madeline,' Jacob continued, and paused for a moment before speaking again, 'I have a proposal for you. The doctor tells me you need to rest here in Germany for at least a week, so I would like to invite you to my cottage on the estate, if that is comfortable for you? I have a spare bedroom, and I'm out on the estate much of the day so it would be quiet.'

Madeline's mind raced as she considered her options. Leaving the oppressive atmosphere of the hospital felt like a blessing, but placing her trust in Jacob, whom she barely knew, was daunting. Yet, there was something undeniably alluring about him – a quiet strength and resolve that drew her in.

'Jacob, I...' she began, her voice faltering as she tried to articulate her thoughts. 'I'm grateful for your offer, but...'

He gently covered her hand with his own. 'Please don't say no out of politeness. You risked everything to take my books to safety; it's the least I can do. You would be safe in the cottage and I will help you get back on your feet.'

The room fell silent, the air thick with unspoken words and heavy with emotions. Madeline's mind raced, torn between gratitude for his offer and apprehension about the implications of accepting. She couldn't deny the allure of Jacob's proposition.

'Thank you, Jacob,' Madeline said finally, her voice barely above a whisper. 'This is very kind of you.'

He continued, 'I have spoken to Elsa; she will give me back the books, and I will go and see the doctor to tell him I have come to take you home.' His gaze lingered on her face for just a moment longer before he turned to leave.

Madeline sank back into her pillow. Beneath her gratitude lingered a gnawing uncertainty, a fear of the unknown that tugged at her conscience. In the midst of war and uncertainty, the prospect of a safe haven – and perhaps something more – beckoned her forward. But at what cost? And could she be around Jacob in such a vulnerable and intimate way? A man she barely knew?

She had very few choices right now. She needed help to recover, so a guesthouse was out of the question. Yet, she remained concerned about this development. Not just as an agent, but as a woman. She had not lived in the same house as a man since her husband had died. And she was aware that, even in their brief interaction, this man had already awakened something deep within her that she had long since buried. And she wasn't sure if she was ready to confront it.

30

SCOTLAND, NOVEMBER 2011

Olivia

When Kurt opened the door, Livi could have sworn she glimpsed a flicker of joy in his eyes at seeing her, but it vanished quickly, replaced by his usual brusque demeanor.

'Olivia, come in.'

Stepping into the functional front room, Livi surveyed her surroundings with a pang of sadness. The house showed the usual signs of his solitary existence, a read newspaper folded on a side table, the TV on but turned down, the aroma of brewing tea filling the air. Nothing more, nothing less. And she wondered how many years he had lived like this.

After an awkward pause, Livi broke the silence. 'Thank you for agreeing to see me.'

'Of course,' Kurt replied gruffly, his expression unreadable. 'I asked you to keep me updated. Would you like a drink?'

'Thank you,' she replied. He poured a cup of tea and they sat down at the kitchen table.

'What is it you've found out that's so important?' he asked.

Taking a deep breath, Livi launched into her explanation,

her voice trembling with emotion as she recounted her discoveries at Eichenwald. She showed him the photographs she had taken, saving the portrait of Kurt as a young boy alongside Frederick Mueller for last. Finally, she pulled up the image of the Gestapo officer with the young boy on his lap, accompanied by the plaque identifying him.

Kurt's hands shook as he stared at the photograph in disbelief. He let out a heavy sigh, the weight of realization settling on his shoulders. 'This... this was always my worst fear. Of course I suspected it. But I had always hoped there had been a mistake. I was so young...' His voice trailed off to a dry rasp barely audible in the quiet room.

Livi's own anxiety spiked as she nervously asked, 'Was I right to bring it to you?'

Kurt's eyes were still fixed on the photograph. 'Yes, you were right,' he replied, his voice now heavy with resignation, 'I needed to know the truth, no matter how painful it may be.'

'What was he like? Do you remember him?' she asked gently, hoping for anything good to hold on to for her own sanity. Any shred of goodness amid the darkness.

But the change that came over Kurt's face was chilling. His eyes turned cold, and his once calm demeanour twisted into one of pure hatred and revulsion.

'Frederick Mueller was a *monster*,' he spat out with venom, his words laced with seething anger. He stood up abruptly and began to pace, his movements erratic as he struggled to contain his emotions.

He turned away from Livi, obviously not wanting to elaborate any further on the subject. And while she burned with curiosity for answers, she also respected his grief. This wasn't just a distant story about an ancestor for him – it was his parents.

He sat back down and looked exhausted. And they sat in silence as the kitchen seemed to grow dimmer, united by the weight of a history they couldn't change. Livi's heart ached with guilt and she bit her lip, fighting back the remorse that threatened to spill out.

'I'm so sorry, Kurt,' she murmured, reaching out for his hand across the worn table. 'I didn't mean to hurt you. I thought it was important to know the truth... but maybe I shouldn't have said anything.' Her words hung heavy in the air, filled with regret and sorrow.

As her fingers gently covered his, he jerked his hand away and she watched him continue to shut down emotionally in front of her.

'Nonsense, you have nothing to be sorry about. That man, I can never call him my father, has something to be sorry about, and my mother has something to be sorry about – she married this *evil* man. But we don't. Now I know the truth for sure, and I will have to find a way to live with that.' Kurt's voice was barely audible, strained by the gravity of the revelation.

Livi's green eyes glistened with her own unshed tears. She didn't try to take his hand again in response, offering him a small, sad smile instead.

Suddenly, Kurt's face contorted with anguish, and he stood up again abruptly, clearly overwhelmed. 'I... I need a moment,' he muttered.

She glimpsed at her phone; it was only seven thirty, so too early to go to bed.

'Of course, I will go and unpack,' she said.

She could tell he needed time to process all he had learned alone. He went to the kitchen window, once again searching in the dark sky for answers.

Upstairs, Livi slowly unpacked her overnight bag and then lay on the cold, hard bed. She wanted to give Kurt as much time as he needed. She tried to read the book she had brought with her, but she just couldn't concentrate and found herself staring absently out the window too. As she lay there her thoughts returned to her trip to Germany and she remembered the way she herself had felt emotionally stirred at the manor.

After an hour of waiting, she used the pretext of fetching water to check on him.

As she made her way down the stairs, it was eerily quiet.

'Hello?' Livi called out, her voice trembling with concern, but there was no reply.

She opened the door to the front room just a crack so as not to disturb him, and gasped with shock. Kurt had collapsed onto the floor, and his body lay unnaturally still.

'*Kurt!*' Livi cried out, rushing to his side. She knelt beside him, shaking his shoulder gently, hoping to rouse him from whatever had taken hold of him. 'Please, wake up!' she whispered, her voice choked with emotion.

But Kurt remained silent, his breath shallow and laboured. His eyes were closed, and his face was ashen, and he looked so vulnerable, a stark contrast to the gruff, hardened man she had known until this point. Panic swelled in her chest as she fumbled for her phone, her fingers trembling as she dialled for help.

'Please,' she prayed silently, watching Kurt's unresponsive form. 'Don't let this be the end.'

Livi's heart thundered in her chest, echoing her rising panic. Her feelings of guilt now swallowed her up with a suffocating silence that enveloped her. Pushing back the dark thoughts that threatened to engulf her, she took a deep breath as she waited for her call to be answered. As she did, a cold draught swept through the house, as if sensing the tension that hung heavily in the air.

'Hello, I need an ambulance!' she choked out, her voice wavering but resolute. 'My grandfather has collapsed, and he's not responding...'

As the emergency services directed her on what to do while she waited for them to arrive, she brushed a lock of grey hair from Kurt's forehead, her hand lingering as if trying to impart some semblance of comfort.

'Grandfather,' she murmured, each word measured with love and concern, 'I'm here, I won't leave you, and help is on the way.'

Ghosts of the past seemed to swirl around them, mingling with the poignant present as Livi slipped her hand into Kurt's cold one, yearning for the sound of his gruff voice. She didn't have much of a relationship with this man. But she had also held out some hope of breaking down some of his walls and getting to know him better, and she didn't want the chance of that happening cut short before it had even started.

'Please hold on,' Livi whispered, her voice barely audible above the distant wail of approaching sirens. 'Please don't die...'

31

BERLIN, AUTUMN 1941

Madeline

The steady rhythm of raindrops pattering against the windowpane filled the dimly lit room as Madeline gazed into the dancing flames of the fire. The warmth emanating from it provided a comforting contrast to the autumn chill in the air outside Jacob's cottage.

Nestled among towering trees and surrounded by nature, this small home had indeed offered a haven – a place to escape the turmoil of the world at war.

It had been five days since Jacob had brought her here from the hospital. During the long days and nights, he had been her constant companion, nursing her back to health with his gentle touch and kind words. Often out on the land, today he was in the main house working.

As Madeline watched the flames flicker, she felt grateful for his care and attention. Tears misted her eyes as she thought of his kindness, and she realised it had been so long since someone had taken care of her. Her family was always there to support her, but to have someone tend to her needs in such a kind and intimate way hadn't happened since... well, since Alex. She stretched out her leg, which was healing well but was still stiff and quite sore.

Memories of her husband flooded her mind, memories she had tried to lock away. But in the stillness of the cottage, they came rushing back with a force she couldn't resist. She remembered the way he would hold her, the way his hands would brush her face, and the way he would whisper, '*I love you*,' into her ear, in the middle of the day with the bookshop full of people.

As Madeline's heart ached at the thought of him, she opened her eyes to see Jacob standing in front of her, holding a cup of tea.

'I thought you might want a drink,' he said softly, taking a seat beside her.

She yawned, her eyes shifting to the clock on the mantelpiece. 'Is it that time already? I didn't hear you come in.' She took a sip of the tea, the warmth of it spreading through her body. 'Thank you,' she whispered, grateful for the distraction.

Jacob gazed at her with concern in his eyes. 'When I came in, you seemed troubled.'

Madeline sighed, feeling vulnerable. 'I was just thinking about someone from my past. It's silly, really.'

His brow furrowed. 'It's not silly if it's causing you pain. Were you thinking about a friend of yours?'

Madeline hesitated for a moment, contemplating whether to reveal more. She had opened up about many aspects of her life in recent days, yet had conspicuously sidestepped any mention of Alex. The reason for her silence on the subject eluded her but as she looked over at Jacob there was a sincerity in his gaze, a genuine concern that beckoned her to trust.

As she steadied herself with a deep breath, the clock continued to thrum gently, a calming, steady rhythm to the backdrop of the crackle and heat of the fireplace.

'I used to be married and my late husband's name was Alex...' she began. Her voice trailed off as she prepared herself to deal with the sadness that was always present when she talked about him. 'He was the most amazing person, kind and funny, passionate about life, about books. When he first came up with the idea of us buying a bookshop, I thought he was mad. But we had some of our happiest times in that little space. It's why it means so much to me, because of the memories.'

Jacob listened attentively. 'It sounds like he was a wonderful person,' he said softly. Madeline swallowed down the brimming feelings that were tightening her throat.

She returned to the flickering flames, lost in thought for a moment, before meeting his gaze again. The question was in his eyes, but he was sensitive enough not to ask it.

'He died so suddenly, of cancer. He was so strong, I couldn't believe how quickly he deteriorated.' She drew in a stuttering breath. 'I nursed him to the end.' Her voice trembled with raw emotion, conveying the depth of her sorrow and longing.

'That must have been difficult for you, losing someone you loved like that,' Jacob said gently.

She dabbed at her eyes with the tips of her fingers. 'I'm sorry, it just you have been so kind, and it has been so long since I stopped, or had a chance to think or breathe.'

He brushed her hand gently. 'It sounds like it was time.'

She agreed.

They both sipped their tea in silence for a moment, before he continued.

'What would Alex think about you being a spy?' he asked, turning towards her.

She chuckled. 'He would have got a tremendous kick out of it; he was a great adventurer and would have signed up for it in a heartbeat. But I think he would be amazed at the fact that I was doing this.'

'I'm sure he would be proud of you.'

'I'm sorry, I didn't mean to burden you with my troubles.'

Jacob shook his head, his tone firm. 'You're not a burden,' he assured her. 'You are risking your life for me. And for the Blumenthal family.'

Glad for a change of topic, Madeline shifted in her seat, pulling up her feet and nestling a cushion against her body. 'Tell me more about them. What happened to them?'

Jacob's face clouded. 'They fled not long after Hitler got into power. With all the propaganda out there, they didn't want to take the chance, with a young family. They didn't tell me where they went, in case it endangered my life. But I think they headed to the south. Mrs Blumenthal has family down there.

'They asked me to stay on and take care of the property. I have some hearing loss in one of my ears, so I knew I would never be called up, and I have such a love for this place. I grew up here you know; my father and grandfather both worked here.

'Before Mr Blumenthal left, he confided in me. He feared that if Hitler had his way no Jewish person, or their history, would be allowed to survive. And he was saddened that, if his children managed to survive this war, there would probably be nothing to come home to.

'He took me into the library. He had such a love for his books, and after the book-burning he was afraid the Nazis would destroy all that history. I promised him I would take care of them and anything else I could save. And that's what I've been doing,' he added with conviction.

'You have a deep connection to this place,' Madeline said softly. 'It's obvious in the way you talk about it.'

'Not unlike your bookshop, it holds powerful memories for me.'

'You've always done this alone?' she asked carefully, not wanting to pry, but still curious.

'You're wondering why I'm not married,' he said, decoding her vagueness, as he piled some more wood on the fire.

She felt herself blush. Was she that transparent?

His soft brown eyes found hers. 'I don't have a lot of time to socialise, and I guess I had some wild romantic notion of waiting for the right person. Does that sound foolish?'

Madeline shook her head. 'No, not at all. I think it's admirable.' She paused, considering her words carefully, thoughts of Alex crossing her mind. 'But it's important to remember that life is short, and sometimes we don't get as much time as we think we will.'

A sombre expression crossed Jacob's face. 'With this war, I know that all too well,' he said quietly. 'But I also believe that everything happens for a reason. Maybe I haven't found the right person yet because I'm meant to be here, taking care of this place, protecting the Blumenthal family's legacy.'

As he looked up at her, for one irrational moment she felt drawn to him. She wanted to pull him into her arms and kiss him. The thought shocked her. She hadn't felt any feelings like this since Alex.

Quickly returning her gaze to her cup, she hoped Jacob hadn't caught the look of longing in her eyes.

He snapped her out of her trance. 'I was hoping you were feeling like a little exercise tomorrow, to start strengthening that leg. After all, the doctor did say before you left that after five days you should start doing more walking.'

She finished her tea. 'Where did you have in mind?'

He sat back. 'Well, the Nazi is off to Poland again tomorrow and the rest of the staff are accompanying the family to the north, to see Mrs Mueller's family. So, the main house will be empty, and I would love you to see it. It's a very special place.'

She noted the admiration in his eyes. 'I would love that, too.'

They played cards, ate dinner together and talked into the

night. He was so easy to be with; it felt as if they were lifelong friends, not someone she'd met just a week ago.

The clock chimed the 11 p.m. hour and he turned to her.

'It's getting late. Would you like some help getting upstairs?'

She hadn't really needed help for the last two days – her leg was healing well – but she hadn't let on; she liked the ritual. 'If it's not too much trouble.'

He got up and reached his hand towards her. As she gripped his arm a shudder of desire raced through her body, taking her by surprise again.

Trying to shake off the feeling of attraction that made her painstakingly aware of the man at her side, Jacob helped her upstairs and into her room. She felt a pang of disappointment that he would be leaving her there alone.

'Thank you for everything, Jacob,' she said, turning towards him. 'I really appreciate all the help you've given me.'

'It's my pleasure,' he said softly. 'I'm just glad I could be here for you.'

She felt a sudden urge to do something bold, to make him stay just a little longer.

'I noticed you have such lovely books of poems here on the bookshelf. Would you mind reading one to me?' She hadn't meant to be that forthright, and her cheeks reddened. 'Does that sound childish, needing to be read to before I go to sleep?'

'Not at all. As I have aged, I have noticed the bedtime stories mean even more to me now than as a child. They give me so much hope.'

He pulled out a slim volume, Rainer Maria Rilke's *Letters to a Young Poet*, and read from it, finishing with, '*Perhaps all the dragons in our lives are princesses who are only waiting to see us act, just once, with beauty and courage. Perhaps everything that frightens us is, in its deepest essence, something helpless that wants our love.*'

'Do you believe that?' she asked wistfully. 'That hardships

are sent to allow our bravery to shine as well as reclaim a part of us that is unloved?'

He closed the book gently, his eyes searching hers. 'I do believe it,' he whispered, his voice soft yet unwavering. 'I believe that every challenge we face is an opportunity for us to find strength we never knew we had. And perhaps, just perhaps, those hardships are there to teach us how to love ourselves more fiercely, to embrace even the parts of us we once deemed unlovable.'

She felt a shiver run down her spine, not from fear but from a newfound sense of hope blossoming within her. In that moment, she saw herself not as a victim of her circumstances, of this war, of her husband's death, but as a warrior ready to face the dragons in her own life with grace and courage.

He continued, 'Without adversity, we are unable to measure our courage. I've reflected a lot on bravery since the war began. I'm starting to think that heroism isn't only about a single grand act. True courage might also be found in the numerous small acts of defiance, driven by an innate need to protect the vulnerable, the unique and the irreplaceable.

'Every book I hide, every photograph you take, are tiny pieces of a larger mosaic of bravery. These small acts accumulate, becoming a force in their own right, a testament to a spirit that refuses to be crushed. And in your quest to find that little Jewish boy...'

Madeline finished his thought. 'Maybe I will reclaim a part of myself that's been neglected and unloved.'

She settled back into the pillows to contemplate these words, thinking of how she had felt about herself since she had been unable to give Alex a child.

'I hope that wasn't too depressing,' he said with a small smile.

Madeline shook her head. 'No, it was beautiful.'

Jacob caught her gaze and she felt a lump form in her throat as he stood to leave. Reaching the door, he turned to her. 'Good-night, see you in the morning.'

As she undressed and got ready for bed, her thoughts were filled with all these new feelings that had suddenly started to emerge this evening, and she was shocked at the intenseness of them.

As she lay in bed, staring up at the ceiling in the darkness, she couldn't ignore the feeling of longing that had taken hold of her. But had it only started tonight? If she was honest with herself, she had been fighting feelings of attraction since the first moment she had entered this house, but had been pushing them away and forcing herself to think about Alex. As she allowed herself to explore these feelings without censorship, she wondered what it would be like to make love to Jacob. Would he be gentle and kind, like he was with her now? She imagined his soft lips brushing hers, his strong arms holding her close, his naked body pressed against her own.

Overwhelmed with desire, she squeezed her eyes shut, trying to push the thoughts away. In the next room she heard the bedsprings creak and felt herself blush. There was just a wall between them. He in his bed, she in hers.

And she couldn't help wondering if he was lying in there having similar thoughts about her.

32

SCOTLAND, NOVEMBER 2011

Olivia

At the hospital, Livi followed the paramedics as they rushed Kurt into accident and emergency. The sterile smell of antiseptic overwhelmed her, and the bright lights were blinding after the darkness of the night.

A nurse approached her and Livi recounted the events leading up to Kurt's collapse, her breath hitching as she spoke. Her words were swallowed up by the frantic motion that had surrounded them.

The nurse took notes from her as other medical staff swarmed around Kurt, taking him behind closed doors, leaving Livi feeling lost and alone in the sterile hallway. She wandered aimlessly, her thoughts in turmoil, as she waited for any news of her grandfather's condition.

Finally, the doctor emerged, her expression grim. 'Your grandfather has suffered a stroke,' she said, her voice gentle but firm. 'He was lucky you were there. If it had been an hour later, he may not have made it. It will be a few weeks, but we expect him to make a full recovery.'

'Can I see him?' she asked, her voice tight.

The doctor motioned for Livi to follow her. They walked down a long hallway and into a dimly lit room. Kurt lay in the hospital bed, his eyes closed and his breathing laboured.

Livi's heart broke at the sight of him, so frail and vulnerable. She took a seat beside him, holding his hand tightly.

Kurt's eyes flickered open, and he looked at Livi with a weak smile. 'You're still here, then? Will I never be rid of you?' His words carried a playful tone, and she sighed with relief. She sat beside him till he fell asleep again before she slipped into the corridor to call her mother and tell her about her dad.

Stephanie answered on the third ring.

'Hello, Livi, is that you? It's late, is everything all right?'

'No, Mum,' Livi said, her voice choked with emotion. 'I am up here in Scotland with my grandfather. He collapsed, and I had to call an ambulance. He's had a stroke, but the doctors say he'll recover. I'm at the hospital now.'

Her mother's voice was filled with concern. 'Oh, no, Livi! Are you okay? Is he?'

'I'm fine,' Livi said, wiping away her tears. 'It's just scary. But I'm here with him now, and he's going to be okay.'

'We'll come up on the first train tomorrow,' her mother promised. 'In the meantime, please take care of yourself, Livi.'

'I will, and I love you, Mum.'

'We love you too, darling.'

Once she had hung up, she quietly made her way back to Kurt's hospital room. The sounds of the machines and the sterile smell of disinfectant filled the room, with only the occasional sound of footsteps from passing nurses breaking the stillness out in the corridor.

Livi sank down and leaned back against the chair, closing her eyes and exhaling a heavy sigh of exhaustion and worry. The weight of the day's events settled on her shoulders as she tried to find some solace in this brief moment of quiet.

The night wore on and the nurses let Livi stay by Kurt's side, but he never stirred as her hand clasped his tightly. She watched the rise and fall of his chest, her stomach knotted with emotion.

She had just got herself a cup of coffee when her parents arrived, early the next day, her mother striding down the corridor, face clouded with worry, her father by her side, trying to keep up.

Livi rushed to them and embraced them tightly, taking comfort in their familiar presence.

'I'm so glad you're here!' she whispered, tears stinging her eyes once again.

'Of course, sweetheart,' her mother replied, holding her close. 'How is he?'

Livi led her mother to Kurt's room, where he lay sleeping peacefully. Stephanie took a seat beside her father's bed and reached for his hand, tears welling up in her eyes as she studied his face.

'He looks so frail,' she murmured, her voice catching in her throat.

'I know,' Livi replied, her own voice thick with emotion. 'But the doctor said he should recover fully.'

Livi's father took his own seat beside Kurt's bed, and when her grandfather awoke his eyes settled on his only daughter.

'Hello, Dad,' she said flatly. Livi knew this had to be hard for her, having no contact with him for so many years and now seeing him so fragile.

'Hello, Stephanie,' Kurt replied, his voice weak but filled with warmth. 'It's been a long time; I'm sorry you have to see me like this.'

'Don't be silly,' Livi's mother replied, squeezing his hand. 'We're just glad you're going to be okay.'

Kurt's eyes lingered on his only child as if capturing every detail of her face to be engraved in his memory forever.

Just then a nurse came in and ushered them out into the hall so she could check on Kurt and administer his medication.

'Why don't you go back to his house and get some sleep or a shower?' Stephanie encouraged her daughter.

Livi suddenly felt the exhaustion catching up on her. 'That sounds like a good idea. I'll come back as soon as I can.'

She knew her clothes were rumpled and her hair a tangled mess as she stepped out into the crisp morning air. But the day was lovely, with the sun high in the sky and the birds chirping their cheerful melodies. Livi took a deep breath, filling her lungs with the fresh air. It felt good to be outside, away from the sterile hospital environment.

At Kurt's house, she took a nap and then a long, hot shower, letting the water wash away the stress and fear of the previous night, and she felt like a new person when she emerged from the bathroom, her hair wet. She caught a glimpse of herself in the mirror and winced. She looked haggard, with dark circles under her green eyes.

She rummaged through her suitcase and found a fresh set of clothes, and dressed. She was too wound up to sleep any longer, so she made her way back to the hospital, stopping at a café along the way to grab a coffee and a croissant.

When she arrived back, Kurt's doctor was in the room talking to her parents.

Kurt was awake and sitting upright in bed, and he greeted her with a faint smile. Her grandfather looked weak, but also relaxed. The usual brusque exterior had been softened by his experience. She listened intently as the doctor discussed his treatment plan and the rehabilitation process he would have to go through.

'We would like to keep him here for about a week, then he can go home, but he will need some help for a few weeks after that.'

Worry shadowed her mother's face. Livi knew she had a lot

of ongoing commitments at home that would hinder her ability to be here for her father.

'I can stay with him.' Livi spoke up, surprising herself. 'I can work in the library at the end of his road – they have internet – and stay here for a few weeks.'

Her parents looked grateful. 'Are you sure, Livi?'

'I'm sure,' Livi replied, her voice firm as she placed a hand on his arm. 'He's my grandfather. I want to be here for him.'

Kurt's eyes filled with tears. He was obviously touched by her care.

'Thank you, Olivia,' he said, his voice barely a whisper. 'I don't want to be a burden to anyone.'

Livi reassured him. 'You're not a burden. I want to help you. We're family, and that's what family does.'

His eyes met hers as though she was speaking a foreign language. And Livi knew this would be an interesting time for both of them. But maybe it would bring them closer in the way she desired.

Her parents stayed the day and left on the evening train. As her mother was leaving Kurt called out to her.

'Stephanie.' His voice was weak but unwavering.

Her mother turned to face him, surprised by the sudden seriousness in his tone.

Kurt took a deep breath, his eyes never leaving Stephanie's. 'When your mother and I divorced, I didn't fight for custody for you because I thought it was for the best. She knew how to love you, do the best for you, and I was no good at any of that. I just didn't know how to...' His voice trailed off before he coughed and continued, 'But I want you to know, you did nothing wrong.'

Stephanie's eyes welled up with tears. 'Thank you, Dad,'

she said, her voice barely above a whisper. 'But we're here now, and that's all that matters.'

Kurt offered a weary smile. 'Yes, we are. And I'm grateful to Livi for contacting me and I would like to stay in touch.'

Livi watched the exchange and, even though it was brief, she could sense a lifetime of regret and sorrow in her grandfather's eyes.

In the corridor Stephanie, her eyes clouded with emotion, said goodbye to Livi.

'Are you sure you'll be okay staying here with him?'

Livi gave her mother's hand a reassuring squeeze. 'I'll be fine, Mum. I want to be here.'

Stephanie hugged her tightly. 'Thank you, Olivia. I'm proud of you. You've been making some brave decisions lately. And it's good to see.'

Livi watched as her mother disappeared down the hallway. She knew this wouldn't be easy, but she was determined to be there for her grandfather, no matter what.

33

BERLIN, AUTUMN 1941

Madeline

The morning chorus of birds woke Madeline from her sleep, a comforting sound that signaled the start of another day in Jacob's company. As she stirred, her mind was immediately flooded with thoughts of him from the previous night. They had stayed up late, playing cards, their laughter echoing in the cozy sanctuary of his cottage. It had been such a simple yet perfect evening, highlighting the genuine connection she felt with him.

He had a way of putting her at ease, allowing her to let down her guard and truly be herself. It had been a long time since Madeline had felt this comfortable and relaxed around someone.

But alongside the budding friendship, there was an undeniable attraction simmering beneath the surface that threatened to consume her.

Madeline pushed aside the urge to get swept away by these feelings. She couldn't afford to let her personal desires cloud her judgment, especially with her life already complicated by the war.

As she dressed and ran a brush through her thick, bobbed hair, Madeline noticed the newfound brightness in her brown eyes.

Descending the stairs carefully, still feeling a slight stiffness in her leg, she found Jacob already in the kitchen, a mug of coffee in hand as he gazed out of the window. His face lit up with a warm smile at the sight of her.

'Good morning,' he greeted her with his usual kindness. 'How did you sleep?'

'Well, and you?' Madeline replied, trying to keep her voice steady despite the butterflies fluttering in her stomach.

Jacob chuckled softly as he poured her coffee. 'Not bad, though it took me a while to drift off. I couldn't stop thinking about our evening.'

Madeline recalled her own restless thoughts about Jacob but was reluctant to share her emotional struggles with him. 'Last night was wonderful. I really enjoyed our game,' she said, avoiding elaborating on her own feelings, as she accepted the cup he handed to her.

His eyes lingered on hers. 'I did too,' he replied, his voice soft filled with tenderness and longing that hinted at something more than just cards.

Quickly lowering her gaze to her coffee, Madeline attempted to shift the conversation to safer ground. 'What do you need to do on the estate today?'

'With everyone away, I want to spend time with *you*,' Jacob said with an intensity that sent a shiver down her spine.

Madeline met his gaze with a warm smile. Trying to swallow down her feelings.

'That would be lovely,' she said trying to sound casual and disguise the tremor in her voice.

After breakfast, they set off on a leisurely walk through the sprawling grounds, Jacob sharing stories of his childhood and the rich history of his family and the estate. Madeline listened intently, captivated not only by his words but also by the passion and warmth in his voice.

As she observed him, she found herself drawing comparisons to Alex. Despite their differences, there was an underlying similarity between them. Alex had been outspoken about his views, while Jacob, though quieter, harbored an equal fervor for what he believed in.

Leading her to the back of the main house, Jacob revealed, 'There's something I would like to show you.' Madeline recalled her unease from her previous visit. Now, with all the staff and Mueller's family away, she could explore the Blumenthals' home without the distraction of Nazi presence. Yet, the pervasive swastikas served as a stark reminder of the house's current significance.

As they wandered through the rooms, she couldn't shake a sense of melancholy. This once vibrant estate, now barren, echoed with Jacob's tales of its former inhabitants. She envisioned the rooms bustling with lively conversations and children's laughter, contrasting sharply with the desolation brought by the war.

Jacob led her into the library, and she remembered the last time she had been here with Mrs Mueller.

'These shelves were filled with Jewish works of literature,' he explained, his voice filled with sorrow. 'I was told to take them away and burn them. But I couldn't bring myself to do it. Instead, I have hidden them away, hoping that one day they could be returned to their rightful owners. Some of the most important works, I asked you to take with you to France.'

'And I will continue to do that for as long as I can,' Madeline said firmly.

Jacob's eyes met hers with admiration. 'Your courage is truly inspiring.'

She chuckled. 'I'm not sure I make the best spy, but I guess I make a pretty decent camel. I'm driven by my love for books and couldn't bear to see all these precious works destroyed. I don't have the commitment that burns in some of the agents I meet, those so willing to die for their cause. But I hate injustice, so I have my own way of fighting, of preserving what I think is important.'

They left the main house and strolled towards the lake, its water glistening in the early morning light. A gentle breeze rustled through the trees, carrying with it the scent of pine.

A sense of peace enveloped Madeline. Despite the weight of her complex life, Jacob had provided a much-needed respite during their time together.

At a small wooden bench overlooking the lake, they paused and took a moment to enjoy the view across the water. They sat in silence for a moment, both of them lost in their own thoughts. The bench was small, and their bodies were so close together a prickle of desire rippled across Madeline's skin.

She turned to look at him and his gaze drifted also towards her. He studied her face for a moment, his eyes lingering on her lips with an intensity that she was sure meant he was contemplating kissing her. It stirred the air between them. Unsure how to navigate this or her own flood of emotions, she turned away, attempting to quell her growing desire.

Jacob's touch on her arm was tender, silently urging her to face him. Slowly, she complied, her stomach fluttering with anticipation.

'I need to tell you something,' he began softly, his voice caressing the tense silence.

'What is it?' she whispered, her response barely threading through the air.

Taking a deep breath, Jacob confessed, 'From the moment we met, I've felt an undeniable connection to you. I've tried to dismiss it, attributing it to mere physical attraction, but it's deeper, Madeline. So much more.'

'I feel it too,' she admitted, her voice quivering, revealing her own inner turmoil. 'But I have to find Ada, and my life is in Paris. Not to mention, I could be arrested at any time if the Nazis found out what I was doing. I need to stay focused. I'm not sure there is much room in my life for a love affair right now. It wouldn't be fair to either of us.'

Jacob's face fell slightly, a flicker of disappointment clouding his eyes. 'You're right. Duty must come first,' he said, his tone heavy with sorrow.

'But,' Madeline added, 'that doesn't mean we can't make the most of the time we have together.'

Jacob's disappointment was evident, but he seemed softened by her touch.

As they made their way back, Madeline's limp became more pronounced, and Jacob, ever attentive, offered his arm. As she drew close to him his whole presence surrounded her, the scent of pine from his cologne, the warmth of his body, and the closeness of his cheek to her own – a dance of proximity that was both comforting and excruciating.

Back at the house, Jacob helped Madeline to a comfortable chair near the fireplace. He disappeared briefly and returned with a tray of tea and small cakes. They sat in front of the crackling fire, hands wrapped around warm cups, but the mood remained overshadowed by their earlier conversation.

Jacob then left her to do some work on the estate, and was gone much longer than usual. She guessed he was taking time to consider all they had talked about, but still she missed him.

When he came back, they ate a slightly uncomfortable dinner filled with emotional tension before retiring to the front room. As the clock struck nine, Jacob stood up.

'I think I'm going to get an early night. Mueller is back tomorrow, and there are things I need to do in the morning to prepare.'

Madeline agreed, feeling a pang of sadness. She yearned to return to the warmth and intimacy they had enjoyed before his confession. But something had shifted between them, and she wasn't sure how they could make their way back.

They climbed the stairs together, Jacob's supporting hand making the heat between them grow with every step. When they reached the landing, their eyes met in silent understanding.

Jacob's voice was husky with desire as he bade her goodnight.

'Goodnight, Jacob,' she replied, her own voice barely above a whisper. As she watched him retreat into his room, her heart ached with the knowledge of their shared feelings.

Madeline closed her door and leaned against it. Caught in a storm of emotions, she paced the room restlessly. The pull towards Jacob was almost unbearable, yet she knew yielding to it could only complicate their lives further. The war had already taken so much from her, and she feared if she let go, let him in, and he was taken from her, she would never recover.

As she undressed for bed, highlights of their week together replayed in her mind – their deep conversations, his laughter, his touch, the way his eyes lingered on her. The memories were visceral and intense.

She got into bed, trying to fight everything burning inside her. Staring up at the ceiling, she knew she would never sleep. Desperate for answers, she whispered out loud to the room.

'Alex, what should I do?'

That was when she saw it. She couldn't believe she had been here a week and not noticed it until now. She got out of bed and padded to the bookshelf. It felt like a miracle and it was all the encouragement she needed.

High on the top shelf was a book titled *Die Elenden*: the German translation of *Les Misérables*.

She pulled it down and smiled. It was a sign, she knew it, and it was all the encouragement she needed. 'Thank you, Alex,' she whispered, tears of relief pricking her eyes.

She placed it back and grabbed her dressing gown, then crossed the landing, and paused in front of his door for just a second to gather herself before knocking and whispering against the wood. 'Jacob, are you awake?'

He must have been, because he answered the door immediately, his face flushed and his clothes slightly dishevelled.

'Madeline...' he sighed, his voice capturing their mutual longing in a single word.

He stood aside and, knowing she was making a choice that would forever change the course of both their lives, Madeline stepped into Jacob's room.

34

Olivia

It had been over a week since her grandfather's stroke and, to prepare for him coming home, Livi decided to clean the house. She found a broom and cleaning materials in Kurt's hall cupboard and set about getting the place in order. As she tidied away piles of discarded newspapers and threw out expired food from his fridge, she wondered who the last person had been who had taken care of him.

She entered his study. There were piles of papers and magazines and, not wanting to anger him by moving too much around, she began to carefully move the piles in order to clean the desk. As she gently transported a stack of letters onto the side table, one without an envelope fluttered down to the floor. She leaned down to pick it up, and caught a glimpse of some of the wording at the end of the letter.

Please, if you are the same Kurt who came from Germany to Paris during the war and ended up on the train with a group of

orphans, I would so appreciate hearing from you. Kind regards,
Esther Walker

The breath caught in Livi's throat as she read the words.
She knew she should just tuck it back in the pile and ignore it.
After all this was her grandfather's personal correspondence
and was none of her business. But as much as she told herself
this, she found herself compelled to turn it over.

The words on the page were neatly written, each sentence
carefully crafted. Esther, the letter-writer, lived in the
Cotswolds and her mother had taken a train with a group of
orphans during World War Two, and Esther believed that Kurt
himself might have been one of them.

You would have been about six or seven during the evacuation
and one of the other orphans talked about a book you had
with you.

Esther went on to describe the book, which sounded a lot
like the book Livi's grandfather had given her during her first
visit. She scanned the date at the top and calculated the days
back in her head.

He would have received this around the date he had called
her out of the blue. She pictured him sitting at this desk, reading
this. Was that what had provoked him to phone her? To finally
put the ghosts of his past to rest?

The chilly air nipped at Livi's cheeks as she walked to the
hospital, her thoughts consumed by what she had learned. Her
emotions were a whirlwind, torn between wanting answers and
fearing the pain it might cause her grandfather.

The door to Kurt's room creaked open softly as she entered,
a dim light casting a pale glow over the sterile walls, creating an

atmosphere of quiet solitude. The distant hum of machines was the only sound, punctuating the stillness like a metronome keeping time.

Her grandfather was sitting up in bed, reading glasses perched on his nose as he read the paper.

'Hi there,' Livi whispered, her voice barely audible, as she took a seat beside his bed. The weight of the letter seemed to grow heavier with each passing moment.

'Hello, Olivia,' Kurt replied, a small smile forming on his lips. 'Do you not have a job at home to go to?'

The question sounded accusatory, but his tone was far from stern.

'I can work from home with my job. My boss is fine with me being up here for a while.'

'Aye, it's all the way now, hey, people on the internet.'

'Yes, I just pop down to the library at the end of your road to do a little work, when I need to.'

'In my day, you had to get up and actually go to work for eight hours a day to earn your living.'

Livi nodded vaguely, her thoughts still far away. Her curiosity gnawed at her insides, making it increasingly difficult to focus on anything else. She forced herself back to the conversation.

'How are you feeling today?' she asked.

'Much stronger. They reckon I can be up and about tomorrow and then head home,' Kurt replied with a smile.

Livi felt a twinge of sadness at the thought of leaving. Despite looking forward to getting home, she had grown closer to him over the past week.

'Have you been keeping busy?' Kurt enquired, pulling her from her thoughts.

'Uh, yeah,' she stammered, 'I've been cleaning your house.' Her eyes darted away from his, not wanting to reveal that she had been in his office and what she had found.

'Ah, thank you,' he said, his voice softening. 'You didn't have to do that.'

'It's the least I can do for you. That's what families do.'

He looked at her blankly, as if once again, the concept was foreign to him.

As their conversation continued, Livi struggled to keep up with the small talk while thoughts of what she had read weighed heavily on her mind. The idea of causing Kurt more pain was unbearable, but leaving the mystery unsolved was equally distressing, and she wanted to explore further.

She began hesitantly, her voice wavering with emotion. 'I was wondering about the reason you called me and invited me here. You had been so adamant about not wanting to see me.'

Kurt's expression became guarded, his eyes flickering away from Livi's for a moment. Amid his hesitation, she also sensed a glimmer of openness, a testament to the trust they had built. She pressed on, resolved to uncover the truth.

'I'm sorry, I don't mean to pry, but I can't help but wonder why you never stayed in touch. Was it something we did, or...?'

Kurt sighed heavily, his shoulders slumping forward with resignation. 'It wasn't anything you did, Olivia. At least not directly. It's more... complicated than that.'

'What do you mean by complicated?' she asked cautiously.

Kurt hesitated before answering, taking time to gather his thoughts. 'There were things in my past that made me wary of being too close to other people,' he said finally, his voice barely above a whisper. 'And soon, that need to keep people at a distance became a habit. Before I knew it, my defensive walls of protection were also isolating me, and I just didn't know how to change that.'

Feeling a surge of empathy, Livi reached out to take his hand and gave it a gentle squeeze. He looked up at her, the vulnerability in his eyes tugging at her heartstrings. She could see the years of pain of that disconnection and how it had affected him. They sat in silence for a few moments, the only sound coming from the machines beeping in the background.

'Something happened after you called me that that might help you understand why I got back in touch,' he said, his voice steady.

Livi's heart skipped a beat as she waited for her grandfather to continue.

'During the war, I was taken to Paris, and ended up on a train with four other orphans. The things that happened to us were horrific, and it changed me, hardened me. There was no one I felt I could trust. And even the adults who were supposed to take care of me let me down.'

As Livi listened to her grandfather's words, a weight settled in her heart, her thoughts racing as she grappled with the depth of his pain. In that moment, she glimpsed the vulnerable little boy within him. It was evident from his struggle to talk about this that Kurt had never opened up about it before. The fact that he was choosing to share it with her now felt like a gift.

'I'm so sorry,' she said softly, her eyes brimming with tears. 'I had no idea.'

He continued, 'None of my family knows. But not long after you called me, I received a letter from a woman who wants to bring the orphans from that train back together. It got me thinking about all the things from my past that had stolen so much from me. And then I remembered your call. I thought that maybe it wasn't too late for me to make a change, starting with you.'

Livi was moved to tears by her grandfather's vulnerability. She reached out and gently squeezed his hand, offering silent support.

'So, does this mean you will go and see the other orphans?' she asked gently.

He shook his head. 'I don't think so.'

Livi could see the sadness in her grandfather's eyes, and she knew that this was a difficult decision for him to make. She wanted to respect his wishes, but she couldn't help feeling that he was missing out on a chance to reconnect with a part of his past that he had been running from for so long.

'Are you sure?' she asked gently. 'I've had my own struggles with trust; I was married to a man who nearly shattered my trust in other people completely. But I've realised lately that facing my greatest fears head-on is the best way for me to avoid being victimised by that past. This could be an opportunity for you to finally find some closure.'

'Closure?' he scoffed. 'That's some modern psychobabble word for people all airing their dirty laundry in public. I can't see what rehashing the past with other people can do, apart from make me feel worse.'

Livi's heart sank at his words. As she left him that day, her mind was consumed with thoughts of Esther's letter and how confronting his past could hold the key to her grandfather's healing.

When she returned to his house, she immediately headed to his study and paced nervously as her eyes kept drifting towards the letter sitting on his desk. Picking it up and rereading it only strengthened her resolve to act. Surely it couldn't hurt to gather more information. Making a firm decision, she grabbed some stationery from his desk and began to write.

35

BERLIN, AUTUMN 1941

Madeline

Jacob took a confident step forward and, without a word, pulled Madeline into his arms. The warmth of his touch and the heat of his breath on her skin made her shiver, igniting the desire that had been building between them for so long.

Their lips met in a fiery kiss that sent a fresh wave of desire coursing through her body, igniting a fierce passion that tightened her stomach and left her breathless.

As he pulled her in closer, she roamed the strong contours of his back and shoulders, sculpted by hours of labouring on the land, before sliding her hand up to the sensitive skin at the back of his neck, causing him to shudder.

With her hands tangled in his hair, she deepened their kiss, craving him with a desperate hunger. He met her passion with equal intensity as they lost themselves in each other, oblivious to the world around them.

When their lips finally parted, Jacob leaned his forehead against hers, their breath ragged and unsteady.

'I've wanted to do that for so long,' he said, barely above a whisper.

Madeline agreed. 'I wanted it too. I never thought I could feel this way again after Alex's death. It was like I died too. I held back from loving again because I felt guilty, as if I was cheating on his memory. But since I've met you, I feel alive again.'

He gently pulled her towards him, his lips trailing down her neck as he whispered in her ear. 'He would want you to be happy, and I want to love you, Madeline. I want to make you so happy.'

Madeline moaned softly as his kisses grew more urgent, her body responding to his touch. She knew that Jacob was right; Alex would want her to be loved. And with Jacob, she felt true joy for the first time since his death.

There was so much to consider, all the complexities of their lives. But in that moment, the only thing Madeline could think of was Jacob and the way his lips felt on her skin.

As he leaned in close and whispered, his words were like a gentle caress. 'Do you remember when we first met? You asked me why I wasn't married.'

She let out a soft moan of pleasure, before saying, 'You said you were waiting for the right person.'

He gazed into her eyes with a tender intensity. 'That person was you, Madeline. It's clear to me now. I love you so deeply, and I have no reservations in admitting it. I've never experienced anything like this before. It's not just the attraction or the desire I have been battling since I met you, but a profound connection that goes beyond words. Every moment without you feels wasted, and every thought is consumed by you.'

'I feel the same way,' she mumbled, her lips pressed against his. 'But how can we even consider being together? You live here in Germany, and I'm in France. And there's still this war raging around us...'

'I don't care. I'd still choose one hour of pure bliss with you over an entire lifetime without you.'

Unable to contain her desire any longer, and their bodies yearning for more of each other's touch, she led him across the room, her heart thudding with anticipation. Sliding onto the bed, their eyes locked in an unspoken understanding of what was to come.

Taking a moment to catch his breath, he looked directly into her eyes, his voice husky with his desire. 'Are you sure you are ready for this?'

'I have never been more certain,' she assured him eagerly.

She noticed his hand shaking as he slowly and tenderly untied her dressing gown and carefully slid it from her body. Then he lifted her nightdress over her head. In the cool night air, she shuddered with both cold and nervousness.

With her own trembling fingers, Madeline frantically unbuttoned his shirt. In her haste she accidentally snapped off a button, and it flew across the room. They shared a nervous laugh before they were consumed by their desire once again.

Soon they were both naked, their lips and hands exploring every inch of exposed skin, leaving a trail of goosebumps in their wake. As their desire intensified their bodies naturally inter-twined, and they lost themselves in the rhythm of their move-ments. Their eyes locked with desire, communicating a profound understanding of the emotions coursing through them.

Madeline had forgotten how intense and satisfying love-making could be, a blissful connection that went far beyond the physical. Every touch, every kiss, every whisper was electrify-ing, igniting a fire within her that she had long forgotten existed.

'You're so beautiful,' he whispered softly, tears in the corner of his eyes as he traced his fingers along her neck. She looked deep within him, and saw his raw vulnerability and just how deeply he truly loved her. As her own walls surrendered to his touch, she knew she loved him too.

Afterwards, they lay there, breathless and panting as they stared into each other's eyes, a silent understanding passing between them, deepening their connection more than words ever could.

They lay in each other's arms until the early hours of the morning, talking and sharing, kissing and caressing, unable to get enough of each other's touch.

They made love again just before sunrise and afterwards as he ran his fingertips down the curve of her back, his voice trembled with emotion. 'You have brought me more joy than I ever knew was possible. I wish we could stay in this room forever.'

Madeline agreed as she pulled him back against her. 'I feel so safe with you,' she sighed as she curled her body around him, both their bodies still trembling slightly from the intense passion that had just consumed them.

'Hold me as close as you can,' she whispered, implying more than just physically.

'I promise you, I will never let go,' Jacob responded as he pulled her closer. And as her body calmed, she never wanted this feeling to end.

As Jacob drifted off to sleep in her arms, Madeline pushed away all the thoughts that threatened to rob her of the beauty of this moment. She closed her eyes and savoured the warmth of his touch, the weight of his body pressed against hers.

In that moment, she was content to feel deliriously happy, and it had been a very long time since she had felt that way.

36

SCOTLAND, DECEMBER 2011

Olivia

It was a few weeks after her grandfather's stroke, and he had returned home and was making a good recovery.

'It helps that he has family around to support him,' the district nurse, who came in to check on him, informed her. 'I see so many people on their own; it breaks my heart.'

Livi felt a pang of sadness as she watched the nurse leave. She couldn't bear the thought of what could have happened if she hadn't persisted in seeing Kurt and trying to get closer to him.

In their weeks together, Livi and Kurt had grown closer, spending time playing cards or chess. She had started to see a softer side to her grandfather and, though she still wouldn't refer to their relationship as warm and fluffy, there had been a definite softening of his demeanour towards her.

Not wanting to halt his recovery, she had stayed away from any other conversations about his past. He didn't seem to be prepared to share any more of his mother's story, and she had proved they were descendants of Nazis; there was nothing they

could do about it. And since sending her letter, she had heard
nothing from Esther.

So, it was a surprise when Markus called her the morning
before she left Scotland, just as she was starting work at the
local library.

His tone was excited as he greeted her. 'Livi, you have to
come back to Berlin! There is someone I want you to meet. He
knows a lot more about members of the estate during the war.'

Livi's stomach tightened with anticipation. Since she had
left Germany, she and Markus had stayed in touch as they had
promised, keeping everything light. And she had been so preoccupied with her grandfather's recovery that she hadn't had
much time to contemplate their growing friendship further. She
had tried to dismiss it as something like a holiday romance, but
would this change if she went back? Was she ready for that?

When she told Damien she was leaving again, he offered to
drive her to the airport. On the way, he looked over at her and
shook his head in disbelief. 'You had not left that flat except to
go to work in the five years I have known you, and now you are
jet-setting all over the place!'

'Yes, thank goodness that Hesse brought in some money.
But I have to go, Damien – he's found something really important, and I just can't let it go. You know what I'm like.'

'Oh, are you sure it's not a certain good-looking *German*
that you can't let go?' Damien joked, and she felt her cheeks
flush because she couldn't wholeheartedly say it wasn't. As
much as she had been preoccupied with her grandfather, she
remembered with a tightening of her stomach the evening she
and Markus had spent together in the snow.

In Berlin, she paused in the doorway of Otto Beckmann's
bookshop, again, and her senses filled with the familiar scent of
old books. She spotted Markus as he leaned over the counter,

examining something with great interest, and her stomach flip-flopped with excitement to see him.

When he turned and saw her, the look of warm affection in his eyes was undeniable. He moved towards her and enveloped her in a hug that sent a shiver from her stomach right to her toes. His skin was warm against hers, and the fresh scent of his after-shave lingered momentarily on her cheek.

He introduced her to the elderly man sitting on a stool beside the counter. 'I'd like you to meet Herr Werner Weiss-man. He's a historian and a Holocaust survivor. He was showing me an old map of Eichenwald from that time.' Markus continued, 'after you left, I couldn't get your book and Eichen-wald out of my mind. Then I remembered an old friend of my father's – Werner.'

Weissman's thinning white hair framed his weathered face, while his dark eyes seemed to bear the weight of the life he had lived. He offered Livi a solemn nod, which she returned with equal respect. 'Ms Stapleton,' he began in a voice that carried the quiet strength of survival, 'Markus tells me you're seeking information about wartime activities at Eichenwald.'

'My family has a connection to the place, and I'm trying to uncover the truth about our past.'

'Then allow me to help you,' Werner said, a glimmer of determination in his eyes. 'I have some knowledge of the manor and its dark past; it is where Hitler announced his plans for the concentration camps, on the twentieth of January 1942.'

Livi shuddered at that thought, as he continued.

'At my home, I have something that might be of interest to you.'

Upon entering Werner's study, Livi felt as if she had entered a sanctuary of knowledge and remembrance. Shelves lined the walls, filled with books, photographs and documents, all serving as silent testimonial to a time when humanity's darkest instincts had reigned supreme. Livi instantly felt at home. History was her world; it was where she spent most of her time, and Herr Weissman's collection was impressive.

As she studied some of the pictures on the walls that brought the war to life in such a vivid way, she became lost in a different world.

Her attention was pulled from the shelves when a petite woman wearing a dark polo-neck sweater and trousers entered the room. She had a kind round face and twinkling blue eyes, and white hair pulled into a loose bun.

'I see Werner has managed to attract new flies into his web of war,' she said with a chuckle, and, by the way she met her husband's eyes, it was obviously a joke between them.

'No, actually, we came willingly,' Livi responded with a mischievous grin.

Werner raised bushy eyebrows in a gesture of innocence as his wife shook her head in disbelief. 'Well, as you may not get out of here for hours, knowing how my husband can talk, would you like a cup of coffee?' They all responded in the affirmative and, after the drinks arrived, Livi and Markus gathered around a rickety coffee table as Werner made himself comfortable in a well-worn leather armchair. As she watched him settle himself down, Livi wondered how many times he had done this to tell his stories.

As Livi sipped her coffee, Werner began. His voice was calm and measured, but there was a deep sadness that lingered in his eyes.

Livi listened attentively, her heart aching at the horrors Werner had witnessed and endured. 'I was just a boy when the war began,' he said, his voice cracking slightly. 'And yet, I saw things that no child should ever have to see. My family was taken to a concentration camp, and only I survived.'

Livi could see the pain that lined Werner's face, and she

knew that his memories were still as vivid as ever as he continued. 'After we were released, at first I wanted to put everything I had known and seen behind me and make a new life for myself. I met Bettina, and we had three lovely daughters, and I tried to live my life the best I could.

'But about twenty years ago, I started to see something very disturbing. Not only were people forgetting what happened during the war, but some were denying the Holocaust altogether. Well, that kept me awake at night, until one day I told Bettina I had to do something about it. By then, I was a history professor here in Berlin, and so I decided to retire and instead spend my time making right that wrong.' Gesturing to the room around them, he said proudly, 'Now, this is the fruit of my labours.'

'It's very impressive,' Livi encouraged.

He was pensive for a moment. 'You asked me about Herrenhaus Eichenwald. What do you want to know?'

Livi cleared her throat, surprised at how emotional she felt starting her story. She handed Werner the photographs she had found at the auction, and he looked them over with great interest.

'This is a picture of my great-grandmother, Ada,' she said, pointing out the picture of her with the rose bush.

'Yes, yes, Ada Mueller.' He nodded. 'She was Herr Mueller's first wife. I know of her.'

Livi sucked in a breath. 'Can you tell me anything about what happened to her?'

The professor sat back in his seat as he thought through the facts he knew. 'From what I remember, Ada Mueller was a victim of the regime, as were so many others, pulled into their propaganda. Her husband, Herr Frederick Mueller, was a high-ranking officer in the SS and head of the local Gestapo. He was known for his brutal tactics and unwavering loyalty to the cause. He helped establish Auschwitz and was responsible for many of the atrocities that occurred there. After they split up, Mueller lived there with his second wife, who had a young daughter from a previous marriage. Ada was believed to have died during the war, but there are rumours that there is more to the story than what was officially reported.'

'What kind of rumours?'

Werner leaned forward, his expression serious. 'Some people say that Ada was murdered by Mueller to avenge his pride after she left him. But no one knows what really happened to her. Because after she left him she... disappeared.'

Livi's mind reeled with the prospect that her great-grand-mother might have been murdered by her ex-husband. No wonder Kurt couldn't talk about it. Her mouth was dry as she sought more clarification. 'Do you think there's any truth to those rumours?'

'There is a story of a woman who was killed by Mueller. Her name was not Ada but, from the stories I have gathered, the reason for the murder seems very personal. A lot of people had false papers back then, and her son was too young for us to trace.'

Livi felt her blood run cold. 'My grandfather,' she said, her voice thready.

Markus leaned forward and covered her hand. She didn't pull back; she needed his comfort right then.

Werner's eyes widened. 'Is your grandfather still alive?'

'Yes.'

'Surely he knows the story of what happened to his mother?'

'He has hinted at it, but seems too traumatised to talk about it.'

The professor sighed. 'It happened to a lot of survivors. Give him time to process the weight of the past, because it can become too much to carry alone.'

Livi took in Werner's words, feeling grateful for his understanding. She knew he was right. Her grandfather had carried the burden of his past alone for far too long.

She took a sip of her coffee and asked, 'The woman who Mueller murdered, do you have any information on her?'

The professor knotted his eyebrows and rose from his chair. 'Let me see.' He pulled down a tattered leather records book from his bookshelves. 'I keep a record of all the mysteries I haven't solved yet. I believe I wrote it down in here... Ahh, here it is,' he said, pulling his glasses down to the tip of his nose as he read the words he had written: 'Gertrud Schmidt, killed by Frederick Mueller in 1942. Then I have added a note: 'Was this Ada Mueller, his first wife who just disappeared?' And I have another note of reference, I call it my "morgue file".' He pulled down another dusty book, opened it and handed it to Livi. 'Look who claimed the body from the morgue.'

Livi peered at the professor's scrawling handwriting and read the name: Jacob Weiss. It was vaguely familiar to her, but she couldn't place it for the moment. She turned to Werner for clarification.

'Jacob Weiss was the caretaker of Eichenwald during World War Two. He worked for the Resistance.'

Suddenly, the picture at the manor swirled back into her mind: the slender man with the dark moustache and the hunting rifle at his side.

Werner continued, 'I don't think it is a coincidence. As far as records show, Jacob Weiss was an only child, with no wife, so was this a girlfriend? What would have been his interest in this Gertrud Schmidt? Whoever she was, it was Jacob who buried her.'

'Do you know where?'

Werner shook his head. 'Unfortunately, I don't know. But I will go back through all my records to see if I have missed anything.'

Livi felt exhausted. Learning all of this had been hard. Was this mystery woman, Gertrud Schmidt, a secret girlfriend of this caretaker, or her great-grandmother carrying false papers? She suddenly had an image of her grandfather as a small boy. Had he been there when this happened?

It was no wonder he was so shut down. She thought of his sad, solitary life in Scotland. Maybe it wasn't a choice. Maybe, because of all he had been through, it was all he was capable of.

After they had said goodbye to Werner, Livi and Markus went out to dinner. He took her to his favourite place, a cosy bistro hidden in a quiet corner of the city. The warm glow of a string of lights illuminated their table as they sat down, and the soft chatter of other diners provided a comforting background noise. They ordered a bottle of rich red wine to accompany their meal, and to eat Markus insisted she try a traditional German meal of schnitzel with a side of creamy mashed potatoes and tangy sauerkraut. Livi took a hesitant bite, but then savoured the flavourful combination that danced on her taste buds.

Markus watched her with a small smile, pleased to see her enjoying the local cuisine. She had thought seeing him again would be awkward, but instead she found herself feeling surprisingly at ease in his presence.

The evening started off well, filled with engaging conversation about the discoveries they'd made. However, as they delved into more personal topics the conversation took an unexpected turn.

They had been discussing past relationships and Markus had been talking about the importance of honesty. As he did, he used a phrase that sent a jolt through Livi's body. It was one that her ex-husband Graham had often used to manipulate her: 'Love should be unconditional.'

Livi's grip on her wine glass tightened as Graham's words echoed in her mind. She recalled his manipulative smile and the way he used those words to justify his mistreatment of her. Her anxiety grew as a cascade of memories flooded back, threatening to overwhelm her.

She remembered the years she had spent believing that love meant sacrificing her own needs and desires to meet someone else's expectations. To Graham, 'unconditional' had meant he could do whatever he wanted, and she had to accept it without question or complaint.

Markus noticed the change in Livi's demeanour and reached out to her.

'Livi, are you okay?' he asked, placing a hand on hers. Livi flinched at his touch, feeling a panic attack coming on.

'I'm not feeling well, Markus. I need to leave,' she said quickly, her voice trembling as she felt the weight of the memories pressing down on her. Markus's brow furrowed in concern as she jumped to her feet.

He paid the bill quickly, but she was already out the door when Markus caught up to her, she was breathing shallow and rapid as she sought the fresh air outside.

'Livi, please talk to me. What's wrong?' Markus asked softly, his eyes filled with genuine worry. Livi shook her head, unable to form any words as tears stung her eyes.

'It's nothing... I just need to breathe,' she managed to choke out, her voice barely above a whisper.

He drove her back to her hotel in silence, his worry evident in his tight grip on the steering wheel. Livi stared out of the window, her chest still tight, her breath coming in ragged gasps, as she began to calm down. Her mind was a whirlwind of emotions and memories she thought she had buried long ago.

When they finally arrived at the hotel, she leapt out of the car and practically ran to the entrance, mumbling her goodbye and something about needing to be alone.

It wasn't until she was in the safety of her hotel room that Livi allowed herself to break down. The dam she had built to hold back years of hurt and pain finally burst, and she collapsed onto the bed, sobbing uncontrollably.

The weight of her past relationship with Graham, the emotional manipulation and scars it had left on her heart, all came flooding back with a vengeance.

What had made her think that she was ready to move on and start a new chapter in her life? How could she have been so foolish as to believe that she had healed from the wounds of her past so easily? Livi curled into a ball on the bed, and cried herself to sleep.

37

PARIS, DECEMBER 1941

Madeline

On the evening of the seventh of December, Madeline rushed home to be with her family. She gathered with them around Bernard's illegal wireless to hear the news of an attack on Pearl Harbor, joining her parents and her sister Charlotte, who were already listening to the reports with somber expressions.

As she settled down beside them, a sense of urgency grew within Madeline – she still hadn't found Ada and her son in Berlin, and, as an American citizen who had so far been allowed to travel to Germany with relative ease, she knew this attack would have major ramifications for her trips there.

Unaware of Madeline's new plight, Bernard lowered his voice to a conspiratorial whisper as they listened intently.

'This changes everything,' he murmured, his eyes gleaming with excitement. 'It's about time the Americans stepped up.'

That night, Madeline hardly slept as her mind raced with thoughts of Ada and her son, still trapped in Berlin. And now there was Jacob. Her stomach tightened with thoughts of him. She had to find a way to still be able to travel to see him.

. . .

The next morning, as the sun began to rise, Madeline ventured out for her breakfast. People hurried about their daily routine, but there was an underlying sense that everything had changed.

She stood at the back of another long queue at the bakery, waiting patiently to buy a loaf of bread. As she glanced around, she noticed the faces of those around her, previously weary but now lifted with hope and expectancy, all in lively debate about the new events and what they could mean, some suggesting the war could be over in a matter of months now that the Americans were involved.

Back at her shop, Madeline inserted her key into the lock and twisted until she heard the familiar click. The door to The Elegance of Ink swung open, releasing the familiar comforting scent of her home. She stepped inside, taking a moment to savour the small respite from the chaos outside.

While waiting in the queue, she had decided what she needed to do.

Madeline quickly scrawled a coded message on a piece of paper and discreetly tucked it between the pages of Les Misérables. It was Thursday, and it was a request for Falcon to arrange new false papers so she could continue her work for the war.

Once that was done, Madeline opened the shop and went through her daily routine of arranging the books on their shelves. As she carefully placed each one in its designated space, her thoughts turned to Jacob, the only bright spot in her dark world. Meeting him had changed her life completely, and she missed him so much whenever she was back in Paris.

The bell above the entrance jangled and Madeline looked up. Her stomach clenched when she saw it was Marcel, still wearing his fascist party armband.

Over the last year, he had grown quite self-important; he

enjoyed exercising the little power he had as a sympathizer of the Nazi party, asserting his authority wherever he went and often intimidating the locals.

Madeline swallowed down her discomfort as Marcel approached the counter.

'Good morning, Marcel,' she greeted him with forced cheerfulness. 'How can I assist you today?'

Marcel smirked, his eyes glinting with superiority. 'I'm looking for a book on German history,' he replied, a hint of condescension in his voice. 'Preferably something that showcases the greatness of that civilisation.'

'I do have some books on German history,' she said cautiously, her tone neutral. 'But they provide a comprehensive view of the subject, allowing readers to form their own opinions.'

Marcel's eyes narrowed as he sensed a hint of resistance in Madeline's words. He leaned closer to the counter, and she could smell the remnants of cigarette smoke and alcohol on his breath.

His voice dropped to a dangerous level as he spoke again. 'I don't need any of that liberal propaganda, Madeline. I'm interested in books that highlight the strength and superiority of our Aryan race.'

Madeline clenched her fists behind the counter, trying to hide her unease as she fought to maintain her composure. She knew the danger of openly contradicting Marcel's beliefs, but she couldn't bring herself to stay silent. Taking a deep breath, she spoke with a firmness she hadn't known she possessed.

'Marcel, as an independent bookseller, I strive to provide a range of perspectives to my customers. However, I cannot support or condone ideologies that promote hate or discrimination. If you're looking for books that perpetuate those ideas, I'm afraid you won't find them here.'

With an irritated huff, he stormed off towards the history

section and began rummaging through the books. Just then, Madeline caught sight of Falcon striding into the shop. She stiffened, hoping the agent would sense the danger. Falcon sauntered around the room, noting Marcel in his armband. She pretended to browse while keeping a close eye on her adversary.

Madeline watched Marcel, too. He had pulled out a pile of books and then, getting frustrated at not seeing anything he wanted, shoved them back onto the shelf with such force that he set off a chain reaction, causing a whole line of books to tumble from the shelves. The loud crash echoed throughout the small shop as Madeline's anxiety skyrocketed.

Looking flustered, Marcel took a step back, his eyes nervously scanning the pile of books on the floor. Madeline could do nothing but watch helplessly from her counter, as the coded message slipped out of *Les Misérables* and onto the ground. But Falcon was already there, bending down to pick it up with practised ease.

'Oh, Monsieur, let me help you,' she purred, batting her eyelashes flirtatiously at Marcel. And as she distracted him with her charm, Falcon discreetly slipped the message into her pocket. Madeline breathed a sigh of relief, grateful for the agent's quick thinking. Marcel seemed oblivious to the exchange, his attention captivated by Falcon's flattery.

Madeline hurriedly knelt beside her, quickly scanning the shop to make sure nobody else had entered to notice her actions. As she gathered the fallen books and placed them back on the shelves, she and Falcon exchanged a brief look of relief.

Once the shop was back in order, Madeline stood up and faced Marcel, attempting her most professional demeanour. 'Is there anything else I can help you with today?'

Marcel straightened himself to his full height, his smugness returning. 'No, you have nothing I want to waste my time on,' he sneered, his tone dripping with contempt. 'I'll take my business elsewhere.'

Marcel stormed out of the shop, and she watched him retreat down the street before turning her attention to Falcon. Other customers had arrived so they only exchanged a knowing glance, silently acknowledging the close call they had just experienced. Madeline could see the relief in the agent's eyes, and she couldn't help but feel a wave of gratitude towards her.

Madeline watched her depart the shop with the message safely in her pocket and thought how, even though technically they were both spies, Falcon was everything she herself aspired to be. Falcon was quick-thinking and cunning and had an undeniable charisma that made her the perfect liaison for the Resistance. Madeline, on the other hand, was overcautious and methodical, struggling to think on her feet. But still, she felt passionate about the work she was doing and was committed to contributing to the fight against tyranny in any way she could.

And, ultimately, she was driven by the plight of a young boy. Her inconveniences were nothing compared to living under the fear of Nazi rule every day, and even though it was taking longer than she had imagined to find him, she had unwavering resolve to follow it through to the end.

38

Olivia

Livi awoke with a start from a nightmare, her heart racing, her hair clinging to the back of her neck, damp with perspiration. As she tried to orient herself, the remnants of the evening with Markus echoed in her mind. Sitting up, she ran a shaky hand through her tangled hair, taking slow, deep breaths to calm herself down.

In her nightmare, she had been desperately trying to get to Markus, but he was always just out of reach. And even when she screamed out his name, he couldn't seem to hear her.

She rubbed her temples and tried to push away the tears threatening to fall. How could she allow herself to even consider the possibility of a relationship when her past marriage to Graham had left her so vulnerable?

As she thought of their exchange the day before, she was terrified that she was broken and no amount of therapy or medication could fix her.

She walked to the hotel window. It was still early. The

moon's soft glow illuminated the quiet neighbourhood below, casting a gentle light on the trees and the street.

Livi glanced around, trying to determine the time, but she had no idea what hour it was; she had purposely turned off her phone so she wouldn't constantly check for a message from Markus.

She boiled the kettle and poured hot water over a peppermint tea bag, relishing the enjoyment of a calming ritual. Taking a moment, she closed her eyes, breathing in the comforting scent deeply, before taking a sip and walking to the table, where she settled herself in with a soft sigh.

As she took another sip, her gaze fell upon the poetry book in her bag, which she had meant to show to Otto in the bookshop in case he was interested in purchasing it for his own clientele.

She pulled it out. '*For the One I Love*,' she whispered to herself. The gold lettering on the cover seemed to glow with a timeless charm in the dim light. She forced back her natural cynicism towards love poems.

She noticed that one of the pages towards the back of the book was creased. She smoothed it out and began to read, only to stop abruptly as a shock of recognition coursed through her. It was the poem that she had found in the endpapers of her grandfather's book.

Disbelief and excitement filled her thoughts. Then she remembered she had read a couple of lines from this poem on the day of the auction, but had been so preoccupied with the photos of her great-grandmother that all remembrance of it had slipped from her mind until now.

Frantically, she retrieved her grandfather's book from her bag, her mind racing as she compared the two poems side by side. In the book *For the One I Love*, the poet sought his lost lover in places they had shared together; the handwritten version of the poem was nearly identical except that some of the locations had been changed.

Why would the writer of the notes alter the poem? Could these places mean something? Her mind worked furiously as she contemplated the implications.

Her thoughts tumbled together, colliding and re-forming as she pondered the hidden connections. *I have to tell Markus*, she thought with a pang of longing, realising how much she missed him already.

Livi spent the next few hours poring over the two poems, researching the book and the poet on the internet attempting to find any connection. But as the first light of dawn crept through her window, she was no closer to finding any answers. Her best guess was that it could have been a message sent between agents.

Unable to put it off any longer, she dialled Markus's number and waited for him to answer.

'Olivia?' Markus answered, his voice thick with sleep but alert nonetheless. 'Are you okay? I have been worried about you.'

She felt her heart melt as he continued.

'I don't know what I said last night, but I'm so sorry if I was inappropriate in any way.'

'It's nothing you said,' Livi replied. 'Just some issues from my past I have to deal with.'

'Well, I'm so glad you called. But why are you awake so early?'

'I found something I want you to see. Could you meet today at the coffee shop in my hotel?'

'Of course,' he agreed without hesitation. 'I'll be there as soon as I can.'

Later that morning, she was working her way through her second coffee of the day, sitting at her laptop, when she saw him approach with a warm smile.

'Hey,' he said softly, 'you look tired.'

'I am,' she admitted, leaning into his touch, as he gave her a friendly hug. 'But I'm also excited. I can't wait to share what I've found with you.'

He bought a coffee, and they sat down opposite each other.

She pushed the poetry book and the handwritten poem towards him, laying them out side by side on the table.

As Markus leaned in, reading them both, she explained what she had discovered. 'You're right – these altered lines could mean something,' he said.

'I didn't give this book a second thought. Which is a really bad thing to do as a historian, but I guess I was so caught up in the photographs and the story of her life that I didn't pay enough attention to the *book*.'

Together, they worked through the morning, brainstorming what it could all mean. They researched codes from the war on the internet, and how agents used them to communicate Resistance activity. Their minds were fully engaged in the task at hand.

Finally, Livi pushed back in her chair. 'I think we need to go back to Eichenwald,' she said with a sigh. 'Someone wrote this who knew my grandfather, and he lived at the manor until he moved to Paris – the museum staff may know something more.'

'Before we discuss our plans for the day,' Markus began, his voice gentle, 'I want to know how you are feeling. About everything... *us* included.'

Livi hesitated, her fingers tracing the rim of her empty coffee cup as she gathered her thoughts. 'I'm scared,' she admitted softly, 'but I can't deny how much I care about you, Markus. You've been so kind. But I'm not sure I can give you what I sense you want. Think happened to me in my past and I think I'm broken. And what terrifies me is what happens if there is no way to fix me.'

Markus reached across the table and gently covered Livi's

hand with his own. 'You may feel broken, but I promise you, Livi, you are not beyond repair. I'm sure of it. We all have past traumas we have to come to terms with. You just need to be patient and trust yourself. And if our relationship doesn't develop into anything else, that's okay too. I'll always be here for you – as a friend, whatever you need.'

'Thank you,' she murmured, her eyes meeting his. 'I just wish I could be more certain. But I want to be honest with you. I don't want to string you along if, for some reason, I can't have what everybody else seems to have. And I hate the thought of us not being friends.'

'You'll never have to find out,' Markus replied, his thumb tracing small circles on the back of Livi's hand. 'I'm here for you, always.'

Livi took a deep breath and smiled. 'Okay,' she said. 'Well, we have a puzzle to solve.'

'Yes, we do,' Markus responded, enthused.

Together, they gathered their belongings, and she followed him out of the hotel. The weak winter sun shone down on them as they stepped into the cool, crisp German air. She followed Markus's long strides to the car. As he opened the door for her, she couldn't help but wonder what awaited them, not only at the old estate but also in their blossoming friendship.

39

BERLIN, SUMMER 1942

Madeline

For the next few months, Madeline continued to travel back and forth to Germany with her new false papers that Falcon had arranged for her. She continued taking photos for Archie, gathering literature and smuggling out Jacob's books.

When in Berlin, she stayed with Jacob at his quaint little cottage nestled amid its towering trees and thatched roof speckled with patches of moss. Inside, they shared their love, each moment feeling like a stolen eternity. The world around them faded away, leaving only their intertwined existence.

One warm night, as Madeline lay in Jacob's arms, a knock at the door jolted them both awake.

In the darkness, Jacob's eyes met hers with concern. Reluctantly, he released her and rose from the bed, his expression troubled.

'Stay here, my love,' he whispered, quickly dressing and kissing Madeline's forehead.

As he descended the creaking stairs, Madeline, wrapped in

the covers, felt a sense of unease. Who could be visiting at this hour? She heard hurried conversation and recognised the voice of Swift.

Standing on the landing, wrapped in a sheet, Madeline listened.

'Is Story Keeper here?'

'Yes, she is,' Jacob replied.

Madeline rushed back to the bedroom to dress, then descended the stairs. She found Jacob and Swift in the kitchen.

'We have found her,' Swift said urgently. 'Ada, the woman you've been searching for.'

Madeline was stunned, tears pricking her eyes as she tried to process Swift's words. Ada had finally been found, after two years of dead ends. Anticipation and apprehension weighed on her, and one overwhelming question: was Alex's son still alive?

Jacob's eyes shone with relief as he grasped Madeline's hand, silently reassuring her.

'She's hiding in slums outside Berlin,' Swift continued. 'Her life was threatened by Mueller, so she's very cautious.'

'Do you have the address?' Madeline asked, her throat tight with her emotion.

Swift handed her a slip of paper with the address. Madeline, relieved, looked at Jacob.

'I'll go tomorrow.'

Jacob turned to her, concerned. 'I can't come. People are coming to the estate to cut down trees, and it would be suspicious if I wasn't here.'

'I'll be fine alone,' Madeline reassured him. 'She may be wary, anyway.'

Jacob offered some of Ada's belongings that she had left with him, to help establish trust. And after Swift had left, he held Madeline tightly.

'Please, be careful, my love,' he murmured, his voice filled with his love and concern. 'I cannot bear the thought of anything happening to you.'

Madeline looked up at him. 'I promise,' she whispered, her voice steady.

They returned to bed, but Madeline found sleep elusive, her mind racing with thoughts of meeting Ada. In Jacob's arms she found solace, yet now she faced the unknown and Ada's story.

The next day, Madeline hesitated at the edge of the crumbling pathways, surveying the shabby neighbourhood. The narrow streets seemed to have been forgotten by time, with buildings in disrepair and unkempt gardens fighting for space alongside each other. She watched as a group of untidy children played with a stick and an old rubber ball, their laughter a contrast to the desperation that hung heavy in the air.

Madeline straightened her shoulders and took a deep breath. The door with the given number loomed ahead, and she hesitated once more, her pulse racing in anticipation. What if Ada didn't want to be found? What if her fears were confirmed and Kurt was not Alex's son? She shook off her doubts, knowing that she couldn't turn back now. With a trembling hand, she knocked.

'Who is it?' a voice called from within, muffled and uncertain. Madeline knocked again, louder this time. The door creaked open, revealing a haggard woman with familiar features. Madeline's heart skipped a beat as she recognised those eyes – the same ones that stared back at her from the photographs she had in her handbag.

'Ada?' Madeline asked tentatively, her voice barely above a whisper.

The woman's eyes narrowed, her body tense like a cornered

animal. 'Who are you?' Ada demanded, her voice strained. 'What do you want?'

'Forgive me for startling you,' Madeline said, trying to calm her own nerves. 'My name is Madeline. Are you Ada?'

The woman seemed about to shut the door in her face, so quickly Madeline pulled out the things Jacob had given her – a bundle of letters and some photographs – and thrust them at the woman.

'Please don't shut the door. I'm a friend – see, Jacob gave these to me, he said you left things with him, these things. I brought them so you would know you could trust me.'

'Who are you?' Ada demanded again, though her tone was less fierce.

'I'm...' She hesitated before settling on the right words. '...a friend of Alex's, from Paris.'

'Alex...?' Ada's voice trailed off, her guard slipping for a moment as she tried to make sense of the situation. A flicker of hope crossed her face. 'Is he here?'

Madeline shook her head.

Ada's eyes turned icy once more. Even through the wall she projected, Madeline could see the longing in her eyes, the pain of disappointment.

'Please, may I come in?' she asked gently, sensing Ada's apprehension. 'I have important things to discuss with you.'

Ada hesitated for just a moment as she looked around the street to make sure there was no one else about. Then with a swift nod of her head she stepped back, allowing Madeline to enter the dimly lit room. The air inside was stale and musty, and heaps of dirty clothes were everywhere.

'I wash to make a little money. From rich women, just like I used to be,' she said with a twist of bitterness and in explanation for the chaos. 'I would offer you tea, but I'm out right now,' she said, squaring her shoulders, as if she was signalling to Madeline that even in her current situation she knew the correct protocol.

'I'm fine,' Madeline responded. The squalor and the smell made her heart break for this woman and all she had obviously been through.

Ada cleared a heap of washing from a rickety chair and offered it to Madeline. As she sat down across from Ada, Madeline got a better look at her.

She was bone-thin, her hands red and swollen, probably from the washing. Her hair was slightly matted and deep rings of dark creased her under-eyes. She had a nervous manner, and she rubbed her painful hands together and her eyes darted about as she spoke, and Madeline tried to picture her with Alex.

Ada asked, 'When is Alex coming? Is he going to take his son back with him? It is important that Kurt gets away from here; it is not safe for him.'

Madeline had so many questions too, but first she would need to provide answers. Answers she always found hard to put into words.

'I am afraid I have some bad news for you. Alex died before the war.'

The effect was instantaneous, as if any hope this woman had was suddenly gone. The hardened expression crumbled, and she looked so distraught that Madeline wanted to take the words back. So she quickly continued. 'I got your letter. I have come to help you instead.'

Ada stared at her with a mixture of disbelief and distrust as she said falteringly, 'Why would you want to help me?'

'I was married to Alex. He would want me to help you and his son.' Madeline swallowed down the lump that caught in her throat. She had come to challenge Ada on Kurt's parentage. Demand she prove that Kurt was Alex's. She had come to take back all she had left of Alex. But now none of that mattered; all that mattered was helping this distraught family, and getting them to safety.

Suddenly, it was as if the penny finally dropped for Ada. 'You are Alex's wife, and you came to help me?'

'Yes, you and Kurt.' Madeline's eyes swept around the room. She hadn't seen anything of the boy yet, and suddenly her heart started to quicken with concern. As if sensing her fear, the woman spoke again.

'Kurt doesn't know about Alex. He believes he is Frederick's son. I married Frederick when I was already pregnant. Alex and I had already split up and were about to be divorced. It didn't seem fair to him, and I had already met Frederick and we very quickly started an affair. At first, I thought I was in love. And because he was in the army, we didn't wait long to get married and, even though I knew by my dates that the baby was Alex's, it was so close to when we started our relationship it just seemed easier to tell him the baby was his.

'He was just in the German army then, not part of the Gestapo. We got married. And for a while it was fine. Then he got promoted into the Gestapo and Hitler offered him a chance to serve him in that way and everything changed. The power he now has, and this war, have twisted him. Made him bitter and so angry towards Jewish people.

'When he finally learned from an old friend, whom I had confided in, about the truth regarding Kurt, he was livid and vowed to kill me and my Jewish son. I fled that night with Kurt in my arms. Since then, I have been in hiding.

'Frederick is a proud and vengeful man. I have brought him great shame; everyone accepted Kurt as his son. When he discovered the truth, the situation could not have been worse. I have no doubt that he is a man of his word and will seek to avenge his honour by killing me and Kurt.'

Madeline reached forward and took Ada's hand. 'We are not going to let that happen. I will get false papers for you and you will travel with me to Paris, and stay with me at my book-shop. You can start a new life in France.'

That was when tears welled up in Ada's eyes. The eyes that were so distrustful, so hardened, softened as, in that moment, she glimpsed her chance at hope.

'I will come back soon. Be ready to leave with Kurt.'

Ada agreed but still appeared to be unsure, exhausted with all she had been carrying; she bowed her head, appearing not to believe the truth of it all, finally saying, 'Thank you,' just above a whisper.

Madeline stepped out of the dimly lit house, her eyes slowly adjusting to the sunlight that bathed the shabby neighbourhood in a deceptive warmth. She took a moment to gather her thoughts, her heart heavy with the weight of all that was before her.

As she looked around, she noticed a little boy playing by himself in the narrow alley, his dirty hands grasping a makeshift toy. He turned, and she caught her breath. The resemblance was unmistakable – he had Alex's eyes, those same intense brown eyes that seemed to hold the world to ransom.

'Kurt?' Madeline called out hesitantly, her voice barely audible.

The boy's head snapped back at the sound of his name, and for a brief moment their gazes locked. Her first thought was that this was what their own child may have looked like had he or she lived, and her heart ached.

Then, as if sensing danger, or maybe afraid of the way she stared at him, Kurt dropped his toy and darted behind a stack of crates, disappearing from sight.

'*Kurt!*' Madeline tried again, desperation creeping into her voice. But the boy was gone, swallowed by the shadows that seemed to cling to every corner of this forsaken place.

As she made her way quickly from Ada's neighbourhood the sun dipped below the horizon, leaving behind a trail of fiery reds and oranges that seemed to set the sky ablaze. But the world around Madeline grew darker, more uncertain, as she centred on what she had to do. Looking into the face of her husband's son had fuelled her desire more than she could have ever imagined. Somewhere in this cold and unforgiving war, a small flame of hope still burned.

She had a way to help these people, and she would do everything in her power to keep them both alive.

40

BERLIN, SEPTEMBER 1942

Madeline

The first light of dawn seeped through the cracks in the boarded-up windows, casting eerie shadows across the small house that had been Ada's home in hiding for years.

Madeline passed the tired-looking woman a small bundle; Ada clutched the false papers to her chest, grateful to her new friend. It had taken a few weeks to organise everything through Swift and her contacts, but now they had a new identity for her.

'My new name is Gertrud Schmidt?'

'Yes. Try to remember it. It is the only way to keep you safe.'

'Thank you, you have no idea how much this means to me.'

Madeline noticed how much better Ada looked wearing the clothes she had borrowed for her. Hopefully she would be inconspicuous enough in Madeline's dark full coat and a headscarf.

'We still have a long way to go; you can thank me once we get back to France,' Madeline reminded her.

Ada's eyes locked with hers. 'Whatever happens to me, promise you will get Kurt to safety,' she implored, and Madeline agreed, an unspoken understanding passing between the two women.

Madeline looked at the little boy. His face was sallow and his brow heavy with worry as he listened to the grown-up conversation. He was dressed in clean but worn clothes that were too big for him, which Ada had managed to get. Madeline could see how this life had affected him, and it tore at her heart. She knew she had to remain upbeat for Kurt's sake.

She tried to reassure him. 'Quite an adventure, hey, Kurt, you are going to go on a train today!'

Kurt turned to his mother for assurance. 'But *where* are we going?'

'You are coming on a little visit to my bookshop in Paris,' Madeline continued.

He turned and stared back at her with large, scared eyes and a hopeless expression. In that moment Madeline caught a glimpse of what living in hiding had cost him. And it hurt her to see that such a small boy had lived through so much upheaval.

Grabbing their things, Ada opened the door, and they headed out.

'Well, I won't miss this life,' Ada said as they hurried away down the road.

The three of them moved out into the cold, desolate streets of Berlin. Each step echoed in the silence, the fear they all felt.

As they hurried through the narrow alleys, Madeline noticed how Ada's eyes darted from one shadow to another, her instincts obviously sharpened by years of living in hiding. As they made their way into the main city it loomed over them, its towering buildings a stark reminder that out in the open like this, away from the twisted alleys of forgotten places, Ada and Kurt were more vulnerable.

The distant rumble of a train signalled their approach to Berlin station, a sprawling mass of iron and stone that seemed to swallow all who entered. Madeline hesitated for a moment, memories of the bomb blast at the station, as always, threatening to consume her. She forced the images away, focusing on the task at hand.

They slipped through the entrance and were immediately swept up in a sea of busy travellers. The noise was over-whelming – the shouts of porters, the screech of metal wheels on tracks, the hiss of steam engines preparing to depart. Despite the chaos, Madeline felt a flicker of hope as she bought their tickets. Lost in the crowds, they were just three more passen-gers, blending into the sea of faces.

'Let's find our train,' she urged, her eyes scanning the station. As they weaved through the crowd, she noticed that Ada gripped Kurt's hand tightly, ensuring he stayed close, her face a mask of determination.

'Here,' Madeline said, pointing to a sign. The train was due any minute. Once on the platform they caught their breath, and Madeline dared to believe they might have a chance at escaping the nightmare Ada had been living through.

As they waited, Kurt offered her a weak smile, and her chest tightened. She wanted to pinch herself; she was travelling with Alex's son. Here beside her was a living breathing piece of her husband that had lived on after his death; she hadn't realised how much love she could instantly feel for a little boy she had barely spoken to.

The sound of the train approaching the platform pulled her from her thoughts and she watched as it chugged into the station.

As they gathered themselves to board, Ada looked exhausted, and Madeline pulled the tired woman's bag up off the floor and threw it over her own shoulder.

All at once, a menacing figure emerged from the shadows of the platform. Ada gasped in terror, her eyes wild with panic as recognition dawned upon her.

'Frederick, how did you know?' she whispered, her voice trembling.

Madeline's breath caught in her throat as she snapped round and also recognised the tall, broad-shouldered man from the photographs Jacob had given her.

Frederick Mueller's cold, calculating gaze seemed to pierce straight through them with a single glance. The air around them thickened with tension and the platform became eerily silent as he stepped closer.

'I am fortunate that many people have been watching for me. I told you I would find you.'

Before either of them could stop him, Kurt lunged forward and raced towards Frederick.

'Papa!' he proclaimed joyously, unaware of the horror that awaited him.

In response Frederick yanked out a pistol and, snatching Kurt by his collar, caught him in a tight grip as he held the barrel against his head.

Blood pounded through Madeline's body and she felt weak, as if her legs couldn't hold her, as Ada screamed in anguish.

Kurt looked up at his stepfather pleadingly. 'Papa, it is me, Kurt.' His voice quivered with confusion and fear.

Everyone on the platform froze in terror, fearing what would come next.

Feeling overwhelmingly protective, Madeline stepped forward. 'Please,' she pleaded desperately. 'Don't do this.'

'And who are *you*?' sneered Frederick, glaring at Madeline, his lip curling in disdain. 'A brave hero here to save the day?'

Kurt reached up to his father, his small hand trembling. 'What's wrong, Papa? What did I do?' he asked, his voice barely more than a whisper.

Mueller turned his attention back to Kurt, his grip on the gun unwavering. '*Quiet!*' he bellowed, his finger tightening around the trigger.

'Frederick, listen to me!' shrieked Ada desperately as she stepped towards him, tears streaming down her face as she pleaded for her son's life. 'You may hate me, but I beg you, let your son go; he has done nothing wrong!'

Frederick's eyes blazed with uncontrollable rage as he snarled his words through gritted teeth: '*Son?* This despicable creature? He's not my son! This child is nothing more than vermin.'

'Please,' Ada pleaded, her body trembling as her voice echoed in the now silent crowd. 'Don't do this. Please remember who you used to be: the man I loved.'

'Love?' he scoffed, his rancour intensifying further. 'That died long ago when you destroyed everything! You ruined it all!'

Desperate to prevent tragedy from unfolding before her eyes, Madeline frantically racked her mind for a solution. Her every instinct shouted for her to act swiftly, to stop this Nazi from harming an innocent child. Taking a deep breath, she spoke again.

'Please don't punish Kurt; he is just a child,' she declared firmly despite her fear and trepidation. 'Let me take him away so you can settle this between yourselves as adults.'

Mueller paused, his eyes narrowing, as he tightened his grip on Kurt's collar, causing him to cry out in pain. In a flash Ada turned and met Madeline's gaze, her look communicating her need for Madeline to keep her promise to protect Kurt. And then she leapt forward, her motherly instinct unable to bear it any longer, and tried to wrestle the gun from Mueller.

In the tussle, Frederick released his grip on Kurt, and the young boy tumbled onto the ground. Quickly, Madeline ran forward and scooped him up, cradling the distraught boy close to her chest.

Mueller easily pushed Ada away, and pointed the gun directly at her heart, yelling, 'Don't think I have forgotten about what you did! You disgraced me in front of everyone I know –

let me believe he was mine all that time, only for him to be some worthless Jew! There is no way I am letting you get away with this!'

The gunshot pierced the air and time seemed to stand still as it echoed through the station. Madeline felt her heart stop for what felt like eternity before it restarted again. Ada did not make a sound as she crumpled to the ground.

After a moment of shock, pandemonium broke out in the station. Ada's life was clearly slipping away as Frederick stood over her body, his face twisted in satisfaction and rage. He lifted the gun once more, aiming it towards Kurt and Madeline. A shot rang out, and a bullet bounced off the stone floor beside them.

Madeline grabbed the boy's hand and began running, following the crowd that was racing for cover.

'Run, Kurt!' she urged. Fear and tenacity fuelled her actions as they sprinted through the sea of chaos, weaving between terrified travellers and narrowly avoiding trampling feet, leaving behind the haunting image of Ada's lifeless body on the platform.

Unaware of the drama, the Paris train belched smoke into the grey dawn as it prepared to depart. Its horn wailed mournfully, a haunting echo reverberating through the station, oblivious to the scene unfolding on its platform. The air was thick with terror; screams and shouts melded together in a cacophony of fear. Madeline's heart threatened to burst out of her chest as she tightened her grip on Kurt's hand, his small fingers hot and clammy within her own as she continued to race towards it.

'Stay close to me!' she shouted over all the noise, her voice urgent and strained. She could see the confusion and panic in Kurt's eyes, but there was no time for comfort or explanations. They had to escape. She had to keep her promise and save him.

Her mind raced, calculating their best route amid the frantic movements of the crowd. As they darted through the mass of people, the train to Paris loomed before them, its wheels beginning to turn, its metal body gleaming beneath the dim morning light as it started to pick up speed. Madeline could feel the weight of their precarious situation bearing down upon her. But she refused to succumb to despair. Ada had entrusted her with Kurt's life, and she would not fail her.

With a surge of adrenaline, she propelled Kurt forward, their bodies straining against the growing distance between them and their only chance of escape. '*Run faster!*' she urged him.

Reaching the last carriage before it left the platform, she yanked open the door, the cold metal biting into her flesh. '*Jump!*' she yelled, launching herself onto the train. Her grip on Kurt's hand was ironclad as she hauled him in beside her, their desperate leap sending them sprawling into an empty seat as the door slammed behind them.

Gasping for breath, she dared a glance back at the station. A group of people had gathered around Ada's lifeless form, a grim tableau amid the chaos. But Mueller was no longer on the platform. Had he seen them? Was he following her?

A cold sweat trickled down her spine as she looked at Kurt's ashen face. They were on the train, but had she led them into greater peril?

41

BERLIN, DECEMBER 2011

Olivia

As Markus and Livi arrived at Eichenwald once again, the snow that had once blanketed the grounds was now gone, but the estate still held its enchanting beauty.

The gardens were now in full view, vibrant with splashes of colour from blooming bulbs and autumn and winter foliage. Beyond the house, the lake glistened under the bright winter sunlight.

This time, the place was bustling with more people and activity, yet it still maintained a quiet atmosphere. The hushed whispers of visitors only added to the solemnity of the space.

Livi and Markus asked a volunteer for help and were taken to the curator. Dr Greta Vogel listened intently as they recounted their journey. They handed over Kurt's book and, as she carefully opened it and examined its contents, Livi and Markus exchanged nervous glances.

'It's rare to come across a new personal artefact with such historical significance for us,' Dr Vogel remarked. 'You say there was something glued under the endpapers?'

'Yes, a poem,' Livi confirmed.

'May I see it?'

Livi reached into her bag again and handed over the hidden poem. Dr Vogel carefully turned the pages and read it aloud. Livi and Markus listened intently.

'This is truly a remarkable find,' Dr Vogel said after she'd finished the poem. 'Not only have you shed light on the mystery of Kurt Mueller's disappearance, but it also adds to the rich history of Eichenwald.'

Then she furrowed her brow as if remembering something important. 'Come with me.'

She led them down the long, dimly lit hallway with its chilling portraits of Nazi leaders. At the end, they reached a heavy wooden door marked with the words 'Do Not Enter'. Dr Vogel produced a key from her pocket, unlocked the door and led them into a room filled with carefully stored artefacts and documents.

'This is our archive,' she said, gesturing to the shelves of neatly labelled boxes and folders. 'Not everything can be displayed for the public, due to their delicate nature or sensitive content.'

She guided them towards a table in the centre of the room, and pulled out a wooden box filled with letters in pristine condition. From a drawer she retrieved two pairs of white cotton gloves, and handed them to Livi and Markus.

'These are letters written by Jacob Weiss,' she explained as she put on her own gloves, opened the box and carefully removed one of the letters. 'He was the caretaker here at Eichenwald during the war. He worked for the Resistance and saved many belongings of the Jewish family who lived here before the Nazis took over.'

Dr Vogel then opened one of the letters for them to read. 'In this letter, Jacob recounts his final encounter with the family before they were forced to leave Eichenwald behind.'

Livi's fingers trembled as she unfolded the yellowed paper. The handwriting was elegant, yet appeared rushed, and a heavy feeling settled in her chest as she read the faint words.

Dear Hans,

I cannot begin to describe the heaviness that weighs on my heart as I write this letter. The family that I have looked after for so long has made the difficult decision to leave their home behind and flee to safety. It was hard saying goodbye to the children. They were scared and confused, and it broke my heart to see them like that.

As you know, the Nazis have been increasing their presence in the area, and it has become too dangerous for them to stay. I fear for their safety every moment of every day. But I take solace in the fact that they have entrusted me with their most precious belongings, belongings like their books, that tell the story of their lives and their struggles.

I am doing everything in my power to make sure that these belongings make it into safe hands, hands that will preserve their history and remember their legacy. It is the least I can do for a family that has given me so much.

Please keep them in your thoughts and prayers, Hans. And know that I will continue to do everything in my power to protect their memory.

With kind regards,

Jacob

As she reached the end, Livi felt tears pricking at her eyes.

Dr Vogel commented, 'Take a closer look at the handwriting.'

Livi furrowed her brow in confusion but glanced back down

at the letter. Suddenly, it clicked. She recognised the neat cursive from the poem in her grandfather's book.

'This... this is the same handwriting,' she whispered, her voice cracking with emotion.

Markus's eyes widened in realisation, and he and Livi exchanged a stunned look before turning back to Dr Vogel, their minds racing with questions and possibilities.

'So, Jacob wrote this. But why?' asked Livi. 'I found a version of the same poem in a published poetry book; it was identical except some of the references to places in Jacob's poem are different. We wondered if it was coded messages for the Resistance.'

Dr Vogel was thoughtful for a minute.

'Maybe there are more clues in Jacob's cottage?' she mused. 'It's not part of the official tour, but we've preserved it as best we could. I can have someone take you there?'

She ushered them outside, where they met another volunteer, who led them through the winding paths of Eichenwald's immaculate gardens, past bubbling fountains and towering statues, until they reached a small gate that opened to a secluded grove of trees.

The cottage itself was quaint and charming, its sagging roof giving it a cosy feel. A small garden bloomed out front, obviously tended by volunteers, and it added to the cottage's picturesque appearance. As they stepped inside, they were struck by how well preserved everything was – from the carefully arranged furniture to the neatly stacked books on shelves. It was like stepping back in time to when Jacob still lived there.

The volunteer waited by the door as they looked through the rooms. Inside the air was thick with the musty scent of age, and faded memories. The creaking floors echoed with each step as they moved through the abandoned cottage. Black and white photographs lined the walls, depicting generations of caretakers at their work tending to the gardens and livestock. Jacob Weiss was in many of the photos, his kind eyes and gentle smile never faltering.

As they ventured further into the house, they found themselves in Jacob's study. It was a small room, with a desk and chair, a bookshelf lined with books, and a fireplace with a worn armchair in front of it. Markus walked over to the bookshelf, curious about the titles.

'He seemed to like poetry,' he remarked.

Livi pulled out and reread the poem. 'Why would he change these words?' she mused out loud.

She gazed out of the bedroom window, which had an amazing view of the estate, trying to decipher the meaning behind the changes. Meanwhile, Markus continued studying the bookshelf.

And just like that, the penny dropped. Livi knew what Jacob had been trying to hide and where, and why he had hidden it in the poem's words.

'I've got it, Markus, I know what it all means!'

Markus turned around, a curious look on his face. 'What?'

'The poem is a *code*. Not for the Resistance, for something else – some*one* else. Maybe a friend he trusted – or, who knows, the love of his life? That's why he hid it in a poem, copied from a book called *For the One I Love*.'

Markus's eyes widened in surprise. 'What kind of code?'

'Follow me, I know what we need to do.'

42

PARIS, OCTOBER 1942

Madeline

Madeline was reading as she and Kurt sat in her dimly lit living room, the heaviness of an unsaid conversation hanging between them. Fortunately, Mueller had not boarded the train, and she had made it back to Paris safely with the child. But Madeline had been terrified for the whole journey of him catching up with them. It had been a few weeks since they had returned, but still Kurt was very withdrawn.

The words blurred on the page as Madeline's thoughts drifted back to Germany, to the last time she had been with Jacob. A deep ache for connection stirred within her chest, not just for time with Jacob but also for some sort of bond with Alex's son.

She glanced at Kurt whose eyes were fixed on the dancing flames. In that moment, he looked so young and vulnerable, his face illuminated by the warm glow of the fire. The little boy had hardly spoken since they returned from Berlin, and Madeline could only imagine the turmoil he was going through.

Tentatively, she set her book down on the arm of the sofa.

She scooted closer to Kurt and placed her hand on his own. Kurt flinched at her touch. His eyes were dark and haunted.

'You don't have to keep it all inside, Kurt. You can trust me, I'm here for you. If you get to know me, you might even like me,' she whispered softly.

Kurt's eyes flicked to hers for a brief instant before he looked away, his jaw clenched tight. He stared at the floor as if searching for the right words to say, but when he finally spoke his voice was laced with bitterness. 'I could never like you. *You're* the reason my mother is dead,' he spat out, his gaze still averted.

She reeled back. His words had struck her deeply, and tears prickled at the corners of her eyes. She winced at the pain of his accusation. 'That's not true, Kurt,' she responded, her voice choking on the words.

Kurt's eyes blazed with anger as he turned to her, his fingers curling into fists. 'We were doing fine until *you* came. You're the one that told her we had to leave. That's why he found us. Because we left where we were safe. I could have looked after her, if you would have left us alone.'

Madeline's heart sank as Kurt's words cut through her like a knife. She knew she couldn't change the past, but she wished she could have changed the events that led to his mother's death, found a different way out of Germany, or been more aware of Mueller and his movements.

'I was only trying to protect you both,' she said, her voice barely above a whisper. 'I never wanted any harm to come to your mother or to you.'

She studied his frightened eyes, trying to figure out what to do. How could she explain all the complications of the dangers of war to a seven-year-old? Before she could continue the conversation further, Kurt jumped up and stormed into his bedroom. Immediately she heard muffled sobbing and her heart went out to him. But she forced herself not to follow; she knew he needed time to himself.

Madeline waited until the room became quiet before she peeked in and saw he was fast asleep. She sighed and leaned against the doorframe, watching as Kurt's chest rose and fell with each steady breath. Like this, he looked so much like Alex, and it made her heart brim with longing. Longing for the husband she'd lost, and the boy she had but couldn't get close to.

Tiptoeing into the darkened room, Madeline slowly began to undress him. As she lifted his shirt over his head, she couldn't help but notice how thin he was; she could practically see every bone in his body. He had strings of bruises across his skin, marking the harshness of a life on the run. And the sight of that made her heart break even more for the pain and suffering Kurt had endured in his young life.

This was Alex's son. She still couldn't believe it. She had meant to tell him as soon as they had arrived in Paris. But he had been so fragile and heartbroken she just hadn't had the heart to tell him she was his stepmother. She would wait until he was stronger, until he trusted her more.

Madeline carefully tucked Kurt into bed, pulling the covers up to his chin.

Sitting gently beside him, she watched him breathing deeply, his face relaxed in sleep. On his reddened cheeks his eyelashes flickered as he dreamed. She dared to run the tips of her fingers through his soft curly hair and with her touch he turned over, muttering, '*Gute Nacht, Mama,*' and her heart broke.

These were the words she would never hear from her own child. And in that moment, she felt the familiar ache of loss and longing that she and Alex had experienced with the terrible pain of her infertility, and she closed her eyes to hold back tears. Now she had this opportunity to finally have what she had always yearned for but could she ever win over this little boy?

Her biggest fear was that the love of a child she so dearly wanted would still be out of her reach.

As she crept back to the living room, the weight of her loss and Kurt's pain sat heavy in her chest. She sat back down in the armchair and picked up her book, but her heart wasn't in it any more. She couldn't focus on anything else but the pain in Kurt's eyes and the ache in her heart. She knew that there was no easy way for him to heal from the loss of his mother and betrayal of his stepfather or to forgive her. But she was willing to wait.

Madeline let out a deep sigh and closed her eyes, letting the warmth of the fire wash over her. Thoughts of Jacob swirled in her mind, as she wished more than anything that he could be here to take her in his arms right now. She missed him so much, even though they had known each other for such a short time. Their relationship was already so intense, it made her gasp when she recollected him. And the pain of not being with him consumed her.

As she opened her eyes, she became mesmerised by the dancing flames. She began to flirt with a thought: maybe some-time in the future she would have a chance to have a child of her own, a brother or sister for Kurt, with the same warm brown eyes and kind nature as Jacob, the man she loved.

But when she went to bed that night, she felt lonelier than she had in years. Even lonelier than after the loss of Alex. Then, there had been family and friends to comfort her. But now she was alone, with no Alex, no Jacob, and the worry of her young charge who wanted nothing to do with her.

She tossed and turned in bed, her mind racing with all the things she wished were different, before finally, exhausted, she fell into a fitful sleep.

The next morning Kurt ate his breakfast in silence, then retreated to his room. Madeline was glad that it was

Dominique's day to work with her in the bookshop; at least she would have someone to talk to. She also expected Falcon to arrive at some time today, to recover the microfilm she had captured while in Germany.

Dominique arrived early and knocked at the apartment door. 'Good morning!' she said as she beamed. 'I let myself into the shop because I wanted to pop upstairs before we started work. I have a little something for Kurt.'

Madeline was encouraged by the sight of Dominique holding a neatly wrapped gift. 'That's so kind of you. I'm sure Kurt will love it,' she said, feeling a glimmer of hope at the thought of seeing Kurt smile. 'He is in his room; I will show you where.'

When she opened the bedroom door, the small boy was lying on his bed, looking forlorn.

'Kurt,' Madeline said softly, stepping into the room. 'Do you remember Dominique, the lady who works with me in the book-shop? She has brought you a gift.'

She saw a glimmer of excitement on his face, before his brow furrowed with the usual distrust.

'What is it?' he asked suspiciously, eyeing the wrapped package nervously.

'It's a surprise. You won't know until you unwrap it,' Dominique responded.

Kurt's eyes widened a bit at the word 'surprise', and he hesitantly reached out to take the gift from Dominique. When he finally revealed the contents, his face lit up with delight.

'It's a model aeroplane! I have always wanted one,' he exclaimed, holding it up to examine it from every angle.

Dominique beamed. 'I'm glad you like it. Madeline told me you'd been feeling down, and I thought this might cheer you up a bit.'

Madeline watched as Kurt's fingers moved over the smooth

surface of the aeroplane, the first smile she'd seen since she had met him playing at the corners of his mouth.

'If you like, and it is all right with Madeline, we could go and try flying it this morning before the shop gets busy?' Dominique continued.

Kurt's eyes widened at the suggestion, and he looked at Madeline with hopeful anticipation.

Madeline was relieved. 'I think it's a great idea.'

Kurt scrambled off his bed and eagerly put on his shoes.

But as Madeline watched the two of them get ready to leave, Dominique telling him of all they were going to do, she couldn't help feeling envious. Dominique was just trying to be kind to Kurt, but she had managed to win him over so quickly. Why hadn't Madeline thought to buy him a gift? She had so wanted to bond with him, for Alex's sake. Now she feared he would forever perceive her as the one responsible for his mother's death. Madeline pushed the negative thoughts away. She had to focus on Kurt's happiness, not her own insecurities.

Hand in hand, Dominique and Kurt made their way down the stairs and out of the bookshop. Madeline walked to the window and watched them leave, Kurt skipping up the road talking to Dominique as they went. But as she turned she realised with a start that she wasn't the only one watching. Marcel, in his Nazi armband, was smoking a cigarette on the corner and watching them go up the street too. He finished his cigarette and came inside.

'Who was that?' he asked Madeline bluntly.

Madeline felt her stomach clench. There was something in his tone that put her on alert.

'A friend's child I am taking care of,' she lied, hoping he wouldn't ask anything further.

'He has never been here before.'

'No,' said Madeline quietly, dropping her gaze to stare at the pile of books on the counter to be filed back away.

'The Third Reich have asked me to keep an eye on this neighbourhood and to report back to them with anything... unusual.'

Madeline stiffened behind the counter. 'Well, I'm sure the Third Reich will find nothing of importance here. He is just a little boy, and this is just a bookshop.'

He stared at her as he slowly smoked his cigarette. His dirty fingers curled around it.

'We will see,' he said slowly, then disrespectfully dropped the cigarette to the bookshop floor and ground it out with his heel, before turning away and striding out.

As he left a new fear emerged. Kurt was half Jewish; would she be able to protect him if the Führer carried out all he had threatened? Watching Marcel heading up the street in the same direction as Kurt and Dominique, she knew she had to come up with a plan. Marcel had known Madeline and Alex a long time. He had known that Alex was Jewish. And Kurt looked so much like his father.

As she tried to come up with a way to protect him if his heritage was uncovered, she became painfully aware with a shudder that she may not be able to keep him any safer here in France than he was in Germany. And that the enemy may be much closer than she had realised.

43

PARIS, NOVEMBER 1942

Madeline

As the war continued, the streets of Paris were often bathed in an eerie silence, the once-vibrant city now reduced to a sombre shadow of its former self as people fought to keep mind and body together. One evening as she was closing up the shop, Madeline felt a strange feeling of foreboding. Outside her window a heavy mist hung over the cobblestones, dampening even the faintest sounds of footsteps to an echo through the cold night air.

Madeline stood in the doorway of her bookshop, her gaze fixed on the deserted street outside as if searching for a glimmer of hope amid the darkness.

In the beginning there had been hope that the war would be over quickly, especially when the Americans had entered the war the year before. But as the days turned into weeks, months and then years, the grip of the German occupation tightened round the heart of Paris. The once warm smiles of the locals had been replaced by averted gazes and furrowed brows, their spirits crushed under the weight of constant fear. New regulations were imposed with alarming frequency, each one more suffocating than the last. Curfews shortened, rations dwindled, and the walls of the city seemed to close in around them, trapping everyone within the ever-narrowing confines of what was left of their lives. As they prepared to celebrate another Christmas under the occupation, Madeline couldn't shake the feeling that things were about to get worse.

She was puttering around the shop, finishing her tasks, when suddenly the door was pushed open with great haste, the little bell above it jangling loudly, jolting her out of her thoughts. She turned to see her old friend Monsieur Deveaux, the Jewish tobacconist, barging into the shop, a look of panic marking his face.

'Please, you have to help me!' he gasped, clutching his chest as he panted. 'The Gestapo, they're after me. They know I'm Jewish!'

'How? Didn't you have false papers? How would they know?'

But before he even answered, she knew. Marcel.

'Come with me,' she said, grabbing Monsieur Deveaux's arm and leading him to the back of the shop. 'We'll hide you until we can figure out a plan.'

Kurt was standing behind the counter, his eyes widening in confusion and fear as he watched the commotion. She could feel her heart racing with fear. She knew that hiding a Jewish person in Paris under the watchful eyes of the Gestapo was a dangerous and potentially deadly move. But she couldn't leave Monsieur Deveaux to face his fate alone.

They had barely reached the counter when the bell jangled again, and with a cold realisation she saw it was Marcel. He strode into the shop.

'Here you are,' he sneered, peering at the old man. 'The Germans are looking for you.'

Madeline felt her blood run cold as she tried to keep her composure.

Monsieur Deveaux's once-proud posture wilted as Madeline stepped towards him, her voice trembling with anger.

'What is wrong with you, Marcel? We are your friends and neighbours! You're French, for goodness' sake – do you really think the Nazis will protect you once they leave?' She gestured towards the occupied streets outside, where armed soldiers patrolled the once-familiar neighbourhood.

'You have never been my friends!' Marcel spat back, his eyes narrow with hatred. 'You and your kind. You deserve to *suffer*.'

Beside her, she thought Monsieur Deveaux might faint at any moment; his face was drained of colour and his breathing had become ragged. She pulled out a stool for him to sit on. But Madeline stood tall, refusing to back down in the face of Marcel's hate-filled words.

'You don't know what you're saying, Marcel,' she said, her voice firm. 'The Nazis don't care about you any more than they care about us. They only care about power and control. And if you keep helping them, you'll be just another pawn in their game. Is that what you want?'

Marcel hesitated for a moment, his eyes flickering with uncertainty. But then he shook his head and sneered once more.

'You're wasting your breath. I know what I'm doing. And I won't let you stand in my way.'

The jingle of the bell drew everyone's attention. Dominique, bundled in a winter coat, stood in the doorway with a shopping bag in her hand.

'I was just passing, doing some shopping for Christmas...' she started to say, then paused, taking in the scene. Madeline saw the confusion and fear in Dominique's eyes as she took in the sight of Marcel in his Nazi armband and Monsieur Deveaux looking as if he might pass out any second.

'Is everything all right?' she asked.

Madeline drew in a deep breath, attempting to steady herself as she looked at her friend. 'No, everything is not all right,' she said, her voice low. 'Marcel has informed the Gestapo about Monsieur Deveaux.'

Dominique gasped. 'Why?'

'He knows why,' spat out Marcel, pointing at the old man. 'He's pretending not to be Jewish, but the truth is out now. And he's going to pay for his lies and deceit.'

And with those words, he turned on his heel and strode out of the shop, slamming the door behind him.

Madeline watched as Dominique's face paled with fear. The Gestapo didn't tolerate anyone who helped Jews, and even the slightest hint of suspicion could lead to arrest and punishment.

But then, she saw something flicker in Dominique's eyes: tenacity.

'We have to do something,' Dominique said, her voice low with emotion. 'We can't just let them take him away.'

'We can't fight the Gestapo—' Madeline began.

'But we can't just give up and let them win,' Dominique replied, her voice rising with passion. 'We have to *try*.'

Madeline met her friend's gaze, seeing the fire in her eyes. She knew that Dominique was right. They couldn't just stand by and watch as Monsieur Deveaux was taken away to face an unknown fate. They had to act, to try to save him.

Madeline thought about Falcon. The agent had mentioned a secret network of people who helped smuggle Jews out of France and into Spain. It was a dangerous operation, but it might be their only hope.

The two young women helped the trembling old man up to Madeline's little sitting room, and Dominique made him a cup of tea as Madeline lit a fire. Once the old man was settled in his chair, the two friends talked in hushed tones in the kitchen as Madeline prepared to leave.

'Where are you going?' Dominique asked.

'I'm going to see if I can find some help for Monsieur Deveaux. To get him out of the city.'

'But isn't that dangerous?

Madeline sighed. 'Probably, but I have to try.'

She caught sight of Kurt in the doorway of the kitchen, his young eyes wide with fear.

'Kurt, you should get ready for bed,' she said, trying to keep her voice calm. 'It's late.'

'But what's happening with that old man?' Kurt asked, his voice tight with fear. 'What does it mean to be Jewish?'

Madeline felt her throat constrict. Kurt didn't know he was half-Jewish, and maybe it was good for now that he didn't know who his real father was.

'It's a grown-up matter,' she said, her tone firm. 'But don't worry, everything will be okay.'

Kurt hesitated for a moment, his eyes darting between Madeline and Dominique, before nodding and scurrying off to his room.

Once he was gone, Dominique turned to her friend. 'Do you really know someone who can help?'

Madeline looked back at the elderly man slumped in his chair staring at his tea as it turned cold, and her heart went out to him. He had no children and had lost his wife, the love of his life, just a few years before, and all at once he looked older than he had in a long time.

'I have a way to contact people who can help in an emergency. I have to go and find them. Can you stay here for a while? I won't be gone long.'

'Of course,' Dominique agreed, her eyes filled with worry. 'Please be careful.'

Madeline gave her friend's arm a small squeeze. 'I will. Take care of Monsieur Deveaux and Kurt.'

With that, she slipped out of the bookshop and into the darkened streets of Paris. As she moved at a brisk clip, she became acutely aware of the danger that surrounded her. Her thoughts filled with Kurt and the way Marcel had asked questions about him. Had he put two and two together about her stepson's Jewish heritage? And would there be retaliation if they managed to get the old man away to safety?

She arrived at the bar where she could leave a message for Falcon. Taking a deep breath, she entered. The bar was dark, with only a few patrons scattered around. She could see the outline of the bartender behind the counter, wiping glasses with a rag.

Madeline approached him. Falcon had told her the barman was a Resistance leader and was safe to leave a message with.

She leaned in so she wasn't overheard. 'I need to leave a message for Falcon.'

The bartender looked up, his eyes wary. 'I don't know what you're talking about,' he said in a gruff voice.

Then she remembered she needed to say a codeword so the man would know she could be trusted.

She racked her brains, then remembered. 'The sun sometimes rises in the west,' she whispered, her heart racing with anticipation.

The bartender's eyes widened in surprise. '*Très bien,*' he said, nodding. 'What's the message?'

Madeline quickly scrawled a note on a piece of paper, detailing in the code Falcon had taught her the situation with Monsieur Deveaux and asking for Falcon's help in getting him out of the country.

The bartender took the note and slipped it into his pocket. 'I'll make sure she gets this,' he said, his voice low. 'But you should leave now. It's not safe for you to be here.'

Madeline felt a wave of relief wash over her. She had done all she could, and now it was up to Falcon and the Resistance to help Monsieur Deveaux escape.

As she walked back to the bookshop, Madeline couldn't shake the feeling of fear and uncertainty. She brushed a strand of dark hair away from her face, feeling the familiar weight of Jacob's absence and how he was so confident in his Resistance work. She wished he was here to offer her advice. But the man she loved was thousands of miles away in Germany, fighting for the same cause, and her heart ached for him every moment they were apart.

But she had to keep going, for Kurt, for Monsieur Deveaux, for the people who needed her help.

When she arrived home, Dominique was sitting with Monsieur Deveaux, holding his hand and talking softly to him.

Madeline leaned against the door, watching them for a moment. She felt a warmth spread through her chest, a sense of comfort and belonging. These people meant a lot to her, and she would do everything in her power to protect them.

'I left a message,' she said softly. 'We'll hear soon.'

The elderly man sighed, a look of relief spreading across his face. 'Thank you, my dear.'

Kurt refused to go to sleep until Dominique had read him a story, and Madeline felt the usual pang of separation as she heard him laughing in his room while her friend spun tales for him.

Madeline and Monsieur Deveaux sat in the small sitting room, talking softly and waiting for a response from Falcon and the Resistance.

At one point the old man drew close and took her hand. 'Do you still have the box I gave you?'

'Yes, I still have it.'

'Good,' he said, his voice faint. 'I need you to promise me something, Madeline. Something very important.'

Madeline leaned in, her heart racing. 'Anything, Monsieur Deveaux. What is it?'

'Promise me that you'll keep it safe, no matter what happens,' he said, his eyes pleading. 'Fetch it for me, will you?'

She went downstairs and retrieved the box from its hiding place. She brought it back up to the front room and sat down beside Monsieur Deveaux. He took the box from her, cradling it in his lap.

'This box,' he said, his voice barely above a whisper. 'It contains something very important.' He carefully opened it, and pulled out the meagre contents. 'These things are the only things I have left of my wife, and they are very important to me.'

Madeline looked down at them. There were a few old photographs, a bundle of letters and a gold locket. She could see the love and longing in his eyes as he held them in his hands.

'If anything happens to me and I suddenly disappear, I want the memory of her to live on. I want her to be remembered,' he said, showing her a photograph of a beautiful woman with dark hair and sparkling eyes. 'Promise me you'll keep them safe, Madeline.'

'I promise,' she said, feeling a lump form in her throat.

She thought about Alex and how she felt the same about the things she had of his.

It was after midnight and Dominique had left when a knock at the back door woke Madeline up. She had fallen asleep in her chair, and her heart jolted with the sound. Was it the Gestapo?

Madeline took a deep breath before she called out. 'Who is it?'

'It's me,' a familiar voice responded, her voice low. 'I got your message.'

She breathed a sigh of relief and stepped back to let Falcon in.

'Where is he?' she asked.

'He's upstairs,' Madeline replied. 'Thank you for your help.'

'We'll need to move quickly. If the Gestapo already know about him, it won't be long before they come and take him away,' Falcon informed her.

Madeline acknowledged the young agent's words, feeling a sense of urgency wash over her.

Upstairs, the old man was awake, his body tense, his eyes wide with anticipation. 'Is it time to leave?' he asked, his voice so small.

Falcon walked over to him, taking his hand. 'Yes, it's time to go. We have a safe house ready where you'll be hidden until we can get you out of the country.'

'I have none of my things.' He said desperately.

'Don't worry about your things,' Falcon reassured him. 'Your safety is our top priority.'

She watched as Falcon helped Monsieur Deveaux to his feet and escorted him down the stairs. He turned to say goodbye to Madeline, his eyes filled with gratitude.

'Thank you, my dear,' he said, placing a hand on her cheek. 'I couldn't have made it this far without you. You remind me of my wife. You truly are a remarkable woman, Madeline.' The full impact of his kind words swept over her, filling her with a mixture of pride and heartbreak.

Falcon turned to her. 'You did the right thing, but you should know that when the Nazis find out, they will not be happy, and you and this bookshop will be on their radar.'

Madeline felt a sense of fear wash over her once more. She knew what she had done was dangerous, but she couldn't just sit back and watch as innocent people suffered under the Nazi regime.

'I understand,' she said, her voice barely above a whisper. 'I'll be careful.'

With that, Falcon led Monsieur Deveaux out of the bookshop's back entrance and they disappeared into the night. Madeline stood in the doorway watching them go, feeling a sense of both relief and dread wash over her.

When she turned, Kurt was standing at the top of the stairs, barefoot in his blue striped pyjamas, his eyes wide with confusion and fear.

'What's going on?' he asked.

'Monsieur Deveaux had to leave,' Madeline said, her voice soft. 'But it's going to be okay. He's going to a safe place now.'

Kurt looked up at her, his eyes filled with tears. 'But why did he have to leave?' he asked, his voice trembling.

She didn't know how to explain it to a child, but she knew she had to try. 'There are people who want to hurt him because of who he is,' she said, her voice gentle. 'But we're helping him so he can be safe.'

'Because he is Jewish?'

'Yes, Kurt.'

She climbed the stairs and, putting her hand on his shoulder, ushered him back to bed.

'Are we going to be okay?' he asked, his eyes brimming with tears.

Madeline squeezed his arm, feeling a sense of protectiveness wash over her. 'We're going to be okay,' she said, her voice firm. 'I promise.'

As she gently tucked Kurt into bed, a wave of despair washed over her. The hurtful words Marcel had said about Monsieur Deveaux continued to echo in her mind, and she couldn't shake the feeling that things could get much worse for them now.

And she had a nagging fear that she had just made a promise to Kurt that would be impossible to keep.

44

Olivia

Livi led Markus out of the cottage towards a majestic oak tree that dominated the main garden of the estate. Despite its seasonal, skeletal state, the tree was a magnificent sight. When Livi reached the oak she pressed her hand against its rough bark, caught her breath and retrieved the poem left by Jacob.

'I think he left us a set of clues, but to what, I don't know,' she said, her voice tinged with anticipation. 'When I stood in his cottage and looked out of the window, that was the first thing I saw. I remembered it was the first thing mentioned in the poem that was changed from the original.'

She handed Markus the poem. 'You see how the oak tree has been substituted for the pine tree in the poet's original version. I think all the changed words in the poem describe a place here on the estate.'

'What do you think that means?'

'I think it's a map to a place he wants us to find. Each changed word in Jacob's version points us in the direction of something.'

Markus furrowed his brow, deep in thought. 'So, we need to find these places on the estate,' he deduced.

'Exactly. The second word that was changed was from "daisies" to "roses".'

They scanned the surroundings, but there were no roses in sight.

Markus shook his head. 'It's winter, and it was seventy years ago. Maybe there were roses back then, but not now. We could ask one of the volunteers or Dr Vogel if they know of any roses on the estate,' he suggested.

Livi had an idea and, pulling out her phone, she scrolled through her photographs. 'Here,' she said. 'I took photos to show my grandfather. I have pictures of what the estate looked like back then.' She expanded an image. It showed the family members sitting in a rose garden, with the oak in the background.

'If the oak is in the background and the house is to the left side, it means that the rose garden used to be in that direction.' She pointed across the grounds.

They hurriedly made their way across to the far end of the estate.

When they reached the spot where the rose garden had once thrived, they found the remnants of a stone bench. Livi began to look around. 'The next changed word is "secret". Something concealed, do you think?' They searched for a while before her gaze landed on a moss-covered stone wall in the distance.

'The walled garden,' she said, 'as in a secret garden.'

With eager anticipation, the pair approached the moss-covered stone wall. Its gate creaked as Markus pushed it open. Inside was revealed a garden devoid of colour due to the winter. The flower beds were empty, and bare branches reached towards the grey sky. Fallen leaves lay scattered across the ground. Standing in the middle, Livi scanned the area, focusing on the next changed word, 'water'. However, there was no pond or water feature here.

'Maybe they removed whatever was here?' she pondered, disappointed.

She closed her eyes to think; and that was when she heard it: the sound of falling water echoing in the distance. She opened her eyes, a spark of excitement igniting within her.

'Markus, do you hear that? It's running water.'

Markus strained his ears, listening intently. 'You're right! There must be a waterfall nearby. I remember the map of the estate mentioning a brook. Let's follow the sound.'

Leaving the walled garden, they followed the sound of rushing water. Finally, they reached a secluded corner of the estate, where a small, hidden path led them through a thicket of overgrown shrubs. Pushing aside vines and ducking under low-hanging branches, they emerged into a hidden oasis.

Before them stood a tiny waterfall cascading down moss-covered rocks into a crystal-clear pool. The air was filled with the refreshing mist, and the sound of the rushing water drowned out all other noises.

Livi's heart soared as they climbed to the top of the hill, and she checked the poem. There was one more changed word.

'Boat,' she mumbled. 'Why would a boat be in the forest?'

Livi's eyes scanned the wooded path ahead, searching for any signs of what it could be. She pointed towards a patch of sunlight filtering through the trees. 'Maybe we should head towards the lake?'

As she turned, her foot caught on a gnarled tree root, and she stumbled forward. In a split second, Markus's strong arms shot out to catch her. The physical contact sent a jolt of electricity through Livi's body, and she felt an instant connection with him. Their eyes met, and in that fleeting moment she saw the same desire reflected in his intense gaze.

The air around them seemed to crackle with tension as they

both realised the undeniable mutual attraction between them that had been simmering just below the surface.

They sprang apart, both flushed with a embarrassment. Markus released his tight grip on Livi's arm, but his touch seemed to linger, leaving behind a tingle of electricity that prickled across her skin.

After a moment he cleared his throat, breaking the spell that had enveloped them.

'Are you okay?' he asked softly, his voice husky with emotion.

'Yeah, I'm fine,' she mumbled, trying to compose herself. 'I just need to watch where I'm going.'

Livi tried to distract herself by focusing on the poem in front of her, pretending to be engrossed in the words even though her mind was still reeling from their close encounter.

Markus turned to her. 'Wait, look! From here, you can just see a glimpse of the lake.'

Livi's eyes followed Markus's gaze, and through the gaps in the foliage she caught a glimmer of shimmering water.

They hurriedly made their way towards the lake. As they emerged from the forest, a breathtaking vista unfolded before them. The sun danced on the ripples of the water, casting a golden glow across its surface. A small wooden dock stood at the edge and, tied to a post, a weathered rowing boat bobbed on the surf. Livi's heart sank as she realised that whatever had been in a boat in the 1940s might be long gone.

'Not boat,' said Markus. 'Boat*house*.' He pointed to where a small structure nestled on the banks.

It was an old boathouse, its weathered wooden planks barely holding together. A surge of hope coursed through Livi's veins as she realised that this could be the answer they were searching for.

They approached the boathouse, and found it locked.

'We should talk to Dr Vogel, tell her what we have found,' suggested Livi.

Markus agreed. The discovery they had made was too significant to keep to themselves. With renewed conviction, they retraced their steps back to the main house, excitement bubbling within them both as they returned to the curator's office.

An hour later, Dr Vogel and a team of trained volunteers, along with Livi and Markus, stood outside the aged boathouse. Dr Vogel, a key in hand, approached the door and inserted it into the rusty lock. With a gentle turn, the lock clicked open, and she swung the creaky door wide.

Inside, the room was dark. Dr. Vogel led the way, dust particles dancing in the beam of her torchlight. It smelled of damp wood and musty air, and Livi carefully avoided stacks of old newspapers and forgotten trinkets. As their eyes adjusted to the dark, Dr Vogel gave them a short history of the boathouse.

Livi's heart sank as she looked around the barren structure. It seemed they had alerted everyone for nothing. Whatever had been in here in the 1940s was long gone.

Dr Vogel, however, was unperturbed. Handing out torches, her eyes gleamed with perseverance as she spoke. 'Don't lose hope just yet,' she said, her voice filled with reassurance. 'Sometimes, the answers aren't found in what's physically here. Look around for anything that might be a clue.'

They started to search, and it was Markus who called out, 'There are two initials here!' They huddled around to see what he was illuminating – it was on a floorboard in the corner where they could just make out the letters 'S.K.' scratched into the wood.

Dr Vogel smiled. 'That might point to a Resistance agent known as Story Keeper who was active here during the war.

There could be something of great importance beneath that floor,' the curator exclaimed with a hint of excitement.

A short while later, the maintenance crew arrived to pry open the decaying floorboards. As Dr Vogel illuminated the newly revealed space with her torch, Livi gasped, her eyes widening in disbelief at the astonishing sight nestled within the hidden depths.

45

PARIS, CHRISTMAS EVE 1942

Madeline

A heavy drizzle fell on the grey streets of Paris as the Valette family prepared for their annual Christmas Eve gathering. The mood was sombre, a stark contrast to the usual festive atmosphere of past years.

As Madeline looked around at her parents and her sisters, Isabelle, Antoinette, Charlotte and Gigi, she couldn't help but notice the toll that war had taken on them. The weariness and worry etched on their faces told their own stories of hardship and struggle. The rules had become harsher, and rationing had become more extreme, making it difficult for them to make ends meet. But they were together, and that was what truly mattered.

Kurt had joined them for dinner, but he was awkward around other people, with his vacant stare and nervous demeanour. Dominique, who had taken on the role of teaching him French, was surprised at how quickly he was learning. Madeline had also placed him in a small school, hoping to provide some stability and structure in his life. But even with these efforts, Kurt seemed lost in his own world.

He sat huddled in the corner of the kitchen in his coat, while the sisters moved around him and prepared food. Benjamin, tried to engage Kurt in a game of cards. But he seemed too preoccupied with his own thoughts to join in. It was clear that his mind was still burdened by the horrors he had witnessed and endured.

As they continued to make their dinner, their father asked Madeline enthusiastically, 'Need a taste tester?'

Madeline beamed at him. 'Of course, Papa,' she said, handing him a spoonful of the stew she had been helping to prepare. He took a small sip.

'Delicious as always,' he said with a hint of pride in his voice, his eyes closed.

She smiled ruefully, her eyes scanning the simple dinner set before them. The absence of all their favourite Christmas foods made her heart feel heavy with longing. But maybe this would be the last one. Maybe this time next year they would be free...

They sat down to their meal, the warm stew with home-made bread. Charlotte had worked tirelessly to create it, adding bits of meat from their dwindling rations for flavour. She had also managed to harvest some vegetables from their garden – swedes and turnips – making the meal at least filling.

'I'm sorry there is no dessert, cheese or fruit,' she apologised with a sigh. 'I waited in the queue for hours, but the jar of jam I wanted was gone by the time I got to the front.'

'Well, then you will be glad of my Christmas present to you all,' Antoinette announced with a grin, and left the table momentarily before returning with a large square of blue cheese wrapped in brown paper.

The family looked at it in shock, knowing how rare and coveted such a delicacy was during wartime.

'Do I want to know where you got that from?' Delphine asked her daughter sternly, eyeing the cheese suspiciously.

Antoinette scooped a spoonful of stew into her mouth,

shaking her head. 'No, not unless you want the Germans to shoot you.'

'Who cares!' Gigi exclaimed, grabbing a knife eagerly. She carefully split up the cheese between the adults, who savoured its creamy and tangy taste that brought a smile to everyone's face, and after that no one could resist joining in as Bernard started singing Christmas carols.

As they ate and sang, the heavy drizzle outside seemed to fade away, replaced by the warmth and joy that filled the room. For a brief moment, they were able to forget about rationing and the struggles of war. They were transported back to a time when Christmas meant decadent feasts and indulgent desserts, thanks to the large square of blue cheese that had miraculously appeared on their table.

After dinner, Madeline sat near the fireplace sipping on chicory coffee, the taste of which she had started to get used to. She felt a sense of melancholy wash over her as her father played carols on his phonograph; she missed Jacob terribly. The thought of spending Christmas without him was almost unbearable. Madeline had not left Paris since she had arrived back with Kurt, not wanting to disrupt the little boy's routine, and it had been weeks since she had received a letter from Jacob.

She tried to shake off the feeling of foreboding, but it lingered like a heavy weight on her as she traced the rim of her mug with her finger, lost in her own thoughts.

Her gaze drifted towards the little Christmas tree in the corner of the room, adorned with ornaments made by Isabelle and being batted at by one of Charlotte's many acquired stray cats.

Her thoughts drifted to all the Christmases she and Alex had spent together. He had been so big on Christmas, and extravagant with his gift giving.

She thought of Jacob alone in his cottage, and wondered if this kind of long-distance relationship was even possible during wartime. She hadn't been prepared for the onslaught of feelings that had come with meeting him, and the pain of being apart was almost as bad as the grief she had felt at losing Alex.

'Are you all right, my dear?' Bernard asked as he leaned close to her, concern on his face. 'You seem lost in thought.' As always, it was as if he could read her mind.

Madeline had not told her family about Jacob yet; she was uncertain of her family's reaction and the barrage of enquiries that might come regarding her spying activities. So, with her eyes misty with unshed tears, she confided a partial truth. 'I miss Alex, Papa,' she murmured, her voice tinged with a deep yearning. 'Christmas just isn't the same without him.'

Bernard reached out and gently squeezed her hand, his touch a comforting presence. 'I know it's hard,' he said softly. 'But I believe that Alex is with us in spirit. He may not be *physically* present, but his love and memories will always be here, in our hearts.'

Madeline took a deep breath and let it out slowly, trying to find solace in her father's words. 'I had hoped that at least I could get close to his son. But he still resents me so much,' she whispered, looking over at Kurt, who had been quiet throughout the evening. He now sat in the corner looking at a book her parents had given him for Christmas. His sombre expression matched her own, his eyes reflecting the same sense of loss and longing. It was his first Christmas without his mother, and she could only imagine how difficult it must be for him.

Her father followed her gaze. 'Kurt has been through so much, and it may take time for him to accept you. Does he know you're his stepmother yet?'

She shook her head. 'I'm waiting for the right time. I'm sure he will have many questions, and the more he knows about his ancestry the more danger he is in. I will find a way soon after Christmas, once he is more settled.'

Her father leaned in closer, lowering his voice. 'Don't wait too long; I've noticed the way he watches you when he thinks no one is looking. There's a flicker of hope in his eyes, as if he wants to believe that happiness can still exist amid all his darkness.'

Madeline's heart swelled with hope. She couldn't bring back his mother, but she could try her best to give Kurt the love and support he needed.

All at once, there was a knock at the door. They all froze. Before the war, they would have been delighted to see who was visiting, but now there was the constant fear of the enemy. They were always worried that the Nazis had detected Bernard's hidden wireless.

Her father stood up with a frown. 'I'll go and see who it is.'

Madeline watched as he cautiously made his way to the door, and the tension in the room was palpable as they all held their breath, waiting, until the voice of their neighbour, Monsieur Ferrand, brought a collective release. Even still, the fear in everyone's hearts had taken hold, and they all remained frozen in their seats.

'Bernard,' Monsieur Ferrand said in a hushed voice. 'A Merry Christmas to you and your family. My wife made some pickles, and we thought you might like some for your Christmas meal. It's not much, but it's something.'

Relief flooded the room as Bernard opened the door wider to welcome their neighbour inside, and the sisters exchanged glances of relief.

The visitor handed over a jar of home-made pickles to Bernard, and one each for the girls, who all thanked him profusely.

As her father opened his own jar to smell the vinegary fragrance, the scent of the pickles filled the room, bringing a burst of freshness and nostalgia. Madeline's mouth watered, and she couldn't help but be touched at the small gesture of kindness.

'Would you like a glass of my home-made brandy?' Bernard asked. 'I made it from fruit Charlotte managed to grow this year.'

Monsieur Ferrand gladly accepted the offer, and, taking off his coat, settled himself into a chair as Bernard poured the brandy, and a sense of camaraderie filled the room.

'Did you hear,' he said, lowering his voice, 'that the Nazis are planning sweeps of the neighbourhood? They're looking for anyone they suspect of aiding the Resistance.' He looked around at all of them, his eyes filled with worry. 'We all need to be careful.'

Madeline forced down the tight knot that had formed in her throat and fought against envisioning the consequences for herself or Kurt if her covert activities were exposed. She looked at Benjamin playing with a train on the floor and Kurt still reading, innocent children caught in the crossfire of this war. It pained her to see their childhoods stolen away from them, replaced with fear and uncertainty. Had she been wrong to bring this innocent boy from all he had known? What if she were arrested for helping Monsieur Deveaux? What would happen to him then?

After Monsieur Ferrand had left, Madeline could see it in her family's eyes. They were all thinking the same thing: what if they were next? What if the Gestapo came for them?

Madeline knew she couldn't take that risk with her stepson; she couldn't have him pay again for another adult's choices. She had been considering something since the night she managed to help her old friend. But after hearing the words of her neighbour, it seemed to her even more important to act on what she was thinking.

'Benjamin, why don't you show Kurt the new toys you have in the other room?' she suggested.

Both of the boys looked hesitant. Kurt still seemed unsure

how to play, and Benjamin wasn't sure how to interact with this German boy. But they sloped off into the other room.

Once they had left, Madeline turned to her family to share what was on her mind. She told them about what had happened to her neighbour and, in turn, each of her sisters shared their own stories of loss and hardship. They spoke about the constant fear they lived in and how they had all been struggling to keep their heads above water. The conversation was raw and emotional, but it was also cathartic.

As they sat there, keeping each other close, Madeline spoke with a voice steady with resolve. 'I know what we are living through is hard, but we have to keep fighting, even if our battle is simply to carry on each day.'

Instinctively, the sisters joined hands to reassure each other as she continued.

'We're a family, and we'll protect each other, no matter what.' Madeline's voice caught in her throat. 'I fear that after they tried to come for Monsieur Deveaux, Kurt could be next. Even though he is a little boy, Marcel knew Alex, and they look so alike. I have been trying to think of a way to keep him safe.'

Gigi's eyes widened. 'Madeline, you can't let Kurt be taken. We have to do something.'

Antoinette, lately preoccupied with her Jewish husband away in a work camp, spoke up, the usual tenacity in her voice. 'We need a plan,' she said, locking eyes with each of her sisters in turn. 'A plan for the children. We can't just wait for the worst to happen. We have to act now. I need the same for Benjamin. I have thought about taking him away on a train, to a place where he would be safe. But I have other obligations here, things I can't leave right now.'

All the women looked over at their middle sister, normally vivacious and charismatic, who had become withdrawn in recent months. The whole family was concerned about what those 'things' could be. Madeline was convinced it was something dangerous.

Gigi spoke too, her voice trembling. 'I have my ballet teacher's twin daughters living with me and my friends at the moment. They are beautiful and talented, but they are also Jewish. Their father's dance studio was raided. Fortunately, he got away and is in hiding, but their mother is dead, and they are all alone. I've been trying to help them, but I fear it's only a matter of time before they're discovered. And the Nazis might try and find a way to bring him out of hiding using them. So, we must find a way to save them too.'

The room fell into silence as the weight of their circumstances settled in.

'I think getting them out of the city would be the best, but I can't leave right now; there is too much going on at the ballet school. It needs my help,' continued Gigi remorsefully.

Isabelle sighed. 'I would do it, but my work at the Louvre is also imperative at the moment, and I'm the only one that can do what needs to be done. So unfortunately, I can't take the children anywhere.'

'But I can,' piped up a timid voice. All the others turned to look at Charlotte, the most reserved of the sisters. 'I could take them all out of the city on a train.'

Madeline's eyes widened in surprise. She always underestimated Charlotte's quiet strength. Now, she recognized a newfound resolve in her sister's gaze. As the second youngest, she had often been the quietest, usually eclipsed by her more vocal siblings. Yet, in that moment, the glint of determination in her eyes was undeniable.

'Charlotte, are you sure? It's a dangerous journey, especially with all the children being Jewish. If you were caught...'

Charlotte straightened, her voice steady. 'I may not be as outgoing as all of you, but I'm not weak. You all have important jobs to do here, but I don't, and I'll do whatever it takes to keep our family safe and help those in need. Antoinette's right, we can't just sit here and wait for the worst to happen.'

The room fell silent as Charlotte's words lingered in the air. Madeline felt a swell of pride for her younger sister.

One by one each sister voiced their agreement, and they formed a united front, ready to face whatever challenges lay ahead.

In the days after Christmas, they met to meticulously plan. All the Jewish armbands would be unpicked from the children's coats, except for Kurt, who still didn't know his true heritage. Madeline was relieved she hadn't revealed the identity of his real father yet. Keeping him unaware might help keep him safe. He wouldn't have to lie, and would be safer travelling without that knowledge.

Fortunately, all the children were under twelve, so they didn't need identity papers. And unless one of the children said something, no one would know their heritage. Also, another child would be joining them; her name was Sophie, and her mother worked at the Louvre with Isabelle.

Charlotte would take them to the South of France to stay with their aunt, who had offered her large home, until they felt it was safe enough to bring them all back. It could be a matter of weeks, but they also knew it could be months before Charlotte returned.

Even though it was dangerous to take Jewish children illegally out of the city, it was a risk they were all willing to take.

46

PARIS, JANUARY 1943

Madeline

The final arrangements were made to take the children to the South of France, though Madeline had continued debating if it was the right thing to do, and dreaded telling Kurt about their plan. She knew it would be difficult for him to understand why he had to go on yet another journey with what were, to him, just more strangers.

But her mind had been made up the day before, when Marcel had come into the shop and seen Kurt sitting on a stool next to Dominique. Marcel's narrowed eyes and intense stare at the young boy had scared her, but not as much as seeing Kurt frozen in fear, his innocent eyes widening as he stared back. Madeline could see the panic in his expression, and it broke her heart. She knew she had to protect him at all costs, even if it meant uprooting his life once again.

She decided to tell him the next day when they were eating dinner. Attempting to steady her own nerves, she took a deep breath, trying to hide her fear and uncertainty. 'Kurt,' she began, her voice gentle yet filled with assurance, 'I need to talk to you about something important.'

The young boy stared up at her, his eyes filled with his usual apprehension. 'What is it?' he asked, his fork in mid-air, the usual distrust furrowing his brow.

She reached out and laid her hand over his, trying to convey all the love and protection she felt for him. 'I made a promise to your mother before she left us,' she started, her voice wavering slightly. 'A promise to keep you safe, no matter what.'

Kurt's eyes widened as he listened intently.

'There are people out there who want to hurt you. And I can't let that happen.'

Kurt's placed his cutlery down and his hand tightened into a fist under Madeline's touch. 'Who wants to hurt me?' he asked, his voice trembling with uncertainty.

She took a moment to compose herself, gathering her thoughts, before she continued. 'There are bad people in this world, Kurt,' she said softly.

'You mean the *Nazis*,' he spat out.

Madeline's heart ached at the loss of innocence in his voice. 'Yes, Kurt. The Nazis.' She paused, searching for the right words to ease his fears. 'But to keep you safe, I need you to go on a journey with a group of children and my sister Charlotte. You're going to leave Paris and go somewhere far away.'

'Leave? Will I have to leave Dominique and my aeroplane?' he asked with concern.

The affection in his voice for her friend stung, but she continued. 'Yes, Kurt, you will have to leave Dominique and your aeroplane behind for now. It's not safe for you here anymore. But I promise, once it's safe again, you'll come back, and you can see them both. I will keep everything safe for you.'

Anger flashed across the young boy's face. His eyes filled with tears and his small fists clenched tightly on the table's edge.

'I don't want to leave Dominique and my aeroplane!' he exclaimed, his voice filled with both anger and despair.

Madeline tried to comfort him, but as she reached forward Kurt jumped up from the table, his chair clattering to the floor. His face contorted with pain and defiance, he glared at Madeline.

'I won't go! You can't make me!' he shouted, his voice echoing through the small kitchen. Tears streamed down his flushed cheeks, reflecting his inner turmoil.

Madeline stood up slowly, heartbroken at Kurt's anguish. She reached out, but he recoiled, stepping back as if her touch would burn him. With that, he turned and ran to his bedroom. Madeline stood frozen in the kitchen, her heart heavy with sorrow. She never wanted to cause her stepson pain, but knew this was the only way to protect him. She had to find a way to make him understand.

As the days passed, Madeline struggled to bridge the gap between her and Kurt. In desperation, she confided in Dominique about the situation and asked if she could try to get through to him. Dominique agreed to speak to him and one evening offered to tuck him in and read him a story. In the doorway, Madeline listened intently as Dominique spoke soothingly to Kurt, reassuring him that leaving was the right decision.

'You know, Kurt,' Dominique began, her voice soft and soothing, 'I heard you are going on a journey, and, sometimes in life, we have to make hard choices. Choices that can be scary and make us feel like we're losing something important. But we have to remember that these choices are made out of love and to keep us safe.'

'But why do I have to go?' Kurt whispered, his voice filled with sadness and confusion. 'Why can't I just stay here and hide?'

Dominique gently brushed Kurt's hair from his face, her

voice compassionate. 'Oh, I wish it were that simple. But hiding isn't enough.'

'It's because Madeline doesn't want me. Nobody wants me because I am German. Everyone at school says that Germans are the enemy.'

Madeline's heart shattered into a million pieces as she heard Kurt's words. She felt a surge of guilt wash over her as she realised that he believed her decision was a rejection of him.

'Oh, Kurt, that's not true,' she said, her heart aching at the wounds she saw in him, the beliefs already taking hold. 'I wish more than anything you could stay with me. You will be leaving with a group of children and staying near the beach,' she explained, her voice gentle and sincere. 'There's a beautiful house there, owned by our aunt, and you will be with my sister Charlotte.'

Kurt looked at both of them defiantly. 'When I grow up, I am going to do what I want to do,' he said stubbornly. 'I won't need anyone to love me or protect me.'

With that, he turned away, pulling the covers up over his head. Madeline and Dominique exchanged a glance, their hearts heavy with Kurt's pain and uncertainty. They left the room and retreated to the kitchen, the silence thick between them. Madeline poured two cups of tea.

'Do you think he'll come around?' Dominique asked softly, her concern evident.

'I don't know,' she replied, taking a sip of her tea. 'I do know that he blames me for everything terrible that has happened to him in his life.'

Dominique's eyes filled with empathetic tears. 'He's just a child. It's hard for him to see beyond his own hurt and confusion.'

'I know,' Madeline whispered, tears welling in her own eyes. 'But I couldn't bear the thought of him being harmed by all of this. He deserves a chance at a safe and happy life.'

'Do you think it would help if you told him the truth about his father?'

Madeline shook her head, her voice trembling. 'I don't know, Dominique. I've thought about it, but I worry that it will only add to his burden. He's already carrying so much pain and confusion. I want to wait until he's more settled and happier. Once he is in the south, I plan to visit him and tell him the whole truth. But knowing he is Jewish right now would only complicate things further for him. I want him to find his own identity first, without the weight of his heritage overshadowing everything else,' she explained, her voice filled with sadness.

Dominique reached across the table and placed a comforting hand on Madeline's. 'You're doing what you believe is best for Kurt. Often the hardest decisions are made out of love.'

In the first week of January 1943, on a foggy morning, Madeline walked with Kurt to the train station. As they trudged through the mist, she kept stealing glances at her stepson. He seemed tiny amid the chaos that surrounded them. She knew this journey was necessary, but it didn't make it any easier to see him leave. Her heart ached as she watched him clutching his small suitcase tightly, his face a mixture of fear and reluctance.

When they reached the train station, she was grateful to see three of her sisters, Isabelle, Antoinette and Gigi, already there, but her heart broke at the sight of the other children waiting with them. They were all wearing tired-looking clothes and carried small bags for their belongings. All young souls who had been uprooted from their homes, children who had lost their innocence long before they should have.

As the train reached the platform, Madeline knelt down in front of Kurt, her eyes brimming with tears. 'Remember, my darling boy, this isn't goodbye forever,' she whispered, her voice trembling. 'I will come for you when it's safe.'

He seemed to stare through her with defiant resignation. His eyes held a despair and weariness that had only deepened since she had met him in Germany. Madeline fought back her own tears as she pulled Kurt into a stiff embrace. The world seemed so cruel and unjust at that moment, snatching away the last remnants of innocence from this young boy's life.

She held on to him as tightly as she could, hoping that her love alone would be enough to shield him from the pain and uncertainty that lay ahead.

'I will see you soon, and will put your plane away somewhere safe, all ready for you when you come home.'

Charlotte and the other children were boarding the train, and Madeline reluctantly released Kurt from her embrace.

He walked away without even looking back, his small form disappearing into the crowded compartment.

Madeline watched as the train pulled away, her heart torn between hope and fear. She had done what she believed was best for Kurt, but now all she could do was trust that he would find safety and happiness in the South of France.

If she had known then that it was the last time she would see her stepson, she would never have put him on that train. She would have held him tighter, fought harder to keep him by her side, to shield him from the darkness that awaited him.

But in that moment all she could do was stand there, her eyes fixed on the disappearing train, believing that she had made the right choice.

47

BERLIN, DECEMBER 2011

Olivia

In the dim light of the boathouse, the dust swirled as four men lifted out the large chest hidden under the floorboards. As it was brought into the light, the anticipation was almost too much to bear. It was beautifully crafted, adorned with intricate carvings and brass fittings. The air seemed to crackle with excitement as Dr Vogel, wearing her white gloves, stepped forward and carefully lifted the lid.

Inside, they found a treasure trove of documents, photographs and other artefacts from the past, along with books, which Livi presumed were the ones missing from the library. Livi's eyes widened in awe as she surveyed the contents. It was like stepping back in time, a glimpse into the lives of those who had come before.

On top of everything sat an envelope addressed 'For Story Keeper'. Dr Vogel opened it and Livi saw that it contained a single piece of folded paper. Dr Vogel unfolded the yellowing paper and read it aloud.

Dear Darling Story Keeper,

If you are reading this, then you have unravelled the tapestry of clues I wove into the poem I recited the night you left. How I have longed to share more with you, to hold you close once again and speak the words that I have hidden within my heart.

The night you departed was the longest of my life; the cottage echoed with the emptiness of your absence. My only fear is that, if you are reading this, something must have happened to me. My plan was to restore all these books to the library before the family arrives back. They are the books that the Nazis told me to burn, Mr Blumenthal's most precious Jewish works. I made the fire as he asked, but burned Nazi propaganda, and in the dead of night I hid the books here in the boathouse and prayed they would not be found until the war was over.

The short time we have had together will last me a lifetime. I know now why I waited so long for you, and I am now convinced that the poets were right; it is not the length of time that you know a person, but the depth of love you experience. I could never have fathomed a connection like ours. It was everything I had waited for, and I don't regret anything.

Also, my darling, I know as his stepmother you will take care of Kurt as I have taken care of his mother. She will be here waiting for him when he returns. Remember the night of the storm that left an indelible mark? Ada is there. I asked Swift that, if anything happens to me, I want the same fate. If I can't be in your arms, it is where I belong. I have placed her in that safe place and I know when you read this you will be clever enough to be able to find her.

I have one final task for you, my dear Story Keeper. Please promise that if for some reason I am no longer here you will restore these books to their rightful place in the library.

*Until the moment when our souls are reunited, I remain,
forever and always, yours.*

J

Livi was so shocked by the mention of her grandfather that
she felt light-headed.

Stepmother. What stepmother?

'Let's take this chest carefully up to the archival room at the
house,' Dr Vogel said carefully. 'There's a specific procedure we
need to follow to protect everything as we unpack it.'

'Dr Vogel,' Livi asked, 'I know this is unorthodox, but that
letter is talking about my grandfather. Do you mind if I take a
photograph of it for him to see?'

The curator looked concerned, but relented. 'You must
promise not to make any of this public until we have had a
chance to do the work we need to do. But as we would never
have found this without you, I think I can allow it.' She carefully unfolded the letter, and Livi took the photograph.

Dr Vogel drew in a breath and suddenly became very busi-
ness-like as she interacted with the volunteers. 'Now, I need to
document the discovery with notes, including the date, time,
location, and my initial observations about the box and its
contents. Plus, assess the condition of the books to determine if
any immediate conservation measures are needed to prevent
further deterioration, as well as determining the appropriate
preservation needs for the books.'

The group of volunteers huddled around the old wooden
box, their voices filled with excitement as they prepared to move
it. Dr Vogel turned to Livi and Markus, gratitude shining in her
eyes. 'Thank you both for discovering this. We will carefully
document everything, and, if we find anything that could assist
you on your quest, I am more than willing to help.'

They left the boathouse, and Livi waited until Dr Vogel was
out of sight before turning to Markus.

'I can't believe what Jacob wrote,' she said, her voice filled
with disbelief. 'About Story Keeper being his stepmother. My
grandfather was a war orphan; there were no known step-
parents in our family.' She paused, trying to make sense of it all.

'Frederick did remarry. Do you think that woman is who
Jacob was referring to?' Markus asked.

'Maybe we should look in the museum.'

They walked back to the manor in silence, and quickly
searched through the museum for any information about Frederick's second wife. There was no mention of Livi's great-grandmother anywhere, as if she had never existed. But there was a
record of Frederick's second marriage, to a wealthy German
debutante who supported the Nazi party and shared her
husband's anti-Semitic views. Livi stared at the portrait of the
woman with her perfectly coiffed hair and fake smile, feeling
confused. 'Something isn't right,' she finally said, shaking her
head. 'I refuse to believe that she is Story Keeper.'

Markus agreed.

'There must be more to this story,' Livi went on solemnly,
her eyes scanning Jacob's letter once again for any clues. 'Plus,
Jacob talks about this woman taking care of Kurt. She never did
that. My grandfather was taken to Paris.'

As she turned her focus back to the letter, Livi suddenly
froze. Something else had caught her attention. She had been so
overwhelmed by the mention of her grandfather that she hadn't
properly taken in the line about Ada until now. In a rush of
excitement, she enlarged the photo on her phone to show
Markus.

'Remember the night of the storm? That left an indelible
mark?' Livi read out loud. Her words trailed off as she made a
sudden realisation. Her eyes widened with excitement, and

tears began to well up. 'It's another clue!' she exclaimed, grabbing Markus's hand and pulling him towards the door.

'We have to go back,' Livi said breathlessly as they rushed back through the manor and towards the woods.

'I saw it, I know I did,' she panted as they approached the boathouse.

'Saw what?' Markus asked, his concern evident on his face.

'The tree he is talking about in here!' Livi yelled, darting into a nearby clearing with Markus close behind.

'A tree? There are hundreds of trees here,' he said, bewildered by her sudden urgency.

'There!' Livi pointed to a specific tree at the edge of the clearing and raced towards it. Markus followed behind, slightly out of breath and confused.

Livi stopped in front of the tree and hunched over, trying to catch her breath. 'I should never have given up jogging,' she said with a slight wheeze as she looked up at Markus.

'What are we looking for?' he asked, trying to catch his own breath.

'In the letter, Jacob talked about a thunderstorm that left an indelible mark,' Livi explained as she searched the ground around the tree. 'I think he was referring to this tree that has been struck by lightning. Help me look!' she pleaded, dropping to her knees as she crawled about scanning the ground.

'For what?' Markus asked, confused.

Suddenly, Livi stopped and fell back on her heels, closing her eyes as she fought back tears. 'This,' she said, returning to the ground and aggressively pulling at the grass around her.

'I don't think you should be doing that,' Markus cautioned.

But Livi didn't listen as she uncovered a round grey stone hidden beneath the grass.

'What is it?' Markus asked, moving closer.

As they both read the words carved into the stone – Gertrud Schmidt – Livi's eyes filled with tears and her voice became hoarse.

'It's my great-grandmother's grave.'

48

PARIS, JANUARY 1943

Madeline

The very next day, Madeline swallowed down her fear as Gestapo officers pushed their way into her bookshop. Their presence was like a heavy weight. It felt suffocating and threatening her safe space. Their black leather trench coats and polished boots oozed intimidation, causing dread to wash over her in an icy wave. She forced herself to stand tall, despite the fear that threatened to consume her.

One of the officers strode forward, his harsh voice cutting through the silence. 'Is this your shop, Fräulein?' he demanded, eyes scanning the room like a predator searching for prey.

Madeline attempted to keep her composure in front of these dangerous men. 'Yes, it is. How can I help you?'

She was trembling inside, but she refused to show it.

'We have received reports that you are harbouring Jews,' the officer continued, his tone growing colder. 'We have orders to search the premises.'

Madeline's heart dropped as she heard those words. But then she thought of Monsieur Deveaux's face, and a fire ignited within her. She was tired of being afraid and at the mercy of these tyrants. Her forced smile disappeared as she spoke with newfound conviction. 'I have no idea what you're talking about. This is just a bookshop.'

The officers shared a knowing look before the taller one stepped forward again. 'We have reason to believe otherwise. We suggest you cooperate with us or face the consequences.'

'I have nothing to hide from you. Feel free to search the place, but I guarantee you won't find anything incriminating.' Madeline took a deep breath and braced herself for whatever would come next, ready to stand her ground.

She cringed as they rifled through her books and overturned her display tables in search of signs of anything illegal. After they had finished destroying her shop, the officers pushed past her and their heavy boots thudded on the stairs up to Madeline's apartment. She was grateful that Kurt had got away to the South of France with her sister just in time.

Through the window she caught sight of Marcel lurking outside, smoking a cigarette and watching the bookshop. How could he betray his neighbours like this? Madeline's mind raced with thoughts of what could happen if they found anything in her apartment. Would they arrest her? Or worse?

Above her head, the sound of shattering glass and splintering wood filled the air, causing Madeline's heart to race even faster. They were up there now, tearing through Alex's belongings, and she hoped that she had hidden Jacob's books well enough.

And then, just as abruptly as it had started, it stopped. Madeline held her breath as she heard footsteps thud back down the stairs and approach the counter where she stood. She turned to face the two officers who had invaded her home.

'Well, well, what do we have here?' one of them sneered, holding up one of Jacob's books in front of Madeline's face. She couldn't bring herself to meet his accusing gaze, mortified she hadn't hidden the book in a better place.

The taller officer grabbed her roughly by the arm and pulled her towards the door. 'You're under arrest,' he spat, his voice thick with disgust and hatred. 'For harbouring Jews and possession of subversive literature.'

The officers bound her hands and dragged her away from everything she knew and loved. As they led her out the door, the world outside seemed to blur. She felt numb, disconnected from reality.

The Gestapo officers shoved Madeline into the backseat of their black sedan, their grip tight and unforgiving. She glanced out of the window, catching Marcel's gaze lingering on her before he quickly averted his eyes. Betrayal burned within her, a searing pain that reminded her she had done nothing wrong.

As the car sped through Paris, Madeline couldn't help but feel a surge of anger. Anger for a world where an act of compassion resulted in this kind of treatment.

She also felt afraid. Afraid for what awaited her at the Gestapo headquarters. She had heard many stories of torture and cruelty that occurred behind those walls. A feeling of dread shuddered throughout her body, but she refused to let fear consume her. She had to stay strong for herself, for Jacob, Kurt, and all those she had tried to protect.

When they arrived at their destination, Madeline was roughly pulled from the car and escorted inside the gloomy building. It was damp and cold, and the frigid air seemed to seep into her very bones, making her muscles shiver involuntarily as they dragged her down a dimly lit corridor.

They reached a door labelled 'Interrogation Room', and she took a deep breath, steeling herself for whatever lay ahead.

The door swung open, revealing a stark room with a single table, and the officer pushed her down into a chair.

'You will wait here!'

Madeline sat in the cold metal chair, her bound hands trembling in her lap. She tried to calm her racing heart and steady her breath, but the weight of the situation was suffocating. The room was bleak, its dim lighting casting long shadows on the cracked walls.

She wasn't sure how long she was there; it could have been minutes, it could have been hours that she sat, waiting in silence, anxiously anticipating what would come next. As she did, she tried to understand how she had got here. She hadn't wanted to be courageous; she hadn't wanted to be a Resistance fighter, being brave like Falcon or Swift. She had just been following her heart. How could it be a crime to protect books or help an elderly man and a child?

The sound of footsteps echoed down the corridor, growing louder with each approaching second. The door swung open again, and a tall figure clad in a black uniform entered the room. His face wore an expression of cold detachment, his eyes devoid of any emotion or compassion.

The Nazi took a seat across from Madeline, his gaze piercing through her soul.

He pulled out a file and looked at the name on it. 'Madeline Valette,' he said. 'You own a bookshop,' he went on, peering up through round spectacles. 'We had a complaint from someone who is working for us that you aided a Jewish man leaving the city.'

Madeline's heart raced as the officer presented the accusation. She knew she had to choose her words carefully, lest she incriminate herself further. With a steady voice, she responded, 'I have no knowledge of any such incident. I run a bookshop, and my main priority is serving my customers.'

'Does that include having them break the law? When the man in question' – he scanned his notes – 'Deveaux, was ordered to present himself to the authorities?'

The officer leaned forward, his eyes narrowing. 'We have

evidence that suggests you helped him defy that order. Is this true?'

Madeline's mind raced as she tried to come up with an explanation. 'The man you are talking about is a regular customer.' Her voice was trembling slightly. 'He often comes by to discuss literature and purchase books. But I assure you, we have never discussed anything illegal.'

The officer's eyes bored into Madeline, searching for any signs of deception. She held his gaze. The room felt suffocating, the silence weighing heavily between them.

After what felt like an eternity, he spoke again. 'We have sources that claim otherwise,' he said, his voice laced with scepticism. 'Your bookshop has been under surveillance for quite some time now by that person. You will face the consequences of your actions,' he declared, his tone final. 'Until then, you will remain in custody.'

Madeline felt terrified. What would they do to her? What would happen to her life and bookshop? Her mind raced with thoughts of Kurt and Jacob, her family. Her mother could never find out she had been arrested.

The man stood up abruptly, signalling the end of the interrogation. Two officers re-entered the room, pulled Madeline roughly to her feet and led her out and back down the dimly lit corridor. She clung to the remnants of hope, desperately searching for any glimmer of a way out.

They reached a small cell at the end of the hallway and the officers shoved her inside, slamming the door shut behind her with a resounding clang.

Alone in the darkness, Madeline tried to catch her breath; her whole body was trembling. How had her life come to this?

As she sat in the darkened room contemplating her fate, her thoughts returned to Jacob and the last time she had seen him. It had been different from her usual visits. There had been a weight pressing down on them, as if somewhere in their innermost beings they knew that hard times were coming.

On the last night before she'd left with Ada, he had read poetry to her and then handed her the book as a gift. It was called *For the One I Love*. 'This book has significance,' he had said. 'Take it with you, and when we are together again I will show you all the secrets it hides.' He had hinted at it being more than just a book of love.

'What do you mean?' she had asked, concern creasing her brow.

'Just trust me. I don't want to put your life in any more danger, but think of it as a message,' he had responded softly, his gaze holding hers. 'In time, you will understand.'

Now that book was back in her shop, probably being ransacked by the Gestapo, and she may never know what Jacob had meant.

49

BERLIN, DECEMBER 2011

Olivia

Livi stood and stared at the round stone, her great-grandmother's grave, with tears streaming down her face. As she tried to come to terms with it all, she couldn't quite believe this was real. It felt like being caught up in some spy movie. Had she really just uncovered a World War Two mystery?

Markus was very respectful and stood a little further back, giving her the time and space to process everything she was feeling. Once again, she appreciated his sensitivity. He just seemed to know what she needed and when.

After a while, she took a long, slow breath and closed her eyes, then opened them, turned and spoke to Markus. 'We should tell Dr Vogel about this find.'

They went to Dr Vogel's office and told her what they had discovered. After departing the manor, leaving the curator still elated, Livi pulled out her phone and called her grandfather. He needed to know where his mother was buried. He would want to know.

But rather than responding in the friendly way she had

expected, Kurt seemed livid. 'Oh, it's Olivia, is it?' His Scottish brogue was harsh and condescending. 'I'm glad you called. I want to know why *you* think you have the right to interfere in *my* life.'

After all that Livi had been experienced in Germany, for a moment she was thrown by his hostility. 'I'm sorry,' she said meekly, 'I'm not sure I understand.'

'Well, let me tell you so you do. I just got a call from Esther Walker, and she told me you wrote to her.' Kurt's voice trembled with anger, his words seething with betrayal. Livi's heart sank as she listened to his accusations, feeling the weight of her actions crashing down on her.

'I... I didn't mean to upset you,' she stammered, her voice quivering. 'I only wanted to help, to find some answers for both of us.'

'*Help?*' Kurt scoffed, his voice laced with bitterness. 'You think digging up the past will *help*? It's taken me years to bury those memories, and you come along thinking you can just resurrect them whenever you feel like it.'

Livi felt tears welling up in her eyes, the pain of her grandfather's harsh words cutting deep.

'I thought you would want closure,' she responded, her voice barely above a whisper.

'Closure?' Kurt spat, his anger unabated. 'What good will closure do? Opening old wounds won't change anything. It won't bring back my mother or erase the atrocities I witnessed! What gives you the right to do what you've done?'

Livi felt sick. She had only wanted to help, to give her grandfather a chance at healing and finding some semblance of peace. But now, all she could hear was the pain and anger in his voice again.

'I'm sorry,' she managed to choke out, tears streaming down her face. 'I will call her and tell her that you are not interested. What is her number?'

He threw the phone down and, when he picked it back up, spat out a phone number.

'Now you call her and tell her this is all your fault and that she is not to be back in touch. Under any circumstances.'

Livi scribbled down the number and then spoke again. 'I didn't mean to hurt you. I thought... I thought...'

'That is exactly what you didn't do, Olivia. You come here for a couple of weeks and suddenly you know everything about me, and everything I need. This is exactly why I have nothing to do with family. Because they interfere and always let you down.' And with that, he slammed down the phone.

She turned to Markus, who was watching her intently. 'Who was that?' he asked, concern on his face as he watched Livi crumble under the weight of her grandfather's anger.

Livi took a deep breath, wiping away her tears with the back of her hand. 'It was my grandfather,' she replied, her voice filled with sadness. 'He's furious with me for reaching out to Esther.'

Markus's eyebrows furrowed in confusion. 'Esther? Who's Esther?'

Livi let out a sob, trying to collect herself. 'She's a woman who wrote to my grandfather, wanting to reunite him with some orphans from the war. I thought it would be a chance for him to find closure and healing, but he sees it as me meddling in his life.'

Markus's eyes softened as he stepped closer to Livi, placing a comforting hand on her shoulder.

'Livi, you were only trying to help. You had good intentions.'

'I know,' Livi whispered, her voice cracked with emotion. 'But he's so angry and hurt. I never wanted to cause him more pain.'

Markus pulled her into a gentle embrace, holding her close. 'You can't blame yourself for his reaction. Sometimes, people aren't ready to confront their past, even if it means finding closure.'

Livi nodded against Markus's chest, finding solace in his comforting presence. 'I just wish he would understand that I only want what's best for him.'

'I know,' Markus murmured into her hair, his voice soothing. 'Perhaps it's best to give your grandfather some space for now.'

Livi sighed heavily, the weight of disappointment settling on her shoulders. 'You're right. Maybe I need to step back and let him figure things out on his own.'

Suddenly, she realised she was in Markus's arms, and it felt like the most natural thing in the world. She couldn't even remember the last time someone had held her like this. She looked up into his concerned blue eyes and felt a sense of comfort wash over her.

The world around them seemed to fade away, leaving only the two of them suspended in a deep connection. Markus's gaze held a tenderness that Livi had never experienced before, as if he truly cared for her. As if sensing her thoughts, he gently brushed a strand of hair away from her face.

'Livi, you don't have to face this alone. I'm here for you, every step of the way.'

'But why?' she asked. 'I have given you nothing. What would you be getting out of all this?'

Markus studied her face as his thumb gently caressed her cheek. 'The last time I checked, this is how relationships work. When one person is going through something, the other is there to support, to listen, to be there. Livi, you don't have to give me anything.'

Livi's heart raced as she absorbed Markus's words, feeling warmth spread through her chest. It had been so long since someone had shown her such genuine kindness and understanding. It was a balm to her wounded soul.

And suddenly, she had a totally irrational impulse. She dropped her gaze to his lips, feeling a flutter of anticipation in her chest. She wanted to kiss him. Wanted to wrap her arms round him and get lost in his embrace.

Before she could stop herself, she slipped her hand into his hair and pulled him down towards her. Their lips met in a gentle yet passionate kiss. In that moment, the weight of her grandfather's anger and the pain of their fractured relationship faded away, replaced by the intoxicating sensation of being wanted and understood.

Markus's arms wrapped around Livi, pulling her closer as the kiss deepened. His hands drew gentle circles on her back, sending shivers down her spine. Livi's fingers tangled in his hair, holding on to him as if he was her lifeline in this sea of uncertainty. Her whole body shuddered with the intensity of the sensation.

This was like nothing she had experienced with Graham. There had been passion in the beginning, of course. But nothing compared with this tenderness, this infinite connection that seemed to transcend everything she had experienced before.

As they gently pulled apart, they were breathless and wide-eyed. He rested his forehead on her own as they absorbed the moment. He slowly broke into a smile. 'What was that?'

Livi's cheeks flushed with exhilaration combined with embarrassment. 'I... I don't know,' she stammered, her voice barely above a whisper. 'It just felt right.'

Markus chuckled softly, his eyes still locked with hers. 'Well, it felt right to me, too,' he admitted, his thumb gently stroking her lips, making them tingle. 'Do you want to go somewhere less public so we can talk about it?'

Livi suddenly realised they were still standing outside of the manor house, and people who were leaving were having to weave around them. She blushed, feeling self-conscious under the curious gazes of strangers.

'Yes, let's find somewhere more private. Maybe we could get a drink at my hotel,' she said coyly, 'so, as you say, we can talk about this.' She just had no idea how to act. She had never really been in a serious relationship as an adult. Livi and Graham had met when they were fourteen. And this was so completely different from snatching a kiss behind the bike sheds at school and she was clueless on how to navigate it.

Markus's eyes were filled with warmth and understanding. 'That sounds perfect.'

50

PARIS, FEBRUARY 1943

Madeline

Madeline lost track of time until the day she was abruptly pulled from her cell and ushered into a room crowded with Nazi officers, their chilling gazes piercing through her. The atmosphere was dense with apprehension, stifling her as she confronted her accusers, bracing for the verdict that would determine her future.

A tall and imposing officer cleared his throat and began to read out the charges against her. He spat out each word, which echoed ominously in the silence of the room. The officer was cold and detached as he detailed the consequences of Madeline's actions. 'For aiding an enemy of the state, Madeline Valette, you are sentenced to one year of hard labour in a German work camp.'

Madeline gasped, her hands clenched into trembling fists, her knuckles paling under the strain. *A work camp* - the words echoed in her mind, sending waves of horror and despair crashing over her. She had heard the stories of the brutalities that occurred within those walls, the labour that drained the life out of their prisoners, the starvation and sickness that plagued their frail bodies.

The walls of the room seemed to press closer, suffocating her as she grappled with the reality of her sentence. Her gaze darted around, seeking a trace of empathy amidst the sea of indifferent expressions.

'Do you have anything to say?' came the cold inquiry.

'I cannot believe you would punish someone for helping an old man,' Madeline protested, her voice trembling with indignation.

The guard sneered in response. 'We also found evidence of you working with other enemies of ours. Jewish literature was found hidden among the inventory in your bookshop during a thorough search. You are not some innocent woman who was just helping an old man.'

Madeline's pulse raced as she listened to the officer's accusations. She hoped that Falcon was safe, and felt devastated when she thought about Jacob's cherished books.

'You will leave tomorrow for the work camp in Germany,' the officer's words sliced through the silence like a knife. 'You will be transported there with other prisoners of war, and you will be subjected to hard labour and constant surveillance. Any attempts to resist or escape will be met with severe consequences.'

They led her back to her cell and she didn't sleep that night. She lay in silence, her thoughts consumed by Jacob and the uncertainty of their future.

In the middle of the night she was startled by raised voices down the corridor, and there was the sound of some sort of explosion. Fear coursed through her veins as Madeline listened to the commotion growing louder. Pressing her ear against the cold metal door, she strained to catch any hint of what was happening. The chaotic sounds of shouting guards and exchanged gunfire filled the air, signaling something significant unfolding.

All at once, her cell door swung open, and a figure stood before her. He wore a dark jacket over a roughly hewn shirt, trousers tucked into worn leather boots, and a beret set at a defiant angle upon his head. Over his shoulder was slung a gun.

'Quickly,' he instructed her, 'we won't be able to hold them long before they bring reinforcements.'

Instinct told her to trust this stranger, to seize this opportunity for freedom. Without hesitation, she stepped out of her cell and followed him down the dimly lit corridor, their footsteps echoing in sync with her racing heartbeat. They navigated through the chaos-filled prison and emerged into a moonlit courtyard outside, Madeline found herself surrounded by a group of fierce-eyed individuals, unmistakably Resistance fighters. Their leader's voice cut through the night, firm yet gentle.

'You are all safe now. Follow us.'

Madeline realised that these brave individuals had risked their lives to rescue her. She fell into step behind them, her legs trembling from a combination of fear and relief. They led her through winding alleyways, staying in the shadows, avoiding any sign of danger.

As they arrived at a building that Madeline assumed was a safe house, she was greeted by more unfamiliar faces. The members of the Resistance moved quickly, organising supplies and sharing plans in hushed tones. 'You can sleep here tonight,' one informed her, and, as she settled into a small room they had shown her, her mind was overcome with a whirlwind of emotions. Gratitude, relief and disbelief washed over her in waves as she lay on the threadbare mattress, too exhausted to even ask any questions. She couldn't believe that she had escaped the Nazis' clutches, that she was now among people fighting against their regime, people just like her.

Tiredness took hold as she closed her eyes. Sleep came

fitfully; she was plagued by nightmares of her time in the prison and the looming threat of the work camp. But what would be her fate now? She couldn't return to her bookshop. Where would she go? Only one place came to mind.

With a scarf covering her hair and face, she knocked on Dominique's door just before curfew the next evening. Her bookshop employee looked in shock as she opened the door.

'Madeline? Is it really you?' Dominique exclaimed, her eyes welling with tears.

Madeline was unable to find her voice. The two women embraced tightly, their silent reunion speaking volumes of their shared relief and joy. As they pulled away from each other, Dominique's eyes were filled with concern.

'What happened to you? We heard rumours that you had been arrested, but we had no way of knowing if it was true.'

Madeline took a deep breath, gathering her thoughts, as Dominique pulled her into the front room and handed her a drink. She recounted the events leading to her capture, her sentence and her miraculous escape. Her friend listened intently, her expression shifting from worry to awe.

'They raided the bookshop. Have you been there at all?'

Dominique's face clouded with sadness. 'Yes, I went back,' she replied, her voice filled with sorrow as she recalled what she had seen. 'They took everything of value, then destroyed what was left.' Her eyes filled with tears as she reached for Madeline's hand, offering comfort and support. 'I'm sorry. Your bookshop was so important to so many of us.'

Madeline caught her eye, her throat tight with emotion. 'What happened?'

'I arrived for work as usual. And they were already there, Nazis like a swarm of locusts. I stood back in the shadows, watching them from a distance, not wanting to draw attention to myself.

'They ransacked the shelves, tore apart the books, and confiscated anything they deemed suspicious or valuable. They even set fire to some of the literature right there in the street,' her friend recounted, her voice heavy with sorrow.

Madeline was devastated as she imagined the destruction, the loss of countless stories and voices silenced by hatred. 'And my personal things?' she asked, her voice barely above a whisper.

Dominique's eyes reflected her concern. 'I'm sorry, Madeline. I don't know.'

Madeline felt a lump in her throat as the weight of her loss settled on her shoulders. The bookshop had been her sanctuary, her refuge from the harsh realities of the world. It had been a place of solace, and it had been her and Alex's home. Tears welled up in her eyes, but she fought against them, refusing to let the grief consume her.

'What will you do now?' Dominique enquired, concern evident in her voice.

'Well, I can't go to my parents. If the Gestapo come looking for me, they will be sure to go there. I will have to go into hiding,' Madeline replied, her tone resigned.

'You can stay here,' Dominique said firmly, offering her support without hesitation.

Madeline grabbed Dominique's hand with gratitude shining in her eyes, appreciating her unwavering support. 'Thank you, my dear friend. I don't know what I would do without you,' she whispered, her voice brimming with emotion.

Dominique's eyes filled with conviction. 'We'll get through this together, Madeline. We will find a way to rebuild and resist. The fight is not over.'

Over the next eighteen months, Madeline settled into a clandestine life, hidden away in the safety of Dominique's home. Her friend got word to her family that she was safe but in hiding, and she wrote to Jacob telling him the same and not to contact her, to keep Dominique safe.

She stayed there until word started to filter through, in the summer of 1944, that there were signs of the Germans retreating from the area. In all that time, the hardest part was not hearing from Jacob. Berlin was being blitzed by the Allies, and she heard through the underground newspapers that Germany was in chaos.

The tides of war were shifting and, with each passing day, rumours spread like wildfire, whispers of liberation and freedom. The Resistance fighters grew bolder with their acts of defiance, launching attacks against German forces and sabotaging supply lines. Madeline felt a surge of pride knowing that she was part of this courageous movement.

As news of the approaching Allied forces reached their ears, plans were set into motion for the final push against the Nazis, and she waited with anticipation until one day the streets were filled with the news of the imminent liberation of Paris.

It was only then that she dared to venture back to her bookshop; but nothing could have prepared her for what she saw. The shop stood in ruins, a mere shell of its former self. The familiar sight of colourful book spines lining the shelves had been replaced with empty, charred remnants. Madeline's heart sank as she stepped over broken glass and debris, her eyes welling up with tears. The destruction was overwhelming. The walls, once bright and welcoming, were now blackened. The scent of smoke still lingered in the air, a haunting reminder of the flames that had consumed so much.

She knelt down amid the wreckage and picked up a fragment of a book cover that had survived the fire. It was tattered and singed, but the title was still visible: *Les Misérables*. A bitter-sweet smile formed on Madeline's lips.

'Oh, my darling,' she whispered into the bleakness.

She still missed her sweet husband, but during her time away her thoughts of him had been replaced by her overwhelming desire to be with Jacob. During her time in hiding, she had made up her mind. Once this war was over, she would sell the bookshop and go to Germany to be with him. She hadn't heard from him in so long, but in that time, her love had not dimmed.

⸻

The liberation of Paris on 25 August 1944 was met with a bitter-sweet celebration in the charred remains of the bookshop. Madeline gathered with friends and fellow Resistance fighters, and they filled the air with both jubilation and sorrow, honouring their hard-won freedom while mourning the loss of countless lives and the destruction of their beloved city.

As wine flowed freely to mark the occasion, a sudden commotion outside drew everyone's attention to a group of men and women herding someone down the road. Shouts of 'traitor' and 'collaborator' echoed through the streets as they pushed their captive forward, bloodied and bruised. The young man's head hung low, but as he passed the bookshop his eyes locked with Madeline's own, and she realised who it was – Marcel.

She knew he deserved everything he was getting, and she thought about the time she had spent in a Nazi jail because of him; and yet, as she stared into his hollow eyes, she couldn't help but wonder what could have been if Marcel had chosen a different path.

In that moment of that strange interplay of longing and loss, she saw another face she had never expected to see again.

However, her happiness was short-lived because, the minute they locked eyes, she knew that something was very wrong.

51

BERLIN, DECEMBER 2011

Olivia

They drove to the hotel in a comfortable silence. Livi's mind was racing, reeling from the sadness of her conversation with her grandfather and nervousness about where things were going with Markus. She couldn't believe what had just happened, but she also couldn't deny the intense connection she felt with him. It had been growing stronger since their first visit to the manor.

In the hotel bar, Livi ordered a glass of wine, trying to calm her nerves. Markus looked equally uneasy. They sat in silence for a moment, each lost in their own thoughts. Eventually, Livi took a deep breath and spoke.

'Markus, I want you to know that I never date. It's a choice I made after my divorce.'

He watched her intently, sipping his drink and waiting, as she thought about how to proceed. She decided to be forthright.

'I didn't tell you the whole truth about how my marriage ended,' she confessed, her voice soft as she met Markus's concerned gaze. 'I said it was mutual, but it was far from that.

My marriage ended because I finally had the courage to leave after years of emotional and physical abuse.'

Markus looked horrified but respectfully allowed her to continue, which she was grateful for.

'I had seen signs of it while we were dating, but I always put it down to adolescent fears. I thought he would grow out of it once we were married, and he had no reason to doubt my love.

'However, after we got married he became even more possessive and controlling. He wouldn't let me go out without him. If I did, he would constantly call my friends' homes and follow me. Then he would sulk for hours when I returned.

'Then he began criticising every little thing I did, berating me for days over the slightest mistake. I thought if I just did everything perfectly, things would get better. But they only got worse,' she continued, her voice trembling. 'Then he started becoming violent, and I was too ashamed to speak up or leave. I carried the weight of his abuse for years, and it slowly chipped away at my confidence until there was almost nothing left.'

Tears streamed down Livi's face as she recounted the final incident that had made her face the truth.

'He came home drunk one night while one of my friends was visiting. I said something he didn't agree with, and he slapped me across the face. The look of shock and horror of my friend made me realise what I had been living with for so long. It was when I saw the abuse through her eyes I understood.

'After I left, I started suffering from depression and anxiety. The depression is under control now, but I still struggle with the anxiety, and it is a constant reminder of what I lived through.

'My doctor believes it will lessen over time, if I continue to get help. But after what I went through, I have been so afraid and damaged that I didn't know how to trust myself, let alone someone else. So, when you and I started spending time together, I didn't know how to navigate these feelings or what to do with them. You've been nothing but kind, understanding and supportive, but I've been holding myself back out of fear. I've rebuilt a life for myself that is safe, albeit small. But I didn't expect anything else, especially another relationship.' She felt a sob catch in her throat. 'But now you're here, and you're wonderful, and I'm... *terrified*.'

Markus reached out and gently took her hand, his thumb softly brushing across her knuckles. He leaned in close, his words a whisper on her lips, sending a shudder down her spine.

'You don't need to be afraid with me, Livi. I won't hurt you. I understand those are just words and I need to earn your trust. And I can't promise to fix everything, but I can promise to be patient and understanding as we navigate this together.' His voice was filled with sincerity, his eyes shining with unwavering support.

Livi felt a wave of relief wash over her. She had finally shared her deepest fears and insecurities, and attached to that was also a lot of shame, even though she knew intellectually she had nothing to be ashamed of. Still, she could hear her ex-husband Graham's voice telling her it was all her fault.

Markus's words broke through her thoughts. 'What do you want from me? I mean, what do you *need* from me right now? Just tell me, and I will do it, anything. Because when I saw you for the first time at Otto's, I was drawn to you in a way I can't explain. It was like something inside me recognised something in you, something that I hadn't even realised I needed. I wanted to be near you, to get to know you no matter what, and to offer you a different kind of relationship than I had ever had before. I'm by no means perfect. I have dated since my divorce, but nothing has ever felt like this. I want you to be happy more than I want my own happiness, Livi, and I want to support you in whatever way I can. If you need time, I'll give it to you. And if you need space, I'll respect that too. Because nothing is more important to me than getting this right.'

Livi took a deep breath, letting his words sink in. She knew that she had to trust him, and this was the first step.

'I know I need to take this slowly, but honestly, what I want right now is for these overwhelming feelings of attraction for you to go away so I can think straight.'

Markus laughed softly. 'I believe I know what you mean. I have found it hard to think about my acting since we met. Speaking of that, I have an audition to prepare for and I should probably go.'

They finished their drinks, and he walked her up to her hotel room door. Livi turned to face him, and hesitated. Everything inside her wanted to pull him in and explore the only way she knew how to deal with the overwhelming physical need for him. But she knew it would be wrong to do so until she had figured out if she could even manage this.

'I'll call you later,' he said, his hand resting gently on her arm.

'Okay,' she replied, her voice barely audible.

She unlocked her door and stood in the doorway, the weight of her past and present choices bearing down.

He slid his hand down her arm, then gently took her hand and squeezed it. He was about to turn and leave when she stopped him. She hadn't meant to; it had been a reflex action. An unconscious desire to keep him with her that she seemed to have no control over.

Markus turned back towards her, his eyes filled with surprise. He studied her face for a moment before a soft smile played at the corners of his lips as he looked at how strongly she gripped him.

'I will probably need to take this hand with me—'

She cut him off. 'I don't want to let you go,' she whispered, her voice barely audible. Shocked at her own confession of desire.

Markus's surprised look quickly reflected his own yearning as he gazed into her eyes. 'Oh, Livi...' he whispered.

Then, before she could overthink it, Livi pulled his body down against hers, again, her lips urgent and passionately finding his, allowing the flow of all the desire that she had been holding back since she met him. Markus tenderly responded, drawing in a long slow breath as he enfolded her deeply in his arms, their bodies melting into each other. For only a second kiss, it was far from awkward. In fact, it was the opposite of awkward. It was a tender, yet passionate exchange that felt like finally coming home after being away on a very long and difficult journey. But this had a little more heat behind it than the kiss in the car park.

Livi could have stayed in that moment for the rest of her life. All the words of reassurance she had heard from Markus had done nothing compared to the safety and security she felt in his arms.

Desire thrashed through her body, and she struggled to control herself. She placed her hand on his chest and could feel the wild beating of his heart, matching her own. She knew she would regret rushing this, so she had to stop before she completely lost it.

She slowly pulled away and instantly missed the warmth of his body against hers. Markus sighed as his eyes found hers.

'Well, that was lovely,' he whispered with a low chuckle. 'I like your idea of taking it slow.'

Livi laughed, feeling her face flush from the intimacy of the moment. She took a deep breath, trying to regain her composure. 'I'm so sorry, I don't know what came over me.'

The tips of his fingers gently caressed her cheek, and slide down her body to take her hands as she fought the desire to know what that gentle caress would feel like on the rest of her body. They stood there, holding hands, taking comfort in each other's presence for a long moment. Taking time to absorb what had just happened. Livi had never felt this vulnerable with another person, and it was a feeling that both terrified and exhilarated her.

Someone came out of one of the other rooms and the spell was broken. The pair quickly moved apart and laughed softly with the embarrassment.

'I'll speak to you soon,' Markus promised, giving her hand a reassuring squeeze, before turning and walking down the corridor.

As Livi watched him walk away, feeling the emptiness of the space around her without him, she caught her breath, trying to process what had just happened. She had just kissed a man, twice, after seven years of being single, and it had felt like the most natural thing in the world. As she stepped back inside her hotel room, she felt a cascade of emotions: excitement, fear and a sense of freedom that she hadn't experienced in a long time.

She lay on her bed, staring at the ceiling, thinking about Markus, reliving their kiss over and over in her mind. It had been so intense and meaningful, and she knew that it would change the way she saw him from now on. She couldn't help but feel nervous about what their relationship would become, but also hopeful that maybe, just maybe, she had finally found someone who could help her break free from the shadows of her past.

52

PARIS, AUGUST 1944

Madeline

As the crowd continued to celebrate, Madeline guided Swift up the creaky stairs to her apartment above the bookshop. The faint smell of smoke lingered in the air but, miraculously, her home had been spared from the worst of the fire.

They sat down at the small kitchen table, each with a glass of wine, while Madeline tried to come to terms with the fact that Swift was sitting in front of her.

'What are you doing here? Why did you leave Germany?'

'I had to,' Swift replied gravely, her voice thick with emotion. 'Our cell was compromised, and I've been on the run since then. I made my way to the South of France, where I've been in hiding. Then as soon as I was able to, I made my way here. I needed to come to see you for Jacob's sake.'

Madeline's stomach clenched at the mention of his name. She feared what news the young agent might have brought with her.

Swift drew in a long, slow breath before she continued. 'I'm sorry to be the bearer of bad news,' she whispered, her eyes filled with sorrow. 'But Jacob... he's gone. Mueller found out about his involvement in helping Ada escape and... he was executed.'

Madeline felt like she had been punched in the gut, her heart shattering into a million pieces as she tried to understand Swift's words, unable to comprehend the loss of the man she loved.

'No,' she whispered, shaking her head in denial. 'It can't be true.'

Swift reached out and took Madeline's hand gently. 'I wish it weren't true either,' she said softly. 'But I was there when it happened. Jacob died a hero.'

A sob escaped Madeline's lips as she clung on to Swift's hand for support. The weight of grief and despair threatened to swallow her whole.

'When? How?' she managed to choke out.

'After you left with Kurt,' Swift replied, her voice heavy with emotion. 'I received word that Mueller had killed a woman on the platform in Berlin – and I knew it could have been Ada. We had a person working at the morgue in Berlin who described the murdered woman's looks, and I recognised the false name we had obtained for her.

'When I told Jacob what happened, he insisted on bringing her body back to the manor and burying it there. He said he would want Kurt and you to be able to visit her whenever you wanted to.'

Madeline found it hard to concentrate as she listened to Swift recounting the events. Tears streamed down her face as the other woman explained how she and Jacob had moved Ada's body under the cover of night and buried her on the estate. She couldn't believe that Jacob was gone, that their plans for a future together had been shattered in an instant. It felt as if the world around her had crumbled, leaving her with nothing but emptiness.

Swift continued, 'Jacob said he would leave you a note about all this.'

'I never got it,' Madeline said sadly. 'But how did Mueller know about Ada?'

'No one could figure out how Mueller had known that Ada was going to be on that platform until after the traitor in our cell was exposed. He had been at the meeting when we first located Ada and knew about her false papers. Mueller had someone watching the station.'

A painful silence settled between them as they both grappled with the weight of their loss. The room felt suffocating, the grief hanging heavy in the air. Madeline's mind raced, searching for answers, for some semblance of understanding amid all the overwhelming sadness.

A surge of anger rose within her. Anger at Mueller, anger at the war, and anger at the cruel hand fate had dealt her.

A ripple of laughter filled the air from downstairs in the shop, where the party was still going on. Madeline looked down at her drink, her mind still reeling from the news of Jacob's death. The sounds from the shop seemed distant and foreign, a stark contrast to the overwhelming grief that consumed her.

Swift continued. 'It took Mueller a while to find out that it was Jacob who had helped her escape, but once we realised what had happened we knew it would only be a matter of time before Mueller would be back for Jacob. So that evening we began arranging his departure. I went over to his cottage to inform him of the plan, but while I was there Mueller came storming in. Jacob acted quickly and pushed me inside a cupboard so he could confront him alone.'

Swift's voice tightened. 'I heard Mueller shouting, demanding answers from Jacob. He accused him of betrayal. Jacob denied it vehemently, but Mueller wouldn't listen. They argued back and forth, their voices growing louder and angrier.'

Madeline imagined the scene unfolding before her. The

image of Jacob standing up to Mueller, fighting against the inevitable, filled her mind. She felt an overwhelming sense of pride mixed with anguish for the man she had loved so deeply.

'And then?' she urged Swift.

Tears stung the other woman's eyes as she continued. 'Mueller told him he would pay for his actions, and then I heard a... gunshot.'

Madeline gasped, her hand flying to her mouth in shock. The room fell into an eerie silence as Swift's words hung heavy in the air.

'I waited in that cupboard till I heard the front door slam. And the sight that greeted me was one that will be seared into my memory forever. I knelt beside him – he was still alive, though barely; the light was fading from his eyes. I held his hand, trying to offer whatever comfort I could, as he whispered his last words to me.'

Madeline held her breath, her heart breaking with each passing moment. She couldn't imagine the pain and sorrow Swift must have felt, witnessing Jacob's final moments.

'He told me to find you, Madeline.' Swift's voice quivered with emotion. 'He said that you were the most important thing in the world to him, and that he loved you more than anything.'

Tears flowed freely down Madeline's cheeks as she absorbed Jacob's final message. The weight of his love for her felt almost too much to bear, knowing that he had sacrificed everything for her safety.

'He asked me to tell you that he would always be with you, no matter what, and that it had all been worth it because, he said, being with you, even for just that short moment, was worth more than a lifetime of empty days without you.' Swift's voice cracked as she finished speaking.

Tears rolled down Madeline's cheeks, her heart breaking all over again. The weight of grief pressed down on her chest, making it difficult to breathe.

'I'm so sorry, Madeline,' Swift whispered, her voice filled with regret. 'I wish there was something more I could have done to save him.'

Madeline shook her head, unable to find the right words to express her pain. Her mind was consumed by memories of Jacob – his laughter, his touch, his unwavering love for her. Now, he was gone forever.

'He told me to give you this. The following week I was gone, I was not waiting around for them to track me down as well. I have spent the rest of the war waiting to find you. He was clear – he wanted me to tell you himself; he didn't want you to hear it from a stranger.'

Swift handed her an envelope.

The words 'For Story Keeper' were scrawled on the outside. She took the envelope from Swift's hand, her fingers trembling as she turned it over in her hands. The weight of it felt heavy, as if holding all the unanswered questions and unsaid words that Jacob had left behind. She looked up at Swift, tears glistening in her eyes.

'Thank you,' she managed to whisper, her voice thick with emotion. 'Thank you for being there with him.'

Madeline clasped the envelope tightly. She knew she needed to open it, to read the words Jacob had left for her. But she was afraid to move forward and face the finality of his death. This was the last tangible piece of him that she had left, a final link to the man she loved, and she was terrified to confront a future without him by her side.

53

BERLIN, DECEMBER 2011

Olivia

The next morning, Livi called the number her grandfather had given her and waited. Anticipation and anxiety mounted, as the phone rang and a woman's voice answered.

'High Street Gallery?'

Livi's voice caught for a moment before she managed to say, 'Hello, is this Esther?'

'Speaking,' the woman replied, her tone professional yet warm.

Taking a deep breath, Livi gathered her thoughts. 'Hi, Esther, I'm Olivia Stapleton, Kurt Armstrong's – granddaughter...'

'Oh, yes, it's lovely to finally connect with you,' Esther said warmly.

Livi hesitated, her voice tinged with sadness. 'I'm calling because my grandfather isn't interested in further communication or connection with you or the orphans. He's not ready to revisit those painful memories.'

'I understand,' Esther replied empathetically. 'The children

I've contacted have been reluctant. Their ordeal, abandoned on that train, was undoubtedly horrific.'

'I really don't know much about the story. My grandfather won't talk about his experience,' Livi admitted.

Esther responded, 'My mother has Alzheimer's, and her memory is patchy. Yet she recalled that your grandfather was a sad child, lost his mother, and had a cruel father. He was one of the older boys, who cared for the younger ones on the train.'

Livi imagined her grandfather's burden, young yet responsible for protecting the other children.

Driven by curiosity, she asked, 'why did you decide to reunite the orphans now?'

'As I have begun piecing together the story, there have been many questions,' Esther explained softly. 'Their memories have gaps – fragments of truth, but nothing the same.

'I consulted my mother's doctor because she's recently become distressed about all of this. He said that repressed memories are common in trauma survivors. The mind protects us from our horrors, but uncovering those memories can aid healing. And he suggested reuniting her with the people who had been through the same experience, to help her.'

'How did you manage to track them down?'

Esther let out a soft chuckle. 'It was no easy task, I assure you. Nearly all of them were adopted and had new names; fortunately, some of them ended up in the UK and Madeline was very helpful with all she knew.'

'Madeline?' Livi enquired.

'She owned a bookshop in Paris during the war. She is very elderly, but she knew them as children, and was particularly keen to locate Kurt.'

Livi's heart skipped a beat at the mention of her grandfather's name. 'Did Madeline say why she wanted you to find him?'

Esther was quiet for a moment, obviously reflecting. 'She

was vague on details, but her fondness for him was very evident.'

'May I have Madeline's contact information? In case my grandfather is interested in being in touch with her.'

After Esther had shared Madeline's details, they concluded their conversation.

'I haven't given up hope on my grandfather yet. He is quite obstinate, but I'm going to keep trying.'

Livi said goodbye and hung up, her heart buoyed by hope. She pondered her grandfather's enigmatic past and his reluctance to face it. She recognised that she couldn't compel him to share before he was ready, and right now her priority was mending their relationship.

A couple of hours later, Markus arrived to drive her to the airport. When she saw him at her hotel room door, her stomach knotted with fresh excitement. Their greeting was awkward, caught between yesterday's kiss and today's uncertainty. But he pulled her close to his chest, and his embrace was reassuring; his whisper of missing her sent a shiver through her.

'Me too,' Livi replied, her voice filled with sincerity as she buried her face into the crook of his neck, inhaling his familiar scent and feeling a sense of calm wash over her.

As they pulled apart from one another, they shared an embarrassed laugh at the newness of their feelings.

'Well, we should probably get you to London,' Markus remarked, picking up her bag.

'Actually, I have decided to go straight to Scotland,' Livi declared, her eyes alight with resolve.

'To your grandfather's?'

'Yes. I need to see him, to talk to him face-to-face. Maybe if I can show him how much I care, how much I want to understand, he'll be willing to let me in. I was wrong to contact Esther when he had asked me not to. I just wanted to help and thought all he needed was encouragement, but I was very wrong to presume, and I need to make it right.'

At the airport, their parting was hard.

'Well, I guess this is goodbye.' Markus's voice was filled with a tinge of sadness as he looked into Livi's eyes. 'For now,' he added.

She fidgeted nervously with the strap of her backpack, feeling the weight of the moment. She reached out and took Markus's hand in hers to assure him, 'For now,' echoing his sentiment.

He looked at her curiously. 'How is this going to work, Livi?' he asked, voicing their shared uncertainty.

Livi sighed, her grip on his hand tightening. 'I don't know; let's just take it one step at a time. Germany isn't that far away.'

She leaned forward and pressed her lips against his, savouring the bittersweet taste of their farewell. Time seemed to stand still as they shared a final, lingering kiss, and afterwards he pulled her in for a hug.

'We'll make it work,' he whispered, his voice filled with unwavering conviction. 'We'll find a way.'

Reluctantly, she started to make her way to her gate.

'Livi,' he called after her, and she turned.

'My grandmother left me some money, and I was thinking of taking a trip. How is London this time of year?'

'London is beautiful any time of year, if the right people are in it.'

'Okay, sounds good, call me when you get home.'

As Livi made her way through the airport, her heart felt light with hope. And as the plane ascended, her thoughts turned to Scotland, to the delicate task of reconciling with her grandfather. It wasn't until they were descending that she realised how calm she had been during the flight itself; with everything on her mind, she had barely had time to be anxious.

Upon landing in Scotland, she made her way from the

airport to the small village where her grandfather lived. The earthy scent of pine filled the air as she walked the narrow road, her stomach twisting with anticipation.

Gathering her resolve, she knocked on the door.

When Kurt answered, he looked genuinely surprised. 'I didn't expect to see you again. What do you want?' he asked, his voice presenting its usual gruffness.

'Look, I was wrong,' Livi began, her voice trembling. 'I shouldn't have reached out to Esther against your wishes. I wanted to help and understand, but I see now that I over-stepped. I'm here to apologise and make things right.'

He paused for a second, then stiffened. 'Okay, you've said your piece,' he replied dismissively, avoiding eye contact, and edged the door closed.

'*No!*' she blurted out, raising her voice, surprising herself by stepping forward to block the door. 'I won't let you shut me out. I care about you, and I want to understand your past. I want to be a part of your life, and your stubbornness won't deter me.'

Kurt glanced up and down the street, concerned about the scene she was making.

Livi softened her tone. 'Please, hear me out.'

He drew in a breath as if considering her words. 'Fine,' he grumbled and grudgingly let her inside.

The familiar coldness of the house greeted her, but she could smell something cooking.

As if reading her mind, Kurt spoke. 'I was making stew. I suppose you'll want a cup of tea after all that shouting.'

While he prepared the tea, Livi apologised again, her voice sincere. 'I never meant to disrespect you. It was wrong to assume I knew best.'

'Yes, it was wrong.' Kurt's voice was gruff, but there was a hint of vulnerability that Livi hadn't expected.

'What I don't understand,' he continued, 'is why you care about all this. You're a young person with your whole life ahead of you. Why would you want to be burdened by an old man's past?'

'Because you're not just any old man,' Livi said, her voice filled with conviction. 'You're my grandfather. And no matter what mistakes you've made or what pain you've endured, you're still my family. And I *care* about you.'

Kurt turned away from Livi, his hands fumbling slightly as he poured the tea. His eyes remained fixed on the task at hand as he spoke, his voice quieter than before. 'You don't understand,' he muttered. 'You can't possibly understand the things I've done, the darkness that resides within me.'

Livi approached him cautiously, reaching out to gently place her hand on his arm. 'Maybe I won't ever fully understand. But that doesn't mean I can't try,' she said, her voice filled with compassion. 'We all have our flaws and our past mistakes, but that doesn't define who we are as people. I believe in the power of forgiveness and second chances.'

When Kurt turned to her, his weathered face was heavy with lines of pain and regret, but there was also a glimmer of hope in his eyes. 'You're a stubborn one, just like your grandmother,' he muttered, a hint of a smile playing at the corners of his mouth.

Livi smiled back at him, a flicker of warmth spreading through her chest.

'Look, can we start again? I promise not to do anything that you don't want me to,' she said sincerely. 'I got ahead of myself after finding out about Mueller. I became a little obsessed with finding out all the truth. It's a flaw I have; I can get really single-minded and find it hard to see anything else.'

'Well, in that way you take after me,' Kurt replied, a wry smile playing on his lips. 'Now drink your tea,' he added, thrusting a mug at her.

Livi chuckled softly and took a sip of her tea. Sitting down at the table, she let out a sigh of relief. 'I promise from now on I will be as good as gold. I won't even contact Madeline if you don't want me to.'

Kurt paused, his eyes searching Livi's with his question. 'Madeline?'

Livi's heart skipped a beat as she realised her slip. She had mentioned Madeline without thinking, forgetting that Kurt had never told her the full story of his past. She hesitated for a moment, debating whether to backtrack or delve further into this unknown part of his life.

She continued carefully. 'She owned a bookshop in Paris and—'

He cut her off. 'I know who she is. Madeline is still alive?'

'Yes. When I called Esther to tell her not to call you again, she told me that she had spoken very fondly of you.'

Kurt's face paled, his eyes widening with a mixture of shock and disbelief, as he sat down to digest this new information. Livi could see the emotions swirling within him, his past suddenly brought back to life by the mention of Madeline's name.

She continued. 'But I promise I won't contact her if you don't want me to.'

He looked straight at her and shocked her with his directness. 'You can contact her.'

Livi stared at him, her mug of tea suspended in mid-air. She had expected resistance, anger, so his unexpected permission caught her off guard. 'Are you sure?' she asked cautiously, her voice laced with confusion.

Kurt spoke slowly, his eyes distant as memories continued to flood back to him. 'I don't want to see the orphans, but I have questions only Madeline can answer. I thought she was gone – she must be in her nineties.'

'Okay,' Livi said, covering his hand with her own before realising what she was doing.

But Kurt didn't pull his hand away. Instead, he looked down

at their hands entwined, and slowly turned his over so her small palm was cradled in his weathered one.

Livi could feel the roughness of his skin against her own, and it felt good. The moment between them lasted no more than a minute before Kurt released her hand and stood up, emotion tightening his voice for a second before he continued in his usual brisk manner.

'Well, as it seems I am never going to be rid of you, I had better try and see if I can make this stew stretch to the two of us.'

Livi watched as Kurt busied himself with the dinner, and right then she couldn't help but feel a sense of triumph.

'Well, don't just sit there,' he continued. 'There are carrots to be chopped.'

'Okay, boss,' she joked as she rolled up her sleeves.

As they worked side by side in the small, dimly lit kitchen, Livi felt a growing sense of camaraderie with Kurt. They had a long way to go to be what she would call comfortable, but it was a start.

54

PARIS, JANUARY 2012

Madeline

Madeline Valette pulled herself slowly out of bed, her joints protesting with every movement. The morning light filtered through the lace curtains, casting delicate patterns on the bedroom walls. At ninety-six, she cherished these moments of quiet reflection, knowing each day was a precious gift.

As she got ready, she thought of all her day would bring. She had never remarried after Alex and her relationship with Jacob. But she still lived above the bookshop. Her grand-niece ran the shop now, and Madeline would go down and perch on a stool occasionally, just to enjoy the coming and going of Parisian life. So much had changed in the world in seventy years. Computers and mobile phones and a world that seemed to speed up every day. She was glad she had her memories to keep her company.

As she moved across her room, the scent of her favorite French lavender from the sachets in her dresser mixed with the faint mustiness of old books. Her fingers brushed against the heart-shaped locket, cool and smooth against her wrinkled skin.

Her mind drifted to the war, and to Jacob. She hadn't thought about him for so long. But today, as she stared out at the bustling streets of Paris from her window, memories of him flooded back with a force that made her heart ache. She opened the locket which she'd found in the envelope from him the day Swift had told her about his death. She pulled out the yellowing paper he had placed there. It read, *Embrace your dragons.* In all these years, she had very rarely taken it off.

She opened a drawer in her dressing table, pulled out the yellowing letter he had written to accompany it and reread it, something she had done countless times.

The words on the page brought Madeline back to that fateful day when her heart had shattered into a million fragments. The day Swift had come to the bookshop. As she read Jacob's final words, the pain resurfaced, raw and visceral, as if it had never left her heart.

My dearest Story Keeper, the letter began, written in Jacob's elegant script.

If you're reading this, then I may no longer be here. I cannot express the depth of my love for you, nor the agony I feel knowing that we will never have the life we dreamed of. But even in death, I know my love for you will remain unwavering.

Tears welled in Madeline's eyes as she traced Jacob's words with her finger. Even though the ink had faded to a light brown, each stroke still seemed to carry his essence, an essence she could still feel, ever-present in her life, to this day. Sometimes she had trouble remembering his face or his voice, but she never forgot how he had made her feel.

She continued reading.

I want you to know that our time together was the most cherished part of my existence. You brought light into my darkest days, and your love showed me that there is beauty in this world even in the midst of chaos and despair. I am eternally grateful for the love we shared, even if it was cut short.

Madeline's tears fell freely now, blurring the words on the page, but she continued to read through her grief.

I know that life will go on for you, my darling. And though it pains me to think of a world where I am not by your side, I implore you to find happiness again. You deserve it, more than anyone I have ever known. Find joy in the simple pleasures, the warmth of sunlight on your skin, the laughter of loved ones, and the beauty of a world that continues to turn despite our pain.

As Madeline absorbed Jacob's words, once again, she couldn't help but feel a glimmer of hope amid her sorrow. His love still resonated within her, reminding her of the strength they had shared during their time together.

I leave you with this necklace, Jacob's letter concluded.

A symbol of our everlasting love. It belonged to my mother, and she meant the world to me. Wear it close to your heart, for even in death I will be there with you. I believe that love can transcend time and space, and because of that I know my spirit will always be with you.

Madeline clutched the necklace in her hand, feeling its weight and the power it held as she closed her eyes.

'I need your strength today, my dear Jacob,' she murmured. 'More than ever.'

The door to her apartment opened and her grand-niece's voice broke her reverie.

'Good morning, Great-Aunty!' Chloe called. 'I've made your favourite tea.'

Madeline beamed at her grand-niece with a sense of deep affection. Chloe had been her anchor in this fast-paced world, always reminding her of the importance of family and love.

'How are you feeling today? Are you looking forward to your visit?' Chloe asked.

Madeline nodded, not wanting to burden someone so young with what this meant to her. She had prayed for so many years for this to happen. Hoped for it, and now she was finally going to see him again. The little boy with the scared brown eyes.

'I've picked out your periwinkle-blue dress for you to wear. I know it's one of your favourites and it brings out the colour in your eyes,' Chloe said, chirpy and upbeat.

Madeline smiled as she watched Chloe pottering about, pulling out clothes and humming to herself. Sometimes she really reminded her of her sister Gigi, Chloe's grandmother. Though she didn't have the impish nature of her most mischievous sister, Chloe had the same flaming red hair and moved in a way that reminded her of the youngest Valette.

As she sat down to have breakfast, Chloe left her to return to the bookshop, and Madeline prepared herself for the day ahead.

She picked up the letter she had received just two weeks before from a young woman called Olivia Stapleton, written on behalf of her grandfather, Kurt Armstrong, once known as Kurt Mueller, asking if Madeline might have more information about his past.

She drew in a breath. Could this Kurt Mueller really be the one she had placed on a train so long ago? Alex's son? The letter had come as a shock, reopening wounds that had never fully healed. And now, seventy years later, fate had finally brought them back together. She thought of all the heartache she had felt in trying to find him after her sister Charlotte had gone missing, and after the war. And the regrets she had about letting him go before he had learned the truth. Would he forgive her after all this time?

She tried to read a book but, after she had reread the same page five times, she gave up and sat waiting nervously.

At 1 p.m., Chloe knocked gently on the door and stepped inside. 'They are here. Can I bring them in?' she asked.

Madeline agreed, and couldn't seem to move, she was so overcome. As she heard their footfalls on the stairs she drew in a deep breath, trying to steady her nerves. She had been waiting for this moment for so long, and now that it was finally here she felt terrified. What if it wasn't him? What if it was just another Kurt? Would her heart be broken all over again?

She pushed herself up from her chair, trying to steady herself against the wave of emotions that began to roll over her.

'Yes, Chloe,' she said, her voice shaking slightly. 'Bring them in.'

Chloe disappeared momentarily, returning with an older man and a young woman by her side.

Madeline had thought she would have trouble knowing for sure. But she recognised him immediately, and her heart skipped a beat as she looked into his warm brown eyes. The same scared eyes that had haunted her dreams for years were now wrinkled and resolute, but she could see the pain marking his face, mirroring the anguish she had carried in her own heart all these years.

They stood there in silence for what felt like an eternity, the weight of seven decades hanging heavy in the air between them.

Finally, Madeline signalled for them to sit down, and then, attempting to fill the silence, Livi explained how she and Kurt had been reunited.

Madeline couldn't take her eyes off Kurt as she blinked away tears. He still looked so much like Alex it took her breath away. She wanted to hold him and tell him how sorry she was.

How she should have looked for him harder. That she had so wanted to give him the home he had needed. And that, even though she wasn't his real mother, she would have found a way to make his pain bearable.

Livi turned to Madeline. 'So, we were hoping you could help us fill in some of the blanks about my grandfather's life.'

While Madeline acknowledged Livi's presence, her focus was primarily on the man beside her. Turning towards him, she asked gently, 'Kurt, do you remember me?'

Kurt's eyes met hers. 'You were the woman who brought me from Germany and put me on that train.'

Madeline closed her eyes, unable to bear the pain of his sadness. 'I was more than that, Kurt. I am your stepmother.'

Kurt looked visibly shocked.

Livi said in a reverent tone, 'Are you by any chance... Story Keeper?'

Madeline smiled with pride. 'I haven't heard that name for many years. But yes, I am Story Keeper, or at least I was during the war.'

Kurt's eyes widened in disbelief and his voice was barely a whisper. 'My stepmother? But how?'

Madeline took a deep breath, bracing herself for the flood of emotions that would surely follow her revelation. She folded her nervous hands in her lap. 'After your mother was killed by that Nazi, I wanted to tell you so many times. That the reason I came to find you was because Ada wrote to me and told me you were the child of my late husband. I didn't want to believe it. But when I saw you, I knew it was true. You look *so* much like him.'

She signalled to Livi to hand Kurt a black and white photo in a silver frame from her sideboard. Olivia reached for it and showed it to Kurt; it was a photo of Madeline and Alex on their honeymoon.

Kurt's hands trembled as he took the photo, and his eyes

welled up with tears as he stared at the image, his gaze fixed on the man standing next to Madeline. His eyes reflected his feelings of a deep sense of loss and longing. Madeline knew he was noting the uncanny resemblance between him and his late father, from the shape of their eyes to the tilt of their chins.

'That's him?' Kurt whispered, his voice filled with a mix of awe and disbelief. 'That's my father?'

Madeline's eyes misted over. 'Yes, Kurt. That's your father, my late husband, Alex.'

'All these years, I have lived fearing I was the son of the monster who killed my mother and countless innocent lives. I have walked in the shadow of that guilt and shame my whole life.'

Tears streamed down Kurt's face as he struggled to process the weight of this newfound revelation. He looked at Madeline, with eyes filled with both longing and pain.

'Why didn't you tell me earlier?' he choked out, his voice trembling with emotion. 'When we first came back here.'

Madeline shook her head, feeling the weight of sadness. 'I wanted to, but you were grieving the loss of your mother, and I feared if I told you that you were half-Jewish someone would find out and take you from me.'

'But I blamed you for everything that happened to me,' he said, his voice hinting at the bitterness he obviously felt.

Madeline drew in a breath. 'I wanted to tell you, and I tried to find you after the war. But it was impossible. I kept hoping you would come back to me. Every time the bell rang on the shop door, I hoped to see your face.'

Kurt's gaze softened; his anger seemed to be slowly giving way to a sense of understanding. 'I never knew,' he said, his voice filled with remorse. 'I was so consumed by my own pain and anger that I never stopped to consider what you might have been going through all these years.'

Madeline reached out and placed a hand on Kurt's cheek,

her touch gentle and comforting. 'I don't blame you,' she said softly. 'You were just a child, trying to make sense of a world that had been torn apart. We were both victims of circumstances beyond our control.'

Tears continued to slip down his cheeks as he leaned into Madeline's touch, seeking solace in her warmth. 'I'm so sorry,' he whispered, his voice filled with genuine regret.

Madeline smiled through her own tears, her heart swelling with love for this man who was once such a scared little boy. 'There is nothing to forgive,' she murmured. 'We have both carried the weight of our own pain for far too long. It's time to let go and embrace the chance for healing and forgiveness.'

Kurt's expression reflected a mixture of gratitude and vulnerability. 'I don't know where to go from here,' he admitted, his voice wavering. 'My whole identity feels shattered.'

Madeline squeezed Kurt's hand gently, offering him a reassuring smile. 'We'll figure it out together,' she said, her voice brimming with love. 'You are not alone any more, Kurt. You have your lovely granddaughter here, and we have each other now, and you have a whole family here in France that has been waiting for your return.'

Livi, who had been quietly sobbing at the emotional scene, nodded her agreement.

A sound at the door pulled them all from their contemplative moment. Chloe wandered in with a tea tray in her hands. 'I thought you might need something to—' She looked at the scene of three people crying and stopped abruptly. 'Is everything okay?' She directed her comment to Madeline, the concern evident on her face.

'It is now,' Madeline affirmed as she gripped Kurt's hand and squeezed it. 'And tea is exactly what we need.'

There was a short pause as Chloe served them, and, as Madeline sipped the warm, soothing drink, she turned to Livi again with a curious expression on her face. 'How did you know my wartime codename?'

Livi recounted her journey to find out about her grandfather's past, and showed Madeline the two books and Jacob's poetry pages.

Madeline reflected as she read the words. 'Jacob so loved riddles and clues. He gave me that poetry book. But I thought everything was taken by the Nazis from my bookshop and sold to a collector. How did you get these?'

Kurt became coy. 'The Jewish book, I took it the night before I got on the train with Charlotte. I was so angry at you, and I saw you hiding it. When you weren't looking, I picked it up, and saw the manor's name in the bookplate. It was the only thing I had of my former life, and I wanted it. Believed it belonged to me.'

Madeline sighed. 'It's strange how life works out, bringing us full circle. If you hadn't stolen that book so long ago, we might never have met again. I am so glad that Esther reached out to find out more about the orphans Charlotte took on the train. It must have taken her some detective work to find you. I look forward to meeting her; she sounds like a very determined young woman. She is bringing all the orphans back together, Kurt, did you know?'

Kurt shrugged. 'I never want to see those people again. Terrible things happened to us during that journey; I don't want to remember.'

Madeline nodded with understanding, then continued resolutely. 'Which is all the more reason for you to go, Kurt. This is your story, and it's theirs too. You were children, victims of a cruel war. Seeing them will help you heal. It's the only way to do that. It's like turning the lights on in a bedroom you thought was full of ghosts. While you're in the dark, they reign over you. But the minute you bring them into the light, they lose all their power to scare you.' She paused and then added, 'I would be willing to go with you for support.'

Kurt seemed moved by this elderly woman's offer. 'I will consider it.'

Madeline turned to Livi. 'What an adventure you've been on, Olivia. Jacob would have enjoyed watching you on your scavenger hunt.' She stopped, feeling the tender pain that never left her. 'I miss him so much, even though we were together for such a short time. It still hurts to this day.' She became wistful. 'I don't even know where Swift buried him. In all the shock of finding out about his death, I never thought to ask her, and I never saw her again.'

'I know where he is,' said Livi, her voice tight with emotion. 'He is buried next to my great-grandmother at Herrenhaus Eichenwald

I saw his grave when I was there a few weeks ago.'

Madeline drew in a breath as she took in the information. She closed her eyes, and a single tear slipped down her wrinkled cheek. After a short pause, she spoke again. 'It makes sense – he loved that estate – but I can't believe that, all this time, he was right there. I could never bring myself to go back there. I knew he was gone, and I couldn't have borne the emptiness there without him. Maybe it's time to also face my own ghosts. Kurt, will you come with me?'

He seemed unsure as he contemplated her words.

She went on, 'There is one more thing I have I want to give you while you are here.' Gracefully, she got up, and brought over a box wrapped with string.

He eyed it warily before untying it. He gasped at what was inside.

Madeline continued, 'I'm sorry to tell you that my old friend Dominique died a few years ago, but I promised I would keep this for you. And I always believed you would come home to me.'

Kurt pulled out the contents of the box and held up his little model aeroplane.

'My plane,' he said, the huskiness of emotion tightening his throat. 'I remember this.'

Livi felt a lump in her throat as she caught a glimpse of the boy he had been in his face.

'I'm not sure it will fly, but it belongs to you.'

He turned to Madeline. 'I will come with you to Eichenwald. You are right, I need to put my own ghosts to rest, too.'

EPILOGUE

On a crisp winter morning, Markus and Livi strolled hand in hand through the backwoods of the Herrenhaus Eichenwald estate. Around them the towering trees cast long shadows over the frozen ground. The air was filled with the sharp scent of pine.

Madeline and Kurt walked ahead of them, their steps slow and contemplative as they reflected on what lay ahead. As they approached a tree marked by a lightning strike, Markus and Livi slowed their pace, holding back to allow them their own moment of grief.

Kurt and his stepmother stood in silent reverence for a moment, staring down at the two weathered stones which bore two names etched crudely into their surface, marking the final resting place of their loved ones, who now lay peacefully beneath the earth.

Markus squeezed Livi's hand in reassurance as she watched her grandfather help his stepmother kneel down to place pink and cream roses on top of one of the graves.

A sob caught in the older woman's throat as she traced the letters on the moss-covered stone.

'Oh, my darling Jacob,' she whispered. 'I found Kurt. After all these years, he came back to me. And I know you had something to do with it.'

Kurt's eyes welled up with emotion as he listened to Madeline's heartfelt words, and he covered her hand with his own as she continued.

'I'm so sorry I have stayed away for so long, but I cherish all the memories we made together in this magical place. I thought it would be hard to come back here, but you are so alive here in the nature all around me. I see your face in the beauty of this landscape, hear your voice in the rustling of the leaves. So much of what you nurtured and created lives on here as your legacy and will never be forgotten. We had such a short time together, but I still feel your love so deeply, and never more than here, in a place that so tenderly held our love.'

A wood pigeon cooed in the distance as, with a tender touch, Kurt placed a bouquet of pure white lilies on the stone next to Jacob's. The delicate petals exuded a sweet, calming fragrance that filled the air around them.

He helped Madeline to her feet and, pushing through his emotion, spoke again. 'It is only now that I realise she is really dead. When we left her on that platform so many years ago, I told myself she was only injured and would follow us soon. That she would never abandon me. From that day on, every time a phone rang, or the door knocked, I hoped it would be her.'

He turned to his granddaughter and gazed at her with watery eyes. 'You look so much like her, Olivia. And that first day you appeared on my doorstep, for a fleeting moment I thought it was her. That she had come back for me at last.' His voice cracked with emotion as he held back tears. 'I thought I would finally have someone who would really love me again.'

He smiled sadly and gestured towards the gravestone and,

with a gentle touch, took Livi's hand in his own weathered one and squeezed it gently.

'In a way, she did come back to me that day,' he said softly. 'Her spirit living on through you, the same unbreakable tenacity of heart that just refused to give up on me, a bitter, angry old man.'

Tears rolled down Livi's cheeks; she had never heard her grandfather speak so openly about his feelings before. It was a tender moment, a deep connection, and she squeezed his hand back, reaffirming her commitment.

Then, as the small party stood in quiet contemplation, a gust of wind rustled the leaves, carrying their whispered words and unspoken emotions into the air. And in that moment, the weight of the past seemed to dissipate, replaced by a sense of closure and acceptance.

Kurt and Madeline stood side by side, bound in their newfound connection at the end of their journey, as Livi and Markus stood a few steps away at the beginning of their own. And all of them with nothing to fear, in a future that held nothing but the hope and promise of better days to come.

A LETTER FROM SUZANNE

Dear Reader,

I sincerely hope you enjoyed reading *The Bookseller of Paris*. If you did enjoy it and want to keep up to date with my latest releases, just sign up at the following link. Your email address will never be shared, and you can unsubscribe at any time.

www.bookouture.com/suzanne-kelman

Writing this book was pure joy. Each day the intoxicating scent of freshly printed pages and the gentle rustle of books filled my senses, whisking me away between the enchanting world of a British antiquarian bookseller and the dangerously thrilling life of a Parisian bookshop owner during the tumultuous 1940s.

As with all my books, the inspiration for the second book in this series is drawn from a real-life heroine. In this case, the incredible experiences of Adele Kibre, a skilled spy for the Allies who serves as the foundation for the character of Madeline.

It was as I delved deep into my research on the preservation of books during the war that I stumbled upon her story. It was a tale that both amazed and inspired me. In a time when men were seen as the leaders and heroes, it was surprising to learn that the best 'man' the Allies had in the field for preserving knowledge was in fact a woman. Adele, an American living in Europe, played a pivotal role in the OSS acquisitions programme – a crucial aspect of the US Intelligence Service, similar to Britain's elite SOE, which I have previously written about in my book *When We Were Brave*.

Throughout the 1940s, Adele fearlessly and tirelessly smuggled over 3,000 reels of microfilm and written material across enemy lines, risking her life daily in pursuit of her mission. Her story was truly captivating, and, although my fictional narrative only scratches the surface of her incredible bravery, I felt it was imperative to spread awareness of this extraordinary woman.

As I pondered how to tell her story, I was drawn to the idea of making 'my Adele' a simple Parisian bookshop owner with a hidden identity as a spy for the Resistance. Setting the story in a bookshop would also serve as a vehicle to shed light on an important aspect of this dark period in history – the banning and burning of books. The phrase 'knowledge is power' is still relevant today despite the decades that have passed since this time. It pains me to acknowledge that, even in the modern era, books are still being banned, a bleak reminder that history continues to repeat itself.

While history may praise individuals like Adele Kibre, there are also other people and places remembered for their infamy and evil deeds. Villa Am Großen Wannsee, located in Berlin, which served as the inspiration for Herrenhaus Eichenwald in my story, represents this duality. This elegant mansion was where the unthinkable was conceived – the horrific plan known as the Final Solution, the systematic extermination of European Jews that was decided upon during a chilling meeting on 20 January 1942.

By setting part of my tale within this villa, I sought to juxtapose the resilience of the human spirit with the backdrop of its most harrowing trials. Today, the Villa Am Großen Wannsee hosts a permanent exhibition recounting the horrors perpetrated during the Holocaust.

To maintain the flow of my story, Madeline's encounters at Eichenwald happen at a different time on my fictional timeline than this infamous meeting. Therefore, I was unable to directly portray the meeting in my writing. So, instead, I allude to it through Mueller's involvement and Olivia's story.

Whereas Adele Kibre was a real person, the character of Mueller is not based on one single person. He embodies the cruelty of multiple Gestapo officers who were responsible for creating and managing the death camps. In weaving together the threads of historical fact and fictional narrative, my aim is to honour the courage of real-life heroes like Kibre while shedding light on the darkness of historical atrocities perpetrated by figures like Mueller.

In creating the contemporary timeline, the inspiration for Olivia's story came about after watching a thought-provoking and haunting documentary on the descendants of notorious Nazi figures. Witnessing the lingering pain and trauma still present in their lives was heart-wrenching. They carried a heavy burden of shame, struggling to reconcile with their inherited legacy. The exploration of guilt, identity and the everlasting impact of the war on their family's history left a profound impression on me. It was a part of the Nazi legacy that I felt compelled to share through my writing.

As I come to the end of this letter, dear reader, I wanted to let you know my heart and mind are consumed by the creation of the third book in the Paris Sisters series. With each word, my attachment to the Valette family grows, the complicated yet lovable protagonists of each book. While their adventures may be born from my imagination, they are rooted in the awe-inspiring actions of real-life heroines.

Every twist and turn of their journey are guided by remarkable women who have left a lasting legacy of courage and resilience. As I continue to write I am in awe of the transformative power of storytelling, from exploring darkness within us to celebrating resistance and hope. My desire is that this journey will inspire you too.

Thank you for joining me on this poignant journey through the cobbled streets of Paris and into the clandestine heart of wartime intrigue.

With deepest gratitude for reading this story and in anticipation of our next literary adventure together,

All best wishes,

Suzanne

www.suzannekelmanauthor.com

facebook.com/suzkelman
x.com/suzkelman

ACKNOWLEDGEMENTS

First and foremost, I am truly grateful to Bookouture, my exceptional publisher, for their unwavering support, dedication and enthusiasm. Their team is made up of incredible individuals who work tirelessly to bring my books to life and I will be forever grateful to them.

A special mention goes to Jess Whitlum-Cooper, my fantastic new editor, whose encouragement and superb editing have elevated my writing to new heights.

I want to express my heartfelt gratitude to Jenny Geras, Peta Nightingale, Lizzie Brien, Mandy Kullar, Hannah Snetsinger, Jen Shannon, Occy Carr, Melanie Price, Alex Crow, Alba Proko, Jacqui Lewis, Becca Allen, Richard King, and all those who have played a role in making my books successful. Your efforts in promoting and spreading the word about my stories have not gone unnoticed.

Also, a special thank you to the amazing trio of Kim Nash, Noelle Holten and Sarah Hardy for their unwavering support and determination in reaching as many readers as possible with my work.

I am deeply grateful for my husband, Matthew Wilson. He has been my unwavering support and patient guide throughout this ambitious project. Without him, I wouldn't have had the courage to embark on this journey. In all eleven timelines of this series, he has kept track and provided valuable insights. He is my rock, always there to keep me grounded amid chaos. I am forever thankful for his presence in my life.

To my son Christopher, I am amazed by the incredible man you have become. Your strength, intelligence and compassion never fail to impress me. Thank you for always lending an ear and providing invaluable feedback on my writing. Your support and encouragement mean the world to me. You are my greatest inspiration and I am grateful for you every day.

I also must express my immense gratitude to my cherished group of close friends: the ever-encouraging Melinda Mack, the wise and witty Eric, the fiercely loyal Shauna Buchet and my trusted writing confidante K.J. Waters. Your unwavering friendship and support have been a steadfast source of inspiration and drive for me throughout this journey. I am eternally grateful for your presence in my life and could not have accomplished this without such a supportive group of friends.

But above all else, I want to express my heartfelt gratitude to each and every one of you – my incredible readers. Your constant support and loyalty are invaluable to me. I am always humbled and deeply appreciative that you have chosen my work amid the vast sea of options that are available. Thank you all.

PUBLISHING TEAM

Turning a manuscript into a book requires the efforts of many people. The publishing team at Bookouture would like to acknowledge everyone who contributed to this publication.

Audio
Alba Proko
Sinead O'Connor
Melissa Tran

Commercial
Lauren Morrissette
Hannah Richmond
Imogen Allport

Data and analysis
Mark Alder
Mohamed Bussuri

Cover design
Debbie Clement

Editorial
Jess Whitlum-Cooper
Imogen Allport

Printed in Great Britain
by Amazon